The
BEWITCHED VIKING

SANDRA HILL

A V O N
An Imprint of HarperCollins*Publishers*

AVON BOOKS
An Imprint of HarperCollins*Publishers*
10 East 53rd Street
New York, New York 10022-5299

Copyright © 1999, 2011 by Sandra Hill
ISBN 978-0-06-201900-4
www.avonromance.com

First Avon Books paperback printing: February 2011

Avon Trademark Reg. U.S. Pat. Off. and in Other Countries, Marca Registrada, Hecho en U.S.A.
HarperCollins® is a registered trademark of HarperCollins Publishers.

Printed in the U.S.A.

10 9 8 7 6 5 4 3 2 1

To all those readers with a sense of humor who relish a hero who can make them smile. And to those women who have their very own rogues . . . men who know the value of a wink and a grin, at just the right time . . . well aren't you the lucky ones!

And to my husband, Robert, who made me smile the first time we met. He was a political aide then, and I a fledgling reporter. We were walking into the governor's office when he did the most outrageous . . . well, that's another story <grin>. Suffice it to say, he's been making me smile ever since.
I guess I'm one of the lucky ones.

And now in Norway
A branch
Of the god's race
Had grown . . .

Ynglinga Saga

The
BEWITCHED VIKING

CHAPTER ONE

M en! Clueless through the ages! . . .
    "The king's manroot took a right turn."

"What? What root?" Blinking with confusion, Tykir Thorksson lifted his head off the alehouse table and gaped drunkenly at Bjold, the royal messenger.

"And he beseeches your service in correcting the . . . uh, problem."

"*Me?* Do my ears play me false?" With a brain that felt like a mashed turnip itself, Tykir scratched the fine hairs on his forearm and wondered irrelevantly how the emissary of his cousin King Anlaf, had even tracked him to Birka. And why, for the love of Freyja, would he go to the botherment of the grueling trek from the far northern reaches of Trondelag to this bustling market town on the island of Björkö in Lake Mälar? To tell him about . . . vegetables? "*Blód hel!* I am inclined to take offense. You see afore you a noted warrior and a trader in precious amber. Since when have I become a farmsteader, with knowledge of roots?"

Bjold's jaw dropped at Tykir's ferocious overreaction. Immediately, he clicked it shut and, with a snarl of impatience, tried again. "The king's *cock* has taken a right turn."

"His rooster?" Tykir was becoming more and more confused. First vegetables. Now poultry. Next this lackwit would be asking him for help in drying *lutefisk*.

"Not *that* cock." Bjold sniffed huffily, clearly repelled by Tykir's mead-sodden state.

In truth, Tykir did not often drink to excess. Though he appeared to have a carefree nature, he detested any lack of self-control. He had reason to celebrate, of course, having just returned from a successful trip to the Baltic lands, where his workers had harvested a crop of prized amber for his trading ventures.

Still, this heavy cloud of depression had been hanging over him for days. No doubt it was just boredom. "A-Viking, a-fighting and a-wenching" had long been his life's motto—leastways on the surface—but somehow those pleasures were fading.

Having seen thirty-five winters, Tykir had garnered more wealth than he could use in a lifetime. He'd lost count years ago of all the beautiful women he'd bedded, but now he no longer felt a youthling's swift rush of enthusiasm at the sight of every comely wench who came within snaring distance.

Then there was the matter of fighting—a time-honored Viking pastime. From the age of fourteen, he'd fought like a wild berserker in the battles of various kingdoms, like his father afore him—*may his soul be resting in Valhalla!* But he found himself questioning of late the motives of leaders who called for the rash spilling of blood from their underlings.

Well, there was a-Viking. Tykir had seen adventure in all his trading and Viking voyages. From the Rus lands to Iceland, from the Baltic Ocean to the English Channel, Tykir had visited and revisited, explored and discovered, even conquered. Never did he stay long in one place, though, by deliberate intent. 'Twas not good for a man in his position to form roots.

What else was there to draw a man's jaded interest? What challenges that he had not already mastered?

Tykir sighed deeply.

"By your leave, Jarl Thorksson, 'tis the king's *other* cock

I refer to." Bjold had been rambling on whilst Tykir's mind wandered. Suddenly, the messenger's words sank in, and Tykir's eyes went wide with understanding. *Manroot. Cock.* He glanced down to the jointure of his thighs and winced in masculine empathy. "The king's cock did *what?*"

"Made a right turn. Halfway down." The envoy thirstily quaffed a horn of ale, then wiped his mouth on his sleeve. He was clearly relieved that Tykir finally understood his message. "Looks like a flag at half mast, it does."

"And he wants *me* to fix it?" Tykir gasped out with horror.

"Not you precisely."

Tykir leveled a glare at the impudent lad. "Who precisely?"

The tone in his icy voice must have caught the lackwit's attention. With eyes darting nervously from side to side, Bjold answered, "The witch."

Odin's blood! 'Twas like pulling burrs from a wolf's tail, getting a straight answer from the dolt. "Just any witch?"

"Nay. One in particular." The messenger shifted uncomfortably under Tykir's close scrutiny.

Tykir rolled his eyes heavenward. "Well, that is clear as fjord fog on a rainy day." *If I were not so tired, I would shake the brainless cur till his rotten teeth rattled for such discourtesy.*

Bjold let out a long whoosh of exasperation and disclosed, "The witch with the 'Virgin's Veil.'"

Tykir made a low growling sound, and Bjold, with belated wisdom, hurried to explain. "The witch's name is Alinor . . . Lady Alinor of Northumbria. 'Tis she who put the curse on Anlaf's manpart. All because Anlaf and his hird of soldiers stopped by St. Beatrice's Abbey in Britain one day last year. The abbey is home to a nunnery where Lady Alinor was seeking sanctuary for a time from her bumbling brothers, the Lords Egbert and Hebert."

Tykir wondered what would constitute "bumbling" in the mind of this bumbling idiot. But he did not dare ask, lest he face another long-winded discourse. Instead, he focused on Bjold's other words. "Stopped by? Anlaf *stopped by* a nunnery? For a bit of raping and pillaging, I wager."

"And if we did?" Bjold bristled, revealing his part in the marauding band. "'Tis neither here nor there whether we were a-plundering or not. I daresay you've done a fair share of plundering in your day, too. At issue here is the fact that the witch waved a relic in the king's face . . . a blue headrail, which she claimed once adorned the Blessed Virgin Mary." He paused, then explained, as if Tykir were a dimwit, "The Virgin Mary is the mother of the Christians' One-God."

Tykir fisted his hands to prevent himself from throttling the fool. "I know who the Virgin Mary is."

"Well, as I was saying . . . that's when Lady Alinor put her curse on Anlaf, threatening, 'Curse you, heathen! May your manpart fall off if you do this evil deed.' Well, his manpart didn't fall off—leastways, not yet—but it took a turn to the right." Bjold took a deep breath after that long explanation.

"And?" Tykir prodded. "What has that to do with me?"

"The king wants you to bring the witch back to Trondelag, with her magic veil, to remove the bloody curse."

"Is that all?" Tykir remarked. But what he thought was, *A Saxon. Anlaf expects me to stop in the midst of my trading voyage, go all the way to Britain to get the wench, who will no doubt be unwilling, take her back to the Norselands, by way of Hedeby, where I must needs drop off the last of my trading goods, then make my way home to Dragonstead. And all this afore the winter ice sets in. Hah! Anlaf ever was an overbearing lout, even when we were boys. But he goes too far this time.* "Nay."

"Nay? Do you say to your liege lord nay? Where is your Norse loyalty?"

Tykir stiffened with affront. "Hah! Anlaf is no more my liege lord than the Wessex King Edred. You know well and good that Northmen pledge allegiance to a particular leader, not a nation. My uncle, Haakon, is all-king of Norway, and to him alone do I pay homage. Further, 'twas Haakon—then fostering in King Athelstan's court in Britain and having seen only fifteen winters—who went back to the Norselands on King Harald Fairhair's death and returned to all bonders the odal-rights to their land. My title to Dragonstead was reaffirmed to me by Haakon and will remain free and clear in my family name for posterity."

Tykir felt an aching tug in his heart at the mere thought of Dragonstead. If he was being truthful with himself, he would have to admit that Dragonstead mattered more to him than anything. And that was dangerous.

Bjold's face flamed with the heat of embarrassment, but still he blundered on. "The king thought you might be reluctant."

"Oh, he did, did he?"

"He said to tell you that you could have Fierce One for a boon if you wouldst do him this favor."

Tykir sat up straighter. "Anlaf would grant me his prized stallion—the one gifted to him by that Saracen chieftain?"

"Yea." Bjold nodded emphatically. "The black devil with the white markings on his hooves. That be the one."

"Hmmm," Tykir said, despite his misgivings. Still, he resisted. "Nay. I have too much to do afore retreating to Dragonstead for the winter."

"In that case, King Analf directed me to offer the slave girl, Samirah, as well. The one with the tiny silver bells on her ankles, and the two silver bells dangling from the pierced rings in her . . ." He cupped two hands in front of his chest to indicate Samirah's most noted endowments.

"Hmmm," Tykir said again, but not because of the slave girl, enticing as he knew her to be. Truth be told, the horse held more appeal. In the end, though, he repeated his earlier refusal. "Nay, I have no time."

Bjold wrung his hands nervously. "I had not wanted to

tell you this, but afore I do . . . well, uh, tell me one thing. You are not the type of man who is wont to kill the messenger with bad tidings, are you?"

Tykir drew himself up alertly. "Speak, wretch, or I will slice your tongue from your mouth and send it to Anlaf on a bread trencher."

Bjold's face went even brighter. "'Tis Adam the Healer," he squeaked out. "Anlaf holds him as friendly hostage till you deliver the witch."

"What?" he roared. "How did Adam end up in Trondelag? I thought he was in the Arab lands. And what in bloody hell is a 'friendly hostage'?" Adam was a young man of no more than twenty years who had been studying medicine these past five years in the Arab lands, where the most noted healers practiced their arts. He was the adopted son of Tykir's half-sister, Rain, and her husband, Selik, who resided in Jorvik. Adam was like family to him, a nephew by adoption.

"Friendly hostage means Adam will come to no harm. He just cannot leave Anlaf's court."

Tykir made a low, rumbling growl of outrage in his throat.

Bjold shriveled under his obvious wrath and concluded in a rush, "It all comes back to the witch and your mission to capture her."

Standing abruptly, Tykir leaned across the table and grabbed Bjold by the front of his surcoat, lifting him off his bench and half-leaning over the table toward him, knocking horns of ale hither and yon. The boy looked as if he might soil his braies, so afeared was he. "Start from the beginning," Tykir said icily, "and leave naught out."

He settled back for what he hoped was not an overlong tale. Especially since his head was pounding like Thor's mighty hammer, *Mjolnir*. Especially since he was in dire need of a bath house to rid himself of the fleas that infested his skin and clothing after a long sea voyage. Especially since his good friend Rurik raised his equally mead-sodden head from the table next to him and grinned, silently mouthing the words, "A witch-hunt?"

Rurik had good reason to relish the prospect of a witch-hunt. Being godly handsome (second only to Tykir, in Tykir's not so humble opinion), Rurik wore his long black hair, as well as his beard, in intricate braids. His mustache was a daily clipped work of art. But Rurik's overblown vanity had been dealt a blow two years past—by a witch, no less—a Scottish witch, who'd dyed a jagged line down the middle of Rurik's face, whilst he slept, from hairline to chin, with the blue woad of the Scottish warriors. Thus far, Rurik had been unable to wash the color from his skin, or find the wily witch.

Yea, Rurik would be encouraging him to undertake Anlaf's witchly mission.

Then things got worse.

Before Bjold could begin to talk, Bolthor the Giant, Tykir's own personal skald—*may Odin have mercy!*—slid onto the bench next to him. Tykir could not suppress the groan that escaped his lips. He needed a skald almost as much as he needed a witch, especially a skald as tall as a small tree.

But what was a man to do when a fellow warrior saved his life in battle? When said life-friend lost an eye at the Battle of Ripon five years past, Tykir had felt compelled to offer work to the despondent knight. Thus far, Bolthor had tried—and failed—as cook, blacksmith and armorer on Tykir's northern homestead. Finally, Tykir's household had revolted at the unpalatable food, burned-down smithy and broken swords.

Tykir gave Bolthor a passing sideways glance, then looked again. Uh-oh! Too late, he realized that Bolthor had that certain dreamy expression on his face that foreboded the verse-mood coming upon him. Too late to escape now.

"Hear one and all, this is the saga of Tykir the Great," Bolthor began. It was the manner in which all of Bolthor's sagas began. They didn't get any better than that opening line, unfortunately.

Rurik's lips curved upward with mirth. With a hand over his mouth, he murmured to Tykir under his breath, *"Hver fugl synger med sitt nebb."*

"Humph!" Tykir said in reply. "Every bird may very well sing with its own voice, but Bolthor's birdsong is the most unmelodious I have ever heard."

Unaware of their opinions, Bolthor adjusted the black patch over his one eyeless socket and took a stylus into his huge hand. Squinting through his good eye, he began painstakingly to press runic symbols onto the wax tablet he had set on the table in front of him. 'Twas not the norm for skalds to write down the sagas, but Bolthor's head was thick, and he often forgot the words to the tales he had composed.

"Methinks a good title for this one would be 'Tykir and the Crooked Cock.' Let me see, how shall I start? Hmmm.

> *"In the land of the Saxons,*
> *An evil witch did fly.*
> *To Anlaf's proud duckling,*
> *She set her evil eye.*
> *Now, alas and alack,*
> *His furry pet can no longer*
> *Quack . . .*
> *Nor with his mate*
> *Fly straight."*

Bolthor paused. "How does it sound thus far?" he asked hopefully.

"Magnificent," Tykir said, patting Bolthor on the shoulder. *Horrible.* Tykir barely stifled a grimace of distaste. *I hope my brother Eirik never hears of this one. He will fall over laughing, almost as much as he did over the "Tykir and the Reluctant Maiden" saga Bolthor concocted last winter. Somehow, Bolthor's overlong tales almost always end with me looking the fool. And best that Anlaf does not hear of Bolthor enhancing his wordfame by referring to his manpart as a duckling, or there will be sword dew spilled aplenty.*

Tykir scratched his unshaven face and wondered idly if he smelled as bad as his companions. Vikings were renowned for their fastidious nature, unlike those piggish Saxon and Frankish men, who bathed but once a season. Lifting one arm, he sniffed under his armpit . . . and flinched.

"How do you spell duckling?" Bolthor whispered in an aside.

"C-O-C-K," Tykir responded dryly. Let Bolthor figure how to translate the word into the futhark alphabet. That should take a goodly amount of time.

He turned to Bjold. "Proceed," he directed him with a wave of his hand. "I doubt me I will like your report from King Anlaf, but spare me not even the smallest detail."

When Bjold finished, at last, a good hour later, a sudden realization came to Tykir . . . one that drew a wide smile to his face, overshadowing the anger that lingered beneath the surface over Anlaf's treatment of Adam. *I am no longer bored.*

He looked at Rurik, then Bolthor, before announcing, "It would seem we are going a-witching."

NORTH YORKSHIRE, SIX SENNIGHTS LATER

Here come the baa . . . d men . . .

"The Vikings are coming. The Vikings are coming."

"Baaa. Baaa. Baaa. Baaa."

"Bleat. Bleat. Bleat. Bleat."

"Ruff ruff, ruff, ruff!"

"The Vikings are coming. The Vikings are coming."

Whether it be her crying sheep or her barking sheepdog or her shrieking, sheeplike maid, Elswyth, who was approaching with the dire warning of yet another Northman sighting, Lady Alinor had more than enough problems for one day. A most unladylike phrase escaped her lips—something to do with an unmentionable exercise the Vikings, the sheep and the dog could do to themselves, or to each other, for all she cared. 'Twas an expression she'd heard her hersir use on more than one occasion when they were ready to explode with ill-temper. And Alinor's temper was very ill, and explosive, at the moment.

Hanging on to a tree root with one hand, Alinor was dangling into a shallow gully infested with briars, trying to extricate one of her ewes, Bathsheba, from the sharp thorns with the crook of her long staff. Her mangy sheepdog, inappropriately named Beauty, was yipping off in the distance as it attempted to steer a small flock of straying sheep back to the stone-fenced pastures of the lower dales.

Continuing to bleat his yearnings nonstop was David, a lusty, overanxious ram of a curly-horned breed almost nonexistent outside Córdoba—a bride gift from her last marriage. Ironically, Sheba was in heat, and she yearned mightily for the mating that would produce new lambs for Alinor's thriving flock come spring, but still the dumb female had felt the need to play games of catch-me-if-you-will with the curly-horned David. That's when the coy Sheba had landed herself in the briar patch.

Not all that different from human males and females in their mating rituals, Alinor supposed.

"The Vikings are coming. The Vikings are coming."

"Baaa. Baaa. Baaa. Baaa."

"Bleat. Bleat. Bleat. Bleat."

"Ruff, ruff, ruff, ruff!"

Alinor paused in the act of cutting away the branches caught in Sheba's matted fur, glanced over her shoulder, and groaned at the sight of her kitchen maid rushing toward her over the heather-blanketed flatlands, headrail flapping in the wind and brown homespun kirtle hiked practically to her knobby knees. Elswyth *always* thought the Vikings were coming, no matter if it was mere wayfarers approaching Graycote Manor from the old Roman road or stray cows from the pastures of Castle Bellard, three miles to the east.

In truth, fighting men from the North had been coming into Britain in droves this past year as news spread of Eric Bloodaxe's campaign to expel King Olaf Sigtryggsson and regain the crown of Northumbria. Recently he had achieved that goal, thanks to the efforts of Archbishop Wulfstan and members of the Norse nobility residing in northern Britain.

Elswyth's fears had started a year past, when she had accompanied Alinor to the nunnery at St. Beatrice's Abbey. Whilst there, they'd had the misfortune to witness a thwarted Viking attack on the good nuns. Alinor had been hiding out at the convent from her twin brothers, Egbert and Hebert, who had come up with yet another marriage prospect for her: Ecgfrith of Upper Mercia, a doddering old lord with one foot in the grave. Actually, Ecgfrith had passed away before Egbert and Hebert even found Alinor at the nunnery. What a birching she'd received for her willfulness! Though she had seen only twenty-five winters, Alinor had wed and been widowed three times since her fifteenth birthday, all to serve the greedy needs of her brothers.

And it would seem her problems were unending, for just yestermorn she'd received a missive from her wool agent in Jorvik, informing her that Egbert and Hebert had been boasting in the market town of a new marriage contract that carried the seal of their third cousin, King Edred—a contract for matrimony between their sister, Lady Alinor of Graycote Manor, and Lord Cedric of Wessex. The sickly king had been plagued by troubles since his reign began six years past. If the Vikings weren't stirring unrest in the north, his own noblemen—not least of whom her own brothers—were constantly nagging at him for favors.

It mattered not to her brothers that the short, corpulent Cedric was as wide as he was tall. He weighed as much as a horse and was old enough to be her great-grandsire. The important thing to Egbert and Hebert would be the estates Cedric owned, which would cede to a wife, and therefore to them as guardians, upon his death.

Well, Alinor could not refuse the king's command, but if she never actually received the royal command of her weak-sapped sovereign, how could she be deemed lacking in proper loyalty? Therefore, she intended to be long gone, into a new temporary hiding place, before Egbert and Hebert's arrival, which she estimated to be two days hence, giving Alinor temporary respite from her brothers' machinations.

"Come, Elswyth," she entreated, now that the maid drew near. "Help me free Sheba."

"But . . . but . . ." Elswyth protested breathlessly, "the Vikings are coming."

"And if they are? What is it to us? We have no riches for them to pillage—apparent ones, leastways." Alinor had willingly given up all the estates deeded to her by three dead husbands, except for this one measly manor in the far north of Britain, precisely so that she would garner no attention from her only remaining family. The fact that she prospered with her thriving wool trade went unnoticed by her brothers since she plowed all the profits back into the sheep folds and hidden chests of gold. Her greatest dream was that one day she would just be left alone.

"But they could *ravish* us," Elswyth cried in a horrified whisper.

Alinor had to laugh at that. They would have to be sorry Vikings indeed to feel the inclination to toss the aging Elswyth's robes over her head. And Alinor had known well and good from an early age that she was not comely to men. With hair of a most garish shade of red and freckles covering her entire body, which was too tall and too thin by half, Alinor held no appeal for the average man . . . and Vikings, renowned for their good looks, were reputed to be most particular.

"Elswyth," she said in a kindly tone, "we are in more

danger of being raped by David than any Viking if we do not soon extricate his lady-love from these brambles."

Grumbling, Elswyth reached forward to assist Alinor, but under her breath she mumbled that famous Anglo-Saxon refrain, "Oh, Lord, from the fury of the Northmen please protect us."

Road trips are sometimes the pits . . .

Tykir was furious.

It had taken him two sennights to complete his trading ventures in Birka, along with some ship repairs, before sailing for British soil. Now, for the past four sennights—twenty-eight wasted, bloody days—he and Rurik and Bolthor had been riding from one end of the British isle to the other, searching for the elusive witch. Vikings were meant to sail the seas, not travel long, bumpy distances on land, atop horses, till their arses were bruised and their moods riled.

And it was all the fault of the Lady Alinor. Rather, the Lady Witch, he corrected himself. An interesting lady, as it turned out. The thrice-widowed sorceress—*and didn't that happenstance of three conveniently dead spouses provoke a thinking man's suspicion?*—owned a dozen wealthy estates across this hellish land, all managed by her brothers, the bumbling twins to whom Bjold had referred. But she chose to live in a poor holding in the bleak, far northern Northumbria, almost up to the Scottish borders . . . no doubt to practice her pagan rites in privacy.

Well, the quest was almost over. When they'd stopped at Graycote Manor a short time ago, her castellan informed Tykir that the Lady Alinor was up in the fells tending to her sheep. *Tending? Was she engaged in some black rite involving animal sacrifice or such?*

The odd thing was the timber and stone keep, with its crumbling ramparts and stockades, was kept neat, but sorely out of date. At the same time, vast fields of cut hay lay drying for winter feed. A dozen cows lowed in a nearby byre waiting to be milked. Piles of harvested turnips, carrots, cabbages and other food items rolled by in heavy carts. It was an ill-kept estate, overflowing with provender. How peculiar!

Well, be that as it may. He cared not if the witch was rich or poor. Soon his journey would be over, and the Lady Alinor would pay good and well for all the trouble she had put him to.

"We must be careful, Tykir," Rurik warned him.

The three of them rode horses side by side up one fell and down the other, following the castellan's directions. Lady Alinor's dim-witted castellan—leader of a scraggly band of troops—had not even thought to question his mistress's safety in sending three Viking warriors after her.

"I am loath to ask you . . . but why?"

"We know not if this witch is a solitary or in a coven."

Tykir nodded, though he had no particular knowledge of witchcraft, solitary or otherwise. He would have to bow to Rurik's greater wisdom in that regard.

"No doubt the witch will take on a most beauteous countenance to draw us under her spell."

"Do you think so?"

"Yea, that is what happened to me, I warrant. Why else would I have let my guard down in a strange country in the presence of a known witch?"

Tykir laughed. "Because the Scottish wench opened her lissome legs for you, that's why. Because the man-lust is always upon you. Because you think with the rock betwixt your legs, instead of the rock betwixt your ears."

Rurik lifted his chin with affront, calling attention to the blue-dyed line down the middle of his face—testament to his foolish entanglement with a witch.

"Since we are so close to Scotland, why do you not go in search of the witch? Mayhap you can rid yourself of her mark once and for all."

"All of last year I spent searching for the wench, to no avail. I refuse to spend the winter months in the Highlands freezing my arse in search of her now. Next summer I will find her, or be damned."

"I for one wouldst like to know if the old tales are true about witches having a tail they hide beneath their robes," Bolthor interjected. "'Tis said that the only way they can lose the long appendage is by marrying a mortal man."

"See," Rurik argued to Tykir, "I was right about witches taking on a tempting form. It makes sense that they would need to be beautiful if they want to snare a man and thus lose their tails."

"You two would believe anything," Tykir hooted. "All I know is that I want to be the one to light the fire under this particular witch . . . once King Anlaf is finished with her, that is. Then, if I never see English soil, or an English wench, again, it will be too soon for me."

"There she is," Rurik said excitedly.

A long, telling silence followed. Finally, Tykir snorted with disgust and said aloud what they were all thinking: "So much for the theory of beautiful witches!"

"Methinks this calls for a saga." Bolthor was already pulling his wax tablet from a saddlebag, muttering something about "Tykir and the Flame-Haired Witch." Then he launched into his usual introduction, "Hear one and all, this is the saga of Tykir the Great."

"How would you like a stylus up your arse?" Tykir responded.

Bolthor just ignored him and began spouting his verse.

"Flames there were
But not of fire.
Wild spume of
Satan's breath
Spilled from

The witch's head
To catch the wary warrior,
Though he be grandson of
The great King Harald Fairhair."

"I saw a fruit that color once whilst a-Viking in the southern climes. 'Twas called an orange, I think." Rurik spoke with awe on viewing the wench's odd-colored hair.

Tykir had seen red hair before—they all had, of course. Even the great Odin had red hair. But never had Tykir witnessed hair quite like this. Rurik was wrong about its orange color, though; it was more like bright rust on a metal shield.

"Oh, for the love of Freyja! Is that the devil's spittle that adorns her, too?" Bolthor shivered with distaste. "Hair like the fires of hell and the mark of Lucifer on her skin . . . Of a certainty, she is a witch."

He was right. The woman *was* covered with freckles, every part of her exposed skin, and no doubt every other place beneath her drab robes. Her headrail and wimple, which would normally cover the hair of a lady of her high birth, hung ignominiously from a briar thatch just beyond where the Lady Alinor was chasing a ram, who was chasing a bleating sheep.

"Dost see her familiars anywhere about?" Bolthor asked in a hushed voice. "Ofttimes witches use cats as their familiars."

They all scanned the horizon. Not a cat in sight.

"Perchance," Rurik said hesitantly, "her familiars are sheep."

"Sheep?" he and Bolthor said as one.

All of their jaws dropped open with amazement at this incredible turn of events.

But then Tykir came to his senses. "I have ne'er heard of anything so ridiculous in all my life."

"Me neither," Rurik and Bolthor agreed.

But they all looked at each other, unsure. If indeed she did use sheep as familiars, she must be a powerful witch. There were dozens of sheep in the area.

"And look," Bolthor added, "she carries a staff. Everyone knows that a witch carries a magic staff. And a bell and a crystal, of course."

A tinkling sound came from the neck of the female sheep being swived by the lusty ram. The fine hairs stood out all over Tykir's body at that affirmation of at least one of the witch's tools.

They all narrowed their eyes to see if she might be wearing, or carrying, a crystal. They saw nothing but her simple, rumpled gown. No doubt she kept it hidden.

"Do you think she dances naked in the forest?" Rurik wondered. " 'Tis a common witch practice."

"Did your witch?" Tykir asked with a grin.

"Yea, she did," Rurik told him, grinning back. " 'Twas almost worth receiving her cursed mark to see that exhibition."

"I'm not sure there would be so much pleasure in seeing this witch naked," Tykir said. They all concurred.

While they were making these observations, Rurik's dog was barking wildly, the sheep were bleating, and the nervous horses were neighing. In the midst of this chaos, a mangy sheepdog galloped over the fells toward them, a flock of bleating sheep following behind. Apparently, the sheepdog had noticed Rurik's wolfhound, Beast, who stood near his horse's right front leg, trying to appear aloof but pissing trickles of excitement.

The jaws of Tykir and his comrades nigh dropped to the ground with this ungodly spectacle.

Just then, the ram finished his rutting and his sheeply mate escaped. But apparently the randy ram had other ideas. He chased after her, then stopped dead in his tracks, did an about-face and began chasing Lady Alinor, who had been shouting at the two of them to desist at once. When the ram bumped Lady Alinor's rump with his curly horns, she fell to the ground, rump in the air.

And all three men stared, transfixed, at one particular spot.

Did she have a tail or didn't she?

CHAPTER TWO

*T*he shepherdess had an eye for good . . . uh, wool . . .
        The Vikings really were coming.
    In fact, they'd come.
    And they were staring at her posterior.
    Lecherous heathens! Bloody libertines! Viking curs! If they dare try to rape me, I'll pull out my shears, and at least one of them will no longer have the lewd inclination.
    Elswyth was whimpering, a continuous "Ooh, ooh, ooh, ooh" of mortal fright. The dog and a half-dozen sheep were circling the whole lot of them, with Beauty yipping an over-exuberant dog welcome to the beautiful wolfhound who'd arrived with the Northmen. Meanwhile, David had already mounted the finally docile Sheba, and the look on his face was pure ecstasy.
    Alinor would have been mortified if these were anything but Vikings, who probably witnessed such crude behavior all the time in their primitive lands.
    "My good men, what do you here on my lands? How may I assist you?" Alinor inquired in the Norse tongue, which was very similar to English. She'd become proficient in the language these past years as she'd negotiated for her wools in the markets of Northumbria, which were heavily populated with peoples of Viking descent.
    Now, as she spoke to them, she scrambled clumsily to her feet and put one hand on her hip, trying to strike a casual pose of fearlessness, at the same time adjusting her headrail

with the other hand. Except that her headrail and wimple had managed to disappear. Alinor raked her fingers through the disarray atop her head. She suspected that she looked like a flaming, long-haired sheep before the shearing. Truth to tell, Egbert had once told her just that, in a lame attempt at encouraging her to improve her appearance to aid their matrimonial pursuits for her. When her ragged nails kept snagging on the knots in her hair, she gave up. "My manor house is over the fells a short distance," she informed the Vikings, pointing westward. "If it is food and drink you seek, my steward will offer you and your fine steeds hospitality. We are a poor estate, but you need not fear. . . ."

Her words trailed off as she tossed her hair back off her face and got her first good view of the three Viking men, who still sat atop magnificent black destriers with finely tooled leather and silver trappings. She shivered, but not from the cool autumn breeze, which was brisk and gaining strength. Deadly sharp swords, pattern-welded in the Viking tradition, hung from scabbards at their sides. On their horses were highly embossed shields. All of the men were uncommonly tall and hugely muscled. *Jesus, Mary and Joseph!* She had to bite her bottom lip to keep from whimpering, just like Elswyth.

All the men wore slim black wool braies and short leather ankle boots, cross-gartered up trim legs. The one on the left was a veritable giant—at least a head taller than the other two, and they were exceedingly long of frame themselves. His white-blond hair hung loose to shoulder-length. He wore a brown wool tunic, belted at the waist and covered at the shoulders with several layers of matching mantles of different length that left one arm exposed, an arm that rested on a long-poled battle-ax, braced now on the ground. He had probably seen no more than thirty winters, but harsh lines etched his face, aging him beyond his years. A black patch over one eye completed the picture of battered soldier.

The Viking on the right was dark haired, and, Alinor guessed, vain as a peacock. At least five years younger than the giant, he stroked his silky mustache. His beard and hair were woven into intricate braids—a habit many warriors adopted to avoid their hair flying into their eyes in the midst of battle—but this Viking's plaits were interlaced with colored beads. Most interesting was the blue jagged line down the middle of his face, which detracted not at all from his appearance; in fact, some might say it enhanced his attraction. He wore a blue wool tunic, matching his eyes and his face design, but instead of a shoulder mantle, a gray fox skin was tossed carelessly from shoulder to opposite waist, front and back, tucked into a wide belt of tanned leather. The animal that had died for his comfort must have been huge. Reaching down nimbly to the ground, he patted the clamoring dog, cautioning, "Shhh, Beast. 'Tis just a scurvy bitch. Beneath your interest for a quick dalliance, my good dog." He grinned at Alinor as he spoke, making it unclear whether he was referring to Beauty or to her.

But it was the Viking in the middle—the apparent leader—who caught and held her interest. Alinor's head had never been turned by a man's pleasing countenance in the past. It was now.

His long hair was light brown streaked with pale yellow strands, giving the appearance of shimmering gold—the effect caused by the bleaching effects of the sun during many years on the open seas, she would wager. He was older than the rest, possibly five and thirty, and godly handsome. Blessed St. Boniface! His years sat well on him, indeed.

His hair, too, was braided, but only on one side, where a silver earring in the shape of a thunderbolt dangled from one exposed ear. Dressed all in black—braies, tunic, belt—he was covered shoulder to ankle by a cloak of magnificent wool of the best quality, lined with black sable. The cloak was pinned off one shoulder with a heavy gold brooch in a design of intertwining snakes with clear chrysolite eyes. Hanging from a chain around his neck was an amber pendant in the shape of a star with a bloodred drop in the center.

"Well?" he said, his honey brown eyes taking her measure with icy disdain.

"Wh-what?" He must have been talking while her mind had been woolgathering.

"I said, my lady," he repeated with exaggerated patience, "*é heiti Tykir* . . . My name is Jarl Tykir Thorksson, and I have not come this great distance for your food or drink."

She cocked her head to the side. "Why then have you come?"

"'Tis for *you* I have come, Lady Alinor."

Where's a magic broom when a gal needs one? . . .

"Show me your tail."

"Ta-tail . . . ?" Alinor reeled inwardly with shock. Oooh! She would like nothing more than to take a wooden trencher off the table and whack the thick head of the crude oaf, Tykir Thorksson. His reference to a witch tail was the latest in a series of outrageous remarks he'd made to her since they'd come from the sheep pasture, the first and most outrageous being that he'd come all the way from Hedeby *for her*.

She was sitting next to him at the high table in her great hall with an iron hand clamped on her forearm, locking her to the arm of her chair. Otherwise, she'd have risen long ago and exited his presence, forthwith. He and his two comrades had refused to leave her out of their sights since returning to the manor house, not even when she'd gone to the garderobe.

"Listen, uh . . ." The brute had informed her from the first of his title, *jarl*, which was one step below a king and similar in nobility to an English lord. He held this rank of the upper Norse nobility, thanks to bloodlines linking his grandsire, the famous, long-dead King Harald Fairhair. As if she cared whether he was a lowly thrall or a high jarl! Or whether he was Viking, Frank or Saxon, for that matter.

The man was still a crude oaf. *But how does one address a Viking of higher station? My lord? My jarl? My barbarian?* "Listen, my jarl—"

He let out a hoot of laughter. "Call me Tykir."

Nay, a wooden trencher would be too mild a punishment for this one. Better a rock. A big one.

"Well, are you going to show me your buttocks and end these bothersome protests? If you have no tail, prove it . . . though I am inclined to believe that a true witch could make a tail appear and disappear at will."

Despite her efforts at restraint, she bared her teeth and made a low hissing sound of affront.

He grinned.

"If I were a true witch, I would put a spell on you right now and turn you into a toad."

He laughed. "Be that as it may, I have wasted more than enough time in pursuit of you. I expect to be aboard my longship in Jorvik three days hence. So end your senseless malingering."

Aaarrrgh! She'd been trying to convince the stubborn blackguard of her innocence ever since he'd told her out on the fells that he'd come to Graycote for the witch who'd put a spell on some Viking king. A likely story! No doubt he was searching for a target to pillage. Well, he'd find naught of worth in her poor keep. Or perhaps he hoped to kidnap her for hostage. Little did he know that her brothers wouldn't pay even a farthing for her return. Her only value to them was in the bride price they received for her every blessed time they arranged another marriage . . . along with the estates that ceded to her on widowhood, of course.

And her aging castellan, Gerald, would be of no hope. She grimaced with dismay as her gaze hit on her supposed protector, leader of her hird of soldiers. He was over there at the end of the high table, nodding off to sleep, and it barely past high noon. These Vikings must think they'd been handed a gift from their heathen gods on viewing the weak protection of her keep. Hah! That was a deliberate tactic on her part. Her prosperous farms and sheep pastures were in sharp contrast to the starkness of her keep, which was well-maintained and stocked with provisions, but with no embellishments or luxurious furbelows, like wall tapestries or silver tableware. If ever Alinor enlarged her timber and stone manor house into a fine castle, Egbert and Hebert would take it from her in a trice. The same was true of her hird of soldiers under Gerald's leadership. Strong fighting men would just draw her brothers' attention.

"Look at it this way, you have no children here that demand your presence," the Viking said.

Huh? She'd been half-attending while the insensitive clod prattled on.

"You are free to leave your estate in the care of minions. Actually, you could consider this a pleasure trip to the Norselands." He folded his arms and puffed out his chest then, well pleased with himself for coming up with that ludicrous justification for his actions.

"A pleasure trip?" She could scarce keep her voice down to a low shriek. "Wouldst that be comparable to plucking out a person's fingernails and calling it good grooming?"

"Probably," he said unabashedly.

She thought a moment. "How do you know whether I have children?"

"Your castellan told me so."

She was going to have a serious talk with Gerald about his loose tongue. In the meantime, if he could bring up children, then so could she. "What will *your* children think of you hauling an unwilling woman halfway 'round the world?"

His face turned a rosy shade of red under his deeply tanned skin. "I have no children . . . that I know of."

She arched an eyebrow at his wording. "That you know of?"

"My family or lack of one is none of your affair," he said

icily and put up a hand to bar any further words. "I have been kind to you thus far, Lady Alinor. We can do this nicely, or not. It matters not to me."

"But—"

"Gather your belongings, I beseech you. Or I will. One way or another, we must be on our way if we are to make camp at Aynsley afore nightfall."

"But—"

He refused to allow further argument. "Know this, my lady: I promised to deliver a witch to Anlaf, and a witch I will deliver."

"I . . . am . . . *not* . . . a . . . witch," she said in evenly spaced words, so the halfwit would understand.

"Prove . . . it," he said, mimicking her pacing.

She bristled. *Say nothing, Alinor. Keep your wits about you. A clear head has gotten you out of worse situations than this.*

"Everyone knows a witch has a tail," the lout continued.

"Everyone?" she scoffed.

"Thus I've been told," he said defensively. His wonderfully thick, brown lashes fluttered with uncertainty.

"By whom, pray tell?"

Tykir's whisker-stubbled face reddened as he pointed ruefully to the side where the one-eyed giant, Bolthor—the world's most unlikely skald—was imbibing great draughts of mead, mumbling something about, "Hear one and all, this is the saga of Tykir the Great, who met a flame-haired witch-shepherdess . . ."

"Tykir the Great?" Alinor asked, unable to stifle a chuckle.

"To straighten a king's tail
Did the brave warrior come.
To lose her tail
Did the bold witch aspire.
Which tail will win
In this battle of the tails?"

Tykir shrugged sheepishly and shared a chuckle with her at his own expense. She liked that in a man—or woman— the ability to laugh at oneself.

"But you must recognize that this whole situation is absurd. I'm no more a witch than you're a . . . a troll." Her lips twitched with amusement at that remark. "On the other hand . . ."

"Why, you impudent wench! Are you implying that I'm a troll?" He squeezed her forearm as punishment, but not very hard. "In truth, I must needs be honest with you, I cannot help but admire your bravery, though it passes all bounds of recklessness. Has no one ever warned you about tweaking the wolf's tail?"

"Don't you mean the troll's tail?" she asked cheekily.

He laughed. "Too bad you are not a more toothsome morsel. I might have enjoyed tasting your charms on the long journey back to Trondelag."

His dancing eyes assessed her form in its clean gunna of fine forest-green wool, with a matching headrail. Her wild hair was tucked neatly under a white wimple, but she knew she held no appeal for him. It was the freckles, of course. They repelled most men, superstitious fools that they were. And if not superstitious, then overly concerned with the traditional standards of beauty, like milk-white skin. "Dost think I care if you find me lovely as a goddess or homely as a hedgehog? Three husbands have I buried. The next man, wedded spouse or not, who tries to sample my wares will do so over *his* dead body."

The Viking's mouth dropped open with surprise. Then he slapped his free hand on his knee with appreciation. "Thor's blood! Your tongue does outrun your good sense. Don't you know I could pull that talksome appendage from your mouth, slice it off with a mere flick of my sword and roast it for dinner?"

Now, that is an image I do not need planted in my head.

She decided to try a different tact. "Dost thou honestly believe in witchcraft?"

"Yea. Nay." He tapped his chin thoughtfully. "Mayhap."

She cocked her head, trying to understand how a seemingly intelligent man—well, leastways, not a drooling lackbrain—could give credence to dark magic.

"You must needs understand that the Norselands are harsh and wild, especially the far north where I live. 'Tis vastly different from Britain, even up here in Northumbria," he explained. "There are times during the summer when there is continuous daylight, and times during the winter when there is continuous darkness. In a land where darkness is a fact of life for long periods of time, 'tis easy to appreciate how my people have a superstitious bent. Out of the deep forest, down from the mountains, up from rivers and fjords they believe that the magical creatures come: the *hulders,* the *nisser,* the *fosse-grimmer*, the *nøkker.* Witches are naught, compared to this. Oh, I forgot. There are also the elves, the dwarfs and the trolls." He waggled his eyebrows playfully at the last word. "These are not all bad beasties, though. Some of them are quite playful, spurred by our god of mischief, Loki.

"Further, I wouldst tell you a tale of King Harald Fairhair. An intense loathing for wizards and magic did my grandsire have, despite the fact that one of his sons, Ragnvald Rettlebone of Hadeland, practiced such. In the end, he ordered his other son, Eric Bloodaxe, to kill his own son. Eric did not only that, but killed eighty other wizards as well, for good measure.

"So, yea, I believe in the black arts."

"Humph!" It was all nonsense, as far as Alinor was concerned. But then a sudden thought occurred to her. This fierce warrior could fight off her brothers with a swat of his hand, if he so chose. What if she went to the Norselands with him, for a short time, just till her brothers gave up on their latest matrimonial efforts? Wouldn't that be a way of solving both their problems—the Viking would fulfill his promise to deliver a "witch" to remove the curse, and she would escape a fourth wedding?

"Unhand me, Viking," she said then, looking down to her arm, still pinioned to the chair by his long-fingered grasp. "I would hear more of your mission. Exactly how long would it be afore you could return me to Northumbria?"

"My duty ends once I present you to King Anlaf."

She tilted her head in puzzlement.

"After the curse is removed, I'm fairly certain Anlaf would send you home with an armed escort, but by then the winter ice would have set in, I predict. So, I would guess you could be home by Easter."

Fairly certain? Then his other words snagged her attention. "Easter? Easter? That's six months from now. I can't be gone for that long. What of the winter weaving? And the spring lambing? And the first shearing? I have more than a hundred sheep to care for here at Graycote." She gave him a fulminating glower, then concluded, " 'Tis impossible."

"You have no choice, my lady."

Well, we shall see about that. I don't want to take drastic measures, but I will if you force my back to the wall, Viking. "Tell me again. Exactly which high Viking personage am I accused of cursing?"

"Are there so many?"

Are there so many? Alinor repeated snidely in her head. "No, there are not. I cannot remember even one." She paused as a quick flash of memory came to her. "Except . . . oh, surely you do not refer to that Viking assault on St. Beatrice's Abbey last year?"

He nodded. " 'Twas King Anlaf of Trondelag."

Her forehead furrowed with confusion. "I thought Haakon the Good was king of Norway."

"Well, yea, my uncle Haakon is the all-king of Norway, but there are many minor kings. My cousin Anlaf is the chieftain or low-king of a region in Trondelag."

"Your uncle . . . your cousin? Kings?" she sputtered.

"At last! Now you understand."

"Understand? Why, that brute—*your cousin*—was about to rape Sister Mary Esme."

He shrugged. "And you put a curse on him."

"I did?"

"And waved the magic veil?"

"Which magic veil?"

"The Virgin's Veil. And, by the by, do not forget to bring the blue veil with you. Anlaf will want to see it when you remove the curse."

Alinor crossed her eyes with frustration. "That blue veil was *my* headrail, and I was not waving it. It fell off my head in the tussle to get the barbarian off of Sister Mary Esme."

"You jest."

"And another thing, I may have cursed the man, but I did not put a curse on him. There is a difference."

"Dost thou try to befuddle me with words?"

That wouldn't take much.

"Did you or did you not proclaim, 'By the Virgin's Veil, may your manpart fall off if you do this evil thing'?"

There was a long, speaking silence during which Alinor let his words sink in. Her face heated with embarrassment, then, as she asked, with awe, "And did his manpart fall off?"

"Nay, it just took a right turn."

"It?"

"His manroot."

"It did *what?* Oh, I can barely credit what you say. His manpart took a right turn?" Alinor choked with laughter.

"It's not funny," he protested, slapping her heartily on the back to stop her choking.

"Oh, yea, it is. But please," she said, wiping at her tears with the edge of her headrail, "please do not tell me that you and that cloddish king think I would touch his . . . *root*."

Tykir waved a hand airily. "I know not of witchly rites for

straightening a man's lance. Touch it or touch it not, for all I care. Just remove the spell."

"And if I cannot do so?"

"There are laws held sacred at the Things—our governing bodies—where witches can be stoned or drowned. If they are bad witches, that is." He slitted his eyes to study her for a moment. "By the by, are you a good witch or a bad witch?"

"Aaarrrgh!"

"It matters not, actually. I misdoubt that Anlaf would wait for a Thing to be called if you cannot remove the curse."

"Oh?"

"Anlaf will, no doubt, just lop off your head."

The fool asked if she had a mood tail . . .

"You don't have to watch me every blessed minute," the witch sniped at him several hours later.

"Do I not?"

"A big, fearsome warrior like you! What have you to fear from a harmless little female like me?"

You were not harmless from the day you came squalling from the womb, I wager. Seems to me, I've heard that red hair and a shrewish temper go hand in hand. Or was that just something Bolthor put in one of his sagas? Enough! I waste my thoughts on nonsense.

"'Tis good you noticed my impressive stature," he said.

Thor's toenails! The nonsense in my head is spewing out my mouth now.

"How could I not? You block the entire door."

He was leaning his shoulder, casually, against the open door frame of the Lady Alinor's bedchamber, his arms folded across his chest. Block was a good choice of word on her part because he suspected she would bolt in an instant if he were not acting as the barrier to her freedom.

He tapped one booted foot with impatience as the wench . . . rather, the witch . . . or the lady . . . arranged a neat pile on her high bed of the garments she intended to take on her journey to Trondelag. Worst of all, there were *four* blue headrails, and none of them looked magical, or, for that matter, old enough to be the Blessed Virgin relic.

I swear, if she folds that gunna into one more perfect square and smoothes out every single wrinkle, I am going to stuff her belongings in my saddlebags and be done with it. Mayhap I will stuff her scrawny body in there, too, all neatly folded into squarish parts.

Clearly, she was employing a delaying tactic, but for what purpose he could not yet fathom. She appeared to be an intelligent woman . . . or as intelligent as any woman could be. She had to know her fate was sealed; she would be delivered to King Anlaf, willing or unwilling.

Still Tykir held his temper in check. A good soldier knew to wait for just the right moment to pounce. Lady Alinor didn't deceive him. The witch was up to some mischief. He saw the evidence in the nervous fluttering of her fingertips, and this was a woman not prone to flightiness. She had given in too quickly, in the end, to his demand that she accompany him to the Norselands. Being a mite stubborn himself on occasion, Tykir recognized a fellow mule. He grinned to himself at that mental picture, and how the missish Lady Alinor would hate that he put her in that animal category.

She cast him a sideways glance through narrowed, speculative eyes. "Wouldst consider a *danegeld?*"

"Aha! You think to bribe me now? With what? Mutton?"

She bristled at his ridicule of her precious sheep. On the way back to the keep, he'd noted with amusement that she had names for each of the bleating animals.

"Perchance I could gather together a few coin," she offered. The furtive cast in her eyes told him clearly that she hid something. Hmmm. Now that he thought on it, the number of sheep and cattle he'd seen on the fells, along with the well-cultivated fields, bespoke a more prosperous estate than exhibited in Graycote's austere keep or in Lady Alinor's jewelless attire. Mayhap she hoarded her gold. But for what purpose?

Really, it was no matter to him whether she was wealthy as a Baghdad sultan or poor as a landless cotter.

He shook his head. "I promised Anlaf a witch, and a witch he shall have."

"All for the sake of a horse?" she scoffed.

He'd told her moments ago about all the trouble he'd gone to since the king's emissary had come to him in Birka, including Anlaf's wily inducements to seal the mission. Her scoffing tone irritated him. Whether he'd been barmy or not to take on this mission was his concern, and whether he did so out of boredom or for a fine stallion did not merit her criticism.

"Do not forget the slave girl," he pointed out in a deliberate attempt to rattle her composure. "The one with the bells." For some reason, he'd mentioned the horse and the jingling Samirah, but he hadn't told her about Adam. The less people who knew the better, especially his sister Rain and her husband, Selik. They would go off in a rage if they discovered Anlaf's perfidy regarding their adopted son. In fact, their rage might cause a whole bloody war over an incident that Tykir could handle by simply delivering a witch.

Her upper lip curled with contempt. "Men are the same everywhere, are they not? It does not matter if they be Norseman or Englishman, men are led by the tail betwixt their legs."

Tykir was startled by her blunt words and realized that she was referring to his slave girl comment. He was not accustomed to such crudity from a lady, but he forced his face to remain expressionless. "My lady, you exceed yourself. You would do best not to earn my scorn. Speaking of tails, how much trouble does yours cause?"

"I . . . am . . . not . . . a . . . witch," she repeated, a refrain that was becoming tiresome to him.

"I would think it could pose problems when you attend your needs in the garderobe," he said, as if she had not even spoken. He'd already noticed that she hated it when he ignored her words. "Or riding a horse. Oh, oh, I thought of something . . ."

"Now, there is a rare event."

He frowned at her impertinent interruption. "I am loath to ask, but . . . do you have a mood tail?"

He could tell she did not want to ask but could not help herself. "A mood tail?"

"You know . . . does it wag of its own volition when you are in a happy mood, like a puppy? And droop when you are in a despondent mood, like when the blood curdles in your witchly cauldron?"

"I find no humor in your foolery." She bit her bottom lip with frustration. There was something appealing about the woman when her feathers were ruffled, but he just could not see past those hideous freckles. And even though a crisp wimple covered her bright red hair, he knew it was there underneath, just waiting to spring forth. Moreover, she had no breasts to speak of, as far as he could tell. His preferences did not necessarily lean toward the buxom, but flatter than two eggs on a hot rock held little enticement, either.

"Keep your eyes in their sockets, Viking," she admonished.

Aha! Another feather ruffled. He liked ruffling her. So he added, "Oh, Holy Thor! How could I have forgotten the most important thing? What do you do with your tail when you spread your legs for the bed sport?"

She gasped, then quickly masked her shock with a bland face. "Since I have been a widow for a year and more, bedsport is hardly something I engage in. Have you all-knowing Vikings found a way to engage in bed sport without a mate?" She batted her eyelashes at him as if she was serious, while in fact she mocked him. "Verily, there was not all that much mating even when I had a mate . . . not that I ever complained about that."

"Oh, lady, that is exactly the kind of provocative remark you should not make to a Viking."

He grinned at her lasciviously.

She glared at him.

"So, do not distract me with tempting propositions. We must be on our way."

"Tem-tempting," she sputtered.

"By the by, Rurik and Bolthor and I were wondering if you ever dance naked in the forest."

"Dance . . . dance . . . oh, you are the most ill-bred, insufferable, loathsome, lecherous lout I have ever encountered in all my life. And believe me, I have met more than a few."

"Well, yea, but enough compliments for now. We have no time for man-woman banter."

She drew herself up with affront. "Turn aside whilst I gather my undergarments. 'Tis not meet that you should ogle my intimate apparel."

"Ogle? Me?" Tykir stiffened. "Lady, despite my mention of temptation, do not delude yourself. Your intimate apparel holds no allure for me. Nor do your intimate *parts*. Your virtue will not be forfeit in my company, I assure you."

Just then, Bolthor approached from the corridor. "I have gathered provisions from the kitchen, and Rurik says the horses are ready."

Tykir looked toward Lady Alinor, eyebrows arched in question of her readiness.

A flush of panic swept her features, causing the freckles to stand out even more. However, before he could assure her of her safety—leastways till they got to Anlaf's court—a loud rumbling came from Tykir's gut, followed by a most painful cramping. At the same time, bile rose without warning into his throat.

Startled, Tykir glanced first at Bolthor, who was gazing at him with concern as he bent over at the waist, clutching his midsection, then at the Lady Alinor, who had the effrontery to grin. He thought he heard her murmur, "'Twould seem I had a choice after all." Without another word, he made a mad rush for the garderobe.

There were two things Tykir heard Bolthor say behind him

as he laid one palm over his stomach and another over his mouth, praying he would make the privy before he embarrassed himself: "Lady Alinor, if you have put a curse on my master Tykir, I will light the torch beneath your stake myself. And it will be a slow-burning fire." Then, "Methinks a good title would be, 'Tykir the Great and the Raging Bowel.'"

Bubble, bubble, toil and trouble, for sure . . .

Two days later, Tykir sat atop his horse in the inner bailey, about to leave Graycote, finally. He was weak-kneed as an untried boy after his first swiving, and he'd lost so much weight he resembled a starvling, but he was alive, praise be to the gods, and there had been times in these past two days when he questioned whether he'd survive the violent heaving and purging.

"I still say you should have let me kill the scurvy witch when first we realized she had laid a curse on your entrails," Bolthor complained. "Mayhap the spell would have been removed earlier."

All of the castle folk—three dozen of them, from the high castellan to the lowly kitchen carls—were barricaded in the stable under Bolthor's stern-faced guard. When Tykir and his comrades reached a village later today, or mayhap even tomorrow, they would make sure someone was sent back to unlock them. There was plenty of water to share with the horses, and it would do none of them harm to go a day without food.

Bolthor left his post and mounted his horse upon seeing Rurik emerging from the manor's great hall. He led the much-subdued Lady Alinor by a rope tied round her neck, though her eyes sparked green fire of outrage at her mistreatment by her three captors, including himself. Hah! He would like to speak with her about *real* mistreatment.

Welt marks stood prominent on her right cheek from Rurik's slap yestermorn when she finally confessed her perfidy, though she'd claimed 'twas a mere herb, not a deadly curse. Furthermore, she'd avowed that the herbal potion was intended to delay his departure from Graycote, not cause his departure from this world. If she'd wanted to kill him, she would have given the tainted drink to Rurik and Bolthor, as well, she contended. Tykir could have accepted that explanation if she hadn't then refused to explain what purpose could be served by a delay.

That's when Rurik had wielded his open palm on her. It had taken both Tykir and Bolthor to hold Rurik back from more permanent injury. No doubt Rurik would have liked to mark the witch's face permanently, just as his had been.

That side of her face was swollen and bluish-yellow with healing—a stark foil against her pale skin highlighted with the ungodly freckles. She was fortunate Rurik hadn't loosened all her teeth with the force of his blow. Rurik's hatred of witches had intensified threefold since their arrival at Graycote.

Tykir stared at her dispassionately. Violence was a common happenstance in a Viking's life, especially in battle, but it was rarely directed at women. He could feel no sympathy for this woman, though, since he had suffered so much worse at her hands.

He supposed they should be fearful in her presence after what she had done to him and Anlaf. But the three of them now wore makeshift wooden crosses hanging from leather thongs on their chests. It was Bolthor's idea. A sure method for warding off evil spirits, including a witch's magic, or so he asserted. Plus, they had put their braies on backwards to confuse the witch—another of Bolthor's bright ideas—something that was inconvenient when visiting the garderobe for a mere piss. Finally, Rurik had brought forth a small vial of holy water he'd been given by a monk in Dublin. Periodically, these past two days, Rurik sprinkled each of them with the blessed liquid. He intended to replenish his supply at the minster in Jorvik.

When Rurik had doused the witch with a generous splash of the holy water, they'd all backed away, fully expecting her skin to sizzle and burn. But nothing had happened, except she resembled a sodden rooster.

Tykir wasn't so sure about all these maneuvers, especially when Lady Alinor snickered the first time he explained their purpose, including the backwards braies.

"Are you an idiot?" she'd asked.

"Nay!" he'd snapped. *Mayhap,* he'd thought.

Two days had gone by without another witchly spell; perchance they were safe for now. And it was past time to leave this bloody Saxon land and return to Trondelag, where witches and trolls and magical events were the stuff of legends. He could scarce wait till this whole witchly mission was over and done. If it weren't for Adam, he would have abandoned the ill-fated assignment sennights ago.

Because the Lady Alinor's hands were bound in front of her, Rurik put his hands on either side of her waist and lifted her up to her saddle, none too gently. She wore loose underbraies so she could sit astride, something she had protested vehemently, but he'd insisted upon for the sake of speed. The lady's snarl was her only reaction to being touched by a man who clearly repulsed her. With good reason.

In a rare moment of consciousness these past two days, Tykir had discovered that Rurik was piling tree limbs and kindling in the courtyard . . . enough wood to feed a huge bonfire. In the midst of this was a wooden stake to which Rurik intended to place the witch the moment Tykir died and went off to Valhalla.

Luckily, Tykir had not died. Lucky for the witch, as well.

But the witch's pyre still stood as a reminder in the courtyard for all to see. And the grim-faced Alinor was all too aware of its continuing existence.

In the process of arranging the woman on the shifting mare, Rurik jerked her restrained hands forward so she would be able to grasp the front of the saddle. Bolthor had already taken her reins in hand and would lead her horse.

"You brute!" the foolish woman commented to Rurik.

"You daughter of Satan!" Rurik countered

"If I had real powers, I would have struck you dead long ago."

"Desist!" Tykir roared. " 'Twill be two or three sennights, at the least, on land and sea, till we get to Anlaf's court. Let me establish here and now that I refuse to listen to you two bickering endlessly the entire time."

"But he—" she started to say.

"But she—" Rurik started to say.

"But nothing!" Tykir growled, rubbing his forehead. It was an ill omen of things to come if he had a headache even before they began their journey. He fixed Lady Alinor with his gaze now. "You do know how to ride, don't you?"

"Hah! 'Tis a fine time to be asking."

The expression on his face must have alerted her that she was treading a fine line. "Yea, I can ride, though I've never done it with my hands tied."

He shrugged. "Either ride thus or on my lap."

She looked as if he'd suggested her riding him, instead of his horse.

"I can ride my own horse," she said in a strangled voice.

"Fine. Let us be off then."

"Come, Beast," Rurik called out cheerily to his wolf-hound, who stood at Tykir's side.

The dog lifted its head haughtily and refused to obey his master's command—something he never used to do. The animal had switched his allegiance to Alinor ever since Rurik had taken her sheep and her mangy sheepdog, Beauty, to a far pasture. Thereafter, Beast had been alternately despondent and mad with frustration, howling till the wee hours of the morning. 'Twould seem Beast was smitten with Beauty. Their constant chasing of each other about the keep these past two days, with a dozen dumb sheep following after, had driven all the servants nigh mad.

"So be it then, traitor." Rurik nudged his knees against his stallion's sides to prompt him into motion. At the same time, he reached over and slapped Alinor's mare on the rump.

The mare bolted.

And Lady Alinor slipped ignominiously to the ground, smack onto her bottom. Since she appeared merely chagrined, not injured, Tykir assumed her tail had buffered the fall.

All three men burst out laughing.

"I thought you said you could ride," Tykir gasped out.

"You could have given me fair warning, you . . . you . . ."

Bolthor was laughing so hard that his one eye was watering, and Rurik smirked with delight.

"Curse you all, you heathen louts," she shouted, scrambling clumsily to her feet. "I hope . . . I hope . . ."

Just then a flock of winter geese came flying overhead, honking loudly . . . and splattered the three men. Lady Alinor had the good sense, or the mental forewarning, to duck under her mare's belly. Thus, she was the only one unanointed by the vile "rain." Tears of laughter were streaming down her face when she emerged from her hiding place.

Tykir exchanged a meaningful look with his two comrades as they all attempted to brush off the goose droppings with scraps of cloth. And then they exclaimed as one:

"She really is a witch."

CHAPTER THREE

⬥

FIVE DAYS LATER

Trouble followed him like . . . sheep . . .

"Tykir! Ty-kir Thork-sson! What in the name of heaven are you up to now?"

Tykir put his face in his hands at the familiar female voice addressing him from the steps of the royal palace in Jorvik. "Eadyth," he murmured under his breath. "Just what I do not need!"

Standing near the entrance to the king's garth, where his uncle, Eric Bloodaxe, the Norse king, resided, was Tykir's sister-by-marriage, Eadyth. All of Britain was under Saxon rule, except for this incessant splinter, Northumbria, which was once more in the hands of the Vikings. And if Eadyth, a Saxon lady, was in Jorvik, the Viking seat of Northumbria, then that could only mean that her husband, his half-Viking brother Eirik, lord of Ravenshire, was close by.

With Eirik and Eadyth as witnesses, he would never, ever live down this misadventure. Never.

"What are you doing with all those sheep?" Eadyth started in on him. "You hate sheep. You always claimed your grandmother's sheep smelled to high Valhalla. Are you trading in sheep now, instead of amber?"

He groaned.

"Who is that?" Alinor asked. The witch was astride the mare next to him.

"My sister-by-marriage, Lady Eadyth," he informed her. "She is married to my brother Eirik, lord of Ravenshire."

"You are kin to a Saxon lord?" Alinor's eyebrows lifted with astonishment. "You have blood links to Norse kings and Saxon lords. What next? A Byzantine emperor?"

He would have said something witsome and biting back to her, but he never got the chance. Eadyth, fists on hips, was railing at him again. "Why are the hands tied on the woman sitting on that horse? Why does she have a rope dangling from her neck? And why is she glaring at you so? Are those fingermarks on her cheek? Did you strike a woman, Tykir? Did you? For shame!"

Lady Alinor did look awful. She'd long since lost her wimple and headrail. Luckily, they were not blue, or he would have had to go chasing back after them, in case it was the Virgin's Veil. Her hair stood out like a curly-leafed fire bush. Though autumn was in full bloom, her pale complexion was sunburned . . . not a pretty picture with the freckles standing out even more. Her clothing was dirty and disheveled since she'd refused to allow him or Rurik or Bolthor to watch—uh, guard—her whilst she changed.

He heard Rurik and Bolthor chuckle behind him.

"Why are you three dolts wearing your braies backwards? Is it some kind of lackbrain jest? And crosses . . . since when have you turned the religious zealot, Tykir?"

Rurik snickered, but not for long.

"Rurik, what happened to your face? Did you fall in a vat of woad dye? Do you attempt to stand out in a crowd? Ah, vanity ever was your weakness, and you no doubt think that silly mark is attractive. Well, it's not."

Now it was Rurik's turn to groan.

"And Bolthor, how nice to see you again. Have you come up with any new sagas?"

"For a certainty, my lady." Bolthor beamed like a bloody moon. "My master, Tykir the Great, has been so busy I can scarce keep track of all his exploits."

"I can just imagine," Eadyth said, eyeing Tykir with dry humor as she silently mouthed, "Tykir the *Great?*"

After five days of riding up one fell and over another, in the company of the most shrewish witch from hell, followed by a smitten sheepdog and a half-dozen sheep who refused to stay in their pens despite being returned to Graycote *three* times, Tykir had thought he'd experienced the worst days of his life. He soon found out that the worst was about to come.

Just then, an arrow whizzed by his head, barely missing his right ear, and embedded itself in a passing cart. Amazed, he turned to see a group of armed horsemen approaching. Just entering the high-arched gates that separated the Norse palace from the Coppergate merchant sector of Jorvik, the attackers were still some distance away—at least twenty paces—way too far for even an expert archer to aim his bow.

Startled passersby strolling the stalls of the tradesmen, as well as personages about to enter the palace grounds, gaped with alarm at the peril entering their midst. Many ran for cover or ducked under the canopies of their trading booths.

"*Helvtis!*" he swore upon seeing that the two noblemen in front had bushy red hair and green eyes. "Damn!"

He and Rurik and Bolthor exchanged looks of incredulity, even as they instinctively went into battle readiness. Reaching for weapons and shields, they prepared to fight off whatever foe threatened them. But what man in his right mind would risk starting a fight in the midst of the business center of the city, or so near the palace and its fighting forces?

One of the red-haired miscreants yelled, "Halt, you whoreson of the North!" He was waving a sword in the air so wildly that Tykir feared he might chop off his own head.

The other red-haired miscreant seemed to have trouble staying upright on his horse and was holding on to the reins with both hands. From the bow and quiver slung over his shoulder, Tykir assumed he was the ill-trained archer who'd attempted to shoot him. The lackwit managed to inform Alinor in a shrill shout, "Never fear, sister dear, we have come to rescue you from the devil's spawn."

Devil's spawn? Is he referring to me?

"Eadyth," Tykir ordered, "get into the palace, out of danger's way." She was staring at the impending action, openmouthed, as if it was a jester's play. "Make haste now!" he roared, and she nigh jumped out of her skin.

Bolthor had already released his halberd, affectionately named "Head Splitter," from its specially designed leather strap at the side of his horse. Grinning with anticipation, Bolthor hefted the long-handled battle-ax in one hand. On more occasions than Tykir could count, he'd seen Bolthor save the day in a fierce fight by severing an enemy from crown to cock with just one swift blow from "Head Splitter."

Rurik pulled a leather helmet with a metal noseguard over his head, lay his favorite sword, "Death Stalker," across his lap, and grinned. He probably relished the prospect of spilt blood, since they'd not exercised their battle skills for a long time.

As the attackers approached, Tykir noticed another nobleman trailing behind—a short, balding man of at least sixty who was as wide as he was tall. His poor horse looked swaybacked with the excess weight. "No heathen barbarian steals what is mine," he asserted. He, too, was waving a sword in a dangerous fashion.

"Halt, if you value your lives," Tykir warned the group, standing up in his stirrups, sword and shield raised high. The whole time, he surveyed the hird: twelve soldiers, in addition to the three noblemen. He and Rurik and Bolthor could handle the lot themselves with ease.

Suddenly, in the midst of his assessment, Tykir understood why Lady Alinor had attempted to delay their departure from Graycote. She'd been hoping for her brothers' arrival. And could that human lard barrel bringing up the rear guard be her latest betrothed? Had she poisoned him so that they would have time to come to her rescue?

His eyes met hers in accusation.

She shrugged.

"And these would be the Lords Egbert and Hebert, I presume?"

"Indeed," she said, with less enthusiasm than should be expected from a woman who'd been saved from a fate worse than death—Vikings.

"And the lord of Lard?"

Her eyes twinkled with merriment at that misname, the first show of genuine pleasure he'd witnessed since their first meeting. She was almost pretty when she smiled . . . if one could overlook the freckles . . . which he could not, of course.

"Cedric," she answered.

"I certainly hope you intend to be on top on your wedding night, lest you be crushed to death."

She made a most unbecoming snarling sound.

Another arrow flew by, far over his head, shot by one of her brothers, the one with the unsteady saddle seat.

He placed his battle shield in front of his face nonchalantly, fixing a questioning glare alternately at the distant archer and then at Lady Alinor.

"Egbert," she answered his silent query.

"Is he trying to warn me off?" Tykir asked.

"Nay. He's just inept."

He and Rurik and Bolthor dismounted quickly and drew their swords, prepared to fight off the attackers, who now galloped into the courtyard of the castle. Hebert almost flew headfirst out of the saddle when his horse came to an abrupt halt.

Lady Alinor sat atop her horse like a bloody queen, oblivious to the impending danger. In truth, these misguided knights would not harm her, not deliberately. But they might accidentally kill the very person they wanted to rescue. With a muttered curse, Tykir pulled her from the saddle and shoved her behind him, where she fell to her knees. Meanwhile the sheep were bleating, the two dogs were barking, Eadyth was screaming into the palace doors, "Eirik, Eirik, come save your brother," and the riderless horses were bumping into each other with fright as they tried to escape the melee.

Even worse, Viking soldiers poured from the guard house and passing Saxon soldiers rushed to their allies' aid. There was a shaky truce betwixt the Saxon and Viking folks in Northumbria, though that might change after today, Tykir thought.

Tykir said a silent prayer then, to both the Christian and Norse gods. "Oh, Lord, and Mighty Odin, please spare me from the fury of bumbling idiots . . . and witches."

And thus the bewitching began . . .

Alinor could not believe the scene unfolding before her in the palace bailey, a short distance from the bustling town center.

Swords were clanking, fists were flying and all around were the sounds of fighting men—grunts, shouts, cries of pain. There were at least two dozen men on either side of the fray now, and more were jumping in by the moment.

The troll and his comrades in trolldom were proving themselves expert fighters. Tykir and Rurik employed swords, while Bolthor swung a monstrously lethal broadax. And all the men on both sides seemed to be enjoying themselves immensely, as most men did. Well, mayhap not her brothers so much. While they relished a good manly fight, they never were much for the spilling of their own blood.

Alinor scrambled to her feet and out of the way, finding herself next to the lady wringing her hands with concern on the palace steps, the one married to Tykir's brother. She was the most beautiful woman Alinor had ever seen. Being at least a half head taller than Alinor, she had wisps of silver-blond hair framing a perfectly shaped face under a white wimple and a pale green headrail that matched an exquisite, darker green gown embroidered with silver thread in a floral design. She was not young—she must have seen more than thirty years—and yet her skin was smooth as silk, the color of new cream, marred by no imperfections, except for a single enticing mole above her lip. Not a freckle in sight.

Alinor didn't care about such things. And yet she felt somewhat like a barnyard hen in the presence of a silver swan. It was not a pleasant feeling.

The fighting was tapering off. Three Saxons and one Viking lay on the ground, wounded, but not mortally so. Egbert, Hebert and Cedric, not surprisingly, were nowhere to be seen. No doubt they'd scurried off at first glimpse of Bolthor's formidable size . . . or his battle-ax, raised high overhead, ready to crack the skull of any foe who crossed his path. Rurik was holding one protesting Saxon to the ground with a booted foot planted on his chest and a deadly sword pressed to his throat. Tykir wiped a sweaty brow with one forearm but ignored the blood streaming from his bruised nose as he continued to engage in the strike-and-withdraw exercise of swordplay with a Saxon unlucky enough not to have been struck down with a minor wound.

Alinor realized in that instant that she was missing an opportunity for escape. Slowly, one sideways step at a time, she sidled away from Lady Eadyth, whose attention was still fixed on an uncommonly handsome, dark-haired knight, presumably her husband, who was rounding up the wounded Saxon soldiers who were able to stand. It must be Tykir's brother, Eirik. *Hell's teeth, did good looks abound in the Thorksson family? Or amongst all Vikings?*

If she could just make it through the gatehouse, she would be able to meld into the busy streets of the market town. Just a few more steps. The guards' attention was diverted to the fight, leaving the entryway without surveillance.

She pivoted abruptly then and bolted toward the open gates.

"Aaarrrgh!" she choked out as the noose around her neck tightened and jerked her head back.

"Were you going somewhere, witchling?" a smooth masculine voice whispered against her ear. One arm wrapped around her waist from behind, drawing her flush against his hard body.

"'Twould seem I'm going to hell," she said in a suffocated whisper.

"For a certainty," he agreed, nuzzling her hair . . . just to annoy her. "Now, you have two punishments to anticipate, my lady. One for the poison spell. Another for calling your brothers down on us. Oh, wait . . . I misspoke. There are three punishments. The third will be for your attempted escape." He licked her exposed ear as a final insult, and Alinor felt the outrage all the way to her toes. And, oddly, some places in between as well.

She struggled against his imprisoning arms. "You bloodthirsty brute! You enjoyed that fight, didn't you?"

"Better to be the crow than the carrion." He laughed and tugged on her neck rope.

Alinor had forgotten about the rope, which still dangled from her neck. She turned slowly within Tykir's grasp. He tickled her nose with the frayed end of her rope, which he must have grabbed while she attempted to escape. If she'd been thinking properly, she could have loosened it with her tied hands and pulled it over her head while all the fighting was going on.

But nay, Alinor realized, escape would have been impossible, even then. Glancing behind Tykir, she saw that the six sheep, one ram and two dogs had been following after her, bleating and barking a traitorous chorus that couldn't have been more clear to the Viking: "There she goes, there she goes, there she goes."

Alinor sighed with dismay. She would have to come up with a new plan, since she obviously couldn't depend on Egbert or Hebert to rescue her. Plainly, they were no match for the superior fighting abilities of these Norsemen. Before she had a chance to think of a new plan, though, Tykir the

Troll bent his legs slightly, grabbed her around the knees and flung her over his shoulder. Then he headed back toward the Norse palace, with the dogs and sheep protesting loudly and masculine laughter and shouts of encouragement surrounding them as they passed.

"I take exception to your hasty retreat, Lady Alinor. Do you not favor my company?" Tykir teased.

"About as much as I favor the company of slime-bellied snakes." She tried to squirm free, pounding his back with her bound fists, missing half the time because she was blinded by her hair hanging down to the backs of his knees. He chuckled at her antics and clamped a large paw over her posterior.

That stilled her . . . for a moment. "You brute . . . you animal . . . you . . . you . . . *Viking*."

"Tykir, tell us true," she heard Rurik call out with an ominous snicker, "does she have a tail?"

He rubbed her entire bottom, side to side, even the crease, before announcing, "Nay, there is no tail, but methinks I will have to examine the situation more thoroughly . . . in private . . . without these cumbersome garments."

More male laughter followed, with ribald remarks on exactly how he might proceed in that regard.

If the blood were not rushing to Alinor's head, she would have told him what she thought of his outrageous suggestion and his comrade's crudity. Instead, she took a good bite out of his shoulder and would not let go.

His howl of pain rang through the courtyard just before his knees buckled at the surprising attack. He tripped forward, causing Alinor to go with him. She landed on her back, her bound hands raised overhead, her legs spread wide, with the hem of her gunna hiked knee-high and the Viking troll on top of her, with his face planted in her midsection . . . laughing.

"How . . . dare . . . you?" she sputtered, not sure if she was more outraged by his position atop her or by his laughter.

She lowered her bound hands and grasped a hunk of hair, forcing his head off her stomach so she could address the lout directly.

His nose was still bleeding. A bruise above his right eye was beginning to swell and turn the socket black and blue. Whiskers shadowed his face, though she knew he'd shaved just that morn before they broke camp outside Jorvik. His blond hair stood up on end where she still grasped it.

Despite all that, the insufferable man was godly handsome.

She released his hair as if it had suddenly caught fire. Hearing a chuckle, she peered up and noticed all the faces staring down at them . . . some in wonder, like the Lady Eadyth and her husband Eirik; some in amusement, like Rurik and the Viking soldiers; some in contemplation, like Bolthor, who was mumbling something about sagas and poems and witchly tales . . . or was it tails?

Alinor groaned, then groaned again as Tykir raised himself on his elbows, still laughing, and adjusted his body over hers.

His laughter stopped immediately.

Alinor's eyes went huge with amazement at the hard object prodding betwixt her legs. It was unlike any of the limp threads she'd experienced in her three mates. More like the whole bloody spindle.

Tykir groaned, too, but his was a decidedly masculine sound.

"My lord, are you in pain?" Bolthor asked.

Tykir shook his head. He appeared unable to speak.

"Dost thou have a wound?" Lord Eirik inquired solicitously. "Shall we send for the healer from the hospitium? Or our sister Rain?"

Tykir continued to shake his head, harder now.

"Is it the witch?"

• Tykir nodded.

"A witch? *A witch?*" Lady Eadyth squealed with horror.

"Yea, the witch with the Virgin's Veil," Bolthor told Lady Eadyth. "Lady Alinor is a witch."

Eirik let out a snort of disbelief. "There is no such thing."

"Hah! You would not say such if you were King Anlaf," Rurik interjected.

"King Anlaf? Our cousin Anlaf?" Lord Eirik seemed genuinely puzzled. "What has he to do with witchcraft?"

"This witch," Rurik said, pointing to Alinor, "has put a spell on King Anlaf."

"A spell?" Lord Eirik asked dumbly.

"Yea, a spell that made his manroot take a right turn," Rurik explained.

Lord Eirik and Lady Eadyth exchanged a look, then burst out laughing, as did all the Viking soldiers and lookers-on who'd gathered at the outlandish scene. The only ones not participating in the mirth were Rurik and Bolthor, who were chagrined at the lack of belief in their tale.

Alinor and Tykir were not laughing either.

Tykir held her gaze the whole time, and finally he whispered in a low, seductive voice, as he insinuated himself more intimately against the cradle of her hips, "I am bewitched."

Rurik must have overheard because he commented, "Oh-ho! She must be a witch then, for never would you be attracted to such a pig-ugly wench."

"Rurik! For shame!" Lady Eadyth chastised.

Alinor was barely aware of all the conversations swirling around her. All she could do was gaze back at Tykir, unable to break eye contact. New, unbelievable sensations swept her body. They were horrible, horrible, horrible. And so wonderful she could scarcely breathe.

I am the one bewitched, she admitted to herself then. And this time when she prayed silently, the well-known Anglo-Saxon prayer took on a new format: "Oh, Lord, from the *passion* of a Northman, please protect me."

* * *

And then he took care of business . . . man-business . . .

"I still say we should ride to Selik and Rain's estate and tell them of Adam's plight," Eirik said once again. He'd been saying the same, in one form or another, over the past hour.

"Nay," Tykir insisted. "You know they would overreact and demand to come with me. They have enough to worry about with the orphanage, Rain's hospitium and their four children, not to mention her being with child again. Besides, Adam will be safe at Anlaf's court till I arrive . . . just restricted a bit."

They both smiled at the image of Adam being restricted. Ever since he'd been a wild youthling, rescued from the Jorvik streets with his sister Adela, no one had been able to hold Adam down. Tykir looked forward to seeing just how Anlaf had managed to confine the man who'd traveled to many foreign lands, despite his young years, in his quest to become a healer, like Rain.

Tykir was sitting with his brother on the stone steps of the king's personal steam house within the palace gardens, now brown and dormant with the coming of winter. A young male house servant lifted a heavy wooden bucket of water and tossed it onto the white-hot rocks, causing more steam to issue forth. Soon, they would wash off their perspiration in the icy waters of the adjoining bathhouse, where female thralls would assist them in shaving off the day's whiskers and donning clean garments.

Vikings did like their personal comforts, cleanliness being one of them. It was why so many females in so many lands fell at their feet and into their bed furs, in Tykir's opinion. Oh, he and his fellow Norsemen liked to boast of their great looks and superior talents in the bedding, but he suspected that ofttimes it just boiled down to their smelling a mite less than other men.

"But why involve the witch?"

Tykir shrugged. "He asked for a witch in exchange for Adam. At the time, it seemed the expedient thing to do. You know I could have gained Adam's release, but it would have involved much coin or fighting. If I'd known then of the excessive delays I would encounter, I never would have bothered."

"But to kidnap a lady of high station, Tykir? Really, 'tis pushing the bounds of propriety, even for you."

"A *witch* of high station," he corrected and took a long sip of mead from the goblet next to him. "And since when have I ever claimed to be proper?"

"Eadyth will try her best at matchmaking, you know."

"With a witch?" Tykir hooted.

Eirik shrugged. "Well, can you blame her? All her best efforts with every other kind of female have come to naught."

Just then, one of the female thralls walked in, carrying a pile of linen towels. She was blond and buxom, and Tykir wasn't certain, but he thought he knew her. In truth, he might have bedded her once or twice in the past. The woman did a little curtsy and gazed at him shyly.

He winked.

She blushed.

Eirik made a grunting sound of disgust. "I think you should come back to Ravenshire with us for the winter."

Tykir shook his head, but his attention was on the woman who was bending over to pick up some items of dirty clothing he and Eirik had tossed on the ground. Her backside was in the air. Yea, Tykir recognized the woman now.

"Why not?"

"Why not what?" He turned back to his brother, who was grinning in a knowing fashion and shaking his head at his obvious distraction. "Oh . . . you mean, why not return to Northumbria? I might have if I'd gathered the witch sennights ago, as I'd planned. Now, there will be no time left, even if I make haste, to get to Hedeby, then Anlaf's court, then home for the winter."

Eirik pressed a hand to his thigh with concern. "Ah, Tykir! Is the leg bothering you overmuch?"

"Just in the winter. 'Tis why I prefer to be snug in my own homestead. Then, too, I want to go to the Baltic lands come spring for the first amber harvest of the season."

"I worry about you, Tykir. I have not always been there when you needed me. I would make up for past mistakes."

"Do not concern yourself over me, brother," he said, rising up stark naked before the servant girl, who still lingered. Without saying a word, he lifted the vixen into his arms and carried her, screeching with delight, into the bathhouse, where cleanliness was not his main intent . . . leastways, not right away.

Just before the door closed after him, Eirik remarked, "We haven't finished our talk. What will you do with the witch?"

Tykir gave a two-word answer, coarse and explicit.

But he didn't mean it.

Really.

Women and gossip . . . a universal pasttime . . .

"Tykir is really not a bad sort at all," Eadyth insisted as she poured a pail of clean water over Alinor's soap-lathered hair. The unruly strands hung down to her waist when unbound.

Eadyth had insisted that Alinor call her by her given name several hours past, when they'd left the company of the men back at the palace, excepting Bolthor, who stood guard downstairs. Tykir, his brother and the other men had spoken of a visit to the bathhouse at the palace, where they would steam off the dirt and grime of "battle." And regale each other with overblown tales of conquest in the little skirmish they'd just ended.

"In fact, Tykir is one of the most charming men I've ever met. And that includes my husband, Eirik, who can be most . . . ah, persuasive, when he wants to be." Eadyth flashed Alinor a secretive smile, as if Alinor would understand perfectly. Hah! No man had ever exerted himself to be charming to Alinor. Certainly not her three aged husbands, who'd believed they were doing her a favor by marrying her.

As to that other assertion . . . Alinor snorted her opinion of Tykir being proclaimed the most charming man in Eadyth's acquaintance. Eadyth must live in a nunnery. "He is a troll," Alinor contended as she parted the wet swaths of her hair to peer up at the woman with disbelief.

Undaunted, Eadyth countered, "Well, of course. All men are trolls betimes."

Alinor couldn't be concerned about Tykir or the Vikings or even her captivity right now. She was taking too much pleasure in her first bath in over a week. Sitting in a copper tub, she sighed at the joy of mere soap and water. They were in the second-floor bedchamber of Gyda, an elderly Viking widow who was a longtime friend of the Thorksson family. As Alinor bathed, Gyda sat in a straight-backed chair, working a hand loom and listening intently to Eadyth's palace gossip.

"I can scarce believe that Eric Bloodaxe is king once again," Gyda commented, her fingers weaving the various colored threads into an intricate Norse pattern. "He is like a pesky fly that keeps coming back, no matter how often swatted away. I have no love of the Saxons, of course," she said, casting an apologetic glance at Alinor, "but he has been a thorn in the side of King Edred off and on for years now. I wish he would either leave or manage to stay in power here in Northumbria."

"King Eric is uncle to my husband and Tykir, but a more ruthless man I have never met," Eadyth explained to Alinor, who was lathering up her hair again.

"Even when they were babes, their father, Thork, could not acknowledge them for fear Eric would come after them," Gyda added. "That is why they lived with me and my Olaf for many years of their youth, apart from their beloved father, who went off Jomsviking to protect them. Orphans, they were, for all purposes, even with living kin."

Alinor paused her hair washing. "I don't understand. How could the father's abandonment protect the sons?"

"Ah! You do not know how Eric Bloodaxe got his name then," Eadyth declared and glanced toward Gyda. Both women shook their heads in disgust. "King Harald Fairhair, one of the most powerful rulers in Norway, was the father of dozens of sons and daughters alike by his numerous wives and mistresses. He practiced the *more danico*. Eric was ruthless from an early age in his pursuit of his father's crown. 'Tis a fact that many of his brothers died under his blade to feed that ambition. Thus the name Eric Bloodaxe."

"And Tykir and Eirik's father—Thork, methinks you called him—how did he fit into the picture?" Alinor asked.

"Thork never had any interest in a kingship, and he was illegitimate, besides. But though Eric's blood was legitimate, he was hated by the Norse people for his cruelty," Eadyth said. "There was the unfounded fear on Eric's part that while Thork disdained a crown, his sons might not."

"And so Thork pretended at first that he had no sons, abandoning the babes to the care of others. They were forbidden to call him father, and never did he give them a warm word or gesture of affection. Then later, when word got out that they were indeed his sons, he was forced to pretend an indifference." Gyda clicked her tongue as her eyes clouded over with unpleasant memories. "And his overprotection was warranted. There was a time . . . I remember it well . . . when an evil Viking villain, Ivar the Terrible, chopped off Eirik's little finger and sent it to Ravenshire in a parchment, all to lure Thork to his death. Which was the final result, in the end. Death. Both Thork's and my husband's, Olaf."

Eadyth reached over and patted Gyda's quaking shoulders.

"What about their mothers?" Alinor was attempting to break the grimness that had overtaken their conversation.

"Thea, a Saxon thrall, was Eirik's mother. She died in the birthing," Gyda answered. "But Tykir . . . well, his mother Asbol was a Viking princess who abandoned the boy when he was still in swaddling clothes. Thork offered to marry her, 'tis said, but she sought a nobler marriage, and never once wanted to see her child over the years."

All of the women exchanged appalled looks at that unnatural behavior for a mother.

"They were such lonely children," Gyda continued, "raised here in Jorvik by me and Olaf, then at Ravenshire by Dar and Aud, their grandparents, till their death, but I think Tykir suffered most, being the youngest. I remember how the little boy would ask every woman he encountered, 'Are you my mother?' 'Twas heartwrenching, I tell you. He was left alone when he was only eight and Eirik ten when Eirik went off to foster in King Athelstan's Saxon court. Eirik was only half-Viking, you recall, but Tykir was pure Viking to the core. I remember how he would proclaim, even when he was too small to lift a mighty sword, that someday he would be a Jomsviking, too . . . just so he could stand beside his father. Then, his father died later that year, when he was eight, and Eirik was off a-fostering. And finally, his stepmother, Ruby, disappeared in a mysterious fashion."

"Gyda!" Eadyth exclaimed with sudden inspiration. "Dost think that is why Tykir has refused to settle in one place all these years? Why he never wed?"

"I am certain of it," Gyda said with an emphatic nod. "The boy was rejected or abandoned by everyone he ever loved. So he protects himself from hurt by never caring deeply for anyone. Even his own brother, whom he visits only on rare occasions."

"Oh, this is too much. You two are trying to turn my anger away from that troll by playing on my sympathies. The *boy* has seen thirty and five winters, and if he fails to care for anyone but himself, 'tis because he is a troll."

Gyda and Eadyth smiled at the vehemence of her response.

"Do you think . . . ?" Eadyth arched a brow at Gyda.

The old woman chortled gleefully. "Mayhap. Mayhap."

And they both gazed at Alinor in the oddest way.

"Here," Eadyth said then, handing Alinor a small soapstone container filled with a rose-scented cream. "Your hair is just like mine—"

Alinor surveyed Eadyth's silken tresses and laughed. The woman must be blind.

"—curly and unmanageable. I have developed a wonderful concoction for the hair that tames even the wildest tresses."

Alinor was skeptical, though the cream did smell wonderful. She usually didn't indulge in such vanities, but mayhap just this once. As she worked the delicious substance into her long strands, Eadyth addressed Alinor once again. "Is it true that you are a witch?"

"Do I look like a witch?" Alinor scoffed, then immediately regretted her words as the eyes of both women traveled over her freckle-ridden body. She was aware of that old wives' tale about freckles being the devil's spittle, and apparently so were they.

"'Tis a well-known fact that a witch cannot be discerned by outward aspects. Take Eric Bloodaxe's wife, Gunnhild, for example," Eadyth said, as she rinsed the lotion out of Alinor's hair and motioned for her to stand so she could comb out the tangles in the wet strands. "Yea, Gunnhild, the sister of King Harald Gormsson of Denmark, studied witchcraft in her early days in Finnmark, and a more beautiful woman there never was. At least from outward appearances. 'Tis said Eric rescued her from a most bizarre witchly voyage into the White Sea and over the years has gained strength from her powers."

"There are good witches and bad witches, of course." Gyda stopped her weaving for a moment and stared at Alinor, attempting to determine in which category she fell.

"I am not a witch," Alinor said, but neither of the women paid her any heed.

"You must talk with Gunnhild this eve when we sup at the palace," Eadyth said. "Mayhap you can share potions and such in the midst of the feast."

"Me? Me?" Alinor stammered. "Why would I be asked to participate in some Viking feast?"

"Because you are Tykir's captive," Eadyth declared, as if that was a normal thing to be. "And you must remain under guard at all times. Tykir insists. Tykir wouldn't want Bolthor or Rurik or any of his men to miss this feast tonight by staying behind to guard you." Eadyth glanced at Alinor reprovingly, obviously deeming her a most selfish female to think otherwise.

"I am *not* a witch," she repeated again, then exhaled with exasperation. Really, it was like talking to a wall, trying to convince people of her innocence. "Do you even know what this is all about? Do you have any idea what they think I have done?"

Gyda shook her head slowly, and Eadyth said hesitantly, "Well, I know what Rurik said back at the palace, but I can hardly credit . . . tell us your version."

When Alinor explained, their mouths gaped with amazement.

"The king's manpart did what?" Eadyth choked out.

"Turned right, apparently," Alinor answered dryly.

"And you put a spell on him to make it do such?" Gyda grinned, rather impressed by that feat.

"There are a few men I wouldn't mind afflicting so." Eadyth grinned mischievously. "Can you teach me the spell?"

"I am not a witch. I keep trying to tell you, it's what they accuse me of, but it's not true."

The women remained unconvinced.

"You know," Gyda said, tapping her pressed lips pensively with a forefinger, "it seems to me that I have heard of this malady afore on a man's private parts. Ofttimes 'tis caused by an injury that scars over and forces the staff to go crooked. The few cases I've heard of eventually corrected themselves."

"So all King Anlaf needs to cure himself is time?" Eadyth offered hopefully.

"Mayhap." Gyda tapped her chin pensively. "Lest the crooked manpart is caused by a witch's curse, of course." She looked pointedly at Alinor.

"I am *not* a witch. Why won't anyone believe me?" Alinor felt like weeping with frustration.

"What of the bowel spell you put on Tykir? Surely you cannot deny that." Eadyth folded her arms over her chest and nodded her head, as if she'd just won some point of argument.

"Well, nay, but—"

"Aha!" Eadyth and Gyda said as one.

"—but it was a mere herb that grows—"

"A poison?" Eadyth lashed out. "You gave Tykir a bane drink? That is as bad as a witchly potion, Alinor. I could kill you myself for that."

"It wasn't a deadly potion . . . oh, what's the use? No one believes me anyhow."

"EA-DYTH!" a loud male voice rang out from downstairs.

Eadyth cringed and Gyda gathered up her weaving items, preparing to leave the room.

"Oh, the brute! He knows I hate it when he yells for me like a cow in the field."

"EA-DYTH!" her husband shouted once again, his voice coming closer. "Where are you? I have something to show you."

Eadyth's face bloomed bright red. "I have seen *it* more than enough times, believe me," she informed Alinor with a wink. "Here," she said, handing her a towel. "Best you dry yourself afore my husband comes blundering in here."

Both Eadyth and Gyda left the room, giggling.

Through the closed door, she could swear she heard Eirik say, "Ea-dyth! I dropped honey on the front of my braies back at the castle. Can you think of any way I can remove it?"

Eadyth said something that Alinor could not overhear, but Eirik let loose with a low, masculine growl of pleasure at whatever it was.

And Alinor decided that Eadyth needed no lessons at all from a witch.

* * *

How could he have been so blind? ...

Tykir leaned against the doorjamb of Gyda's house and watched with amusement as his brother greeted his wife with a familiar pat on the behind and a deep, noisy kiss.

Seven years they had been wed, and still they acted as lovestruck youthlings. Three children they'd had together— Thorkel, Ragnor and Freydis—and three others they'd brought into the marriage betwixt them ... Eadyth's John, and Eirik's Larise and Emma. Ravenshire rang with the joyous sounds of children of all ages, and yet these two behaved as children themselves.

There was a Norse legend about a golden apple and how adventurers searched for this treasure a lifetime and more, across many lands, risking life and family. The moral of the tale was that often the precious fruit was growing in one's own orchard.

Eirik had found that golden apple.

Tykir was pleased for his brother, truly he was. There weren't many men fortunate enough to find a lifemate who was steadfast and loving. He never had.

"Have you left any mead for me back at the castle?" Bolthor asked as he passed by him through the doorway.

"Yea, I did. Not as good as Eadyth's home-brewed ale, but sufficient. There is Frisian wine, as well. And Rurik discovered a group of thralls bought by the king's steward from a Nubian slave trader. He said for the price of a gold coin, one of them has a surprise for you." Tykir jiggled his eyebrows meaningfully.

Bolthor laughed. "Good thing I have a gold coin." He hesitated, then added with a chuckle, "I will see you aboard ship at dawn when we set sail."

Eirik and Eadyth came next.

"We have decided to dine with the king, then come back here to sleep tonight," Eirik informed him. "Eadyth has no inclination to sleep under our uncle's roof. Nor do I."

Tykir nodded.

"Will you come with us?"

"You go on ahead. I wouldst get the witch first."

"Why not leave her here tonight?" Eadyth suggested.

He shook his head. "Nay, the witch does not leave my sight till we are asea. Even then, I cannot be sure she will not put a curse on my ship if I do not watch her closely."

Eadyth began to protest, but Eirik laid a warning hand on her arm. "Leave be, Eadyth. 'Tis Tykir's concern, not ours."

They left then, and Tykir waved aside Gyda's tsk-ing reprimand when he took the steps two at a time, attempting to locate Alinor. The night was wasting, and he had much mead to imbibe afore dawn.

"Alinor, where are you, witch?" he called out, at the same time he opened a bedchamber door. "'Tis time to . . ."

His words trailed off at the vision that greeted him.

A woman was standing knee-deep in a hip bath. Her arms were raised overhead, pushing long strands of wet, rust-colored hair off her face. The sleek tresses hung in a silky swath down her back practically to her buttocks, which were round and smooth and most enticing. With a start, the woman turned quickly, arms still upraised, and regarded his shock with her own.

It mattered not that her creamy skin was covered with freckles from forehead to knees, and probably to toes under the murky water. Her body was spectacular. Small breasts, yea, but they were high and firm, with raspberry tips. A trim waist and narrow hips. Long, slim legs joined by a thatch of reddish-blond curls dewed with droplets of water. In all, a perfectly proportioned body that would put the finest goddess to shame.

My very own witch goddess.

Bloody hell! When did I start thinking of her as mine?

The witch blinked at him through green cat eyes, as if she was held in the same spell that immobilized him. Mere seconds had passed since he'd opened the door, but it seemed like a lifetime. Only then did he admit what he'd already come to suspect earlier.

He was bewitched.

And he didn't care.

CHAPTER FOUR

❧

Just your average, everyday, royal Viking feast . . .

"Stop it," Alinor hissed at Tykir.

They were sitting on long benches in the vast great hall of the Norse palace, along with hundreds of other noble, and not so noble, personages. Everyone of high station in Northumbria, whether Norse or Saxon by birth, had come with their entourages to pay self-serving homage to the newly reinstated king, Eric Bloodaxe Haraldsson, and his wife, the witch-queen Gunnhild.

The royal couple was ensconced at the high table up on the dais with those of highest rank. Tykir, his friends and family, along with Alinor, his captive, sat just a short ways below, definitely a position of favor.

"Stop what?" the insufferable Viking knight inquired with exaggerated concern, as if he cared what was bothering her . . . which he did not, of course. The troll braced his shoulders back against the wall behind them, sipped at his goblet of mead and regarded her with lazy amusement.

Alinor felt as if she'd landed in a Viking version of hell. Especially since she was practically joined at the hip, and other places, to the man who had become her nemesis of late.

"Stop moving your hand about, for one thing." She glanced pointedly at their bound hands—his left tied at the wrist to her right. At the moment, the pair of appendages were sitting high on his thigh. Very high!

"Oh! I beg your pardon, my lady," he said solicitously.

Then, with total lack of social grace, he raised his hand to scratch his belly. Which placed her hand just about square on . . .

"You crude clod!" She jerked her hand away from his . . . bulge. "You dumb dolt! You slimy swine! You . . . you . . ."

"How about loathsome lout?" Eadyth offered from across the table. "It always works well for me."

Her husband looped his arm around her shoulders and squeezed. Presumably in punishment, but more like affection. Married couple though they be, the two could not seem to keep their hands off each other's persons. Alinor had never witnessed such spousal behavior. For a certainty, she'd never yearned to touch any of the slimy maggots she'd been handed in matrimony.

Well, mayhap she would feel differently if she was as beauteous as Eadyth, with her luxurious silver-blond hair lying wimpleless about her shoulders under a gossamer-thin headrail of palest lavender, held in place by a gold circlet of twisted flowers. Her headrail matched her misty violet eyes and her darker lavender gunna, which was embroidered at the edges in the orphrey style with gold thread.

Then, too, she might feel differently if she'd ever been wed to a man as young and roguishly handsome as Eadyth's husband, Eirik, who was a few years older than his brother Tykir. God's mercy! He was a sight to behold, with his black hair and blue eyes, bedecked in a deep blue wool tunic over black braies, belted at the waist. A short mantle was pinned back off one shoulder with a most unusual gold brooch in the form of a twisted dragon with amber eyes.

Tykir made a coughing noise, recalling her attention to him. "'Tis not polite to ogle another woman's spouse."

"I was not ogling. I just wondered how such a comely man as Lord Eirik could have such a homely troll as you for a brother."

"Some women like my looks." The grin on his face told Alinor how much he cared whether she considered him ugly or not. And she had to admit that even with a blackened eye and bruised nose, he was far from ugly.

"Some women cannot see past a man's money pouch. And speaking of looks, I would appreciate it if you would stop looking at me in that manner." She said this in an undertone. Ever since he'd come barging into Gyda's bedchamber, he'd been staring at her in the strangest way. And smiling.

"What manner?" he asked with a knowing chuckle.

She must have spoken louder than she realized because Rurik, who sat on the other side of Tykir, leaned forward around the buxom Viking maid who sat on his lap and commented, "Yea, Tykir, you have been gaping at the witch like a tasty sweet from a sultan's harem. Are you *drunkkinn?*"

"Not yet," Tykir said, taking another long swig of mead from his cup, his eyes holding Alinor's the entire time. No man had ever looked at her in quite that way before, and she found it discomfiting.

Even more annoying was Tykir's appearance. No man should be so beautiful. Or so rascally.

He was wearing a buttery brown tunic of the softest wool over a pair of dark brown braies. The star-shaped amber pendant hung by a gold chain against his chest. She assumed that he had bathed in the palace bathhouse that afternoon because the flaxen strands in his light brown hair glistened, resembling threads of spun gold. One side of his hair was braided so that his thunderbolt earring was exposed, as it had been the first time she had seen him. His sword was in the scabbard at his hip, and his sable-lined cloak lay on the bench, on his other side.

Tykir winked at her.

And Alinor wished she could sink into the rushes to hide her mortification. It was one thing to be caught ogling Eirik of Ravenshire, but quite another *unacceptable* thing to be caught ogling the troll.

"You must not let the witch cast her spells on you, Tykir," Rurik warned. "Are you still wearing your cross?"

In answer, Tykir pulled the wooden cross on a leather thong from inside his tunic and settled it on his chest next to the amber pendant.

"Well, if you are going to take risks by engaging in eye contact with a witch, you must exercise every precaution." Before anyone realized what he was about, Rurik stood, dropping his lap companion unceremoniously to the floor. She shrieked with outrage before scurrying off indignantly.

Annoyed at the interruption, Beast shifted in the rushes at his master's feet, growled, then immediately went back to sleep.

Still standing, Rurik pulled a vial out of a flap in his tunic and commenced to sprinkle holy water all over Tykir. Except that he was feeling the effects of about a *tun* of mead, and the water came out in a splash, instead of a sprinkle, all over Tykir's meticulously groomed hair and forehead.

"*Blód hel,* Rurik! I'm not bewitched . . . well, I probably am bewitched . . . but not because of some dark spell." He stood abruptly, forcing Alinor to stand as well, and shook his head like a shaggy dog, thus causing her and everyone else around them to be anointed as well.

"What do you mean?" Rurik asked. "Bewitched, you say, but not by the witch's spell?"

Yea, I truly am in Viking hell. Or a Viking madhouse.

"I saw the Lady Alinor . . . *naked,*" Tykir confessed, as if that was any explanation at all.

Everyone gawked at Tykir in shock, not the least of all Alinor. Quickly regaining her wits, she swung her free arm in a fist to land on the lackbrain's chest. It was like hitting a stone wall. The man didn't even flinch.

"What?" He put his free hand up in surrender.

"You're not supposed to tell people *that.*"

"I'm not?"

"Most definitely not."

"You can look at my nude body if you like," he offered magnanimously. "Then we will be even."

"You *are* drunk," she accused.

"Nay, I am not."

"Well, what does that signify?" Rurik wanted to know. "Seeing a nude witch . . . I have seen such, as you well know."

As one, everyone stared at his blue face marking in sympathy, including Bolthor, who'd just come up and sat next to Alinor. He'd been off with the Nubian slave girl, for the fourth time that evening, by Alinor's count.

"That design appears to be made by woad, much like the Scottish warriors adorn themselves with in battle," Eadyth remarked, "but I have never known it to stay permanently."

"'Tis not just woad. The dye had essence of zephline mixed with it, I warrant," Alinor observed, flicking at some crumbs on the table in front of her.

"You . . . you know how to remove this mark?" Rurik sputtered incredulously. "You *are* a witch, then."

"Nay, I'm not a witch. I am a shepherdess and weaver, with a talent for dying fabrics. In truth, I make the best wool fabric in all Northumbria."

Eirik let out a whoop of laughter.

Eadyth jabbed him with her elbow. "Behave yourself, husband."

"My wife has spouted similar such *modest* claims on occasion," Eirik elaborated.

Eadyth clucked her disapproval at Eirik and explained to Alinor, "I make the best mead and honey in all Northumbria."

Rurik cared not about wool or mead or honey, however. "Can you remove the mark, witch?" he demanded impatiently of Alinor.

"Mayhap I can, and mayhap I cannot."

"Mayhap I can lop off your head, and mayhap I cannot," was Rurik's response as he made a low, primitive sound of outrage. He would have jumped over Tykir, to decapitate her no doubt, if her rope-mate had not raised a hand in caution.

Grumbling with frustration, Rurik stopped a passing

housecarl and took another jug of ale from his tray. "And you find attraction in this bitch . . . I mean, witch?" He took a long draw, from the jug, then swiped the back of his hand over his mouth.

"I never said I was attracted," Tykir protested.

The harsh sentiments smarted, and she could not keep her face from heating up.

"Tykir! I'm disappointed in you," Eadyth remonstrated. "Surely you above all others know to look beneath the surface. Remember the lecture you gave your own brother at our wedding feast about good Viking men knowing how to judge a woman fairly?"

"Det er ikke gull alt som glimmer," Eirik added, nodding his head in agreement. "All that glitters is not gold. And some of the glitter you have been sniffing after of late has the lackluster of brass, if you ask me."

"I do not recall asking you," Tykir said huffily. "And 'tis unfair of Eadyth to remind me of things I said seven years ago."

Alinor cringed and felt like putting her face on the table. She abhorred the idea that these people were discussing her as if she was not there . . . as if she was of no significance.

"All I said was that I had seen the witch naked," Tykir objected. "And it was a surprise. A *big* surprise." He rolled his eyes in emphasis.

"Oh! I am beginning to understand, Tykir. Did you finally see *the tail?*" Rurik said those last words in a whisper . . . the inference being that if he spoke aloud she might do something witchly, like levitate and ride out of the Norse castle on a broom or a black cat.

Dumber than dung, the whole lot of them!

Just then, an older Viking nobleman could be seen approaching their table. He was accompanied by a finely garbed woman—a Saxon would be her guess, by her mode of dress—and a daughter of no more than fifteen years . . . a girl of passing fair appearance, buxom and pretty.

"Oh-ho, you are truly snared now, Tykir," his brother teased. "Earl Orm and his lady have been trying to contrive a marriage betwixt you and his youngest daughter, Eneda, for the past two years."

"You could have warned me," Tykir mumbled but stood as a courtesy when the nobleman stepped closer with his family.

He must have forgotten that his left hand was bound to Alinor's right because he raised his arm in greeting, which caused her arm to raise as well, like a puppet. And as he gesticulated while talking with a wave here and a wave there, Alinor's arm was forced to follow suit. In the end, she grumbled with disgust, tugged on his wrist in reminder and stood beside him.

Tykir had the nerve to wink at her. Apparently, he had remembered their bound hands the whole time and chosen to embarrass her. The troll!

She saw the lips of Lord Orm's wife flatten with disdain as she noted their tied wrists.

The young girl, though, twittered shyly with a hand fluttering coyly to her face. Clearly, she would favor this union, if it could be arranged. Her mother was not so predisposed, if her clenched fists were any indication.

And Alinor noticed something else. The woman was as condescending in her demeanor to Eadyth as she was to her. Eadyth caught Alinor's eye and pulled a face to show her opinion of the haughty lady.

Alinor startled herself by feeling an unaccustomed roil of annoyance at the fuss Tykir was making now over the young girl. Could it be jealousy?

Nay. Never.

Mayhap.

I'm losing my mind.

When the couple and their marriageable daughter walked away, finally, with Tykir's promise of a visit to their Northumbrian estate sometime soon, Tykir sat down with a long sigh, dragging Alinor with him. "Whew," he said.

His family and friends were grinning at his discomfort.

"So, would you like my help in finding a bride gift for the fair Eneda?" Eadyth inquired cheerily.

"Not bloody likely," Tykir responded, taking a long gulp from his cup of mead.

"Tell me," Alinor deliberately paused, "would you be taking a wet nurse with you to the bridal bed?"

Everyone laughed at that, except Tykir.

"Are you saying I'm too old for the maid?"

Alinor gave him a look that said, "What do you think?" But then she had to concede, "Actually, I was her age when I was first wed. And my husband was a bit older than you."

"How much older?"

"He was five and sixty."

Tykir began to choke on his ale. "A bit? *A bit?* I am only five and thirty."

"Ah, well," Alinor declared with a shrug, "men do deteriorate quickly. 'Tis why they buy young wives, to put on a false front to the world that they are still virile."

Tykir's face flushed with affront.

Eadyth reached across the table and patted Alinor's hand. "I am developing a fondness for you, Alinor. You and I appear to be cut of the same cloth."

"You must admit that the maid had a fine set of breasts," Rurik commented with his usual crude bluntness.

"Rurik! Mind your tongue in the presence of ladies," Eirik cautioned.

Rurik ducked his head. In truth, the wretch was so often in the company of men that he probably forgot himself. And Alinor didn't mind all that much. She'd heard much worse in the company of Egbert and Hebert's troops.

But she quickly changed her mind when Rurik added, "Do not be gloating so, Tykir. You were the one back at Graycote who said that the Lady Alinor had a chest so flat her breasts probably resembled two eggs on a hot rock."

It was Tykir who chastised Rurik now. "Such talk is not becoming amongst ladies, Rurik." To Alinor and Eadyth, he apologized for Rurik by saying, "'Tis just the mead talking."

"Did you say that?" Alinor blurted out, and immediately wished she could take back the words.

Tykir shrugged. "Mayhap. But if I did, I have surely changed my mind."

"I never have been able to understand a man's over-fascination with the female breast," Alinor opined, before she had a chance to bite her tongue. "Really, if you men are so fascinated by that particular portion of the female anatomy, I have a good milch cow with a fine set of udders that would no doubt set you to drooling."

Rurik reared up, as if he would strangle her.

Bolthor held him back, chuckling.

Tykir saluted her in congratulation for having won this particular bout of cross-wills.

Meanwhile Eirik and Eadyth were laughing heartily.

Eadyth wiped tears of mirth from her eyes with the edge of her headrail. "Yea, Alinor, I do believe you would suit."

She didn't say for what precisely Alinor would suit. Still, her words heartened Alinor.

But then, their attention was drawn to another quarter.

"Wouldst look at that," Eirik said suddenly, pointing to the high table, where a group of Saxon nobles were talking animatedly to the king and his castellan. "The nerve of the villains!"

It was Egbert, Hebert and Cedric, along with a few of their high-born associates.

Alinor groaned.

"'Tis naught of concern." Tykir waved a hand airily in voicing that opinion. "The king told me earlier that Alinor's brothers are protesting her abduction to the Saxon King Edred."

Alinor should have known that her brothers would not give up so easily. "That's Edred's Northumbrian toady, Earl

Oswulf, who is addressing Eric Bloodaxe's son Maccus over there to the side," she informed them.

Everyone gawked at her with surprise, wondering how she would know such.

"Edred is my cousin."

"The king of England?" Eirik exclaimed and gave a reproving glare at his brother.

"Oh, Tykir!" Eadyth said on a sigh. "When will you learn to exercise caution?"

"You didn't tell me that the king of all bloody Britain, excepting Northumbria, was your cousin," Tykir accused her.

"Well, he's my cousin thrice-removed," Alinor amended.

"That makes me feel better," Tykir said with dry humor.

"Once, twice, thrice . . . it matters not. King Edred will surely send an army to rescue one of his kin," Eadyth insisted on a wail of dismay. "What have you gotten us into, Tykir?"

Alinor would have liked to rub the salt of their disapproval into Tykir's wounds, but she had to be honest. "I have no illusions about Edred's motive in helping me . . . if in fact that is what's happening. Edred isn't much older than me, you know, and I have five and twenty years. But the king is so weak of digestion at times that he can swallow only the juices of food he has masticated, to the great revulsion of his guests. 'Tis a disease that afflicts many in the House of Wessex."

"Well, thank you for the fine saga," Tykir said sarcastically. "Is there a point? Or an ending?"

Alinor shot the troll a sideways scowl and continued. "While I might sympathize with Edred's maladies, I am not so naive as to believe my cousin exercises familial concern. There are two sides to Edred, as most Englishmen know. He is a devoutly religious man who suffers his bodily pain with stoic acceptance. His palace in many ways is a school of virtue. On the other hand, he can be brutal as . . . well, as a barbaric Viking."

Alinor got a number of glowers for that remark, including from Eadyth. Though a Saxon herself, she clearly defended her half-Norse husband and his countrymen.

"Recently, Edred destroyed the entire town of Thetford just to avenge the death of the local abbot. Every man, woman and child," Alinor said, in explaining the king's brutal side.

The question was: Which side was Edred acting from today?

Edred's emissary could help her, if he wanted. Of that there was no doubt. But was she important enough? What were Egbert and Hebert, or even Cedric, offering in return?

Alinor's heart lurched with sudden hopefulness, but then an odd depression settled over her. She was betwixt and between in this situation. Two choices, and both of them bad. Be rescued by her brothers and end up with—what was it Tykir had called him—yea, she remembered now . . . the lord of Lard. Or be carried off to some heathen land to face a Viking king who expected her to remove a nonexistent spell.

Tykir squeezed her hand. "Never fear, Lady Alinor. The king won't interfere in my business. He plays with your brothers and the Saxon king's emissary. He will bleed as much coin in ransom from them as he can, but in the end you are mine."

You are mine.

What a disconcerting thing to say! A shiver ran through her body from head to toe. If he meant to reassure her, he was sadly misguided. Especially since one of Eric Bloodaxe's housecarls came up and notified them that the king wished to speak with Tykir Thorksson and his captive, the Lady Alinor. Soon Tykir, Alinor, Eirik, Eadyth, Rurik and Bolthor were walking toward the dais in a group.

"Like a swarm of bees, we are," Eadyth said under her breath.

"You should know, dearling. You should know," Eirik told his wife, with a pat on her rump.

Her squeal of consternation was drowned by the din of hundreds of revelers enjoying the feast.

Alinor had been in this very hall years ago with her second husband, and it actually looked much better now. The Vikings were great ones for decorating their door and window surrounds, not to mention the roof beams, with intricate carvings. And the Vikings themselves were certainly an attractive lot, with their colorful clothing, magnificent jewelry and meticulously groomed hair and beards. These were a people taller than the average Saxon, and cleaner, too. No wonder so many Saxon men and women fell in love with their Norse counterparts.

All these observations Alinor made as they moved along the aisle separating the long trestle tables. Their passage was barely noticed, except for a few guests who huddled their heads together, whispering and pointing at Alinor's nether end.

Except for Egbert, Hebert and Cedric.

"Alinor!" Egbert cried out and hugged her warmly, which was an odd experience since she was bound to the grim-faced Tykir, who was forced to move with her. He didn't appear pleased to be in such close proximity to the man who'd tried to shoot him with an arrow earlier that afternoon. It was also an odd experience because Egbert had never hugged her a day in her life. He'd applied a birch rod on more than one occasion, but a hug? Never.

"You're safe!" Hebert added, taking his turn in hugging her. "We were so worried about you, dear sister."

Worried? Hah! Their only worry was that they might lose their bride money.

Egbert wore a huge bandage wrapped around his crown, presumably from an injury sustained that afternoon, and

Hebert had a split lip. They'd probably wounded themselves rushing away from the fray.

Cedric waddled forward and seemed about to take her brothers' place in the embracing business, but Tykir soon put a stop to that with a halting hand. For one insane moment, she wondered if Tykir might be jealous. But then she took another glance at his furious face and decided otherwise.

"Tykir, Eirik," King Eric Bloodaxe greeted them. "We give you welcome. Have you had enough to eat and drink?"

Both men nodded to the king, who was dressed sumptuously in purple wool, from braies to belted tunic to overmantle lined with white fur. He must have seen more than fifty years, if the gray streaks in the dark hair that lay about his shoulders under a thin gold crown were any indication. He was clean-shaven, otherwise, and still handsome, in a cold-eyed way.

"Gunnhild, come forth and greet our guests," the king invited his queen.

Alinor gasped with appreciation at her first close-up view of the queen. An uncommonly beautiful woman, Gunnhild had to be of the same age as her king, but her skin was unlined, her thick blond hair untouched by gray. She wore an embroidered gown of the same purple fabric as the king's and a veritable fortune in jewelry, including gold and silver rings on every finger, wide rings that extended from knuckle to knuckle.

Her intelligent eyes took in Tykir's amber pendant and Eirik's dragon brooch in a greedy glance. "Have you brought me any fine amber trinkets this time, Tykir?" the queen asked.

"I have many a jewel *for purchase*," Tykir said.

She frowned.

"All fit for a queen of your renowned beauty."

She preened.

"I will bring them by for your inspection later tonight."

Queen Gunnhild nodded, then turned to Alinor and gave

her a quick, dismissing assessment. With an air of boredom, she inquired insolently, "You are the witch, I presume?"

Alinor started to nod but caught herself. God's teeth! She was beginning to think of herself as the witch now, too.

"Yea, she is the witch I am taking back to the Norselands," Tykir answered for her. He held up his hand to demonstrate that she was his prisoner.

"There is much I would like to discuss with you," Gunnhild said enigmatically to Alinor. Before she could say more, Egbert and Hebert interrupted, pushing themselves in front of Alinor.

"Nay, she is not a witch," Egbert asserted. "She is our sister, the betrothed of Lord Cedric here, the cousin of the king of all Britain, a gentle-bred lady who should not be handed over to this . . . this heathen."

King Eric raised an eyebrow at the word *heathen*, asking without words whether they put him in the same category. Then he homed in on another part of what Egbert had said. "Dost claim that Edred is king of *all* Britain?"

Egbert realized his mistake immediately. "All Britain, except for Northumbria," he corrected himself.

"Are you really cousin to King Edred?" Gunnhild queried Alinor.

"Thrice-removed," Tykir pointed out.

Alinor glared at him for speaking on her behalf, but he just grinned at her.

"We demand that you hand our sister back to us, and pay *wergild* for the soldiers sorely wounded by you and your barbarians this afternoon," Hebert said. "Is that not so, Earl Oswulf?"

The Saxon nobleman, adviser to King Edred, had been standing quietly in the background. He gave his assent with a curt nod of his head.

"Nay!" Tykir said.

After that, the king heard both sides of the argument. In the end, he offered, "We could call for a Thing in a sennight or so to decide the issue." Alinor knew from what Tykir had told her previously that a Thing was the governing body for Norsemen, similar to the Witan in Britain.

"I can't wait that long," Tykir roared. "Already I am a month late in getting my trading goods to Hedeby. 'Tis a two-week journey to Trondelag in good weather. With autumn advanced now, another sennight of malingering could mean my being unable to return to my homestead for winter. That I cannot accept."

The king addressed Oswulf then. "Is the witch worth drawing swords? Mayhap a full-fledged battle?"

Oswulf's face went pale, and his beady eyes scanned the great hall, noticing the many Norse fighting men. "Not at the present," he conceded. "But I will have to report back to King Edred your refusal to intercede on behalf of Egbert and Hebert. I guarantee he will not be pleased."

"So be it," King Eric said, clearly unafraid of a fight.

Egbert, Hebert and Cedric, muttering curses and vows of revenge, were being led away by an angry Earl Oswulf. For now, her fate was decided, a stunned Alinor realized. She was still the captive of the troll. Everyone would continue to think of her as a witch, including the king, who'd just listened to some hushed message from Rurik and was gazing speculatively at her buttocks.

Gunnhild came forward to give a parting kiss to Eadyth, and then to Alinor, much to her astonishment. Even more surprising was Gunnhild's words in Alinor's ears, "Do not mind my husband looking for your tail. He has been searching for mine nigh on twenty years now, and he still has not found it." With a chuckle, she turned away and walked regally back to her seat at the high table.

As they returned to their benches, Alinor noticed, to her chagrin, that a great number of people were glancing at her backside. Apparently the word had spread since her passage up to the dais a short time ago. She was certain she had Rurik to thank for that. One of these days, she would like to twist Rurik's tongue into a knot . . . a blue knot to match his face design.

Just then, when Alinor thought things could not have gotten worse, they did.

Beast, who'd been sleeping at their table the whole time they were away talking with the king and queen, sat up with sudden alertness, his black ears standing up like sentinels. With an ominous growl, then a bark, he watched the open doorway on the other side of the great hall. A wild barking ensued, followed by a familiar bleating. Beauty came galloping across the great hall, her broken neck chain trailing after her, with David and Bathsheba following close behind, and after that a half dozen more baaing sheep. A stunned silence overcame the entire great hall, in a rippling fashion, as the interlopers trotted by. Soon Beauty and Beast were reunited, with much licking of faces and sniffing of intimate body parts.

It was a scene right out of Alinor's worst nightmare.

She pushed aside the manchet trencher of congealing sliced boar and pressed her forehead to the table. Laughter started low, then crescendoed as the Norse assemblage roared their mirth at the antics of Alinor's minions.

Bolthor mentioned something about a new saga, "Tykir the Great and the Nude Witch," immediately followed by, "Tykir the Great and the Lustful Dogs."

"Oooh, Bolthor, I forgot what a wonderful skald you are," Eadyth enthused. "Please, wouldst thou honor us with a saga?"

Everyone at the table turned a shade of green, repressing the need to groan. Bolthor, however, looked as if he'd been handed the Holy Grail.

"Hear one and all, this is the saga of Tykir the Great," Bolthor began. "In the year of our Lord nine fifty-two, in the land of the Midnight Sun, there was a king with a crooked cock. Anlaf was his name. And he was mightier . . ." On and on Bolthor went, and for the first time Alinor wished she really was a witch. Her first act would be to fly away.

"Never fear, sweetling," Tykir whispered in her ear. She could tell that he was barely stifling a laugh. "I will take you away from all this soon enough."

That was what Alinor was afraid of.

CHAPTER FIVE

&

FIVE DAYS LATER . . .

Row, row, row your longboat . . .
    "It wasn't my fault," Alinor contended. "I tell you, I'm not a witch."

"You fed the seagulls. The seagulls died. The evidence speaks for itself." Tykir exhaled loudly with exasperation. "Never have I seen birds fall from the sky like snowflakes afore. 'Twas . . . well, magical. You are a witch, and that is that."

He turned his back on her and was about to stomp away. How the man managed to keep his balance aboard ship, Alinor couldn't figure out. They'd been five days into their voyage, and she still didn't have her sea legs. Nor her sea stomach, for that matter. No wonder she'd been unable to digest that horrid *gammelost* . . . old cheese . . . which the Vikings favored on their sea journeys, along with the even more unpalatable salted cod known as *lutefisk*. Hard bread and an occasional apple were the mainstay of her diet these days.

"Wait a minute," she called out, and stood, about to follow after Tykir. "I'm not done explaining—"

He pivoted abruptly and shoved her in the chest, forcing her to sit back down on the large wooden storage box under a tented area in the center of the ship. The look on his face was so mean and vicious that she recoiled. She could scarce remember the softer glances he'd been casting her way back at the Norse castle—not that she wanted such—because all the brute had been doing these past five days was glare at her.

"Sit!" he ordered. "Did I not just tell you to sit? Did I not warn you about moving from this spot? Did I not say that my men are threatening mutiny if you pull one more witchly trick? Did I not say I would lop off your head and feed you to the sharks if you opened your mouth one more time?"

"Did I not? Did I not? Did I not?" Alinor murmured.

"Are you mimicking me?" he growled.

"Nay, I'm saying my prayers," she snapped back.

"Prayers? Hah! 'Tis likely more of your incantations."

"Oh, that's unfair. I wasn't performing some dark rites when we were in the midst of that storm yestereve. I was wailing with fear. I've never been on a ship afore. How was I to know that we weren't going to sink to the bottom of the North Sea? How was I to know that bulge water was normal? How was I—"

"Bilge," he said.

"What?"

"It's bilge water, not bulge water."

"Oh, for the love of Mary! Bilge, bulge, barge . . . it matters not to me. I was standing in water ankle-deep. I still have mold on my shoes."

Tykir leaned down and pointed a forefinger at her. "You did a chant and the storm stopped."

She pointed a forefinger back at him. "Chant? I was moaning, 'Oh, oh, oh, please, God, oh, oh, oh, oh!' "

He made a harrumphing sound of disbelief. "My men are already sore mad at you. Because of you, we are six sennights late in returning to the Norselands. They have homes and families to attend to afore the ice comes and the fjords freeze over. One more delay could mean our being stuck in Anlaf's court for the winter months. Worse yet, in Hedeby, where we must stop first to unload the last of my market goods."

It was true. Autumn was on the wane and winter fast approaching. Even with the sun shining brightly overhead, the air was brisk and chilly to the bone. She was wrapped in one of Tykir's thick wool cloaks, lined with fur, but the cold air still whipped through her. Some of the men rowed naked to the waist when the sun was high, but mostly they were garbed for the cold.

And it was true, as well, that the Norse sailors—big, brave warriors that they were—feared her greatly. All of them wore handmade wooden crosses on leather thongs around their necks, and they were seen to sprinkle themselves with holy water on occasion. Rurik must have purchased a barrel of it from the good monks at the abbey in Jorvik.

Worst of all, when the men weren't sneaking peeks at her bottom—they still harbored this silly superstition about a witch's tail—the men were scowling at her, forcing her to keep a distance. Part of that was due to mere coincidences that seemed to crop up over and over in her vicinity. "'Twas not my fault that the milk curdled in the vat the first night out. Or that the wine barrel had a loose stave causing the precious cargo to seep out overnight. Or that Rurik's dog Beast has been crying without end, ever since you sent Beauty and the sheep back to Graycote. Coincidences! That's all!"

She knew he was still angry over her refusing his request to slaughter one of her sheep over the bow of his vessel as a pagan sacrifice to the sea people for weather-luck and good voyage. She'd informed him in no uncertain terms that all her sheep were valuable, but the curly-horned ram was nigh priceless, coming from Córdoba, a land that rarely allowed that species to leave its boundaries, except as royal gifts. How her third husband managed to obtain one of the rare beasts she had no idea, but it had almost been worth putting up with the marriage to gain her prized ram.

Tykir hadn't even smiled when she'd jested with him, "Besides, sacrificing my sheep would not bring you luck. They are Christian sheep, you see."

"You have an answer for everything, my lady. But the fact is, my men believe you are a witch."

"Of course they do. They are encouraged by Rurik's rancor and Bolthor's skaldic imagination, not to mention your constant grumbling. And speaking of men, who knew there would be so many of them? 'Tis not proper that a lady should travel, unchaperoned, in the company of so many men."

"Didst think that Rurik, Bolthor and I would row the ships ourselves?" he answered with undue sarcasm.

"Mayhap I should have known a great number of sailors would be required . . . to man *one* vessel. But how was I to know the number of ships you own?" The longship on which she traveled now, *Swift Dragon,* was one of a fleet of seven dragonships, each manned by more than sixty Viking warriors. The other ships were *Fierce Dragon, Bold Dragon, Brave Dragon, Savage Dragon, Mad Dragon* and *Deadly Dragon,* all of them owned by Tykir. Apparently, it was necessary to travel in convoy to fight off pirate ships, which lurked off the coasts of the northern market towns.

"Didst think I was a pauper?"

"Nay. I know you for what you are. A troll."

He bared his teeth in a gritted smile, and she knew she pushed him dangerously.

To her surprise, the number of ships and the treasure trove of market goods they carried bespoke great wealth on Tykir's part. It was a good thing her brothers didn't know about Tykir's affluence. They'd probably try to make a marriage pact with him. But, nay, he was too young for their devious designs. They would want an old man, soon to die. Besides, Tykir would never agree to wed such as her.

Where are these horrible thoughts coming from? "Tykir," she began in a conciliatory tone, "I was standing at the prow of your ship, avoiding the sailors, as you told me to do. I was trying to eat the midday meal, as you told me to do. But I just could not stomach that revolting *gammelost.* So I fed crumbles of it to some passing seagulls. And before I knew it, there were dozens of the birds taking the bits of the smelly stuff right from my fingers." She sniffed first one hand, then the other. "I still stink."

"It is just old cheese."

"*Old* cheese?" she scoffed. "That cheese could walk by itself."

Despite his best efforts, a grin tugged at his lips. "Actually, there is a legend that says *gammelost* contributed to the victory of King Harald Fairhair, my grandfather, at the Battle of Hafrsfjord in 872," he disclosed with a sheepish smile.

She arched a brow in question.

"The story goes that the king fed his warriors *gammelost* for the breaking of fast in the morn, prior to battle, thus transforming them into berserkers."

"See, it wasn't my fault. The seagulls just went berserk."

"I . . . don't . . . think . . . so," he said with a short laugh. "In any case, stay here and enjoy this beautiful day. We may not have another. Weather changes abruptly during this season."

He rolled his shoulders then, by pressing his elbows backward till they almost touched at his spine, then crossing his arms in front. Several times he did this, as his men were wont to do on occasion, to remove the kinks that came with cramming so many bodies into such a small space.

The man was godly handsome, Alinor had to admit. Even now, wearing a salt-stained leather tunic over black braies, with a wide leather belt tucking in his waist, his body was the embodiment of manhood. His blondish brown hair was tied back into a queue, but its silken texture was still apparent. Women must make much ado over him.

Unaware, or uncaring, of her scrutiny, he stopped rolling his shoulders and leaned down to rub his upper thigh. Eadyth had told Alinor of Tykir's grave injury at the Battle of Brunanburh several years ago, where he'd almost lost his limb.

"Does your leg hurt?" she asked.

His head jerked up. "Which one has the running tongue? Bolthor or Rurik?"

"Eadyth."

He shook his head with disgust. "Yea, my old wound rears up on occasion."

"I have no sympathy for you. A man your age has no business riding across several countries in pursuit of a non-existent witch."

"A man my age?" he sputtered indignantly.

"Yea, do not pretend to be a youthling. You are just like all the other men approaching their middle years, trying to be younger than you are. Cavorting and fornicating till your heart, or other body parts, give out."

"Ca-cavorting?" He was doubled over with laughter at her words. "I am thirty-five years old. I am not yet in my dotage, I assure you, my lady."

"Be that as it may, I could prepare a potion for you that would help. Applied directly, it soothes on contact."

"Lady, your last potion put me on intimate terms with the garderobe. Thank you, but I will decline your offer." Taking a deep breath, he scanned his ship and those following in an arrow formation behind them. The pride on his face was unmistakable.

"You love this life, don't you?"

He turned to her with wariness. "Yea, I do. There is no better sight this side of Valhalla than a dragonship with her sail hauled up and the wind filling it. 'Cloaks of the wind,' we call our sails. A good longboat, a strong breeze and cloaks of the wind . . . surely these are gifts from the gods."

As he walked off to assist the helmsman maneuvering the tiller on the steering oar, Alinor had to agree with him. These long, slim ships, with their carved prows and big, single square sails of red and black stripes, were works of art, as well as being functional . . . a credit to some of the finest craftsmen in the world. The oaken vessels were low in the center, rising gracefully like a swan's neck at prow and stern, soaring high above the waves. They were light in weight—in fact, they could be lifted overhead by the men for portage on reaching stretches of dry riverbeds—yet the ships sailed equally well in shallow waters or rough seas. Rich carvings in the form of intertwining dragon beasts etched the sides of Tykir's ships where the black and yellow battle shields of the warriors hung majestically on the outer edge. Those colors, and red as well, were picked out on the carved dragon heads that embellished the prows, as if the fierce animals were leading a bold path through the dangerous seawaters.

The crew, tanned by the sun and burned by the wind, their clothing stained with salt, were brawny examples of prime manhood. The sailors had to have dexterity to step adroitly about the moving ship, where two men sat on personal seachests at each of the sixteen oar holes lined up on either side of the ship—one to row and the other to spell. At the same time, great strength was needed to raise the long mast and to row in a continuous, back-breaking rhythm.

One of the smaller Norsemen, a nimble-footed lad, was performing a feat he'd done on one other occasion . . . dancing over the ocean atop the shafts of the spears. It was a contest the bored seamen engaged in on occasion, betting to see who could perform the oar dance without falling into the salty depths.

Alinor had to smile. It *was* a beautiful day, just as Tykir had said. There weren't many occasions on which Alinor had the free time to just sit back and admire God's nature around her.

But what she did, instead, was start to weep. First one tear, then another escaped her brimming eyes. With a muffled sob, Alinor used the hem of Tykir's cloak to wipe her cheek. But no sooner did she sop up one tear than another replaced it.

It was untenable. Alinor did not cry. Long ago, when she was no more than eight or so, she'd realized that tears did not move her brothers one whit, and crying gave her no real satisfaction. She'd resolved then to be stronger than they were, sharper of wit, more devious. And her strength of determination had served her well. Until now.

The situation in which she found herself was ludicrous. That anyone would seriously think her a witch defied logic. If only Tykir had spoken with her servants and the villagers at Graycote. She was not the first woman to be abducted . . . for ransom or rape, or spoils of some raid, even to be sold into slavery. But to capture her for sorcery was so far beyond belief that Alinor had not taken the situation seriously enough while still in her home territory . . . while there was still time to alter her circumstance.

How will I ever escape now?

What will happen to me in that heathen land?

Will I ever see my beloved sheep and Graycote again?

More tears slipped down her cheeks, unchecked now.

What am I going to do?

She said a silent prayer then, though Alinor was not much prone to zealous religious practices. She rather favored doing good work every day as a form of prayer. But desperate times called for desperate measures. *Please, God, help me in this desperate situation,* she prayed silently, sniffling back a sob.

Just then, on the other side of the ship, Tykir laughed at something one of his shipmates said to him.

Alinor's eyes went wide with surprise.

Could it be . . . is it a sign?

Has God sent Tykir to save me from my brother's evil machinations?

Could this trip to the Norselands be a celestial vehicle for God's plan to rescue me?

Then the most outlandish question of all assailed Alinor, and she groaned with dismay.

Could Tykir be my guardian angel?

He refused to be her Viking guardian angel . . .

"The witch weeps," one of his men said warily, as if

Tykir had not already noticed. And the burly sailor's words were repeated down the row of oarlocks, and back up the other side, like a whisper on the wind. "The witch weeps, the witch weeps, the witch weeps . . ."

Apparently tears on a witch must be rare, or have some significance. He would have to ask Bolthor or Rurik. They were the sorcery experts. This witch business was all new to Tykir.

Then a new refrain began. "What does it mean? What does it mean? What does it mean? What . . ."

His men looked to him for answers.

"Weeping is naught but a witch's trick," he decided.

His men nodded hesitantly, bowing to his greater wisdom. He was certain—*well, fairly certain*—that the witch hoped to snare them with her ploy for pity.

Did Alinor take him for a fool, that he would be swayed by such blatant feminine wiles? Hah! He had been turning up the hems of female robes since he was twelve years old. There was not a fluttering of the eyelash, sway of the hip, bounce of the buttock, exposure of a breast, exaggerated sigh, or silly sob he had not witnessed in his many encounters with the weaker, though more devious, sex. Women were so transparent. They had not the subtlety of men.

Tykir stalked back to the area where a canopy had been set up for Alinor. Looming over her, hands on hips, he demanded, "Stop it!" *Is that subtle enough for you, my lady?*

"Stop what?"

"Crying." *What do you think I mean? Dancing?*

"I'm not crying," she said, peering up at him through watery green pools, shaded by thick fringes of reddish-gold, glistening with wetness. Remarkable, really, how beautiful her eyes were in a face mottled with those ugly freckles.

"Ert me mjg falleg augu," he murmured. "You have very beautiful eyes." *Now, why would I feel the need to tell her that?*

"What did you say?"

"Your eyes are crossed," he lied. "When you weep, your eyes look crossed." Her beautiful eyes set on him, but not with sorrow. He suspected that she got so few compliments in her life that his rude criticism rang true with her. No doubt her One-God exercised fairness in giving the woman one single mark of beauty to make up for all those other less beauteous attributes.

But, nay, that wasn't quite true. There were other attributes. Like that naked body he had seen. *Nay, nay, nay! I promised myself not to think about that.* "Not crying? My lady, you are making more water than a war horse. Soon we will have to bail out the bilge again." He thought she would smile at that jest, though her smiles were infrequent, and reserved only for Bolthor, or for her bloody sheep. Mayhap that was what caused her sudden dispirit. She missed her sheep.

"Do you miss your familiars?"

"My *what?*"

"Familiars. Don't all witches have familiars?" He felt rather silly now and could feel his face heat up.

"And my familiars would be . . . ?"

He hated that superior attitude she exhibited betimes. Like now. "Sheep."

"Sheep?" Stunned, she blinked at him.

No doubt his perception stunned her. Perchance if he made a baaing sound that would cheer her up. Better yet, he could butt her derriere like that randy ram of hers.

He couldn't help but grin at that.

"Stop smirking. I am not crying. I never cry. 'Twas just the wind. Furthermore, you have strange objects rattling about in your skull if you think my sheep are familiars."

"Your freckles are growing." *Now where did that half-brained observation come from? Humph! I guess I'm just trying to avoid noticing those magnificent eyes. Or thinking about her naked. Nay, nay, nay! I have wiped that image from my mind.*

"What nonsense do you speak now? Do you think to

disconcert me with your idle remarks? Well, you can forget about that nonsense. I care not if you like my freckles or not."

Truly, your tongue wags more than a puppy under the high table at a drunken feast, My Lady Blabberer . . . rather, Blubberer. "I am wounded at your unjust criticism, my lady. What I meant was that your freckles grow larger when you blubber . . . or leastways, they appear to do so when your nose reddens and your face splotches up." *Well, I feel better now.*

"You are a troll."

"So you have said afore." Leastways, *she* must be feeling better, if sniping at him caused her to stop sniveling. Tykir puffed out his chest with pride. He ever did have a talent for brightening the spirits of fair maidens. Not that she was fair, but . . . "Just so you stop your watery show. It bothers my men."

She suggested he do something to himself that he knew for a fact was nigh impossible. And she said his *bothered* men could bloody well join him in the exercise. He put a hand over his heart with exaggerated shock. "I have never heard a high-born lady use such words afore. Of course, you are a high-born lady *witch;* mayhap the rules of your society are different."

"Go away," she said with a slump of the shoulders.

He hated it when she slumped her shoulders. It made him feel as if he was responsible for her woes, which he was not.

Instead of going away, he hunkered down in front of her, his forearms resting on his widespread knees. Instinctively, she shifted her body so they were not touching.

That annoyed him. So, of course, he moved in closer. Now his inner knees bracketed her tightly closed thighs, under the enveloping cloak. *His* cloak, by the by, he noted with a clutch of unreasonable warmth that she was wearing his garment. Almost as if she were under his protective shield.

Nay, nay, nay. She is a mere captive. To be delivered and

be done with. Do not get involved, Tykir. But he was never one to listen to good advice, especially his own. "Tell me why you weep," he urged.

"I was not weeping," she said with a break in her voice. "But if I were . . . weeping . . . which I'm not . . . well, I have good cause, do you not think?"

"And why, pray tell, is that?"

Alinor wore no wimple or headrail today, but her rust-colored tresses, held in place by a braided silk cord around her forehead, did not fly about, as was their norm, because she had taken to using a pomade that Eadyth had given her, causing her hair to lay in gentle waves. The rose fragrance of the cream wafted out to him in delicate enticement.

"Why are you sniffing like a hedgehog?"

That brought him back to reality with a rude jolt. Lopping off her head was gaining more and more appeal. Or, leastways, lopping off her tongue.

"And would you mind moving?" she snapped, trying unsuccessfully to shuffle backwards, away from his legs' embrace. "You are blocking the sun."

He smiled at that. He was a large man, but not *that* big.

"Lady, you avoid my question. Why would you have good cause to weep?"

"I was not—"

He held a forefinger to her lips to prevent her further protestations.

A big mistake, that. Touching her body. Her lips parted with surprise under his finger, which lingered in place. And he noticed for the first time that her lips were full and puffy. And kiss-some, truth be told. Furthermore, they were raspberry-colored, just like her nipples.

Aaarrrgh! Forget I thought that. 'Twas a mistake. I have forgotten entirely how the wench looks naked. It has been so long since I've seen a raspberry, I no longer even remember how they look, or taste. Taste? Bloody hell!

"Oh, good Lord, not that again!" she said, swatting his finger away.

"What?"

"You are staring at me naked, *again.*"

"I am not," he lied.

"Yea, you are, and I will not stand for it."

He wondered how she could stop him. In truth, he would like to know so he could stop himself. Then his reckless tongue took on a mind of its own. "My lady, do you deliberately remind me of your raspberry nipples, which match your raspberry lips, by the by, to avoid speaking of your tears?"

"And to think I was envisioning you as my guardian angel!"

Now, that remark surprised him. The woman did have a knack for catching him off-guard. "What? Who? Me? Ha, ha, ha!"

"Yea, it *is* humorous, isn't it?"

"Humorous? It is preposterous." He thought a moment. "Why is it so preposterous? Dost think there are no Vikings in your heaven? Dost think we have no godliness in us? Dost think you Christians hold the rights to goodness? Dost forget that many of us Vikings practice both the Norse and Christian religions?"

Her mouth gaped open with incredulity at his vehement words. Her lips were not quite so kiss-some when sucking air like a North Sea puff fish. *Thank the gods!*

"What? You *want* to be my guardian angel?" she asked, once she'd clicked her teeth shut.

"Nay, I do not want to be your guardian angel. I do not want to be your . . . anything." Now, that was a near mistake. He'd almost said that he did not want to be her lover, which was a lie, he admitted to himself now. Yea, ever since he'd seen her naked, the thought of wetting his wand . . . rather, whetting his sword . . . at least once . . . had been hovering in his head like a tiresome headache. Once? Hell, in his mind pictures he was wetting and whetting endlessly.

"It was a foolish notion, I admit."

What is she talking about? I am so busy thinking about sex I've lost the thread of her talk. Now I remember. Angels, that was it. She thinks I'm her guardian angel, of all things. "Aha! So that is why you wept. They were tears of relief that your One-God had sent you the most handsome, bravest, perfect guardian angel." *I swear, my tongue has gained a mind of its own.*

"Are you really as lackwitted as you appear betimes?"

Yea. "No more lackwitted than you . . . that you would insult a fierce warrior as you do, *constantly."*

" 'Tis just that you provide so many instances of idiocy."

"Aaarrrgh! Your head must be like a pond and your thoughts like little frogs, jumping from one lily pad to another."

"How poetic!"

He made a low, snarling sound of exasperation. "Could you just once finish one subject before hop-hop-hopping to another?"

"If you insist," she said demurely. *What a farce! The woman wouldn't recognize demure if it smacked her in the middle of her freckled forehead.* "What would you like to know?"

"Why did you think I was your guardian angel?"

"Well, not precisely a guardian angel," she amended. "More like a protector sent by God."

"Sounds like a guardian angel to me," he argued.

She waved a hand dismissively. "Leastways, this was my logic . . ."

Logic and women are an impossible contradiction.

". . . you know how some people believe that if you save a person's life, they are forever beholden to you? Well, I was thinking that mayhap God sent you to Northumbria for me to—"

"Anlaf sent me for you. Last time I checked he was no way close to being a god."

"Stop interrupting me, you clod."

"Tsk-tsk. Is that any way to speak to your guardian angel?"

She made a scowly face at him, which made her resemble an angry rooster. Not an attractive picture.

"As I was saying . . . mayhap God sent you to Northumbria for me, *by way of King Anlaf,* so that you could rescue me from my brothers' latest outrage. In truth, I suspect He sent King Anlaf to that Northumbria nunnery in the first place to set His plan in motion. And further, I was thinking that mayhap you are now responsible for protecting me. So, really, I should not be worried anymore about what will happen to me in Trondelag because you will be there as my personal . . . well, Viking angel." She flashed him a brilliant smile of satisfaction at her deduction.

Incredible! The gall of the woman! "And that is why you wept?"

"Yea, in relief." She shifted her eyes, avoiding direct contact, and he suspected she twisted the truth more than a bit.

He put a hand to his forehead and rubbed out the furrows. "First off, methinks you think too much. Second, you surely jest if you say your One-God sent Anlaf a crooked cock in order to lure me to your side. Third, I am in no way responsible for your safety. Get that through your muddled head. Once I deliver you to Anlaf, I am done with you. And, finally, do not for one minute think of me as an angel, Viking or otherwise. Believe me when I tell you that I have led a less than saintly past, and believe me when I say that the picture of you, naked, in my head does not prompt visions of me flapping my wings about you in protection. More like I am flapping another body part, *in you.*"

She gasped at his crudity.

Good. 'Tis best to set the witch straight from the start.

"You . . . are . . . a . . . troll." It was a favorite refrain of hers.

"Well, then, just call me Saint Troll."

"I don't care what you say. You won't abandon me to some wretched king who might . . . who might—"

"Lop off your head?" he offered.

"Yea."

"You have the wrong opinion of me, my lady. The wrong opinion, by far. I know I jest overmuch, but do not be mistaken in thinking I am soft. I am not. From the age of fifteen till recently, I was a warrior in the armies of any king paying the price, whether it be Jomsviking or Byzantine, it mattered not to me. I cannot count the men I have killed."

"So?"

"So? What do you mean, 'So'?"

"I never questioned whether you had been a stalwart soldier, or are still. But I misdoubt you ever killed a woman, leastways not without some great provocation."

"Oh, my lady, best you think about how much provocation you have given me thus far."

"You will *not* abandon me to some tyrant if there's the least chance of his killing me," she insisted.

"Well, that is no longer the issue."

She tilted her head in bafflement.

"Now that I have seen you naked, and once Anlaf sees you naked, I know that the king would take you on as his sixth wife."

He could see by her fisted hands that she barely restrained herself from clobbering him . . . or trying to. "Even if I am a witch?" she asked in an overly sweet voice.

"Even if you have a tail."

"Well, I still say you won't abandon me. I'm your responsibility now," she persisted.

He used a very coarse word in connection with responsibility.

She raised her chin and glared down her nose at him. "I'm going to say a prayer for you tonight. Among other things, I intend to beseech the Blessed Lord to cleanse your foul tongue."

"Hah! When you tell your beads this eve, best you pray that this image of you, naked, leaves my head. Otherwise you will have a lot more than my foul tongue to worry over."

"And that would be?"

A warrior, such as himself, knew when to charge and when to retreat. A trader, such as himself, knew when to bargain and when to accept defeat. The wench, who apparently had the skills of a rock, did not have the sense to stop when she was ahead.

He raised up on his knees with a palm braced on either side of her hips on the storage box. Leaning closer, he pressed his manhood against the joining of her thighs. Layers of clothing separated them, but his message was clear. His lips were almost touching hers. He felt her breath against his gritted teeth as she inhaled and exhaled with some strong emotion. Their eyes held the entire time, his in challenge, hers in irksome defiance. He stayed in that position for only a moment before rising to his feet. It was enough time . . . for both of them.

He proceeded to leave her then, and the lady called out in a foolish attempt to have the last word, "Well, speak up, you oaf. What do I have to worry about *with you?*"

His final words—rude and provocative and, yea, just a little bit enticing—lingered on the sea breeze long afterwards:

"You do not want to know, my lady. Truly, you do not want to know."

You could say it was a Viking mall . . .

Several days later they approached the land of the Danes and its famous market town at the base of the Jutland peninsula. Hedeby, which the Vikings referred to in their Northern tongue as *æt Hæðum*, was located at the junction of several major trade routes, by sea and land.

Despite being more than a thousand miles from home

and in the heart of Viking territory, Alinor had more than one reason to feel a vast relief . . . and not just because she would finally be stepping on land again.

It was only noon, but already, three times that day, they had encountered vicious-looking pirates. Seamen often put their long shields on the mast-top with the point turned downward to indicate that they came as friends. Not these sea wolves! With their scarred faces and burning eyes, these scavengers of Zealand put a bone-deep fear in Alinor, as Tykir and his Vikings had not thus far. Bolthor had explained that these particular sea outlaws, led by a man called Hord the Rat, maintained a den somewhere between Zealand and Funen . . . a place of terror to one and all. They had gained much success of late in terrorizing the southwest coast of Norway, the Øresund Passage and the Baltic.

The pirate leader had bidden his sailors heave to and grapple the nearest of Tykir's ships. Fortunately, they had given up their attempts quickly on getting a closer view. The mere presence of the fierce fighting forces on Tykir's ships had convinced the pirates to keep their distance thereafter and let them pass by unmolested. Alinor wondered if her prayers in regard to her fate in King Anlaf's court hadn't helped in this regard as well. Or perchance it had been the sight of Tykir and his tall, imposing Northmen, their muscles well honed by battle, donning chain or leather shirts and pulling out sharp swords and battle-axes.

One thing was certain: With each passing pirate sail, Alinor's respect for Tykir as a leader had risen a notch. She didn't have much respect for him as a man, since he'd captured her and disrupted her life on a whim and still declined responsibility for her fate. But as a ship's captain and a chieftain of fighting men, she'd never met better.

There had been times when Tykir's longships rode close to shore, and on some of these promontories and river mouths she'd sometimes seen bearded heads on pikes, indicating that the peoples of that particular land did not welcome seamen

from the north. Even when they'd been Northmen themselves.
Fortunately, Tykir seemed to know how to choose his battles,
and when to ride away from a fruitless fight . . . though Alinor
suspected that he enjoyed a good fight like any other man.
'Twas the nature of the beast.

Now Alinor was leaning against the ship's rail near the
prow, with Bolthor at her side. He was the only one of Tykir's
men who would speak with her. Though even Bolthor, giant
as he was, made sure that his wooden crucifix was visible
and that he was doused with Rurik's holy water. As a further
precaution, he kept making the Christian sign of the cross on
his chest when, in the midst of conversing with her, he recalled that it was a witch with whom he made discourse.

Yestereve, Tykir had doled out small sacks of coins in
payment to his men, though he'd cautioned them that a wise
seaman never counted his wealth till he was home. Some of
Tykir's sailors would be disembarking in Hedeby, staying
with two of the longships that would be beached there over
the winter. Amongst those men, some would take ship on
other vessels leading to their homelands, to return next spring
for the amber harvest in the Baltic. The other five ships would
travel to Trondelag in a day or two, first to King Anlaf's court,
then onward to Tykir's home.

Tykir was busy with the ships' last-minute business, and
he had ordered Bolthor to stand guard over her, which was
ridiculous. How did they expect she would escape here? Jump
overboard and swim in the frigid waters? Fly away on one of
the blustery late autumn breezes? And to what safe haven? A
shark's teeth? The pirates' den?

Now the seven ships were making their way across the
smooth lake at the head of the river Schlei. It was a beautiful
day with clear skies and only a faint breeze, the kind of day
when autumn is shiveringly over but winter's icy blanket not
yet covering the land. The lake resembled a blue-tinted mirror, broken only by the wake of the long-ships as they rowed
smoothly across its calm surface.

"It's spectacular," Alinor said, staring at the unbelievable sight before them. Hedeby.

A huge timber rampart and a lengthy moat surrounded the trading center in a rough semicircle. To the east it was bounded by the waters of Haddeby Noor, with its notably shallow and therefore protective entrance from the Schlei. There were three wide gateways or tunnels—paved with stones—one south and one north for the transit of men, horses and wagons, and one on the west, where a thin stream ran between its piled and strengthened sides down to the fjord.

"Have you never traveled much with your brothers?" Bolthor asked, no doubt amused at her gaping at every new vista like an awestruck child.

She gave the giant a sideways glance of disbelief. "My brothers took me nowhere . . . lest it be some estate or royal gathering where they might barter my body for yet another marriage bed. Never outside Britain."

Bolthor shrugged, as if it was the lot of women. Not worth discussing. Alinor thought about filling the oaf's head with a thought or two about what it was like to be a young woman . . . an *uncomely* young woman with freckles and unmanageable red hair. Could he imagine the humiliation of being rejected, over and over these past ten years and more, since the age of fourteen, as a mate by all the eligible men below the age of fifty of suitable lineage and wealth? No, she guessed that this thick-headed fool—like men of all nations—would fail to see the unfairness of a system that placed women lower than thralls and fine-bred animals. He would consider it a woman's lot, and that was that.

"I've been to Jorvik many a time, of course," she said, instead. "I have an agent there who sells my raw wool and fine fabrics for a good price in the trading stalls of Coppergate. I go into the market town at least twice a year. 'Tis best for a person to keep a hand in her own business."

Bolthor smiled down at her. "You sound like Lady Eadyth. She is ever protective of her honey and mead interests, as well. In truth, Tykir carries many of her products with us this trip to see if he can get a better price for her in the north lands than she does in her native England. Mayhap the jarl will do the same for you when . . . if . . ."

His words trailed off, and Alinor knew he stammered because he was unsure whether she would be returned to her home and her sheep. It was disconcerting to know that Bolthor shared her reservations about her fate.

I am not going to think doomful thoughts. I will return. I will trust that God placed me in the Viking's hands for a reason. It was hard keeping the niggling doubts at bay, however.

"Tell me about Hedeby," Alinor urged.

Bolthor nodded. "There are more than twenty-four hectares enclosed between the ramparts and the sea. See that long, narrow strip of flat land on the open side of the ramparts, facing the water? It is here that some ships and small boats are beached. And here, too, are slips for shipbuilding and repairing."

"It's not as big as Jorvik. Still, it looks intriguing."

"Yea, 'tis. You can find anything of value in Hedeby, whether it be human flesh or fine gold adornments. Next to Jorvik, Tykir sells most of his amber here. In fact, he maintains a house and market stall here year round, watched over by a most trusted craftswoman, Rachelle of Frankland."

"A woman? Tykir trusts his business interests to a woman?"

"Yea? And why not?"

Alinor shook her head. Tykir ever did throw roadblocks in her condemning assessment of him. "And do you come here often?"

"Nay, twice a year at most these past five years or so. Tykir was not always a merchant, you know. He has much word-fame as a soldier and leader of fighting men. Kings of many countries still seek his services. Alas, his injury at Brunanburh harmed him more than is visible to the eye.

And in the winter months, or in seasons of heavy rain, the leg wound pains him sorely, to the point where he becomes almost lame." His head jerked up. With a startled expression on his face, he remarked, "You have a knack for making a man run at the mouth, without caution or discretion. Is it a witch thing?"

Alinor laughed. "Nay, 'tis a woman thing." She jiggled her eyebrows at him, and the big man laughed back at her. Turning more serious, she said, "It was at Brunanburh that you lost your eye, wasn't it?"

He nodded. "Holy Thor! Never have I been engaged in a battle like that one. It marked the end of Viking domination in Britain, for one thing, and amongst those who fed the vultures that day were five kings and seven earls from Ireland, not to mention the son of the king of the Scots. I was left for dead, but Tykir came back for me. To his own peril. 'Twas then a bloody Saxon struck his sword into the jarl's thigh, clear to the bone. Still, he carried me off the battlefield. The surgeons wanted to remove his leg, but fortunately his sister Rain, a healer of much note, was able to save the limb for him."

"Tykir's sister is a healer?" Alinor was astounded. What else did she not know about the dolt? "So how did Tykir get involved in the amber trade?"

"Well, the master was fascinated years ago when he witnessed amber harvesting whilst visiting the Baltic lands. At first, he just engaged in the trading end. Now, he has his own workers there to harvest for him."

"And is there a woman who handles this, too?"

Bolthor laughed. "Nay, 'tis Arnor No-Teeth who heads that enterprise."

Tykir walked up then. "Are you regaling Alinor with another of your wondrous sagas?"

Alinor could see that he was in a rare good mood. No doubt he was as relieved as she to finally set foot on soil. And be one step closer to the end of his mission. "Yea, he was," she answered cheerily, "and I was helping him get the words right."

Bolthor's lips turned up with amusement at her lie.

Tykir made a face of mock horror.

" 'Tis called 'Tykir the Troll Angel.' "

CHAPTER SIX

$\circledcirc$

They were bound to fall in love . . .

More than two hours later, the seven ships were anchored a short distance from shore, the products to be offered in the trading town had been unloaded, and all the men, except one guard per ship, had disembarked and gone off to enjoy a night of drinking and wenching before going to their winter abodes.

Tykir approached Alinor with a loop of rope in his hand.

"Nay," she protested, backing away from him.

"Yea," he insisted, stern-faced and unyielding. "Do not gainsay me now. I have much to do afore nightfall, and no patience have I for your balking."

"But there's no need for you to tie my hands . . . nor my neck. I have nowhere to run here."

"That doesn't mean you wouldn't try." He moved in closer and waved the end of the rope in her face. "I give you two choices, my lady. I tie you to the masthead till the morn, when I return to the ship. Or I tie your hand to mine."

"Or you could just let me walk freely at your side."

He wagged a forefinger in her face. I give you to the count of five. *Einn, tveir, þrir, fjórir, fimm—*"

"Oh, give me the bloody rope." She grabbed the rope from his hands and tried to tie her own wrist.

With a smirk, he took the rope back from her and proceeded to bind their hands tightly together at the wrist. There was no way she would be able to undo the knots without attracting his attention, unless he was drunk, or asleep, or dead.

"I suppose you are so thirsty you could drink a tun of ale," she commented casually a short time later as the oaf dragged her after him down the rocky shore, toward the edges of the town.

"At least a tun," he called back to her, "except I have to meet with Rachelle, and there is much produce I need to stock up on for the winter months."

Hmmm. It appears drink is out of the question.

"Well, you will have to sleep sometime," she offered brightly.

He gave her a sideways glance of suspicion as she did a little skip and caught up to his side.

"Where will I sleep tonight, by the by? Back on the ship?"

He shook his head. "In my home here, behind the market stall. 'Tis cramped quarters they will be, and you will have to share my bed furs."

Alinor's head came up with alertness. "You jest."

"I'm not letting you out of sight, my lady witch . . . not even in the dark." He grinned, aware of her shock. "I am loath to ask, but do you snore? I cannot abide a snoring bed partner."

Alinor's upper lip curled back and a most unfeminine growl emerged from deep in her throat. If he hadn't held her at bay with his outstretched free hand, she would have lunged for him. "Do not think for one minute that you are poking me in the dark with that . . . that thing."

"What thing?" Tykir asked, dancing back when she swung an arm to slap his laughing face.

"That limp wick you and all other men carry around betwixt your legs. That's what."

"Limp? Wick?" he hooted. "Oh, milady, you have obviously never seen a Viking . . . wick."

"You . . . are . . . a . . . troll," she seethed at him, then stomped ahead of him, jerking him along behind her by their bound hands. The most alarming thought occurred to her then. She'd already exhausted the first two possibilities for escape: him being drunk or asleep. That left only dead. She wondered briefly if she would have the stomach for that. But then who would be her guardian angel?

She glanced over her shoulder at the brute, who deliberately hung behind, forcing her to tug on him. Then she glanced again, and wished she could sink into the ground with mortification.

The troll was staring at her bottom. And smiling.

The irksome troll made her tingle . . .

Even wearing Tykir's heavy fur cloak, Alinor shivered. The air had turned blustery and the winter harsh. Suddenly gray skies portended snow or, at the very least, an early frost.

She and Tykir were walking toward the town of Hedeby, the fingers of their bound hands laced together like lovers. It was not really a loverlike body contact, however. First of all, Tykir had forced it on her. Secondly, Tykir was gazing ahead, stone-faced and tight-lipped. He was "sore bedeviled," or so he said, at Alinor's constant hammering away at his less-than-admirable virtues:

"Stop picturing me naked."

"Why do you walk so fast? Dost think me a giant like you?"

"Stop picturing me naked."

"Where did you get that silly earring? And why do you braid your hair on one side only? To show off the ornament or your winsome face? Ugh! You are so vain, you . . . you prideful fop."

"Stop picturing me naked."

"I am hungry . . . but not for *gammelost*. I'd give anything for roast woodcock and a loaf of fresh-baked manchet bread and a . . . why are you smirking? Do not dare suggest what I think you are about to, you . . . you lecherous troll. I didn't mean *anything*."

"Stop picturing me naked."

"Best we find a garderobe . . . *soon!*"

"Hver fjandinn!" Tykir cursed finally. "Damn it, damn it, damn it!" He halted abruptly and turned on her. Taking a deep breath, he conceded with ill grace, "I must yield to your sharp tongue. A truce, my lady?"

Actually, it *was* rather tiresome to nag away at someone who wouldn't respond to every little jibe. She nodded hesitantly.

"I will consent to stop ogling your . . . uh, tail"—he grinned at that last word—"if you will stop pecking away at me like a demented wood-pecking bird. Peck, peck, peck! 'Tis enough to drive a sane man mad."

"And what an appropriate choice of birds! Especially since your brain is naught but a block of wood."

He chuckled, obviously enjoying their banter.

"A truce," Alinor agreed then.

Which was a mistake.

On the one hand, there was what he said next . . . in a low, nimbly drawl. "Ah, sweetling, I knew you and I could get on together if we tried."

Sweetling?

On the other hand, there was what he did. Even as he spoke, Tykir swooped down to seal their bargain with a kiss. It was just a light brush of his lips across hers, but, oh, they were so warm and firm and persuasive. With just that fleeting touch, Alinor felt such a fierce yearning . . . for things she could not even imagine, or had never considered within her grasp.

Tykir jerked back, as if she'd passed poison from her lips to his. But, intuitively, she knew. He was experiencing the same frightening emotion that she was.

Who knew? Alinor thought. *Who knew?*

She did her best to hide her traitorous reaction from Tykir, and he did his best to blanket his demeanor of incredulity. Their hands were still joined, though, and where his palm pressed against hers, skin to skin, she felt an odd connection.

Mayhap he truly was sent to her, by her God or his gods. 'Twas an outlandish idea, of course. But it stayed in Alinor's head and nestled in her heart, giving her momentary hope.

Fortunately, her unwanted thoughts were interrupted by the loud barking of a dog. Beast came galloping toward them, yipping and yelping happily, much to the consternation of Rurik, who was being dragged along by his pet, clutching a length of rope. Rurik was grumbling mightily in the Norse language—foul words, no doubt.

Beast flew through the air with an ambitious leap, from three arm-lengths away, and stood on his hind legs, putting his paws on Alinor's shoulders. He almost knocked over both her and Tykir, who was laughing uproariously. Then he licked her enthusiastically in greeting.

"Oh, aren't you the friendliest dog in the world?" she cooed. "Must be you have Saxon blood in your veins. For a certainty, there is no sign of the ill-tempered Viking in you. Nay, there is not. And, praise the Lord, 'tis a comfort to know that at least one male amongst you plunderers has good taste."

"Come back here, Beast," Rurik demanded. "*Now!* I mean it. Make haste, or you will be sorry."

Still propped against Alinor's body, his tail wagging and his tongue lolling with ecstasy at her ruffling of his head fur, Beast looked back over his shoulder at Rurik with an expression that could only be translated as, "Go away, Viking. I'll come when I'm bloody well ready."

"See . . . see . . ." Rurik sputtered to Tykir. "The witch put a spell on my dog. Five years I have had Beast at my side. My closest companion he has been . . . excepting you, of course," he added hastily. "But now the witch has taken him from me with a spell. Lop off her head, Tykir. 'Tis the only remedy."

Rurik stood glaring at her with misplaced outrage. A dozen magnificent animals must have given their lives for the various furs that adorned his body in layered mantles, and his head was topped by a high black bearskin hat. Gold and silver jewelry bedecked his neck and chest and arms and fingers. Truly, the man was bone-meltingly handsome, even with the woad face mark, in a vicious, overbearing sort of way. With a snort of scorn at her scrutiny, he placed a hand on each hip and tapped a booted foot impatiently, as if he seriously expected Tykir to comply with his order to behead her.

He wouldn't, of course.

Would he?

"Rurik, I swear, you are the world's greatest dunderhead. Didst your mother drop you on your head as a babe?" Sometimes Alinor questioned whether she might have been dropped, as well, especially when her witless tongue raced hither and yon.

Rurik clawed his hands and stretched them out toward her neck. The low, ferocious growl that emerged from his throat would have done Beast proud.

Tykir took Beast by the scruff of the neck and set him aside. Then he quickly shoved Alinor behind him and warned, "Have caution, wench. Push a man too far and even the greatest warrior will be unable to protect your head." He raised his free arm to impede Rurik's approach.

"But the man is deranged," she protested, Still forced to stand behind Tykir, she peered around his right shoulder as she spoke. Meanwhile, the dog thought they were playing a game and ran circles around both her and Tykir. "Beast comes to me, Rurik," she explained, "because he can smell the scent of Beauty on my clothing."

With a hiss of exasperation, Tykir put a palm on her face and rudely pressed her back again so she was hidden totally by his body. Beast thought that was a wonderful trick, apparently, because he jumped up and tried to put his paws on her face, too. Between trying to peer around Tykir to reason with Rurik and trying to calm the dog, Alinor had trouble standing upright.

"That makes sense, Rurik," Tykir said, his one arm still upraised to halt his progress. At the same time, he squeezed her hand tightly with his other hand in a silent message that she was not to interfere anymore.

Alinor peeked under Tykir's uplifted arm and saw Rurik's face soften somewhat, but he continued to insist mulishly, "I still say she is a witch. She stole my dog. 'Tis a crime for which she must pay. The *wergild* for stealing a man's horse is the thief's life. I demand the same for the loss of my dog."

"You can hardly equate a dog with a horse, Rurik," Tykir argued. "Be reasonable." A mischievous chuckle escaped his lips as some thought occurred to him. "Mayhap Alinor could wag her tail for you in recompense for the loss of your dog's devotion."

"Ah ha!" Rurik exclaimed. "So, you have seen her famous tail, after all, Tykir."

"Well, not precisely," Tykir admitted. He was clearly enjoying his ridiculous jest.

"God's teeth! I didn't steal your dog, Rurik," Alinor asserted. "Beast merely shifted his affections."

"Affections?" The sound of mirth was in Tykir's voice.

"Affections?" Rurik shouted, not a hint of mirth in his voice. "I will give you affection. I swear, woman, I could cleave you to your clacking teeth with a single blow and feel not a lick of remorse. With a swing of my sword, Death Stalker, you will get affection."

"Yea, affection, Rurik. You should learn to be more affectionate. Mayhap then your dog would love you again. Furthermore, if you had shown a bit more affection to the Scottish witch, you might not be wearing her mark for life. And personally, I do not think that woad design is half so unattractive as the scowl you wear all the time."

"I am going to kill her, Tykir. I am sorry if that offends you, but I cannot help myself." He was already releasing his sword from its scabbard.

"Nay, Rurik, leave off. The witch will be with us only a

short time longer. Then Beast will gladly come back to you. Go now, find yourself a wench. You know 'tis the best way to cool a hot temper. That and a tun of mead."

After Tykir soothed Rurik with more cajolery, he proceeded to leave, reluctantly. At the last moment, though, he shot daggers of icy promise at Alinor from his blue eyes. Beast stayed behind, unrepentant at his lack of loyalty.

Soon Alinor and Tykir and Beast were walking purposefully toward his home and place of trade in Hedeby. The wood-paved streets cut in an orderly fashion at right angles or parallel to a channeled stream, which ran through the center of Hedeby, west to east. Some of the buildings on these streets were small, less than three-by-three ells, while others were as much as six-by-fifteen ells. The neat dwellings were stave-built with vertical or horizontal planking, or frame-built with wattle-and-daub panels. All of them had reed-thatched roofs and uniformly low doorways. In general, the buildings were placed so that the gable end faced the street, and the attendant outhouses stood behind them. The structures were fenced-off neatly from their neighbors and had their own gates and pathways.

Large numbers of men and women passed by, but Tykir assured Alinor that this was a much-diminished number. Winter approached, and many traders had already left for their homelands. Even so, Alinor could see that a large contingent of people lived here year-round, as evidenced by the young children scampering about at some of the residences. Visible in the backyards were small vegetable patches, bare now of their autumn harvests.

Hedeby was a center for craftsmen who had quarters of their own, much like the Coppergate sector of Jorvik. In front of some of the structures, both homes and businesses, rude stalls had been erected—wood tables with cloth canopies overhead. Here were offered for sale the foods of many lands. Hares, pigeons, chickens, joints of venison, mutton, pork and wild boar, and every fish conceivable. There were also sticky sweets from the east, breads of many different grains, pots of honey, exotic dried fruits from the warmer climates, jugs of the much-prized Norse mead and potent wine from Frisia. There was even *gammelost* and *lutefisk*, which Tykir pointed out with a laugh.

"People actually pay good coin for *that?*" Alinor turned her nose up with disdain.

Many people addressed Tykir by name as they passed, and a few came up and clapped him heartily on the shoulder in welcome. They gave almost no attention to the fact that she was bound to him with rope, but they did stare at her backside. Rurik, or Bolthor, or the seamen from Tykir's ships must have already spread witchly tales of her tail. No doubt the passersby deemed her a personal thrall, or a slave about to be sold in Hedeby.

In fact, on one street, Alinor saw a group of chained men and one woman being led toward a large structure with a wide yard. The men were of dark complexion, possibly of Moorish background, but the woman's skin was pale. Her wails of anguish rose above the din of the crowds as she told her beads and sang psalms aloud in the Frankish tongue.

"Oh, blessed Lord!" Alinor cried. "That woman could very well be a nun." She attempted to rush forward to offer aid but was pulled back short by her restraint.

"You will not interfere," Tykir said firmly. "'Tis none of your affair."

"But . . . but she is clearly a woman of religious conviction . . . a Christian."

He arched a brow at that. "Ah, so you are saying that it is acceptable for only non-Christians to be slaves?"

"That is not what I am saying." *Is it?*

"Nay?" he inquired mockingly. "Then you must be implying that your fellow Christians do not keep slaves."

"Well, yea, they do, but—"

"Slavery is a fact of life in every land. Accept what cannot be changed," he advised.

Alinor would have argued that point with Tykir, except that an even more outrageous event was taking place before the eyes of one and all. In the courtyard of the slave mart, where dozens of slaves were restrained in chains or tied to vertical posts in the ground, a young woman was being offered for sale. But worse than that, her clothing had been stripped from her body and the prospective buyer, a seamen—mayhap even from one of Tykir's ships—was examining her intimately. All the while, he was being encouraged by the guffawing crowd of men.

Tykir dragged her away from the scene, cursing under his breath at her kicks to his shins and her attempts to scratch him with her free hand. When they were far enough away from the slave mart, Tykir slammed her up against the side of a building and used their bound hands as a brace against her neck. "I'm going to release my hand from your mouth now, and if you so much as let a whisper escape your lips before I am done talking to you, you will be next in line at the slave mart. This I swear on my father's grave. Furthermore, whilst my men may have avoided you and your witchly aura like the bloody flux, there are many men who would pay highly for the unique privilege of tumbling a sorceress. Do not doubt my word on that. Are you listening to me, you stubborn witch?"

She nodded her head, fighting back tears of pain at the constricting press of his forearm against her neck.

"You are not in your own land, foolish lady. Nor in mine. What you see and hear may not be to your taste, but no one—least of all me—bloody well cares. I can protect you whilst here . . . to a limit. If you step over that line, you are on your own." He inhaled sharply, as if to control his roiling temper. His smoldering eyes met hers. "Have I made myself clear?"

She nodded again, and he released his arm. Her knees felt soft as butter, and she almost sank to the ground. Tykir caught her with a hand on each side of her waist.

In the distance, she could hear the continued sound of male laughter and a woman's scream.

"Come," he said, more gently now. "There is an ale house over there, which I recall to be reasonably clean. We will have a cup of mead and a plateful of *gammelost.*"

She refused to laugh at his rough attempt at jest. Never would she forget that scene at the slave mart, but she couldn't really blame Tykir for failing to intervene. Slaves were sold in Britain, as well, though she'd never witnessed it firsthand. At the back of her mind was the thought, *It could be me.*

Alinor thought she wouldn't be able to drink or eat, but she had been wrong. Despite her horror at what she'd witnessed, the mead tasted cool and honey-rich. And she ate three slices of warm manchet bread, their centers hollowed out halfway and swimming with chunks of rabbit and leeks in a thick broth.

Afterwards, Tykir led her through the craftsmen's quarters.

A woodworker, maneuvering a foot-treadled pole lathe, was making cups from solid pieces of wood. As the wood spun around, the woodworker held a chisel that gouged and shaped the bowl of the cup.

"This is Sone the Woodworker," Tykir told her. Then he addressed the craftsman. "Have you completed the items I commissioned last spring?"

"Yea," Sone said, nodding enthusiastically. He led them to the back of his shop, where two armchairs and a matching side table sat, all intricately carved in the Viking style with gripping dragon beasts interwoven with the more traditional motif of vining acanthus leaves.

Tykir paid the woodworker with coins from a pouch he carried at his belt and gave directions for the furniture to be delivered to one of his ships.

At another stall, a leatherworker was making boots, shoes, belts and sheaths for knives. The stench of the tanned hides being stretched and processed behind his property took any pleasure out of inspecting his products, to Alinor's mind.

Tykir laughed at her when she crinkled her nose with

distaste. "Living as you do amongst animals on your estate, I would have thought you'd be accustomed to such earthy smells."

"In Coppergate, 'tis a common sight to see skins cured with chicken dung. That does not mean I have to relish the odor."

He laughed again, and it was with much alacrity that they moved on to the comb maker, where a skilled artisan carved his product out of the antlers of a red deer. Once he had the comb itself cut out, he used a fine saw to form the teeth. Finally he decorated his wares. There were also craftsmen working in other types of bone, making ice skates, knife handles, spindle whorls, dice and playing pieces. "I have a herdsman at Dragonstead with an even finer talent for carving," Tykir told her in an undertone, and bought nothing.

Dragonstead, Alinor thought. Tykir had previously mentioned to her the name of his estate in Norway. Now that she knew him better, she deemed the title fitting. Big lumbering beast who blows hot air.

Next, they stopped to watch a jewelry maker melting gold and silver and other less precious metals in small crucibles. He poured the molten metal into stone molds, and it was like magic watching the liquid cool into shiny brooches or coins, with the patterns already on them. Especially interesting to Alinor were the fine filigree pendants he was working into delicate designs, like gold or silver spiderwebs. Some jewelry makers, whose booths they visited next, displayed samples of beautiful ornaments made of amber, ivory, jet and silver. And many of the jewelers carried the colored beads that were so prized by the Viking women . . . not to be worn as neckrings, but as signs of affluence, strung between the utilitarian brooches that rested on either shoulder, holding needle, thread, miniature scissors and keys. The more beads, the wealthier the woman.

"Oooh!" Alinor sighed again and again when they came upon the gossamer-thin silks from the Orient, patterned fabrics called brocades from Byzantium, soapstone products from the Norselands, rich furs of sable, fox and the rare white bear from the Baltic, Frankish glass of jewel-like colors and swords with ornate hilts, millstones of basalt from the Rhineland, quern stones from Koblenz and fanciful harness mounts and jingly spurs from the dark-eyed Saracen craftsmen.

Tykir smiled at her unrestrained appreciation for such frivolous objects. "You should see my treasure room at Dragonstead," he boasted.

"Will I see your treasure room at Dragonstead?" she asked.

"Nay, but you *should* see my treasure room at Dragonstead," he corrected. "These baubles that impress you so here," he said, fingering a length of gold-threaded silk, "are naught compared to my collection."

What an arrogant, overbearing, prideful man! I will see his home, and then he will return me to my home, she decided with an emphatic uplifting of her chin. *He is my guardian Viking angel, no matter what he says.*

In the back of Alinor's mind, however, lingered the image of the naked slave girl, and Tykir doing naught to help. *He will not stand back and let Anlaf harm my person. He surely will not.*

In many stalls could be seen the strong ropes made of walrus or seal skin that were popular with seamen. "Look at that," Tykir said, picking up a huge length of strangely twisted rope. He explained how it was made, by cutting the beast's hide in a single continuous strip, in a spiral, from the shoulder to the tail. Tykir bought three of the ropes—all that the craftsman had on hand—and ordered three more to be picked up next fall.

But there were even more wondrous sights to behold, including live birds in gilt cages and collections of bird feathers, which fascinated Alinor to no end, till finally Tykir pulled her away with a laugh.

"Someday you may meet Abdul, the talksome parrot I

gave to Eadyth as a wedding gift." The secretive smile on his face bespoke some mischief, but all Alinor could think of was his implication once again of life for her beyond Anlaf's court.

"Better yet, I should show you the collection of bird feathers I purchased from a Baghdad sultan who was disbanding his harem. There are at least fifty different feathers, of all sizes and textures, in their own satin-lined chest of gold." The mischievous smile grew more mischievous.

"I never could see the sense of collecting useless objects. My brother Egbert collected rocks as a youthling. Rocks, I tell you. And Hebert collected birds' eggs. One of them was rotten and it took three sennights to get the stink from his bedchamber."

Tykir smiled at her sudden sharing of tidbits from her personal life.

Her curiosity got the better of her then. "What use would there be for feathers in a harem?"

Tykir laughed aloud and nudged her playfully in the side with his elbow. "Alinor, Alinor. For a thrice-widowed, worldly woman, your innocence astounds me."

"I never claimed to be worldly," she blustered, and elbow-jabbed him back.

They moved on, comfortable with the silence between them.

Many different accents and languages could be heard as the customers and merchants argued over price and quality. Instead of coin or barter, most of the buyers used hack silver for their purchases—pieces of silver that could be cut and weighed on collapsible bronze scales. The merchants were often seen scratching the pieces to make sure they were pure silver before putting them on the scale.

She could see that Tykir was amused by her amazement at the scene. He smiled as he said, "Most Viking wealth comes from trading, as you see here. Not pillaging and war."

In truth, the Norse traders *were* well-dressed and well-behaved and prosperous. Just like their Saxon counterparts in Jorvik. Oh, some of the seamen looked as if they might engage in a bit of plundering and pillaging on occasion, like the rapist back at the slave mart, but in this more peaceful setting, she could find no fault.

Tykir stopped abruptly, and Alinor realized that they'd arrived at his residence and place of business. He put a finger to his lips, cautioning silence, as he perused the workings of his enterprise from a short distance away. His long house was one of the larger designs in Hedeby, framed with wattle and daub and roofed with thatch. Its roof extended forward in the front about two ells to form a permanent canopy for the trading wares.

Beast, realizing that they were not moving on, dropped to the ground under the table near Alinor's feet, with his muzzle propped on his front paws, and immediately fell asleep. She and Tykir watched the goings-on at his booth, which held a tantalizing array of amber in all its forms . . . from the raw stone to finely crafted jewelry.

A huge dark-haired Viking man wearing a full-length cloak of wolfskin pelts, drawn back off one shoulder with a silver pennanular brooch, was examining some jewelry set out on the table before him. Waiting on him, behind the table, was a young man of no more than fifteen. To the side of the building, with her back to them, sat a woman using fine cutting and abrasion tools and polishing cloths to fashion lumps of raw amber into workable sizes and shapes. A guard, arms crossed over his wide chest, stood beside the open doorway of the house, watching over the youth and the woman and the expensive wares.

"This would suit Drifa, my first wife," the customer said, taking a string of amber beads in his big pawlike hands.

"A good choice," the boy exclaimed. "See how the beads are of uniform size and color. And they are strung on the finest silk thread, with knots betwixt each bead to prevent chipping."

The Viking nodded. "I will take that. And Grima, my second wife, should favor the pendant over there . . . yea, that's the one . . . seeing as how she already has enough glass beads to prove my wealth." As an afterthought, he added, "But the beads and the pendant must be of equal value, lest I have to listen to their jealous bickerings all winter long." The pendant he chose was an oval filigree frame containing a pale yellow stone, hanging from a dainty silver chain.

"Your two wives will be well pleased, I assure you," the boy said, his eyes twinkling with delight at the two sales.

"Hah! Think you that I only have two wives? You do not know much about a Norseman's virility if you think one woman would satisfy. Three more wives have I besides Drifa and Grima, not to mention five wives long buried." He winked at the boy. "Hard swiving wears down some weak-sapped women."

The boy clearly restrained himself from smiling widely with anticipation at the prospect of additional sales.

"My helpers get a commission on each sale," Tykir whispered in her ear. To Alinor's dismay, she felt the rippling effect of his breath all the way to her toes . . . and some disconcerting place in between. "'Tis an incentive for them to work harder."

The lout was continuing to talk to her, unaware of the effect he was beginning to have on her.

But then the lout blew softly in her ear.

Every tiny hair on Alinor's body, from scalp to toe, stood at attention. In truth, her freckles were paying attention, too.

The lout *did* know that he had an effect on her.

Quickly, the boy spread out three other objects in front of the Viking, presumably of equal value: an exquisite three-cornered brooch of heavy gold, with an amber stone in the center the size of a raven's egg; an armlet of intertwined daisies made of gold petals with amber centers and a set of silver wire ear ornaments with dangling amber gems.

The Viking waved a hand in agreement to the additional purchases, and the boy's eyes nearly popped out at the casualness with which the Norseman spent his money.

"Five wives!" she hissed then in a whisper to Tykir.

He just grinned at her.

"Oh, and one other thing. I must needs have a special gift for Lita, my newest concubine. Only sixteen she is, but ah . . . the things her nubile body can do!" The Viking made a smacking noise of appreciation with his mouth.

Alinor would have liked to smack him, to be sure.

The boy brought forth a delicate finger ring with a tiny amber stone.

"Perfect," the Viking said.

"It's worth more than the others," the boy advised.

"Lita is worth more than the others."

Alinor made a low, snarling noise.

Tykir chuckled softly and squeezed her hand tightly. "Say naught, my witch," he warned, sensing her desire to lash the brute with a piece of her mind.

"Trolls . . . you are a nation of trolls!" Alinor grumbled indignantly.

"Come over here," he said with a laugh. "I will give you a quick education in amber."

The boy glanced over to where they now stood at the far end of the tables, noticing them for the first time. His eyes went wide on recognizing Tykir. "Master Thorksson, I did not see you there," he apologized. He made as if to come to them.

Tykir waved him back. "Finish your transaction, Karl."

Alinor looked down at the table where Tykir had led her, which displayed unmounted pieces of amber.

"We call amber 'The Gold of the North,' but it comes in many colors. Most people think of amber as yellow, like this," he explained, pointing to a stone the size of a hen's egg, "but as you can see, it comes in many colors . . . yellow, orange, red, white, brown, green, blue and even black, which is actually dark shades of the other colors. Those cloudy stones are raw amber, untreated and unpolished. After being heated in oil, the bubbles and fissures will disappear and the amber turns transparent." He moved his hand over the table in a sweeping gesture to illustrate.

"I never realized," she murmured, picking up the egg-shaped piece of amber and closing her fist over it. Immediately, she raised surprised eyes to his. "'Tis warm, as if it has a life of its own. In fact, it seems to pulse."

Tykir smiled, and she could tell that he was pleased by her interest. "That is why so many cultures believe it has mystical, even medicinal, attributes. As to that, I cannot verify, but there is something otherworldly about the stone, methinks."

She cocked her head in question at his fancifulness. This was a side to Tykir she had not seen before. "Were you always interested in amber trading?"

He laughed. "Nay, I only dabbled in trade betwixt battles for one king or another. In those days, wines and furs held more appeal for trade. But then one day, about seven years past, I saw some horsemen in the Baltics harvesting a crop of amber from the sea waves. From then on," he said, shrugging with some embarrassment, "I have been fascinated by this gem."

Amazing, she thought. Both Tykir and the stone.

"Didst you know that amber is naught more than tree sap from millions of years ago?" he went on.

"I had heard such."

"Consider this: Many millions of years ago, when there were great stands of forests reaching almost to the sky, huge globs of resin seeped from the bark, catching in their path various seeds, leaves, feathers, insects, even whole animals. Over the years, the resin hardened, preserving the object. Like this butterfly here." He handed Alinor a chunk of rock, which shimmered with a rainbow of translucent yellows. Inside was a tiny butterfly . . . perfect in every detail.

"Oh," she sighed, putting a hand to her mouth in awe. "Never have I seen such a wondrous object."

"Yea," he agreed in a soft voice, staring down at the object with equal awe. "Once, I had a piece with a honey bee in it, but I gave it to Hrolf the Ganger, first Duke of Norsemandy." He took the pendant which hung round his neck on a gold chain in his hand and showed it to her. The reddish-gold amber had been cut and polished into a star shape, and inside was what appeared to be a drop of blood. "Look closely," he said. "What appears to be wound-dew is the petal of a flower . . . mayhap some ancient rose."

Alinor peered close and saw that it was so. "How old do you think this stone is?" she asked, pointing once again to the remarkable amber-encased butterfly.

He shrugged. "No one can say for sure. Mayhap back to the time when the world was created."

"Before Adam and Eve?" she breathed.

He smiled at the childlike wonder in her voice. "Or the time when the Norse gods and goddesses formed the beginning of our civilization."

"Oh, my!" Alinor said then, her attention diverted to a piece of jewelry lying on a scrap of blue velvet. Alinor had never been one to covet expensive body adornments, but this neck ring was the most magnificent bit of vanity she had ever seen. Surely fit for a queen. The thick gold band would fit snugly around a woman's neck, above the collarbone. From it were suspended a dozen tear-shaped amber stones, starting with a large one in the center and decreasingly smaller ones on either side, down to the size of tiny human tears.

"You like that, do you?" he said, with a laugh. "'Tis the most precious item of jewelry I have, and it is not for sale. It was given to me by an Arab goldsmith, in return for a favor I rendered him. Ahab recommended that the neck ring be given to my bride on our wedding night, as a charm ensuring marriage-luck. Since I do not intend to wed, I will give it to one of Eirik's daughters on her wedding day."

Alinor couldn't help herself. She reached out her free hand and touched the neck ring with her fingertips, very gently. "Dost know what this reminds me of? A poem I heard once. 'Twas written by one of the ancient Romans . . . Ovid, I think his name was. The poem was called *Metamorphoses*, and in it he described how the daughters of the sun god were overwhelmed by grief over the death of their brother and somehow they became transformed into trees. Their tears crystallized into amber, and from then on the people referred to amber as 'The Tears of the Gods.'"

Tykir was watching her closely, a strange expression on his face. "That is exactly what I call this neck ring," he said in a low voice, "and I have never heard that tale afore." He laughed then, as if embarrassed. "You and Bolthor are cut from the same ell of fabric, I swear. Both of you are storytellers."

She'd been thinking the same thing about Tykir and his whimsical affection for an enchanted stone. "You misjudge me. I am not fanciful, at all. Never have I had the inclination or the talent for weaving stories. I weave fabrics, instead. As to Bolthor, I must tell you, Tykir, he is a horrible skald."

"I know," he said unabashedly, then confessed sheepishly, "sometimes when I see the verse-mood come upon his face, I pretend to be asleep." The whole time, his eagle eyes watched as she reluctantly removed her fingertips from the "Tears of the Gods" neck ring with a last, lingering caress.

He shook his head, as if to clear it of unwanted thoughts. "Since you know of the amber legend in the Roman poem, does that mean you have coffers full of amber jewelry? Mayhap you have even bought one of my pieces in Jorvik."

"What?" His question jarred her. Where would he get such an idea? He had visited Graycote and seen that it was a property not given to excess. The man had only to scan her plain attire to know she was not the kind of woman who amassed ornaments, costly or otherwise. But all she said was, "Nay."

"Nay?" he persisted. " 'Nay,' you have no particular liking for amber? 'Nay,' you have no coffers? 'Nay,' you prefer jewelry of another type? 'Nay,' you collect—"

"I have *no* jewelry. Why do you ask these questions?"

"All women of station have jewels, whether they be gifts from a parent, brothers or husband . . . in your case, husbands."

"Tykir, this subject is becoming tiresome. My parents died of the bloody flux in the year of the great cattle disease when I was but eight years old. My brothers have never given me aught but trouble, and that commenced even afore my parents left this world. As to my three husbands . . . nay, there were no gifts. They considered themselves gift enough." Finally, when her emotions had calmed down, she concluded, "To tell you the truth, I would rather have a sheep than a bauble."

Tykir threw his head back and laughed . . . which was fine with her. He'd been studying her closely, seeing overmuch, especially the way her eyes kept returning to the special neck ring.

Alinor was spared further words on the uncomfortable topic just then as a feminine voice called out, "Tykir!"

"Rachelle!" Tykir rushed behind the tables, dragging Alinor with him toward the jewelry maker, who had been working to the side of the building. With a whoop of delight, he lifted the woman into his embrace with his free arm so her feet dangled above the ground, and he hugged her tightly. It was an indication of Tykir's great strength that he could do so one-armed, whilst still restraining Alinor at his other side. The woman's unbound raven black hair swirled forward, covering both her face and Tykir's like a frothy nimbus.

At first, Alinor thought the woman was sublimely beautiful, petite and fine-boned, with perfectly formed, delicate facial features . . . until she tossed her hair back and turned her face in profile. Then Alinor realized that the tip of the woman's nose had been cut off . . . not enough to be grotesque . . . just enough to make some hideous point. It was the sign of the harlot, imposed betimes by barbaric communities in the sanctimonious name of morality, often under the direction of clerics.

Oh, Alinor held little regard for women of no virtue, but she abhorred the practice, which punished the women but not the men who availed themselves of a harlot's services.

"Alinor, I would have you meet my business partner, Rachelle the Jewelry Maker." Tykir had lowered the woman to the ground, but still had an arm wrapped around her shoulders, tucking her close to his side.

Rachelle looked at Alinor with interest, especially at the rope that bound her wrist, then up to Tykir in question.

"This is Alinor the Witch . . . my captive."

Alinor gave the brute a scowl of disgust and told Rachelle, "My name is Lady Alinor of Graycote."

Rachelle was startled at first by Alinor's defiant words. Then she laughed gaily and extended a hand in welcome. "Come, you must crave a bath after your journey. I will fire up the stones in the bathhouse. Meanwhile, I am most anxious to hear how you came to be Tykir's . . . *captive*. And a witch, of course."

Tykir undid her ties, seeming to take way too much time touching her wrist and palm and fingers, even her forearm, in the process of untying the tight knots. Everywhere he touched seemed to grow warm and tingly. Then, seemingly unaware of his effect on her, he turned to help the boy by serving some additional customers who had come up since the big Viking had departed. Rachelle took her arm, about to lead her into the doorway of the longhouse, when Alinor stopped short.

She shouldn't have been surprised. She really shouldn't have.

Standing in the doorway, rubbing sleepily at his eyes, was a small boy of about four years. Apparently, he had just risen from his nap.

"Mother," he whined, reaching his outstretched arms up to Rachelle.

"Oooh, my sweet little Thibaud. Did you just awaken, heartling?" She lifted the child easily so his face was tucked into her neck and his skinny legs wrapped around her waist.

The boy had long blond hair and honey-brown eyes.

A mirror-image of Tykir.

Alinor swung around to glare at Tykir, who was weighing a customer's silver on a brass scale in exchange for some purchase. He must have sensed her stare because he turned. At first, he tilted his head in question; then his eyes took in the scene with Rachelle, Thibaud clinging to his mother, and Alinor's flaming face. As understanding dawned, a slow grin tugged at his lips and spread into a wide smile. No shame or apologetic demeanor.

The man was a troll.

CHAPTER SEVEN

🏵

Mayhap the troll was not so bad, after all . . .

"Thibaud is not Tykir's child," Rachelle informed her all of a sudden.

Alinor hadn't realized that her thoughts were so obvious. She closed her eyes and groaned inwardly. Rachelle had been so nice to her these past three hours, and how did she thank her? By making judgments.

Since their arrival, Alinor had bathed, laundered her dirty clothing, which hung wetly from pegs near the central hearth, and was now helping Rachelle prepare the evening meal, with the assistance of Maida, a servant from Dublin.

Although it was barely late afternoon, dusk already enveloped the skies. Having only a few shuttered windows, the long house would have been dark and gloomy save for the dancing shadows from the raging cookfire. The warmth of the flames turned the house cozy and secure against the blustery winds. Winter was, indeed, on its way. In this warm atmosphere, Thibaud sat at the trestle table playing happily with a set of carved wooden animals from the eastern lands, which Tykir had brought for him. The fanciful creatures had their own gaily painted, compartmented chest.

Tykir had bathed hours ago, then gone out to arrange the restocking of his ships with supplies to last him and his men over the winter months. Karl, the young boy who had been serving customers on their arrival, was outside with the guard, Ottar the Strong, closing up the trading stall for the day. Ottar had been advised not to allow Alinor outside the longhouse. If she disobeyed, Tykir gave Ottar permission to bind her to a support beam.

Tykir had said he would be back in time for the evening meal but was unsure whether Rurik and Bolthor would return with him. Just in case, Rachelle said she would prepare extra food. Maida was chopping leeks and carrots and turnips to add to the cauldron bubbling over the fire, which Alinor was stirring with a long-handled copper ladle. Already, the smell of simmering chunks of venison filled the air, and Alinor's stomach rumbled with hunger.

"Did you hear what I said, Alinor? Thibaud is not Tykir's child." Rachelle was in the process of taking some wooden trenchers and spoons off a shelf near the hearth, about to set the table.

"Yea, I heard." Alinor had found herself looking involuntarily at the child and noting over and over the remarkable resemblance to his father. For some reason, she didn't want to examine the exhilaration she felt now over Rachelle's words, disclaiming Tykir's paternity. "I never thought . . . I mean, it's none of my affair."

"Yea, you thought," Rachelle said with a chuckle. "Everyone does. And, furthermore, I suspect it is very much your affair."

"I have no idea what you mean."

Rachelle laughed softly. "Just do not let him charm you into some ecstasy, without the benefit of the marriage vows . . . assuming you are not already wed. . . . Ah, I can see by the indignation on your face that you are not."

"Charm? Tykir has the charm of a bullfrog, as far as I'm concerned. And you must be jesting with me about any ecstasy to be gained from a man's attention."

"Nay, I am not jesting." Rachelle cocked her head in puzzlement. "Do you not find Tykir exceedingly handsome?"

Alinor was about to say nay but chose the route of honesty instead. "Well, not *exceedingly* handsome. He is not charming, though. Leastways, not to me. He tries to prick me into a temper at every turn."

"Yea, he is a charmer, for a certainty." Rachelle nodded her head, as if Alinor had agreed with her. "Beware when he stops the teasing and turns the tables suddenly to give you compliments or sweet caresses or soft words." Rachelle stopped in the midst of her short walk between the storage shelf and table, and her eyes went dreamy with some remembrance. Was she calling to mind Tykir, or Thibaud's father?

"I am not so porridge-brained as to be taken in by the slick words of a man like Tykir Thorksson."

Rachelle grinned, unconvinced. "Do not be offended by my words of surrendering to the woman-lust, Alinor. I am a perfect example of how not to handle the pretty words of a man in heat."

"Oh, oh . . . you have said so many things I do not know where to begin discrediting them. Woman-lust? Hah! There is no such thing. I should know. I have been wedded and widowed three times in the past ten years. When it comes to lust, men have the sole rights. With their overblown egos, most of them consider women honored just to get a poke from their sorry danglers."

"Danglers?" Rachelle choked out.

"Yea, those appendages that dangle from men in a most ludicrous manner," Alinor explained, and continued with her tirade. "I've yet to meet the woman who brags that she needs five spouses to satisfy her bed needs, as that Viking lord did outside earlier."

Rachelle laughed. "Ah, you have much to learn, my lady. *Much.* Methinks you are in for a sorry awakening if the right man comes along. Pray God it is not Tykir, because there is no future there, I fear."

"I have no need of Tykir or any other man," Alinor asserted stormily. "Why are women so weak that they feel the necessity for a man in their lives to give them strength?"

Rachelle's eyes went wide before she set the trenchers on

the table. "Mayhap you are right," she admitted shakily, putting the fingertips of one hand to her disfigured nose, then glancing over to her son, who was still playing with his wooden animals. All laughter was gone now. "I stand as physical testimony to where woman-lust can lead a weak woman."

The sad expression on Rachelle's face shamed Alinor.

Putting the ladle aside, Alinor went to Rachelle and laid a hand on her forearm. "Forgive me if I gave insult. It is not my place to judge anyone. In truth, I have been speaking my mind, unbridled, from an early age, living as I did with the two biggest lackwits in all Britain. It mattered not how many times they whipped me for my impertinence. I always thought I knew best." She shrugged, with a wry grin. "I still do."

Rachelle smiled weakly. "I *am* deserving of judgment, though. You see, I was married at the time. Thibaud is the result of an adulterous affair."

Alinor tried to contain her surprise. For herself, she could never understand a woman willingly parting her legs for bedsport, but she knew there were women of little virtue who did such to attain some goal, whether it be coin or status or marriage. Rachelle seemed to fit none of those categories.

"My husband, Arnaud, was a cruel man, subject to unreasonable bouts of temper at the least provocation. Even though he was a merchant in Frankland with much property, he made me continue to work at my jewelry craft, even after we were wed. He was so tightfisted with his coin that his household nigh starved to death for lack of food."

That didn't sound so different from her brothers. Or other men of higher station who treated their women as mere chattel.

"I was so lonely. Oh, I know that smacks of a poor excuse for breaking the Lord's commandment, but Toste the Tall was a Northman of such merry temperament that he melted my foolish young heart with a single smile."

That sounded way too close a description of another Viking with a roguish disposition. "And where did you get the opportunity to meet this Viking? Did he come to your keep in Frankland or your husband's trading stall?"

Rachelle shook her head. "Arnaud had taken me to Rouen for the christening ceremony of the new Duke of Norsemandy's first son, assuming there would be numerous business opportunities there. As you know, the Northmen have been in control of Norsemandy for many years now, starting with Hrolf, the first duke. Toste was a mercenary in the employ of the visiting King Haakon from Norway."

"Tykir's uncle, Haakon the Good?"

Rachelle nodded.

"Was it a momentary . . . uh, lapse with this Viking? Or something more?"

"Something more . . . leastways, on my part. I could not have committed adultery lest I loved the man . . . or thought I did."

"And Toste?"

Rachelle rolled her shoulders with reservation. "I know not. He professed to have deep feelings for me, but that may have been the bedlust speaking. All I know is that I was happier with him those few days than ever I have been before or after."

"Did your husband find the two of you together?"

"Nay, but he suspicioned that something was amiss. Mayhap it was a long look that passed betwixt us in the great hall. Or mayhap some talk amongst the servants. In any case, one day he announced without warning that we were leaving for home, despite riches to be gained whilst trading with all the dignitaries."

"And you never had a chance to speak with Toste again?"

Rachelle shook her head sadly.

"Does he know that he has a son?"

"I am not certain. Nay, I think not." She exhaled wearily. "Perchance I delude myself. He may know and not care. He never searched me out. Yea, deep inside, I suspect his professions of love were mere words."

She put a gentle hand to Rachelle's maimed nose. "And this?"

"Ah, this," Rachelle said with a mournful sigh, touching the same spot that Alinor had. "At first, Arnaud was jubilant over my pregnancy. He treated me almost lovingly, and I was overcome with such a soul-deep remorse that I had betrayed him so. Mayhap Arnaud's ill-treatment all those years was my fault. If I had given him a child. If I had been a better wife—"

"Rachelle, stop . . . stop this instant. Do not try to excuse your husband's brutality by taking on the burden of guilt."

"To make a long story not quite so long," she continued, "the proof of paternity was evident the moment Thibaud came crying from the womb. His blond hair and blue eyes were giveaways, considering that Arnaud and I share the same black hair and dark eyes."

"Would he not forgive your . . . indiscretion?"

"Forgive? 'Twas Arnaud who dragged me by the hair from the birthing sheets, down the manor steps, to the chapel, where he pronounced my crime afore the priest and all our churls. The villagers were invited to toss the first stones, and in the end 'twas Arnaud himself who sliced the harlot mark on my nose."

"Oh, Rachelle," Alinor lamented, taking the weeping woman into her arms.

Rachelle soon calmed down and concluded her story. "After several weeks of care in the hut of a forest midwife, who took pity on me, I made my way with Thibaud to Rouen. But, of course, by then all the festivities had ended, and the guests long departed. It was there that I met Tykir, who took pity on me and brought me to Hedeby. He claimed to be in dire need of a jewelry maker to sell his products here, but I suspect I was such a pitiful sight he could not help himself."

Alinor gave her a disbelieving look. She did not want to contemplate what this said about Tykir. He was a troll. She had to remember that. Where was his concern for *her* plight?

"So, now you are in reduced straits here, stranded in a Norse trading town?"

Rachelle laughed gaily at that. "Nay, I am a woman who has survived a horrible marriage and vicious punishment. Now I am self-sufficient. Tykir allows me a portion of his profits, and they are ample. I am a wealthy woman, dependent on no man. And, best of all, I have my most beloved son."

Alinor thought about that for a moment. "I must confess, I envy you."

"Me?" Rachelle backed away slightly, as if Alinor had become unbalanced.

"Yea, I do. I really do, Rachelle. All my life I have yearned just to be left in peace. I raise the best sheep in all Northumbria. Truly, I do. My weavers produce the finest wool under my direction . . . soft as silk. I could easily support myself . . . I do now, without my brothers' knowledge. But a woman has no power in my country, or any other. Whatever wealth I gain belongs to my brothers, or my husband when I am wed. Whatever improvements I make to my estates benefit them, not me. They can sell it all right under me. In fact, they can sell me, as well. And they do . . . over and over."

It was Rachelle's turn to hug Alinor.

"You will think me barmy when I tell you of the fantasy I have harbored of late," Alinor said. "I have been wondering if perchance God sent Tykir to rescue me from my brothers."

Instead of laughing, Rachelle gave Alinor's idea serious thought. Tapping her pressed lips with a forefinger, she pondered her words. "But Tykir says he will deliver you to King Anlaf and be done with you."

"Does that fit the character of a man who would rescue a stranger and her child?"

"Do not put too much credence in that seeming generosity. I am a trained craftswoman, and he was in need of just such a worker at the time. Also, he had a passing acquaintance with Toste, and felt somewhat responsible for the orphaning of a Norse child . . . even one not of his blood."

"Well, actually, he might not be all that softhearted as I would like," Alinor conceded, and related the story of Tykir's refusal to intervene with the slave girl earlier that day.

Rachelle made a clucking noise of dismay, but all she said was, "It is a hard life for women."

With spirits dampened, Alinor reflected on her fate. "Dost thou really believe Tykir will abandon me to possible death in Anlaf's court? All for the sake of a horse and a slave girl?"

"A horse and a slave girl?" Rachelle frowned with confusion.

Alinor explained the reasons Tykir had undertaken this quest to capture a witch for King Anlaf.

"Ah, you do not know the real reason Tykir captured you?"

"The *real* reason?" Alinor shook her head dumbly.

"Anlaf is holding as friendly hostage the healer, Adam of Arabia. Adam is the adopted son of his half-sister Rain and his brother-by-marriage, Selik . . . a man who fought side by side with Thork Haraldsson in the battle many years past with Ivar the Terrible that eventually led to his death. The family connections are complicated, but the heart-bonds are not."

Alinor put a hand to her forehead in puzzlement. "So, Tykir had no choice?"

"He had a choice. Adam is in no real peril. Anlaf wouldn't risk enraging so many Northmen in high places by harming Adam, but neither will Anlaf release him till his malady is cured."

"Well, why didn't the troll just tell me all this?"

Rachelle waved a hand with dismissal. "Tykir is a man. Men do not deign to share their plans with women."

"But he told you," Alinor argued.

"Only because I badgered him to justify his conduct. And, actually, 'twas Bolthor who filled in most of the picture."

"So, dost thou think there is any chance of Tykir being my guardian Viking—"

"Guardian Viking?" Rachelle choked out a laugh.

"—sent by God to champion my cause against my brothers?" Even Alinor had to smile at how foolish her words sounded.

"Who can say? Who can say? I do not believe Tykir will release you and jeopardize Adam. But mayhap God has a finger in this porridge. Yea, in reflecting on it, I am beginning to suspect you will play a pivotal role in the unraveling of this mess."

"But there is the chance that Tykir will sacrifice me for Adam . . . that he will leave Trondelag with Adam, and me behind to handle my fate with my own devices, such as they are."

"Yea, there is that chance." Rachelle studied her for a moment. "Do you have . . . devices?"

Alinor laughed at that. So, even Rachelle was not altogether sure she was not a witch. "There are devices and there are devices," she answered enigmatically. Suddenly, a marvelous plan occurred to Alinor. Stepping away from her newfound friend, she paced back and forth along the hearth. "Is it possible," she asked Rachelle, "that Tykir might be convinced to set me up in business?"

"Hah! And what business might that be?" Rurik asked, coming through the doorway, bringing a gust of frosty wind with him. So tall was he that the roof beams of the low ceiling grazed his head, as they did for Tykir and Bolthor. "The witch business?"

Alinor glared at Rurik. Then, slowly, she let a slow grin slip across her lips. Her eyes dropped deliberately to the region of his precious manparts and, surreptitiously, so no one else would notice, she waggled her fingers.

"Did you see that? Did you see that?" Rurik raged. "The witch just put a spell on me."

Tykir, who came in behind him, looked from Rurik, who was peering inside his braies, to her, and back again, then shrugged, seeing nothing amiss. "As to businesses, you'd best not be thinking I'd get involved with sheep, My lady of the Freckles," Tykir remarked to her as he proceeded to the hearth fire, where he rubbed his hands briskly over the flames . . . and winked at a giggling Maida—*the lecherous lout*. "I had more than enough of those smelly creatures on the journey from Graycote to Jorvik."

"My sheep do not smell," Alinor said indignantly and brushed her gown aside with repugnance when Tykir stepped too close to her, giving her one of those lascivious I-can-see-you-naked looks.

Bolthor was the last to come in, along with Ottar and Karl, who washed their hands in a bucket on a bench near the door. "I have a thought for a new saga," Bolthor began. Everyone rolled their eyes, but not so the giant could see. "How Tykir the Great Came to Be a Sheep Herder."

That wasn't my knee, sweetheart . . .

Hours later, Tykir prepared to slip into his bed furs, where the Lady Alinor awaited him.

Well, "awaited" was not precisely the correct word.

He could practically hear the grinding of her teeth from halfway across the room.

Despite his softening toward Alinor in some regards, considering that she had tried to poison him with one of her potions, he did not trust her any farther than he could see her. As a result, he'd informed her an hour past that she would share his bed furs or be trussed up against one of the roof support beams, where she would, no doubt, turn into an icicle once the hearth fires died down—a uniquely speckled icicle, at that.

She'd raged, nagged, cajoled, then raged again, to no avail.

Finally, Rurik and Bolthor had gone out, griping mightily, to seek quieter sleep companions—well, mayhap not so quiet . . . most men, and they were no exception, relished a woman who was vocal in her bed-pleasures. And Viking men were known for their abilities to give women bed-pleasures. In any case, Rurik and Bolthor had contended that they would be unable to rest in this longhouse with their ears ringing from Alinor's screeching voice.

Of course, Rurik had no choice but to depart anyway since Rachelle had slapped his face—not once, but twice—for suggesting she engage in some perverse activity with him.

Then, too, when she thought no one was looking, Alinor had taken to waggling her fingers in the oddest way at Rurik's manparts, which made Rurik turn nigh green in the face.

Tykir thought he might go mad before he ever reached Trondelag.

Now Ottar and Karl snored lustily at the far end of the long house, near the front door. Rachelle had long since gone to her bench bed on the other side of the raised hearth with Thibaud, who was exhausted by an hour of wrestling on the rush-covered floors with Tykir, Rurik and Bolthor. Holy Thor, how the straw had flown!

Rachelle had just smiled at their rough antics. But Alinor had tsk-ed and tsk-ed, calling them all "naught but little boys" themselves . . . to which he and Rurik and Bolthor had grinned in agreement, and crossed their eyes at her . . . which just made Alinor tsk some more.

Now he banked the hearth fire and yawned, openmouthed, as he approached his bed furs on the other side of the hearth, where Alinor lay on her back with the skins pulled up to her chin. He suddenly realized how bone-weary he was. It had been a very long day. Good thing he had not succumbed to Rurik and Bolthor's exhortation that he accompany them to a bawdy house. He doubted he would be up to the bedsport tonight.

With another robust yawn, he began to remove his clothing. First, he hopped about on one foot, then another, as he unlaced his cross-gartered ankle boots. He thought he heard Alinor make a teeth-sucking noise of disgust at the ruckus he was making. No one else seemed to notice, though, apparently being fast asleep.

Alinor's disapproval annoyed him, along with her constant complaints all the evening long . . . in fact, these past two sennights. What kind of captive was she that she felt free to berate her captors? What did that say about him as the captor?

He would turn the tables on her, he decided. He would undress in front of her, slowly, and imprint an image on her brain of him, naked, just as he had of her. That would show her.

He hoped.

But the witch defeated him by keeping her eyes scrunched tight. He was fairly certain she did not see his naked form—which was magnificent, if he did say so himself—because he watched her closely. She did not once blink or peek.

That annoyed him, too.

With a muttered curse, he slipped into the furs beside her. She squealed with outrage, unable to maintain her cool composure. Mayhap she had seen him after all, and was now swoony with concern over the size of his . . . form. Some women were missish in that regard, not realizing that the female body was made to accommodate any . . . form.

"Your toes are cold, you brute. Don't touch me. Move your feet."

Well, mayhap not so swoony . . . or missish.

She waggled her bare toes against his bare toes, and he experienced the shock of it all the way to the top of his scalp, the ends of his fingers and the very tip of his manhood. The last time he'd felt such an immediate jolt was when Bolthor, who weighed as much as a midsize horse, had stepped on his big toe. Blessed Freyja! He had seen stars then. But that had been different. This shock was painful, too, but in a most delicious way. *Who would have thought toes could be such an erotic body part?*

"Stop squirming," he grumbled, trying to make himself comfortable, "lest you arouse me." That last disclosure was an impulsive inspiration, for which he congratulated himself.

She stilled immediately. "You lecherous lout! Are you naked?"

"Of course I'm naked. 'Tis how most mortal men, and women, sleep. Aren't you?" He reached out a hand to check, and encountered her underchemise. *Helvtis,* he thought, though why he should care, he could not say. *Damn, damn, damn.*

"No, I'm not naked," she snapped, slapping his hand away. She rolled over to her side and turned to face the wall, taking most of the bed furs with her.

He grinned and pulled his half of the bed furs back. Then, risking bodily damage, he nestled against her, spoon-fashion. She had no place to go. Thank the gods!

"Stop pressing your knee into my backside," she ordered in an icy voice, which, no doubt, had a chilling effect on her sheep. But none whatsoever on him.

He chuckled. "My knee is nowhere near your rump," he told her. And it wasn't.

When understanding dawned, she bolted up into a sitting position and tried to flee the bed furs. "You loathsome wretch!"

"Shhhh," he cautioned, pushing her down so she lay on her back. "You'll wake everyone." With that, he rolled over onto his side and threw one leg over her thighs and an arm across her chest, thus imprisoning her.

But what he accomplished, instead, was a soul-searing blow to his senses. With his legs, through her night rail, he perceived the shapeliness of her thighs, causing the very hairs to stand up on his legs, and everywhere else. Under his forearm, the nipple of her breast budded, begging for his touch. The witch felt so damn good in his arms that the very breath seemed to stop in his lungs, and his heart skipped a beat.

She gasped, as if equally affected, and stopped struggling.

With a groan, he nuzzled her rose-scented hair and whispered, "You should stop using Eadyth's hair ointment."

"Why?" she whispered back.

He felt her breath against his cheek as she turned to speak to him. It was warm and fresh and dangerously enticing. "Because I like it too much," he answered.

That gave her pause. The lady would not like him liking anything about her . . . not her naked body, not the smell of her hair, not her sweet breath and definitely not the imprint of her nipple on his flesh.

I am doomed, he thought. *The witch has ensorcelled me with her spells. And I do not care. All I care about is—*

"All you care about is your lustful impulses," she charged, trying to shift out of his embrace. "You are just like every other man, thinking only of yourself."

"I am like no other man," he assured her, tightening his arm and leg across her.

"If I lie still, will you leave me alone?"

Smart woman! Knows when to fight and when to negotiate. "Mayhap."

"I would like to offer you a bargain . . . one that could be very lucrative for you."

His mind went suddenly alert. What was she up to now? "Lucrative in what way? I have more than enough wealth."

"Nobody has too much wealth."

"I do."

"Nay, you do not," she argued.

"Make your damn offer and be done with this foolishness. But know that if it involves your release and an exchange of money, I am not interested."

"Loosen your hold on me first. I'm suffocating."

"I'm not on top of you. You do not bear my weight. And my arm and leg are only resting lightly on you. How can you be suffocating?"

"Your nearness suffocates me."

Ah, so she was aware of this strange connection betwixt them. He couldn't quite explain it. It was more than a spark, but less than a flame. Was her body making ready for the bedsport, even as her stubborn mind resisted? He did have that effect on women betimes. He smiled widely with satisfaction.

"Stop smiling," she chastised.

"How can you tell I'm smiling?" The room was dark, but not totally black due to the brightness cast by the banked fire.

"I sensed it."

"You sensed a smile?"

"Aaarrgh! Let us get back to the subject at hand. I will not ask that you release me now—"

"Good thing," he interrupted, "because I would not."

"—not this instant, I mean. I know that you are honor bound to deliver me to King Anlaf's court. Your nephew Adam's safety is important to you, and—"

"Adam? Who told you about Adam? That god Loki must be stirring trouble again in the form of a certain someone who has a loose tongue in my company."

"It does not matter how I found out. The important thing is that you deliver me to King Anlaf's court, *and* that you offer me your protection there. Most significant, you will promise to return me to my home at Graycote . . . let us say, by Christmas."

"Let us say . . . not in my bloody lifetime."

"Now, do not be hasty. Do you not want to know my terms?"

"Nay."

He thought she said something foul in an undertone before speaking aloud. "I can give you three hundred marks of silver, if you will agree to my safe return to Northumbria."

He wondered how she was able to lay her hands on that considerable sum, but he'd been truthful in telling her he had wealth enough. "You would ransom yourself?"

"No one else will."

Any other woman would moan and bewail her misfortune in making that statement, but not Alinor. She just brushed it off as a fact of her life. He did not want to admire the shrew, but sometimes he could not help himself.

"Well?"

He laughed at her persistence. "'Twould not be worth the aggravation."

"Aggra-aggravation," she sputtered.

He rather enjoyed making her sputter.

"Five hundred marks, then."

Now that surprised him. "Alinor, how in the name of your holy saints would you obtain five hundred marks to give me?"

"You do not need to know the how of it. But if you must know, sheep."

"Sheep," he repeated drolly. "Your familiars would bring the coin here?"

"Familiars? Blessed Lord! You can't be that lackwitted. I have many folds of sheep . . . just animals. Nothing magical about them, except the fine fabrics to be gleaned from their fur."

"There is *that* much to be gained from those smelly beasts?"

"My sheep do not smell, I tell you." If she'd been standing up, she would have stamped her foot, Tykir would warrant.

"I don't want money from you," he said.

"Well, what do you want from me?"

Oh, she should not have asked that. She really should not have. "Let's make love," he blurted out in a voice that sounded husky, even to his own ears.

She inhaled sharply with shock, then scoffed, "That is lust speaking."

"Yea."

"Really, what is it about men and sex? Three minutes of bouncing atop a woman—one minute of which is spent in trying to get the wick to stand up properly—and they're in a swoon."

"Three . . . three minutes?" he sputtered. "Oh, Alinor, you have been cheated."

"Humph! That's another thing about men. They always deem themselves better than all others in the bedsport. Well, let me tell you, if they think to impress women with such boasts, they are sorely mistaken. Women do not care one whit about the size of the wick, or how long it can burn."

"Do not cast me in the same mold as all men, my lady. As to wicks, I am more like a whole candle. And I assure you, I can burn for a looong time."

"Talk, talk, talk."

"You know what they say, don't you? It's not the size of the stick, but the magic in the wand. Luckily, we Vikings have the size and the magic."

"Oh, really! Wicks, sticks, wands, it matters not to me. I am not impressed, or moved to any great rapture."

"Well, you keep on talking like that and you may find more than you wagered for."

"You wouldst take me without my free consent?"

"Nay, I would arouse you till you begged for my . . . *wick*."

"If you are so desperate for a woman, why didn't you go with Rurik and Bolthor?"

"Desperate would be too strong a word. It's been more than a sennight since I have lain betwixt a woman's thighs, and—"

Her body went rigid with alertness. "A sennight? How could that be? You have been nigh plastered to my side every minute of every blessed day for two sennights now. The only time you were out of my sight was the afternoon I went to Gyda's house in Jorvik to bathe . . ." Her tirade dwindled off as realization struck. Then she punched him in the arm. "The afternoon? You rutted with a woman in daylight? You are a pig."

He had to laugh at that bit of ignorance on her part about

the mating habits of men and women. "So, do you want to make love or not?"

The only answer he got was a grinding sound, like the gnashing of teeth, which he took to be a refusal. "'Tis just that my body is tense and restless. I doubt me I will be able to fall asleep. So, I thought—"

"—you thought to poke at me, to relieve your boredom." Her contemptuous tone didn't bode well for his prospects. "What am I? A receptacle for your seed? I . . . think . . . not!"

"You would enjoy the *poking*, this I guarantee."

"Oh, I swear, you have conceit enough for a dozen men!"

"'Tis not conceit. 'Tis a fact. I know . . . secrets." He would have waggled his eyebrows at her, but he misdoubted she would be able to see them.

"Secrets?" She burst out with a light, ripply laugh. "Is it just you who has these secrets, or all Northmen?"

"Well, I cannot speak for every Viking. But, yea, 'tis said all have the knack. I merely polished it to perfection."

This time she didn't even try to hold back her laughter. "Have a caution, Viking. Keep your *knack* on your side of the furs, or you may find your knack taking a right turn . . . but not from any witchly spell. 'Twill be from a knock with my fist."

"A knack-knock? I like it when you talk fierce to me. My *knack* does, too."

"Ooooh, this is the most ridiculous conversation I've ever had in all my life."

"You started it."

"I did not," she declared indignantly. Then, "Did I?"

"You did." He misremembered whether she had or hadn't, but that mattered neither here nor there. It was always good policy to make a woman feel guilty. They did all kinds of delicious things to make amends.

"Are you seriously saying that you would agree to my terms if I would agree to rut with you?"

Rut? He cringed at her vulgar word. "Nay, I am agreeing to nothing. I merely answered your question."

"What question?"

"You asked what I wanted from you, and I said the first thing that popped into my head."

"Well, pop this into your head, my Lord Lech. I will not, now or ever, make love with you. Not for coin. Not for lust. Not for any reason whatsoever."

Tykir grinned. "Is that your final word?"

"Nay, these are my final words . . ."

He waited expectantly.

". . . you are a troll."

Yea, I am. Else why would I be considering what I am considering? 'Tis foolhardy. 'Tis a mistake in the making. 'Tis like jumping off a cliff into a stormy sea.

'Tis bloody damn tempting.

Her lips were a hairsbreadth away from his, close enough for a kiss. His *wick knack* took particular note of that fact, too, and he had to clench his fists to keep from grabbing for her. Best he change the subject, with all haste. He forced himself to yawn widely. "Well, best we get some sleep. I would like for us to be on our way afore midday."

"Can't we stay at least another day?"

He shook his head. "Nay. The rowing will be hard as it is for my seamen, especially if there is ice on the oars. Winter is truly on the horizon. I can tell by the ache in my leg tonight. When my battle scar throbs, that usually portends cold weather. Methinks there may even be frost on the bracken come morn."

"Would that be the leg that has moved into forbidden territory?" she asked waspishly.

He groaned inwardly. He hadn't realized that his knee had moved instinctively upwards. But what a feckless maid she was to call his attention to the fact. Now, if he moved it, he would appear guilty. But if he did not move it, he would not be able to stop thinking about the heat that seemed to emanate from her *there*. He chose the latter course. "That would be the leg," he admitted. "And best you watch your tart tongue, my lady, or you may provoke other of my body parts to move into other of your forbidden territories."

"Your crudity knows no bounds." She tried, unsuccessfully, to squirm out of his grasp. "Only you would find a way to bring a discussion of the weather back to . . . to . . ."

"Sex?" *Oh, that was very intelligent of me. Bring back the unwanted subject.*

"Yea, sex, you bloody fool. Sex, sex, sex, that's all you men think about. Mention plowing, you think of sex. Mention weaving, you think of sex. Mention horse riding, you think of sex. Mention sheep, you think of sex—"

He laughed so hard then that he began to choke. "Sheep? Sheep?" he sputtered. "Oh, Alinor, you are unbelievable."

"Don't think that I don't know what you're thinking!"

"There are a goodly number of thinks in there," he quipped. "I'd best think about that for a while."

She slapped at his chest in remonstrance. "You are thinking that I may be mud ugly in the daylight with my brash hair and freckles and other uncomely attributes, but in the dark, one female is the same as any other."

"You have me all figured out, do you?"

"Yea, I do. 'Tis just as Egbert and Hebert used to say when they came home late, after a night of wenching. It matters not the beauty of the sky when you are plowing a field."

"We Vikings have a similar saying," he said. *"I mø er all katterå."* He paused for only a moment before translating with a laugh, "All cats are gray in the dark."

She punched him.

Which was a mistake, because he laughed even harder.

Then she made the biggest mistake of all. She shifted abruptly to confront him, thus causing her breasts and upper legs to abrade his forearm and thighs, but, most alarming, putting her lips within kissing distance of his. And if there was one thing he relished in the lovesport more than any other, it was kissing. Long and deep, short and soft, demanding and persuasive, wet and dry. Good kissing was almost equal to good sex. Not quite, but almost.

So, without considering the consequences, he put a hand to her nape and drew her to him. Her lips parted with surprise, and he took advantage by slanting his mouth over hers in a perfect fit, with her lips forced to remain open.

Then he proceeded to show her, well and true, that all men were not alike.

CHAPTER EIGHT

❧

Kisses sweeter than mead . . .
    A kiss.
  So this is a kiss.
  Hmmm.
  Ummmmm.
  Tykir had caught her unawares, lips parted, about to protest, when first he pulled her to him. Now the gentle pressure of his lips forced hers to remain open for his plundering. Shifting and shaping, he plied an age-old expertise till he won her pliancy.
  Then he started over again.
  It should have been embarrassing, but it was not.
  It should have been an assault, but it was not.
  It should have been repulsive, but—*oh, sweet Mary!*—it was not.
  By the time she realized that she lay quiescent, surrendering to the seduction of his kiss, it was too late. Her curiosity was aroused, her senses enflamed.
  A kiss is like an exploration, she marveled. *Man of woman. Woman of man. And of oneself.*
  And it is a dance. She smiled inwardly at such uncharacteristic whimsy on her part. But truly it *was* a dance—a lyrical movement of the body set to the music of the senses. An erotic play of slow rhythms and subtle nuances.
  She wanted to know more.
  There was a clean, musky fragrance to his skin, contrasting

with the lingering scent of the animal furs and the wood fire. His breath tasted of honeyed mead.

But, nay, it was madness to continue on this path. She should push him away now. Stop this insanity before the lout deemed her smitten with him . . . which she was not. It was the kiss that held her in thrall, of course, not the man. Instead of resisting, she dug her fingers into his shoulders and lay back to give him easier access.

His body stilled. Then he murmured one word and one word only against her lips: "Alinor." There was wonder in his voice, and surprise, and raw, frightening promise.

Blessed St. Jude, patron of hopeless cases, come to my aid. I fear I am becoming the most hopeless case of all.

Leaning over her, he placed one hand to her throat to hold her in place, with his wide thumb resting on the pulse spot on her neck. Could he feel the thundering of her heart? The roaring of her blood?

His kiss changed then, reclaiming hers with a shocking hunger. Before Alinor had a chance to register the significance of this switch and realize that now might be the time to call a halt to this risky game, Tykir forced her lips wider with his own, and his tongue pushed slowly and deeply into her mouth. Stunned, she allowed him this invasion. His tongue withdrew, then plunged again.

Tongue kissing, of which Alinor had heard but never quite believed, was deliciously revolting, she decided. The slickness in her mouth—whether hers or his, she could not tell, to her horror—should be distasteful. The rhythmic thrust and parry of his tongue should have caused her outrage. The command of his lips that she respond should have caused her consternation. But, oh, what a traitor her body proved to be! Her breasts peaked into hard points and ached with the need for . . . something. Heat curled into a strange knot at the pit of her stomach. In that secret place between her legs a throb started, clenching in slow, progressively stronger counterpoint to the cadence of his tongue's sheathing and unsheathing.

Just when she was starting to discover the intricate steps of the tongue sport, he broke the kiss and whispered against her ear, "Did you like that kind of kiss, witch-ling?"

She couldn't have answered if her life depended on it, so mortified was she at his guessing her appreciation; so she did something even worse. She moaned.

To her amazement, he didn't laugh, or make some biting remark about lustful widows. What he did was moan back at her—a low, masculine rumble of pure arousal.

She ducked her head against his shoulder to hide her shame.

He tipped her face back up with a forefinger under her chin. "Do not hide from me. Your eagerness excites me."

Before she could deny his ludicrous claim, she saw his head descending. This time his kiss was a gentle act of controlled aggression. He nipped her bottom lip with his front teeth and tugged lightly. He showed her with soft, sexual words of encouragement how to glide her own tongue into his mouth, and how to draw on his tongue when he entered hers. He angled her head and settled his mouth over hers again, murmuring, "'Tis time to get down to the *serious* business of kissing."

God's teeth! What had they been doing thus far, if not the *serious* business of kissing?

He was rapacious then. His mouth closed on hers again and again, entreating, claiming, playing, persuading. His molding, unending kiss changed patterns like rain in a summer storm, alternately rough and tender, harsh and wonderful.

Her breath caught in her throat, then came out in a thready exhalation.

His breath was a hot, ragged reminder that he was male and dangerous.

Alinor never knew a kiss could be so many things.

He tore his mouth from hers and pressed his forehead against hers, panting. "I want to make love with you," he said in a thickened voice.

Who knew what she might have replied if St. Jude hadn't come to her aid then in the form of the most unlikely angel: Rurik.

Water was dripping down on Alinor's face.

At first she thought it was a leak in the roof where rainfall might have started while her attention had been diverted elsewhere. But, nay, the droplets were coming off Tykir's hair because of the holy water Rurik was drizzling from above.

"Have you lost your bloody mind?" Tykir shouted as he reared up, off of her and out of the furs.

The loudness of his voice awakened Rachelle, Ottar and Karl. Rachelle lit a soapstone lamp and Ottar rushed forth with raised sword, not knowing if there was an intruder.

Rurik was raising a fist, as well as his voice, as he berated his friend. "But I saw you kissing the witch and knew you must be under her spell. Did she give you another potion?"

"Nay, lackbrain, she gave me nothing . . . no thanks to you."

Rachelle raised her lamp high, took one look at Alinor's kiss-swollen lips and whisker-grazed face and laughed so hard and long that everyone turned to stare at her in question.

No one except Alinor seemed to be aware, or care, that Ottar, Karl and Tykir were nude. Totally. In fact, Alinor couldn't keep her eyes from stealing glance after glance at the hard evidence between Tykir's thighs that bespoke just how much he had wanted to make love with her. *Now, that is a magic wand if I ever saw one . . . which I haven't, of course.*

She was glad now that they had been interrupted, but glancing down one last time, she felt the tiniest twinge of regret. And curiosity.

What would it be like to make love with this man?

Did she really question the size of his wick? . . .
What would it be like to make love with this woman?
That thought and many others in a similar vein were keep-

ing Tykir awake. At least an hour had passed since he'd called out, "Sleep well!" to everyone, and they had returned, "Good night!" and gone to their rest, again. From the sounds of snoring and even breathing, he assumed they were all asleep.

Except him.

And Alinor.

What was she thinking that kept her awake? Probably ways to cut off certain of his body parts in retribution for the embarrassment he'd dealt her a short time ago. Who knew she would be so missish over a little exposed male flesh? Or teasing about swollen lips? With the distance she put between them now, he assumed she was not entertaining the same erotic thoughts as he. Nay, she practically hugged the wall so that not a hair on his body could touch a hair on hers.

Holy Thor! Just that "hair" image caused his staff to lengthen a tiny bit more . . . as if any more was possible! He was rock hard and more than eager. Much more of this and he would have to go dip his staff in the water bucket, after first cracking the ice that formed on top. Now there was a thought to dampen a hard man's "enthusiasm."

"Alinor . . ." he said tentatively.

"Nay."

"Nay? I didn't even ask the question yet."

"The answer is still nay. Nay, nay, nay."

He chuckled.

"Smirk all you want, lord of Lech."

"Lord of Lech?" he gasped out.

"We are not going to resume those kissing games. You are not going to touch me. I am not going to touch you. I may have lost my senses there for a moment, but I have them back now. And this *witch* is not making love with yon *troll.*"

"Would *yon* troll be referring to me?" he said, choking with laughter.

"If the name fits, Viking."

"The witch and the troll. It has a nice ring to it, don't you think?"

"Aaarrgh!"

"You wanted me," he pointed out. "Do not try to deny it."

"'Twas just curiosity."

He thought about that for a moment. "Wouldst there be any chance you are curious about how my staff would feel in—"

"Do not even think of suggesting such! I was curious, but now my curiosity has been satisfied. That is the end of it."

"You are satisfied?" he inquired incredulously.

"I'm not talking to you anymore. So do not bother flapping your tongue at me." She made much ado over the process of turning her back on him.

She wants me, too, he decided with a grin. He was a man well versed in female ways. He sensed when they were attracted to him. And when a woman protested this much, 'twas a sure sign she was weakening. Yea, 'twas only a matter of time till Alinor crept closer to his tempting form. He'd best make ready.

He arranged one arm under his head, striking a casual pose. With the other hand, he flipped the bed furs on his side down to his waist, exposing his shoulders and chest. Some women had told him, on more than one occasion, that he had an impressive upper body. Well, actually, many more of them had commented on his lower half, but he didn't want to shock Alinor with that much male virility too soon. Not that she hadn't seen it all already, but not from this close vantage point.

He should be thinking about the consequences of what he was about to do, but he couldn't care right now. All reason was being directed by the organ between his thighs, not the organ between his ears. Which was not a bad thing, in his opinion. Still, he assured himself, making love with Alinor did not mean he was committed to her, or that he was responsible for her care beyond delivery to Anlaf. She would understand that before he dipped his sword in her sheath, that she would.

Odin's breath! It's cold in here. With his body half exposed to the night air, Tykir was beginning to shiver . . . and not from the bedlust. *And speaking of breath, I can see my own breath. There will surely be frost on the oars come morn.*

Then the most amazing thing happened. Well, amazing for Tykir, who prided himself on his allure to women. He heard a sound. A soft sound.

Alinor was snoring.

She had bloody well fallen asleep on him.

"Alinor," he whispered.

Nothing.

Lightly, he touched her hair, which was the only thing showing above the furs.

Nothing.

He glared at her.

Nothing.

With a grumble of disgust, he pulled the bed furs back up to his chin and turned his back on her, as well.

Mayhap she didn't want me quite as much as I thought.

That was a close call . . .

From the other side of the bed furs, Alinor stopped her fake snoring for a moment.

And what she thought was, *Whew!*

Now she was imagining him naked . . .

Eight days later, they finally entered the wide fjord leading to King Anlaf's royal palace in Trondelag. The blowing of a horn pierced the air, announcing the arrival of new ships.

The crew was nigh frozen to the bone. All of them were bundled up in huge furs or heavy woolen cloaks, even when rowing. Their hands were cracked, and bloody at times, from the harsh elements and the harsher task of maneuvering the ship on winter seas with ice-crusted oars and ropes.

Alinor had lain, practically the entire eight days, curled up under Tykir's sable cloak, shivering. She would have been bored to the point of insanity if she hadn't been so cold . . . and frightened, for her fate would soon be decided.

In this last leg of their ship's journey, they had been hit with frigid weather—rain, snow, sleet and gusting winds—all of which the men managed to blame on Alinor's witchly curses. In truth, she had been doing a fair amount of "cursing," both inwardly and outwardly, but mostly in the form of complaints, not some impossible black magic.

To make matters worse, the farther they traveled north into the region known as The Land of the Midnight Sun, the shorter days became. In just a few sennights, Tykir had told her, it would be dark all the day long, and this would last for several of the winter months. What a dismal prospect!

Assuming she would be there that long.

Rurik had taken to checking his manparts a dozen times a day because he contended that Alinor had been looking at him *there* with evil intent. She'd smiled at that idiocy, and waggled her fingers in a fey manner, which only made him madder.

One of the seamen had complained that his loose bowels started the night the witch wished him "Good eventide" in passing. Alinor had told him it was probably the *gammelost*.

Another had developed a fiercesome itch in the hair under his arms, on his chest, in his eyebrows and beard, but mostly between his legs, where he discovered crab lice with claw-like legs. Alinor must have caused the tiny creatures to suddenly inhabit his skin, the superstitious man had wailed. Never would he believe that the poxy wench he'd bedded back in Jorvik could be at fault. Soon the lice spread like wildfire—no doubt lured by all that Viking hair—but this, too, was blamed on Alinor.

Two days out of Hedeby, some of the men had adopted the practice Tykir and Rurik and Bolthor had engaged in at Graycote. They were wearing their braies backwards as a charm against her potential spells. This was a particularly lackwitted exercise, not to mention laughable in appearance, in Alinor's opinion, and she told them so every opportunity she got. For the seaman with the loose bowels, this new fashion custom was more than demented.

Naturally, they all kept checking her backside on the odd chance that her tail would emerge. And they wore wooden crosses, and splashed themselves with holy water repeatedly, which immediately froze into icicles on their beards and noses. Alinor suspected that Rurik had run out of his cache of holy water long ago, and was filling his vials with sea water, which he sold to his fellow shipmates.

Bolthor had come up with so many sagas involving a witch and her evil doings that he constantly bemoaned the fact that his head was becoming fuzzy and the stories getting mixed up. Although he wasn't much nicer to her than any of the other men, Alinor was developing a fondness for the gruff giant.

Worst of all in Alinor's ongoing travail was the Troll-Kisser.

Despite Tykir's warning to desist, Rurik relished the re-telling of how he'd come upon Tykir kissing her in the bed furs. Each time he retold the tale, the details got more exaggerated, to the point where now he claimed to have seen them both naked, down to the freckles on her buttocks and Tykir's mighty "prow," which had been just about to dip into her "waves." The very fact that Tykir would kiss a witch was proof that she'd put a love spell on their master, according to Rurik's ill-logic.

Alinor didn't need any reminders of Tykir's kisses. They were firmly imbedded in her memory. Just the thought of them—and there were far too many thoughts—turned her hot and strangely restless. Never in her wildest imagination, even as a young girl with dreams still intact, did Alinor suspect a man's kiss could be so . . . well, exciting. And the last thing she needed in her life was more excitement, she told herself over and over again.

To make matters even worse, Tykir's leg was bothering him. With the cold dampness that pervaded the air, he could scarce put his full weight on the limb without wincing in pain. He'd taken to limping slightly and often rubbed the scarred thigh through his thick braies. She might have been able to help him, to prescribe some herbal plaster or exercise regimen or—*oh, sweet heaven!*—massage it herself. On second thought, she misdoubted she could bear exposure to his bare flesh . . . *again* . . . without some dire consequence. She trembled involuntarily at imagining what form that dire consequence might take . . . and whether it would affect her, or him, or both of them.

She'd been avoiding Tykir as much as he avoided her since the unfortunate kissing incident. But there had been times when she glanced up suddenly to find Tykir watching her, and she knew he was remembering, too. Once he even licked his lips while studying her.

She'd felt like leaping across the ship to slap the wretch.

Or kiss him.

"Well, have you decided how you will handle the situation?" Tykir asked, limping up beside her now.

She stood at the rail, watching the men steer the longships into berths along the banks of the wide river fronting the palace grounds. Hundreds of other longboats, along with smaller vessels and the larger knarrs used for transporting massive cargoes, were anchored midriver or turned upside down along the shore, beached for the winter.

"What situation?"

"The curse. How will you remove the curse from Anlaf's manroot?" Idly, he reached a hand out and flicked a big snowflake off her eyelashes. Then, to both of their amazements, he put the same forefinger to his mouth and licked.

Alinor felt that lick like an erotic arrow to the pit of her stomach. Luckily, she was able to stifle a groan.

He blinked those big brown, disgustingly thick lashes of his at her, equally affected, she would wager. Or else he played a game with her . . . a game for which she was sorely ill-equipped and woefully mismatched. Forget about her being a witch. This man had beguiled her, good and proper, with a few measly kisses.

Well, not measly.

Concentrate, Alinor. Forget the kisses. Forget his nude body. Start remembering that he's your enemy.

"You're imagining me naked," Tykir teased with a little playful tap to her chin.

"Me? Me?" she sputtered.

"Do not worry, though. I like it."

"You are the expert on naked looks, not me," she asserted.

He just grinned, and gave her a quick once-over assessment that clearly did not involve any clothing.

"To answer your question—"

"Which question?" He was fingering the edges of her hair and sniffing. The man did have a fondness for the rose-scented hair cream Eadyth had given her.

She slapped his hand away. "The question of how to handle 'the situation.'"

"Oh, *that* question."

"I have decided to do nothing."

"What?" Tykir looked magnificent in a rust-colored wool cloak lined with red fox fur, despite a sennight's worth of whiskers shadowing his face. None of them had been able to bathe or change their salt-crusted clothing these past eight days, but Tykir had managed to braid the one side of his damp hair and don the thunderbolt earring and amber pendant in preparation for being received in the king's court.

Alinor, on the other hand, suspected that she looked like a dirty-faced, speckled hen, even in the luxurious sable mantle of Tykir's that she still wore.

"I will do nothing," she repeated. "I am not a witch. 'Tis no fault of mine that Anlaf suffers . . . an affliction. 'Tis no fault of mine that I have been subjected to kidnapping and tortures, and forced to endure indignities befitting a mere thrall. 'Tis no—"

"Tortures?" Tykir's right brow raised. "Name one."

"Kissing. Having two hundred men staring at my posterior all the time. Eating *gammelost*."

He grinned at her, and, Blessed Lord, he was nigh irresistible when he grinned. "Torture by kissing?" he scoffed.

"Yea," she insisted, raising her chin defiantly in the face of his laughter. "Therefore, it is your fault that I am here. So I leave it to you to solve the problem."

"Me? *Me*?" He thought a moment, then narrowed his eyes at her. "We are back to the guardian angel theory, aren't we?"

She shrugged. "It makes no less sense that you have a set of hidden wings than me having a hidden tail."

"I refuse to be your guardian angel," he said, then realized how ridiculous that sounded. "I mean, I refuse to be responsible for your well-being after today. I will present you to King Anlaf. I will make him promise to treat you with the respect due your high station. I will ask him to return you to your home once you have straightened his staff. But I will not be your protector after today."

"Aaarrgh! Have you heard one word I've said the past few sennights? I . . . can't . . . straighten . . . a . . . a . . . a . . . *cock*. There! I've said the word. Are you happy now?"

He smiled.

Yea, he was happy.

The troll!

"Never fear, witchling. You will think of something."

The man had a moat between his ears.

"If all else fails, you could try kissing Anlaf. Believe me, you have a talent in that arena. Yea, that might be the perfect solution. Kisses to cure a curse. I know your kisses *straightened* me out."

She gave him a look of utter disbelief at his callousness and swung her arm in a wide circle before clouting him in his grinning mouth.

He barely winced at her blow. But he did concede, "Then again, mayhap not."

Turns out they didn't need a penis straightener, after all . . .

Anlaf's castle stood on a high *motte,* or earth mound, overlooking the joining of two rivers. At the base of the flat-topped hillock was the usual water-filled moat. There were hutlike homes and small longhouses down by the piers, but most of the people lived within the royal ramparts and the vast surrounding stockade. It appeared as if it could accommodate hundreds, even as many as a thousand inhabitants.

"Are there always so many people here?" Alinor asked Tykir.

"Nay, it must be a feast of one sort or another."

"'Tis the marriage celebration for Anlaf's oldest daughter, no doubt," Bolthor said in passing, with a huge wooden chest on his shoulder. "Yea, methinks I heard that Signe was to wed this season." He grinned at Tykir. "She finally gave up on you."

Tykir grumbled something in the Norse language . . . probably a foul expletive.

But then she considered Bolthor's news. *Wonderful. I get to have my head lopped off during a wedding feast.*

Stop it, Alinor. Naught will happen. You are under the protection of a fierce warrior . . . an important merchant prince.

A troll.

Oh, God!

Having already passed through the gatehouse, Tykir led her with a hand under her elbow. With the onset of the cold weather, his leg wound continued to bother him, and Alinor could see that he fought against limping, or letting anyone see him limp. Prideful man! Most of his men had gone on ahead, or scattered in various directions. For many of them, this was home for the winter. Others would be traveling on to Tykir's homestead, or to their own homes in this immense northern wilderness. The huge double doors were opened by a guard who in turn signaled to another guard who blew a horn announcing their arrival.

The earth and timber castle was enormous, like a palatial fort. It had no clear architectural style, having been added to indiscriminately over the years. But the doors and lintels and various crenallations, even those of stone, were highly carved in the Norse style. Everywhere, there were fierce-looking sentries of tremendous size, carrying swords and shields and battle-axes.

They entered the vast great hall, which at present surely seated more than five hundred men and women, though the latter were in much shorter supply. A dozen enormous free-standing, raised hearths were arranged down the long center of the rectangular room. Mostly, they were intended for warmth during the interminable winter months, since cooking was done in a separate kitchen wing, but with all the body heat being generated by the eating and drinking crowd on this festive occasion, the fiery blazes were hardly needed. On either side of the hearths were arranged three very long rows of trestle tables, starting at the dais, where the high table stood, and leading to the far end of the room, where the lesser guests were seated.

"Come," Tykir said, taking her hand in his and leading her along the right wall toward the dais. Rurik and Bolthor followed behind them, having tied Beast to a post outside. Many friends and acquaintances nodded and greeted the three men along the way, giving Alinor only a passing glance of curiosity. She had the hood of Tykir's cloak pulled up over her head, so there was naught about her appearance to spark any interest.

"Tykir! When did you get back? Did you bring that case of Frisian wine I ordered?"

"Come tell us the news of that weasel, Edred! Is he still nipping at Eric Bloodaxe's heels?"

"How was the amber harvest this year? My third wife has a yearning for one of your baubles."

"Come share a cup with us when you have finished with your king's business, Tykir. We would hear again about the time a sultan's harem was opened to the Varangian Guard."

"Bolthor, is that you? Have you any new sagas to regale us with? I still chuckle betimes over that 'Tykir the Great and the Spitting Contest' tale that you related last year at Gudrik the Glutton's funeral feast."

"Stay here," Tykir told her when they finally reached the head of the first table. He didn't even frown at the reminder of one of Bolthor's sagas, which invariably poked fun at him. The solemnity on his usually open face scared Alinor. Why wasn't he jesting and teasing her in his usual manner? Why wasn't he smiling at all his laughing countrymen who greeted him? Why did he act as if her head was already on the chopping block?

Rurik stepped to the side, about to speak to a group of half-drunk Norsemen dressed in the rich cloth of Norse nobility.

"Keep your teeth shut for a change," Tykir warned Rurik, who was no doubt about to spread his stories about Alinor the Witch.

Rurik seemed about to argue with Tykir's command, but then came back to stand next to Alinor. Glowering at her, he pulled his wooden cross from inside his tunic and waved it in her face.

She crossed her eyes at him.

His face turned bright red under the woad design and he looked as if he might be choking on his tongue.

Good.

"Would you two stop?" Tykir hissed, then proceeded to walk up the steps to the dais.

"Tykir!" The enthusiastic greeting came from a regally

dressed Viking man with an ornate gold circlet sitting on his forehead holding back his long blond hair. His luxurious beard was braided with precious stones and his mustache was full and drooping practically to his jaw. *King Anlaf,* she presumed from his appearance and his position at the head table. "Welcome! Welcome, my cousin! You have come to help celebrate Signe's wedding, eh?" the king roared jovially, giving Tykir a bone-crushing clap on the back.

The two men were of the same size and age, though Tykir was by far the more handsome. *Aaarrgh! I do not care about such things. Leastways, I never did afore hooking up with the beauteous troll.* Somehow, Alinor had thought Anlaf would be much older, especially with a daughter of marriageable age, but then she reminded herself that a man of five and thirty was certainly capable of siring a daughter of seventeen or so winters.

But Alinor was woolgathering whilst events were taking place which could affect her destiny. Tykir was kissing the new bride now . . . a petite, flaxen-haired girl with even features and a dimpled smile. She was not beautiful, but comely nonetheless in a wholesome sort of way. He was also speaking his good wishes to her groom, an attractive young man of about eighteen winters. No elderly husband for this precious daughter.

"'Tis Torgunn . . . a younger son of King Sven Forkbeard of Denmark," Bolthor told her. He had to bend over at the waist in order to place his mouth near her ear.

"Tykir!" a dark-haired man shouted from across the room. He stood abruptly, knocking over the ivory pieces of the Viking game *hnefatafl* that he had been playing with several other men. The sinfully attractive man, no more than twenty, with skin burnished a dark brown like those of men residing in a desert clime, rushed across the room and up the steps. He wore the oddest garment, a sort of long white robe, highly embroidered along the edges with an ornate foreign design she could not identify. It was belted at the waist, with a burnoose hanging at the back of his neck. The attire was much like Alinor had seen on the Arab traders in Jorvik. He did not at all resemble the Vikings in this great hall, though they apparently accepted him as one.

"Adam!" Tykir said with a wide smile, taking the young man into a tight embrace.

So, this was the infamous Adam the Healer . . . the nephew for whom Tykir went to so much trouble.

After much back thumping, Tykir said to the young man, "You don't seem much the worse for wear, despite having been a hostage these many months." Alinor was fortunately able to hear their conversation, standing as they were at the bottom of the dais.

"A hostage?" Adam inquired, clearly puzzled.

Tykir quickly scanned the hall, his eyes latching on to the messenger, Bjold, who was slinking toward one of the exterior doors. With an expression of growing suspicion, Tykir turned on the king. "Did you not send a messenger to me several months past, urging me to deliver a witch to you?"

"Well, yea, but—" the king blustered.

"And did you not offer me your finest stallion, Fierce One?"

"Well, yea, but—" Anlaf shifted from foot to foot, obviously embarrassed about something.

"And did you not promise me the slave girl of the bells?"

"I did?"

"You did." Tykir narrowed his eyes at the wily king. "Most important, did you not say that you would hold Adam hostage here till I delivered the witch?"

"Anlaf!" Adam accused the king. "Did you say such? 'Tis a lie, of course, Tykir. What kind of man dost think I am that I could not escape such 'captivity'?"

A low growling sound began deep in Tykir's chest and was rising upward, like an angry bear.

"The malady went away of its own accord. Is that not a miracle?" a beaming Anlaf informed Tykir. "But there is no harm done. Come share the feast with us." He waved a hand magnanimously. "Mayhap I can even find the jingling bell maiden for you. Ha, ha, ha."

"No harm done?" Tykir sputtered.

"Yea, no harm done." Anlaf's brow furrowed with bafflement over Tykir's anger. "Dost thou disbelieve me? Wouldst thou like to see my newly straightened staff?" He turned his back on the great hall and dropped the front of his braies for Tykir's perusal.

"Very nice," Tykir observed with droll humor as his face flushed purple with fury. Meanwhile, Adam was laughing so hard tears streamed down his face.

These Vikings are the crudest men in the world.

"Anlaf, you have to be the bloodiest fool in all the world," Tykir raged, not at all amused. "You did some lackbrain things to me when we were youthlings, but this time you have pushed the bounds of kinship. Have you no idea what you have done?"

"Me?" Anlaf asked, putting a palm to his chest in affront. "By the by, why do some of your men wear their braies backwards? Is it the new fashion in the Saxon lands? I always thought they were assbackwards. Now I know for a certainty. Ha, ha, ha."

Tykir crossed his eyes with frustration. "You asked me to deliver to you the Saxon witch," he pointed out, as if speaking to a dimwitted child.

"And?"

"You have her." Tykir pointed in her direction.

All eyes turned then toward Alinor.

Uh-oh!

Rurik, the mean-spirited oaf, flipped Alinor's hood back so that her bright red hair sprung forth. By the light of about a hundred candles and an equal number of wall torches, her numerous freckles were no doubt evident, too.

"There is your witch," Tykir announced, his voice dripping with exasperation. "Lady Alinor of Graycote."

Throughout the hall, like a ripple in a fast-moving stream, the word passed. "A witch. A witch. A witch. A witch . . ."

Alinor cast pleading eyes on Tykir then, her only hope in this sea of Vikings.

He remained stern-faced and unmoved.

Please God, she prayed.

Just then, the flames of a vast wall-hearth behind the dais roared brighter as some knotholes sizzled. The radiant light cast an aura behind Tykir's head . . . almost like a well, a halo.

It was a sign.

CHAPTER NINE

※

*I*f *he had to look at the king's wick one more time! . . .*
There is your witch.

Tykir's callous words echoed in his own brain, like a hammer of guilt. He had not intended to blurt out Alinor's identity for all to hear . . . leastways, not in such a premature manner. He knew better than most that timing was critical in all matters, whether it be battle, cajoling a woman into the bed furs or arguing before a thick-headed king. But he'd been caught off guard on learning from Adam that all his troubles of the past two months had been for naught. Cured! Anlaf had been cured, and never bothered to inform him.

And Alinor . . . look at her. Standing near the foot of the steps leading up to the dais, she resembled a child, enveloped as she was in his huge sable cloak, which pooled in the rushes at her feet. Even from here, atop the dais, he could see that her hands trembled, though her stubborn chin was held high. *God's blood!* The foolish woman still harbored the notion that he was some sort of guardian angel, personally sent by her One-god to protect her. Why else would she stand, stricken, staring at him with wide, tear-brimmed eyes at his seeming betrayal?

Betrayal? Hah! She is not my charge any longer. I have delivered her to King Anlaf. I have done my duty.

Why then do I feel as low as a snake's belly?

Nay, I feel no guilt. Nay, nay, nay! I will not be sucked into that mire of responsibility. Keep a distance . . . that has

*been my philosophy since I was a mere child of eight
years, and a wise course it has been. Never stay in one
place too long, and never, ever, let the people-bond become
too important . . . whether it be with family, friends, soldiers and seamen or women.*

*I do not care. That is the key. Caring overmuch about
anyone or anything is a dangerous tightrope for any man to
walk. Too much and his most vulnerable soft areas are exposed. Too little and his soul ices over and dies from lack of
warmth.*

He *did* care about Eirik, of course. And Eadyth. And their
children. Well, 'twas true, there was Selik and Rain and
their children, too, including Adam. And he held just a tiny
bit of affection for Gyda and his uncle, King Haakon, and
Adam's younger sister, Adele. But that was all. Nay, he must
include Bolthor and Rurik, to some extent.

*Good Lord! When did I start caring about so many
people? It has to stop. 'Twas time to draw the line with this
woman. I will not care for her. At all.*

There, it was decided. He felt better now.

That did not mean he was hard-hearted. On the contrary,
he would ensure the witch's safety afore he left . . . or leastways the opportunity to get fair trial. Not that he was obli-
gated to do such, but it was the noble thing to do.

Noble? Since when have I become noble?

*Nay, I am spending too much time worrying over the
wench. 'Tis a sign of weakness. Mayhap 'tis best just to leave.
Anlaf will treat her impartially.*

*Impartially? How impartial can any man be when his
most precious part has been curved by a curse? Yea, Anlaf
must blame the witch for his manly woes these many
months . . . even if he is cured now. Will he not feel the need
for punishment? And what form will that retribution take? A
flogging? Thralldom? Torture? Rape? Burning at the stake?
Beheading?*

Aarrgh! I am not going to think about this anymore.

I do not care.

Truly, I do not care.

Hell, where's the mead?

All this he thought in the seconds following his blunt announcement.

"You brought a witch here?" asked Adam incredulously. Still standing at his side on the dais, Adam looped an arm around his shoulder in comradely fashion and chuckled. "Good Lord, Rurik! What is that blue mark on your face? Is it a beauty mark? You always were too vain. You should take humility lessons from me."

Rurik said something rude about male body parts.

Adam grinned and called his attention back to Tykir and the subject at hand. "Do you and Rurik have a particular taste for witches as bedmates?"

"She's not my bedmate," Tykir snarled.

"Well, that's too bad," Adam said.

Tykir narrowed his eyes at Adam, who still held his shoulder in a brotherly embrace, patting it in exaggerated sympathy. "Too bad? Why is that? Has the desert sun burned out your eyesight? Obviously, you have not looked closely at the wench."

"Are those freckles I see?" Adam slitted his eyes, as if to see better. "I knew a sultan once who claimed every freckle on a woman's body was an erotic spot."

"What?" Tykir fixed his gaze on Alinor, whose head was tilted in puzzlement at their scrutiny. By rough estimate, he figured the woman must have about a thousand of those marks on her body, if he could recall her naked body properly. Hah! That image was imprinted on his lustful brain for all time.

But, as to Adam's correlation betwixt freckles and sex, could it be possible? He turned to question Adam further and was met with a wide, white-toothed grin. Realizing he'd been taken in by the rogue's foolery, he shoved Adam's arm off his shoulder. The lackwit bent over at the waist, laughing his fool head off.

"What the hell are you wearing anyway?" Tykir grumbled,

flicking the fingertips of one hand at the loose white, hooded robe Adam wore, with all the flair of a royal courtier.

"What? You do not like my caftan?"

"Like has naught to do with it. It appears to me you have borrowed some bed linens."

"Methinks you are jealous, Tykir. Tell me true, do you not think I resemble a desert prince? Can you not picture me riding the sand dunes atop my camel?" He waggled his eyebrows at Tykir.

Tykir jabbed him with an elbow to behave. "I certainly hope you are wearing braies beneath. 'Twould be unseemly otherwise."

"Hah! When have I aimed to be seemly?"

The two men grinned at each other.

"Actually, there's a certain freedom in letting your nether parts breathe."

Tykir had to laugh aloud at the rascal then. "If you do too much *breathing* in this part of the country, you will end up with frost on your arse."

A feminine scream rent the air then. At first, Tykir thought it was Alinor, but she stood silent, staring at him as if he were some archangel, about to slay her dragons.

"Why does the witch gaze at you as if you are the raisins in her porridge?" Adam asked.

"She thinks I'm her guardian angel," Tykir replied dryly.

"You?" Adam hooted and doubled over again, resuming laughter.

Another loud scream ripped through the din of the great hall.

This time, Tykir jerked around to see Signe, her fingers clawing at her own hair. "A witch! A witch! And she is covered with the Devil's Spittle . . . and hair like Satan's fire," she wailed. "'Tis a bad omen to have a witch attend one's wedding. Do not let her look upon me, Father, lest I have a clove-footed babe nine months hence." With one last scream, she fell into a faint in her new husband's arms.

"Oh, for the love of Mary!" Alinor muttered with disgust at Signe's spectacle.

King Anlaf could not be concerned about his daughter, however. "Guards, take the witch away. Make haste afore she renews the curse on my manroot."

Tykir drew his sword instinctively, not about to let Anlaf's guards mishandle the wench . . . rather, witch . . . till she had a chance to defend herself. Not that he'd heard a single word from her mouth these many sennights that would weigh in her favor.

Fortunately, Anlaf's personal guard was nowhere to be seen, having the good sense, or the non-sense, to leave the range of Alinor's witchly powers. None of them wanted a crooked staff. With a cry of distress, Anlaf pulled his battle shield off the wall and held it in front of his midsection. Many men throughout the hall did likewise.

"Oh, for the love of Mary!" Alinor reiterated.

"Mary? Who is this Mary the witch keeps calling upon?" Anlaf inquired. "Is it perchance the high-witch?"

"King Anlaf! For shame!" the priest who'd been sitting with Adam exclaimed. Tykir had met him before. Father Caedmon was his name. "Did you not take your baptismal vows seriously when I christened you last year? Mary is the mother of God."

"Oh, *that* Mary." Anlaf's face turned red under his blond beard. Leastways, what could be seen of his face behind his shield, which he still held in front of his body.

"Enough of this prattle!" Tykir roared, waving his sword in the air. "Assure me of Lady's Alinor's safe passage home, and I will be on my way to Dragonstead."

"Sheath your sword, Tykir," Anlaf ordered, his eyes peering above his massive shield. "Is the witch worth losing your life?"

"What makes you think I will be the one spilling wound dew?" he said icily.

"That is why the butter would not come this morn," one slovenly maid servant called out from the doorway leading to the scullery. "I knew there was a bad aura in the air. 'Twas a sign of the witch's approach." As she talked, she was scratching her head, which was no doubt lice-ridden. In Tykir's opinion, the butter probably had not come because the lazy wench had not churned hard enough.

"Beware of her familiar," one man cautioned. "Where is it?" He and others at his table were pivoting their heads this way and that, trying to discern the familiar.

"Her familiars are back in Britain," Bolthor informed them. "They are sheep."

"Do you say she has more than one familiar, and that they are sheep?" asked a powerfully built woman sitting at the high table. 'Twas Anlaf's older sister, Gudny. "She must be a very powerful witch."

"A spell she has put on my dog, Beast," Rurik noted, despite Tykir's warning that he hold his tongue. "Methinks she may have made Beast one of her familiars, too."

Gudny seemed impressed, and was assessing Alinor through narrowed, speculative eyes. Everyone knew that Gudny, who was as tall as a man and as strong as a horse, had been searching for a love potion these many years in hopes of luring her wayward husband Alfrigg back to the bed furs. 'Twas said she had an insatiable appetite for swiving—though Tykir could hardly credit that, more like an insatiable appetite for eating—and Alfrigg had chosen instead to live amongst the monks on a leper island.

Throughout the great hall, a murmur of fear and outrage was passing in waves, emanating from the spot where Alinor still stood with Bolthor and Rurik. People who had been sitting closest stood and moved away, putting hands or arms over their faces so the witch could not give them the evil eye . . . and over their private parts, as well.

"Is she the witch who put the mark on your face?" one

Norse maiden asked Rurik in an awestruck voice. Tykir couldn't tell if the awe was for Rurik's winsome face or the power of the witch.

"Nay," Rurik answered, his interest caught by the maiden's fair face and even fairer bosom. " 'Twas another witch."

"Another witch!" Anlaf roared. "Didst thou dare to bring *two* witches to my daughter's wedding feast? Oh, Holy Thor! Do we perchance have a coven in our midst?"

A number of the wedding guests could be seen ducking under the trestle tables at that alarming prospect.

Alinor had the nerve to snicker.

"Nay, I did not bring two witches," Tykir said wearily. In truth, he wasn't sure he'd even brought one. But that was not the issue. Nor one for him to decide. "Anlaf, you had a . . . problem," Tykir began to explain in a deliberately patient voice, though he was losing his patience by the minute. "You sent a messenger asking for my help, and I agreed . . . to gain the release of Adam."

"But I was never a hostage," Adam interrupted. "I came to Trondelag several months past, planning to go home to Britain for a brief visit. Come spring, I will be returning to the Arab lands, where the study of medicine is more advanced than in any other part of the world. In the meantime, I decided to stay in Anlaf's court for a few months in order to study with his healer, the good priest, Caedmon." Adam's eyes shifted involuntarily as he spoke to the far side of the hall, where Tykir saw Father Caedmon nod his head in agreement. But wait. Tykir thought he heard the slight tinkling of bells at that table. Instantly, he connected that sound with the dark-haired maid shifting restlessly there, next to the priest.

Tykir stifled a laugh. So, Adam was delayed by the slave girl of the infamous bells, not coercion by King Anlaf, and not his scholarly endeavors, either.

It was not surprising to see a Roman priest in a Viking assembly. Many Norsemen practiced both Christian and Norse religions, and the bishops willingly sent priest healers into their heathen midst in hopes of gaining souls at the same time they salved wounds and splinted broken bones.

Adam, on the other hand, ever did latch onto any person who could teach him something new in the healing arts. And women ever did latch onto the fair Adam, who claimed to have learned things, other than medicine, from the Arabs.

Tykir clicked his teeth with disgust at Adam. "You are lucky your father and Eirik did not come with their troops to storm Anlaf's castle for your return."

Adam's face went pale. "I did not think," he murmured.

That was an understatement.

Tykir turned back to Anlaf. "Whether Adam stayed here of his own accord is not important. You led me to believe he was a 'friendly hostage' and that you would release him if I delivered the witch. Well, I have fulfilled my part of the bargain."

Anlaf thought a moment, then smiled widely. "You are free to go, Adam," the king said magnanimously. "See, Tykir. Now we are even."

"Not bloody likely."

"Når enden er god er allting godt," the king said, urging peace. "All's well that ends well."

Tykir balked. "I see no satisfactory end here."

"How so?"

"You know not for certain that the lady is a witch, Anlaf. If she is not, 'twas unfair of you to have brought her here."

"Well, take her back then."

Tykir gritted his jaw. He really did not want to fight with Anlaf. He was tired. He was angry. He was itching to knock out a tooth or two. "I am not going back to Britain till next autumn," he said, pacing his words slowly. "You demanded. I delivered. End of story."

"Story? Story?" Bolthor jumped into the conversation. Tykir hadn't realized that he and Rurik had drawn swords as well and just waited for his word to defend him, if attacked. "Dost want a saga about this? How about 'Tykir the Great and the Uncrooking of the King's Crook'?"

"Once crooked was the king's wick
After a witch caught him playing
With fire in a nunnery.
Now the candle dost burn again.
But for how long?
If the witch remains,
Will Trondelag become
The land of the crooked tapers?"

Tykir and Anlaf both made growling sounds at the same time.

"You played me for the fool, Anlaf. No man does that without consequence, not even a king."

"I did not," Anlaf protested. "I *did* have a crooked cock. I have witnesses to that, and the dire pain I suffered, not to mention the lack of bedsport for three whole months. But now it is hale and hearty. Dost thou want to look at it again?"

"Nay! I do not want to look at your hairy manroot."

"Hairy? Didst see hairs there? Oh, this is too much!" He turned to glare at Alinor. "Didst put a hair curse on me now, witch?"

Tykir had to smile at that idiocy.

Alinor was shaking her head from side to side, murmuring, "Vikings! Dimwits, one and all!"

"At least mine is not hairy," Tykir informed her with a grin.

"How do you know? Have you checked lately? Mayhap I put a hair curse on you, too."

"Sarcasm ill-suits you, my lady." Bile rose in his throat, even though he knew she was just teasing. Leastways, he hoped she was. He barely stifled the impulse to rush to the privy and check for certain.

Adam was laughing so hard that tears rolled down his face.

"I'm in a generous mood today, Tykir. I might have played a small part in this misunderstanding, that I concede.

I'll gift you Fierce One and Samirah, after all, for your trouble," Anlaf conceded. "A horse and a wench. What more could you want?"

"I'll tell you what else I want. I want an apology. I want recompense for my trouble. I want to leave this castle today. I want you to provide safe conduct for the Lady Alinor back to her home in Northumbria."

"You want much for a mere misunderstanding," Anlaf sputtered. "None of my ships leave for Britain for another three or four months. I cannot harbor a witch in my castle all that time. My troops would rebel. My wives and concubines would avoid my bed furs. Who knows what calamities would befall my household. You take her."

"Me? Oh, nay, do not try that trick with me. She stays with you till you return her to her homeland."

The abject horror on Anlaf's face was almost comical when it was considered that the king had faced down legions of fierce soldiers in battle with less fear than he exhibited now. Apparently the loss of one's manpart was more fear-inspiring than the loss of one's life. Anlaf's protests echoed throughout the great hall, where others insisted that the witch could not stay.

"Stone the witch," one man suggested.

"Burn her at the stake," another urged.

"Let us torture her secrets out of her first," Gudny exhorted.

"Does she dance naked in the forest? Mayhap we could watch her dance naked first," one young soldier proposed. "'Twould be good entertainment for a wedding feast."

Others nodded enthusiastically.

"Or trial by water. That would be worth watching," another person offered.

More vigorous nodding.

"Trial by water? What's that?" he heard Alinor inquire of Bolthor.

"They hold you under water for ten minutes or so. If you

survive, you must be a witch. If you drown, then your good name is clear."

Alinor thought for a second. "And that is Viking justice?"

"We learned it from the Saxons," Bolthor told her.

Meanwhile, the Norse revelers were continuing to throw out suggestions to the king regarding the witch's fate.

"Has anyone checked for a tail yet?" one man cautioned.

The murmuring throughout the hall was ominous, to him as well as Alinor, whose face had gone bone white under her horrible freckles. He saw that Rurik's fingers were wrapped around her wrist in a vicelike grip.

He stomped down the dais steps, stormed over to Alinor's side, smacked Rurik's hand aside with a hissing sound of rage at the blue finger marks already marring the delicate skin and dragged her forward with him, an arm protectively draped around her shoulder. Though they stood at the bottom of the short stairway, everyone at the high table rose from their seats and took two steps backward. The bride, who had regained consciousness, was whimpering. The bridegroom was comforting her with a sweeping hand across her back that kept returning to the rump region. Tykir didn't think he was searching for a tail.

"Enough!" Anlaf dropped his shield to the floor and shouted in a roaring voice, which carried across the great hall like thunder, causing waves of silence to follow in its wake. When all was quiet, Anlaf announced, "I have come up with a solution. Tomorrow we will hold a Thing to decide the witch's fate."

The only thing worse than one Viking lackwit is four Viking lackwits . . .

The Thing was about to start by midmorning the next day.

If Alinor had expected a disorganized governing body run by an unruly bunch of primitive Vikings, green-faced from overdrinking the night before, she was woefully mistaken.

The Norsemen apparently held their laws in great respect, for they were groomed and dressed accordingly. Many of them had bathed and donned clean clothing, shaved or trimmed mustaches and beards and combed or braided their long hair. They must have risen at dawn to prepare for this event. Either that or they'd stayed up all night, though none the worse for wear, except for a few bloodshot eyes and breath odor that could wipe out a troop of soldiers with one mighty exhalation.

There were spaces for twenty-one men to sit in a half-circle at the head of the room, facing toward the empty dais . . . three each, including the chieftains, from the seven "tribes" or geographical regions in attendance at the gathering. Tykir, Rurik and Bolthor would sit there, as well, once the Thing began. The rest of the free men were seated on benches behind their chosen representatives. King Anlaf, dressed in his full royal regalia topped by a narrow golden circlet banding his forehead, was to act as the Thing-Leader. He sat in an armed chair in the center of the half-circle.

There were few women present in the assembly itself, though they could be seen in the background, moving about their chores, or eavesdropping on what must be mostly a male event.

She and Tykir were sitting on a bench off to the side, along with other parties who had disputes to be settled by the Thing. Bolthor, Rurik and Adam sat on either side of them on the bench.

Primitive wooden crosses abounded on the chests of many. Alinor suspected that Rurik was doing a prosperous business in crucifixes and holy water. She wished him a bad case of splinters.

An ancient, gray-bearded man rose from the assembly and was making his way slowly toward the front, his progress impeded by those who stopped him along the way in warm greeting. He wore a full-length coat of marten skins. His neatly combed white hair hung about his shoulders like a silken mantle. In his right hand, he carried a long, wooden staff intricately carved with runic symbols. It resembled a bishop's crozier.

"Who is that?" Alinor whispered to Tykir.

He just stared ahead, stone-faced. This was the first she'd seen him since last night, having been taken forcibly to a storage room, where she'd been locked in alone till this morning. It was clear that Tykir blamed her for the whole predicament.

Was it her fault she found herself in the middle of Viking lands? Was it her fault they'd declined to allow Tykir to dump her there whilst he went on his merry way? Was it her fault a storm was brewing outside, turning the skies black and it not yet noon? Was it her fault a threat loomed of their being snowbound at Anlaf's court for the winter?

Adam leaned forward from his seat on the other side of Tykir and informed her, "That's Styrr the Wise, the Lawspeaker. The Norse people have many law codes, but they are seldom written down. It's the responsibility of the lawspeakers to commit those laws to memory and recite them before the Thing begins."

Tykir gave Adam a piercing glare, labeling him traitor for speaking to Alinor when he would not.

Adam ignored Tykir and graced Alinor with a roguish smile that had probably melted more than one maiden's heart. "I am Adam the Healer, by the by. We've not been properly introduced."

Tykir made a snorting sound of disgust.

She smiled back at Adam, more to annoy Tykir than to respond to the younger man's seductive grin. "I am Lady Alinor of Graycote . . . victim of this oaf's ridiculous mission," she said, rolling her eyes toward Tykir. "He wants to blame me for this turn of events, but deep down he knows he is at fault."

"It must be *real* deep," Tykir mumbled.

"What did you say?" she asked.

"Nothing. I am not speaking to you."

"Don't you think that's a trifle immature?"

"Adam, will you be coming with me to Dragonstead for the winter . . . assuming we get out of here afore the fjords freeze?" Tykir inquired, speaking over her. "Or will you stay with Father Caedmon at Anlaf's court?"

"I know not for certain. It depends on whether it comes to combat here at the Thing. If we have to fight our way out of this mess . . ." he shrugged, ". . . then there will be no choice."

"Combat?" she protested. "I thought this was a law court."

Before anyone could answer—not that anyone was rushing to attend to her concerns—Rurik leaned forward from the other side of Adam and addressed Tykir. "Methinks you should let me take the wench outside and lop off her head. That would solve everyone's problem. What say you? Shall I unsheath my trusty sword?"

Alinor told Rurik what he could do with his trusty sword; it was that selfsame vulgar expression she'd used on rare occasions afore. All four men, including Bolthor, on her other side, gaped at her as if she'd sprung three heads.

Hell's teeth! Had they never heard a coarse word from a lady's tongue afore?

Apparently not.

"That is not the first time she has used that expression with us. Is that not so, Tykir?" Rurik curled his upper lip with distaste. "It must be a trait of Saxon women to speak with the roughness of men. Mayhap 'tis just Saxon women who live with sheep. Ones little inclined toward meekness."

Alinor said nothing, but she waggled her fingers in the direction of Rurik's manparts and muttered some nonsensical words. "Mimje hwan ziba-ziba."

Rurik stood at once and sputtered, "See . . . did you all see her put a curse on me?" With a gasp, he rushed from the hall.

"Where is he going?" an amazed Adam asked.

"To the privy to check for curves," Bolthor replied with a dry humor she hadn't known he had. "He does it at least thrice a day." He seemed to catch himself then. "Begging your pardon, my lady, for my crudeness."

Then Bolthor launched into one of his sagas. "Hear one and all, this is the saga of Rurik the Beautiful:

> *"Rurik was a Viking*
> *Who had a grand passion.*
> *But he chose a witch*
> *To dip his wick.*
> *And now he regrets*
> *The ill-fated lesson."*

Tykir and Adam's slack jaws clicked shut with a resounding snap. Truly, Bolthor was not the world's best skald.

"What were the words of that curse you put on Rurik's manpart?" Adam wanted to know, turning his attention back to her.

"God spare me from blue-faced lackwits," Alinor answered.

It took only a moment for Adam to realize that Alinor was not serious. He threw his head back and laughed heartily, uncaring of the Vikings who turned to stare at him. "I like you, Lady Alinor. Mayhap we could . . . ah, talk later, if things work out with the Thing."

"Talk? Hah!" Tykir observed. "She's too old for you, Adam. Why don't you go jingle some bells or something."

"Too old? Tsk-tsk, Tykir. Where are your manners? A chivalrous man does not comment on a woman's age. You must forgive Tykir's testiness, m'lady. He is not himself today."

"Really? He is always testy, as far as I can tell."

"Uh, just to satisfy my curiosity, how old *are* you, Lady Alinor?" Adam posed the question with studied casualness.

Now where did that come from? Oh, I see. The rascal probably thinks I'm a centuries' old witch. "Twenty-five."

"Hah! That is only five years' difference. Besides, I have always liked older women." Adam jiggled his eyebrows at Alinor.

She couldn't help but smile at the outrageous rogue.

"She nags incessantly," Tykir said of a sudden, startling them all. "And her voice! Blessed Freyja! Betimes it is so shrill it makes your ears ache. In truth, I would wager she nags even in the midst of bedsport."

Alinor gave him a sharp jab with her elbow, which did not even budge the immovable lout. "What makes you think I would participate in the bedsport with him, or any other man?"

"What? Did you think Adam was interested in *conversing* with you? About sheep? Or the black arts?" He pondered a moment. "Or freckle cures?"

Freckle cures? Ooooh, that was a low blow. There are black arts I would like to employ with this wretch.

"I like to talk with women," Adam countered defensively. "Sometimes."

Tykir and Bolthor exhaled with a communal, "Hah!"

"And disasters follow her everywhere," Tykir divulged. "Whether it be her witchly arts or just coincidence, I cannot say for certain, but it gets tiresome after a while, I can attest." Bolthor nodded in agreement.

"Disasters? Like what?" Adam scoffed.

"Manparts curving, seagulls dying, twins a-birthing, wine souring, bowels fluxing, storms brewing, even geese shitting on hapless travelers—"

"What hapless travelers?" Adam asked, clearly confused by Tykir's recitation of her supposed ill-doings.

Tykir and Bolthor looked at each other, turned red-faced, and refused to respond.

Adam hooted with laughter. "God's blood! 'Twould seem I have much to catch up on. Mayhap I will go to Dragonstead with you, after all, Tykir. Have you committed all these happenstances to sagas, Bolthor?"

Bolthor beamed at Adam. "Yea, I have. Most of them, leastways. I intend to recite all winter long at Dragonstead."

"I cannot wait." Adam beamed innocently as he spoke.

Everyone else groaned under their breaths.

"Now let me see, Tykir." A mischievous grin crept over Adam's lips. "You have told me the wench—I mean, witch—is not for me because she is too old, too talksome and too magical. Is there aught else I should fear afore taking her off your hands?"

"Who said I wanted you to take Lady Alinor off my hands?" Tykir snapped.

"You did," Alinor declared, baffled by his change of mood.

"I did not. I said that Anlaf must take responsibility for you now. I never said Adam should take on that irksome duty."

"What's the difference?"

"You wouldn't understand," he answered enigmatically. "Being a woman, 'twould be hard for you to fathom the deeper workings of a man's mind."

"Did it take you a long time to think up that nonsense?"

He cast her a sheepish sideways glance. "Nay. It just came to me. An inspiration."

She rolled her eyes heavenward.

"Well, if you do not want her . . ." Adam began, studying the two of them with lips twitching with mirth. The thick-headed Tykir obviously failed to see the teasing that underlay Adam's words. "I guess I could be her protector . . . for a while."

"Please, Adam! Spare us your whims. You would be her protector only till the next winsome maid strolls by . . . not that Lady Alinor is winsome. I mean . . . I did not mean . . ." Tykir slanted an apologetic look at Alinor, as if she did not already know how little appeal she held for him. Tykir let out a whoosh of exasperation. "Face the truth, Adam. You would not like the freckles that cover her from head to toe," Tykir blurted out, and seemed surprised at his own words.

She gasped. The dolt!

But wasn't it odd how Tykir was trying to deflect Adam's interest away from her? Here was a perfect opportunity for him to be rid of her, and what did he do? Sabotage his own plan to relinquish responsibility for her.

She reached over for his hand and had to pry the fingers apart before lacing it with hers. And, oh, how good it felt to press her flesh against his! He was her anchor in this sea of danger. He would save her. She knew he would. "Do not mind the lout," she told Adam. "He is my own personal guardian angel, but he fights his fates mightily."

"Tykir . . . an angel?" Adam shook his head with disbelief. But then he homed in on Tykir's words. "How do you know she is covered with freckles *from head to toe?*" Adam asked, chuckling.

"Because he saw her naked, back in Jorvik," Rurik explained. He'd just returned from the privy, apparently satisfied with the shape of his beloved staff if his swagger was any indication. He dropped down into his seat next to Adam. "And he has not been the same since. Smitten he is with whatever it was he saw."

"I am *not* smitten," Tykir said with consternation, as if that would be the most horrible thing in the world. Well, it would be, of course. She did not want him smitten. Still, he was a brute for saying so with such vehemence.

"As I recall, 'twas the raspberry belly button that got his attention when first he saw her naked. And he cannot get that image from his mind now," Bolthor interjected, tapping his chin with a forefinger thoughtfully. "Nay, 'twas a raspberry birthmark on her belly."

"Raspberry nipples," Tykir corrected.

Oh, the humiliation of such talk! Alinor pulled her hand out of its clasp with the lout and buried her face in her hands.

"This is the story of 'Tykir the Great and the Raspberry Feast,'" Bolthor began.

"Tykir the *Great?*" Adam questioned.

"Shut up," Tykir retorted.

And Bolthor shared his latest creation:

"Viking men have many a yearning
Some cravings liken to a burning.
A-viking, a-plundering, a-swiving
Are but a few that be tormenting.
But Lord spare the maid when
The Norseman gets a yen
For raspberries in his bed."

A long silence ensued. Finally curiosity gave way, and Alinor peered up between her fingertips.

All four men were grinning.

And staring at her chest.

CHAPTER TEN

⬙

If he had to look at the king's vegetable . . . uh, manroot one more time! . . .

Tykir felt as if his feet were planted in quicksand and his upper body were being assailed by buffeting winds. He was being pulled in a dozen directions at once, but somewhere along the way he'd lost his inner life-compass.

How could he have thought this mission for Anlaf would be a simple matter? He must be as lackwitted as Alinor always said.

He wanted to be rid of her.

And he did not.

He wanted to trust her fate to the fairness of a Norse Thing.

He feared what that fate might be.

He swore the whole misadventure was her fault for hurling a curse in the first place.

Yet guilt nagged at him like an aching tooth.

The most alarming revelation had come to him moments ago when Adam had offered to take responsibility for the witch. Oh, he knew the scamp had been half-jesting, but he was the one who'd reacted like a green youthling. For the first time in his life, he'd tasted the bile of jealousy, and that scared him mightily.

At what point had he stopped noticing the ungodly color of her hair or the overabundance of skin splotches? In truth, the witch was starting to look good to him. Yea, to his horror, he was developing a taste for coppery hair and freckles. Other women, even some comely ones at Anlaf's court, appeared pale in comparison.

Tykir was going mad. His life was unraveling, thread by thread. In the midst of this royal assembly, he fought the compulsion to pull at his hair and roar like a wild bull. *That is it,* he concluded, *I have gone berserk.*

He needed to get away and think. Alone. Once he was home at Dragonstead, his mind would become clear once again. He would remember why it was essential that he shield his emotions because, for the life of him, he couldn't stop the ice around his heart from melting now. Much more of this and he would be as vulnerable as a wingless bird.

Besides that, his thigh wound was throbbing with more pain than he'd experienced since the Battle of Brunanburh, when it had been inflicted. He feared he was doing irreparable harm to his leg, hobbling around on it when the limb needed to be elevated and the scarred skin packed with hot poultices. His sister Rain would flail him alive with angry words if she saw how he'd abused her good work in saving his leg fifteen years earlier.

"Tykir," Alinor said softly with a little sigh of sympathy.

Sympathy now? Aaarrgh! He glanced up to see her staring at his thigh, where he was unconsciously kneading it.

Before he had a chance to rebuff her, she swatted his hand aside, laid his cloak over his lap and began to massage the sore muscles underneath herself. At first he was too shocked at the boldness of the wench. But then he could only melt as her expert ministrations brought blessed relief. It was as if her flexing fingers imparted heat to his tortured flesh.

"You must, indeed, be a witch," he murmured, but there was admiration, not condemnation, in his voice.

She shrugged and smiled shyly at him.

Shyness? From the boldest wench in all England? His heart lurched and expanded with a most disarming fullness.

Fortunately, their attention was diverted by the banging of the lawspeaker's staff on the floor at the head of the room.

"Hear one, hear all," Styrr the Wise called out in a surprisingly strong voice for one of his age. "Peace be to you, freemen of Trondelag. Come ye to judge your fellows according to the ancient laws laid down by good Norsemen through the ages."

"Hear! Hear!" the crowd roared.

"Remember our gods and their great esteem for wisdom. Remember how Odin sacrificed one eye to drink from the well of knowledge."

Many nodded at that reminder of their High-God's reverence for law and order.

"But I am remiss. Many of you follow the Christian religion, as well. Dost your God-book not say, 'The tongue of the just is as choice silver'?"

"Amen!" some of the men responded loudly.

"It is the custom that all men differ in opinions. But the goal of all is justice, and in this Thing, justice will prevail."

A loud clamor of assent rang through the assembly.

"All freemen will have a vote. No army will there be enforcing the decisions of the Thing . . . not Anlaf's, nor any other's. Order depends entirely on the willing acceptance of those in judgment, which will be shown by the *vapnatak*, or weapon clatter."

Hundreds of men rattled their swords against shields to demonstrate the method by which votes would be cast.

"This, too, I pronounce. The decisions of the Thing shall be final and accepted by one and all, in peace . . ."

Again, the assembly voiced their agreement with shouts of "Yea!" or yipping yells.

". . . unless the need arise for verdict by combat."

The assent this time was a wild cheer.

Alinor stopped massaging his thigh and snickered. "As if a bloody nose proves anything."

"Or a dead body," he added with a grin.

"I hope they don't expect me to wrestle Anlaf to prove my innocence." 'Twas her feeble attempt at humor, he supposed.

Damn, but he was developing a fondness for her sharp tongue . . . and her brave front in the face of what had to be the most frightening ordeal of her life. "Nay, they would expect you to have a champion fighting in your stead."

He immediately wished he could snatch the words back. Too late! He braced himself for trouble.

Her trembling lips stilled, then spread into a wide smile, just before she slipped her hand in his.

Trouble . . . I am in big trouble.

You could say it was trial by lackwits . . .

Alinor listened carefully as the lawspeaker enumerated all the various crimes and their respective punishments, as dictated by Thing ritual. Adam sat at her side.

Tykir, Rurik and Bolthor had taken their seats in the half-circle of chieftains. Those of his hird who remained at Anlaf's court—about seventy men—sat behind them, awaiting the Thing.

Apparently, Things handled a wide variety of disputes: murder, robbery, land ownership, divorce, rape, grazing and hunting rights, even such mundane conflicts as the wooing of bees or collection of firewood.

The lawspeaker would enumerate the punishment for whatever the crime. In some cases, the punishment was death or banishment. Sometimes the punishment involved the "eye for an eye" mentality. For example, the rape of one man's wife could result in the rape of the rapist's wife or daughter, or both. Most often, though, elaborate *wergilds* were levied, involving the payment of silver, wool, cows or other items of equivalent value.

"The *wergild* in the case of woman-theft demands the payment of bride-money," the lawspeaker was explaining. "For a farmer's daughter in prime with a maidenhead, fresh and strong and without blemish, the *wergild* would be thirty marten skins . . . and they must be winter pelts with no arrow holes. If the daughter be of a chieftain, however, there would be treble bride money paid, equal to up to ten quarter marks of silver."

"And what would the *wergild* be for a Saxon lady?" Alinor asked Adam in an undertone. "A widow, thrice over, who is *past* her prime and *with* blemish, but still fresh and strong."

"Thrice?" Adam exclaimed, then immediately ducked his head when he saw Tykir frown at them for conversing while the lawspeaker was still speaking. In a lower voice, he informed her, "A widow, even of high station, would bring less than the virgin farmer's daughter. Unless she carries vast estates, that is."

Alinor made a snorting sound of disgust. Actually, she had expected no less. Even her brothers did not place all that much value on her when bartering her in the marriage mart.

"Shhh," Adam cautioned then.

The lawspeaker was detailing the various punishments that could be levied for witchcraft, and they were gruesome, indeed. Flaying the skin off the back. Death by sword drink. (She assumed that meant a sword through the heart or lungs, which caused blood to gurgle up through the throat.) Skewering the head on a pole. *Nice image, that!* Burning at the stake. Splitting the witch in half at the buttocks to search for the hidden tail. And something called the Spear Death, whereby twenty spears were planted in the ground and the witch was thrown onto the points of the lances, where she would lay till death overcame her, or she succumbed to the pecking of vultures.

"A bloodthirsty bunch, these Norsemen are." Alinor murmured the words in a jesting way, but inside, she quivered with fright.

Adam patted her hand, and she could have kissed him with thanks.

Finally, it was time for the Thing to hear Alinor's case.

"What crime has been committed here?" the law-speaker asked.

"Witchcraft," Analf answered, "by Lady Alinor of Gray-cote."

"Deception. Failure to honor a commission. Betrayal. Theft," Tykir answered at the same time, "by King Anlaf."

Anlaf glared at him, and Tykir glared back.

Alinor was not about to sit back and let them do all the accusing. She stood, to the shock of those surrounding her, especially Adam, who was tugging on her gunna, trying to force her back to her seat. She dodged his grasp and announced her complaints. "Kidnapping. Torture. Starvation. Seasickness. Assault by constant sexual looks. Improper touching."

Her complaints were met with hoots of laughter and congratulatory shouts directed at Tykir. Tykir, on the other hand, appeared as if he'd swallowed a barrel of *gammelost*.

"Improper touching? That is the best type," one man pronounced, clapping his knee with glee.

"Can you show us how to give a sexual look?" another man made mock of Tykir, the whole time contorting his face into a ridiculous moon-eyed expression.

Adam managed to pull her back to the bench and told her with a short laugh, "Women aren't supposed to address the Thing, unless given specific permission to do so."

"Oh, now you tell me! I suppose my outburst will count against me in the voting."

"I don't know about that. Laughter is always a good sign."

"Proceed," the lawspeaker said, pointing his staff at Anlaf to go first. Easing himself tiredly into a nearby chair, the lawspeaker shook his head slowly from side to side, as if he knew this was going to be an impossible case.

Analf took a pose of arrogance, with wide shoulders thrown back and thumbs looped in his ornate belt, then commenced giving his distorted version of the events at St. Beatrice's Abbey last year. He claimed that he and his men had merely stopped for food and drink and to rest their horses when the witch had placed her infamous curse on his man-parts.

Alinor started to rise again to give the correct version of the encounter, but Adam placed a cautioning hand on her forearm.

"I but wish to tell the truth. The king is lying."

"You will get your chance later."

"Why would the woman curse you if you were doing no harm?" asked one burly Viking with gray-streaked black hair and piercing blue eyes.

Anlaf shrugged. "Mayhap she is a man-hater. Or an enemy of all Norsemen, as many Saxons tend to be. Why else would they recite that foolish prayer to their One-God? 'Oh, Lord, from the fury of the Northmen please protect us.'"

Several men preened, as if engendering fury were a good thing.

"King Anlaf!" Father Caedmon spoke up. "You have taken baptismal vows yourself."

"That I own," Anlaf said, waving a hand dismissively. It was obvious his conversion to Christianity was in name only.

Next, Anlaf detailed the affliction he'd sustained as a result of her supposed curse—the notorious crooked man-part. By the time he was done describing the curvature, the horrific pain, the inability to bury his bent sword into the straight sheaths of his wives and mistresses and the blow to his pride, the majority of the men in the great hall were cringing and tutting with commiseration. Alinor, on the other hand, felt like throwing up the meager contents of her breakfast—gruel with a side of gruel.

Then, the men all oohed and aahed on viewing the new— *better than ever, to hear Anlaf tell it*—manpart. Alinor tried not to look, except for a quick peek through her fingers, which she held to her eyes. Her stomach roiled again. "As far as I can see, it's just an ugly old thing. And purplish, for the love of heaven! Certainly nothing to make such a fuss about."

Adam was bent over, quaking with silent laughter.

"Excuse me for a moment," Tykir said and stood abruptly, interrupting Anlaf's discourse on his remarkable organ, which didn't please Anlaf very much because he was right in the middle of expounding on something called "staying power," or was it "staying up power"?

Men took their manparts entirely too seriously, in Alinor's opinion, and she told Adam so in no uncertain terms, which caused him to sputter with continuing laughter. "Oh, oh, oh . . . I do not believe this."

That was just before Tykir stomped—or as close to a stomp as he could manage with his limp—over to their bench, where he snarled in her ear. "Shut your teeth, you foolish wench, or I may not be able to save your head." To Adam, he just shook his head and muttered, "Fool!"

Before she could ask if, indeed, he intended to save her head, he was stomping/limping back to his judgment seat.

Next Anlaf brought forth his witnesses. His healer, Father Caedmon, a witch expert (though how the old hag gained that expertise was never explained) and finally, three wives and two mistresses, who attested to the severity of his affliction and the pain and deprivation he had suffered, not to mention their own unsatisfied state for many months. That latter was almost laughable to Alinor, but she did not dare show her amusement in the face of the unending glower Tykir sent her way.

Next, Anlaf called on some of Tykir's men, who reported, reluctantly, on the dead seagulls, the shower of goose dung, the bowel fluxes, crab lice, soured wine, sheep familiars and, worst of all, the potion that almost killed Tykir.

The mouths of some of the hardened Vikings were hanging open with amazement. More than a few looked as if they were barely holding back belly-quaking mirth, at Tykir's expense.

It was the strangest experience of her life . . . a wildly preposterous trial in a wild land of wild, wild men. Bolthor was mouthing some words to himself, no doubt composing a new saga, "Tykir the Great and the Wild Thing."

To her amazement, when King Anlaf called on Rurik to give testimony against her, he refused to say anything. Instead, he sat with his elbows braced on his widespread knees, staring glumly downward. The only explanation Alinor could come up with was that Tykir had threatened him with some dire consequence.

Now it was Tykir's turn to present his complaint. He told how King Anlaf's messenger, Bjold, approached him in the market town of Birka. The young man was sitting behind King Anlaf, ready to be called to testify, if necessary.

"First, Bjold offered me the Saracen stallion, Fierce One, if I would complete a mission for King Anlaf."

There were many ooohs from the Viking men, who were clearly impressed with Anlaf's generosity. If Anlaf had any thought of rescinding that offer, it was now locked in place by the approval of his peers. He chose the higher road and nodded graciously at the compliments being showered on him.

The toad!

"My mission was to search out the witch, Lady Alinor, in Northumbria," Tykir continued, "and bring her back to King Anlaf's court so she could remove the curse on his manpart."

"But I'm not—" Alinor started to say.

The lawspeaker ignored Alinor's outburst and waved for Tykir to proceed.

"When I declined to take on Anlaf's mission, even for such a fine horse, Bjold added to the pot another morsel." A slight grin tugged at his lips—*the lecherous lout!*—as he pointed to a far corner where the slave girl, Samirah, of the silver bells, huddled in conversation with several other women. The girl, no more than eighteen and beauteous of form and face, smiled coyly at Tykir. And Alinor felt tears brim her eyes.

Adam noticed. "Besotted, are you?"

"I . . . am . . . not!" she asserted, giving him a look that would have withered one of her housecarls back at Graycote but merely drew a smirk to Adam's lips. But, oh, despite her protests, she feared she *was* starting to care about the rogue. Untenable as it was, she was jealous of a mere girl with bells on her breasts.

Tykir stood silent for a moment before commencing afresh. "I declined both offers that Bjold brought on Anlaf's behalf because I had important work to do afore winter. But then he made me an offer I could not in good conscience refuse. He told me that Adam was being held hostage at his court and would not be released until I delivered the witch. He called it a 'friendly hostage,' but a hostage just the same."

"Is that true?" the lawspeaker demanded of King Anlaf. "Did you deceive Tykir thus?"

"You say me wrong," Anlaf whined to Tykir in a wounded voice. When he saw that Tykir was unmoved, he spoke to the lawspeaker. "Nay, he misunderstood. I merely told Bjold to inform Tykir, as a last resort, that Adam was *visiting* at my court, and Tykir might want to join him here afore retiring to Dragonstead for the winter."

"You lie!" Tykir yelled.

"You overstep yourself," Anlaf yelled back. "Remember to whom you speak."

"King you may be, Anlaf, but that does not give you leave to lie, or deceive."

"It was a misunderstanding, I tell you. We are not foemen, Tykir. Blood kin we be, and comrades. Do not test those bonds with ill-chosen words."

"It is no small matter to deceive blood kin or comrade, be you king or cotter."

The lawspeaker held both hands high to halt their argument.

Bjold was called forth then, and he supported the king in a shifty-eyed, stuttering way.

Tykir and Anlaf started hurling accusations back and forth again, while Bjold scurried away. Norsemen within the half-circle of twenty-one, as well as freemen throughout the hall, were muttering amongst themselves.

Finally, the lawspeaker stood and banged his staff against a nearby shield, calling for attention. Quickly, with a rippling effect, quiet descended over the crowd.

"Let the witch come forth," the lawspeaker said.

Tykir flinched.

Not a good sign, she thought. A moan escaped her lips.

Adam helped her to her feet and whispered in her ear, "Do not go fainthearted now, my lady. Hang firm with the mettle you have shown thus far."

Alinor's legs felt wobbly as she walked to the center of the room, where she was directed to stand, facing the assembly. She glanced toward Tykir for encouragement, but he just stared at her, his face angry and unsmiling. Whether he was angry at her, King Anlaf or the whole proceeding, she could not tell.

"You have been accused of witchcraft, Lady Alinor," the lawspeaker said. "What say you?"

She shook her head. "I'm not a witch."

"How do you explain the hair of flame and Devil's spittle?"

She shrugged. "God's choice, not Satan's."

Father Caedmon stiffened, unsure if she were uttering a profanity or not.

"Did you put a curse on King Anlaf's manroot?"

"Yea," she answered truthfully, and there was a loud murmur of "Aha!" that resounded through the assembly. "But it was not the curse of a witch. Merely that of an outraged woman upon seeing a man about to rape a nun."

"I . . . I . . . I . . . never . . ." Anlaf sputtered.

"Yea, you did, King Anlaf. You and your fellow Vikings entered the abbey of St. Beatrice in Northumbria, where you raped and pillaged the good nuns. When I saw you spread the thighs of Sister Mary Esme, I became outraged. When my efforts to dislodge you proved fruitless, I shouted, 'By the Virgin's Veil, may your manpart fall off if you do this evil thing.' That does not mean I am a witch."

"She cursed me, and my cock took a turn, halfway down," Anlaf argued. "I am confirmed a thousand times she is a witch."

"If I were a witch, why would I not place a curse on this whole bloody assembly and be done with it?" she scoffed. "Then I would not need a Thing to gain my freedom. I would just fly off with the aid of magic arts."

A number of the men shifted uncomfortably at her reminder that she could conceivably curse their dangly parts, as well. Some of them crossed their legs in protection, and a few reached for nearby shields.

"And is the headrail you wear now the Virgin's Veil?" the lawspeaker asked.

"Aaarrgh! Are you people listening to me? I am not a witch. There is no curse that could curve a man's staff, as far as I know. 'Tis said a certain malady can cause such symptoms, which go away of their own accord, in time. But Father Caedmon, or Adam the Healer, would know more of that than I."

"That is of no significance," Anlaf contended, examining his fingernails with unconcern.

"Yea, it is. I believe you had a physical ailment, not a magical one."

"That will be for the Thing to decide," the lawspeaker said sternly. "Now continue, Lady Alinor."

"I have no knowledge of a relic known as the Virgin's Veil. This is one of five blue headrails I own, all cut from the same English cloth. 'By the Virgin's Veil' is an expression, that's all."

"What explanation have you for all the frightful events that occur in your vicinity?" Anlaf asked belligerently.

"Coincidence."

"Hah!" Anlaf responded. And under his breath he muttered, "Bloody witch!" She could see equally dubious grimaces on the faces of many of the men.

The lawspeaker stared at her for a long moment, then sighed loudly. "This is a dilemma. We have three versions of a dispute, all different. Let us think on this problem and come up with a just solution."

About five minutes of contemplation followed then, as the men presumably thought through all aspects of the case. Some of them spoke to neighbors. There was much nodding and shaking of heads.

Those five minutes felt like five hours to Alinor, whose fate weighed in the balance. Surely, in the end, Tykir would come to her rescue . . . if rescuing became necessary. Her instincts about him as her God-sent champion—her guardian Viking angel, ludicrous as that sounded—could not be so far off the mark.

Finally, the lawspeaker's crinkled face brightened, as if inspired. He banged his staff on the floor for attention. "All good men know when to compromise," Styrr the Wise began. "It occurs to me that we have been told how a witch attempts to seduce mortal man so she may lose her tail. And I remind you that Tykir has told us he does not believe the Lady Alinor is a witch. Therefore, I suggest that Tykir prove his claim by marrying the witch." He smiled broadly through his toothless mouth at what he obviously considered a brilliant settlement.

Tykir's face first went pale with shock, then purple with rage. He sputtered with disbelief.

"Those are wise words Styrr has delivered . . . and well worth pondering," King Anlaf offered quickly. After only a moment of contemplation, he shouted, "Yea! A perfect solution!"

And the entire body of free men and chieftains voted their favor with whooping cheers and the raucous clatter of their weapons against shields, the *vapnatak*. "Prove she is not a witch, Tykir. Marry the wench," many of them hollered.

"Nay! I refuse," Tykir bellowed.

"You refuse a decision of the Thing?" the lawspeaker inquired stonily. "Do you choose decision by combat instead?"

"Wait a minute. Wait a minute," Alinor said. "Let me talk to Tykir in private for a brief moment."

"I have naught to say to you," he said in an ice-laden voice when she pulled him off to the side. "This is all your fault."

"My fault?" she snapped, but then softened her voice. She needed to have him on her side, not alienate him further. "Listen, Tykir, marrying me is a perfect solution."

He made a snorting noise that was most offensive. She would have whacked him on the head if she did not need his help in this matter. "Really. Marry me to end this absurd problem with Anlaf. You take me away to Dragonstead for the winter, and I will return to Graycote come spring. It's a perfect solution for me. We will be wed, but not really wed. My brothers will be forced to end their marriage machinations. And I will not have to worry over having a bothersome husband about...." Her words trailed off as she realized how insulting her plan sounded.

Tykir was shaking his head at her, as if she'd lost her mind. "And what would I gain from this so-called marriage?"

"Well... well..." she faltered. "It would be the noble thing to do."

"Hah! More like the angel thing to do."

"That, too," she said brightly.

"I am not a saint."

"I know."

"Nay, Alinor. You do not know."

"I could... you know..." Her face burned hotly.

"Nay, I do not know. Tell me." He was not making this easy for her at all.

"Well, I could be your... um, bedmate for the winter."

At first his mouth dropped open with surprise. Then he laughed. The lout laughed. "What have you to offer that Samirah, or some other wench, could not provide . . . without all the bother?"

"You wanted me before . . . in Hedeby."

"A moment of madness."

"Mayhap I have hidden talents." *By the rood! Did I say that? The only talent I have in bedsport is gritting my teeth.*

He laughed mirthlessly and walked away from her, shaking his head and muttering something about having "gone berserk." He then addressed the lawspeaker, Anlaf and the freemen. "This I will agree to. King Anlaf will give me the stallion, five hundred marks of silver—"

"Five hundred marks of silver!" King Anlaf exclaimed.

"—and I, in turn, will take the Lady Alinor with me to Dragonstead for the winter, to prove I do not fear her witchly powers. I will not marry her, though. That is asking too much. Even Anlaf must admit that." He hesitated, then added, "You can keep the jingling girl."

Alinor cringed inwardly at his vehement refusal to wed her. She understood. She really did. Still, it hurt.

"Methinks it a reasonable compromise," the lawspeaker opined.

King Anlaf tapped his bearded chin thoughtfully. Finally, he nodded, and the weapon clatter of the assembly gave the final stamp of approval to Tykir's solution.

"At least I walk away with my head, if not my dignity," she said to Tykir as he took her by the upper arm, nigh dragging her from the great hall. She was trying to lighten his dark mood.

Bolthor followed behind, along with the seventy or so of his men who still remained. The men, armed with swords but no casting weapons, formed a tight phalanx as they withdrew from Anlaf's court, wary of any treachery. Farther behind, Adam sprinted along after them, his robe raised to his knees to facilitate flight. Rurik came last, weighted down by cloth sacks of the coin he'd amassed from his cross and holy water transactions.

When they got to the doorway of the great hall, Tykir turned on her and said, nose pressed to nose, "Attend me well, lady. You are going to pay dearly for this trick you have played on me, in ways you cannot possibly imagine."

"'Tis nigh impossible I could even think up such a trick."

"Shut . . . your . . . teeth."

She would have liked to express her opinion of his nasty manner, but she was free, thanks to him, and she decided to show her gratitude by remaining silent. Not that she had a choice.

As they all walked toward his longship in the falling snow, Alinor pondered Tykir's words. *You are going to pay dearly for this trick you have played on me, in ways you cannot possibly imagine.* In that moment, she discovered that she had a really good imagination.

And she thought, *Hmmm.*

Beware of Vikings bearing gifts . . .

An hour later, two of Tykir's longships prepared to set sail on the winding fjords north to Dragonstead.

The weather had turned bitter cold, and sleet was coming down in a steady fall of wet, biting pellets. She could tell by the nervous efficiency that the seamen expended in their tasks that they were worried by the coming storm, and about whether they would be able to make the two-day trip home before the streams froze over.

Alinor sat huddled under several layers of fur rugs. The horse—a beautiful beast of sleek-as-satin black—was firmly ensconced on the other vessel, despite Anlaf's offer to buy the animal back from Tykir.

Tykir wasn't talking to anyone, most especially her. He went about his duties stoically, overseeing his ship's departure. His usually full lips were thinned and bluish, and not just from the cold. She could tell that he was in tremendous pain from his old leg wound but would not stop and rest, or he might not be able to go on.

They were ready to set sail now.

Tykir walked up to her and shoved a pile of five flat boxes into her hands. They were finely carved in some foreign style and gilded along the raised edges.

"For me?" She was puzzled by the contradiction of gifts and his icy demeanor.

"For you."

"But . . . but why?"

"These, my lady witch, will mark the first stage of your payment to me of the huge debt you now owe me."

"I . . . I don't understand. You give me gifts so I can pay you?"

"Yea," he said. The smile that stretched his lips never met his eyes, which regarded her coolly. "And your debt is huge."

The fine hairs stood out at the back of her neck. "You are talking about punishment, not payment, are you not?"

"Yea, but you have a few days to ponder your future, my lady. I will not begin to collect till we are settled in at Dragonstead for the winter . . . *the whole bloody winter.*"

"I'm not afraid of you," she said, even though she was beginning to be just that.

"Then you are a bigger fool than I thought." With those words, he walked off and signaled his men to begin rowing.

A short time later, Adam walked up and sat down beside Alinor. "Why are you frowning so?" Adam asked. "I would think you would be jubilant. You won."

"I did no such thing. This wasn't a contest. And no matter what Tykir says, it wasn't my fault, either."

Adam laughed. "He is a mite perturbed with you."

"That's an understatement. It's why I was frowning. I don't understand these gifts he gave me. Oh, he spouted some nonsense about their being my first installment in paying him back a huge debt. But I've examined them and . . ." She handed them to Adam, and he opened the largest one first. It was a silk-lined shallow box containing dozens of feathers of all sizes, colors and textures. "Aren't they magnificent?" she commented.

He nodded, deep in thought, and opened the next flat chest. This one contained ten flagons of various scented oils. "He has commented on the rose-scented hair cream that his sister-by-marriage, Lady Eadyth, gave to me, but I am deeply touched that he would grace me with these."

Adam was beginning to grin enigmatically.

"Why are you smirking?"

"I am beginning to understand the method of payment Tykir plans to exact from you." He opened the next box, which held the oddest objects, short lengths of velvet ropes . . . four of them. "Yea, I am beginning to understand."

A very small box held a magnificent amber cabochon, about the size of a bird's egg. "This is beautiful but has no backing to be used as a brooch, and no metal loop through which a neck chain could be run."

"It's a belly button stone," Adam said with a chuckle.

"A what?"

"It's a special gem, favored by many of the houris in sultans' harems. The woman wears naught but this stone in the navel."

It took a moment for comprehension to dawn. When it did, she gasped. "He's mad if he thinks I would . . . well, suffice it to say, he's mad." She turned the gem this way and that, trying to picture it in place. Finally, she put it away, making a tsk-ing sound of disapproval. "Is the man perverted?"

"Probably." Adam winked at her and reached for the last box.

"Oh, that one's a mistake," she said, trying to pull it back. "Tykir must have meant it for Samirah."

He opened it, and out spilled the most scandalous garment, made of near transparent red silk scarves, edged with tiny jingling bells. "Nay, you are mistaken, Lady Alinor. He intends it for you. I am certain of that."

She stared at him, aghast.

"Lady Alinor, I predict this is going to be the most interesting winter of your life."

CHAPTER ELEVEN

❦

Wanna see my tail, baby? . . .

They arrived at Dragonstead two days later as snow began to fall in a steady blanketing of puffy flakes.

Alinor and all the other seafarers were exhausted, frozen to the bone and barely able to find their land legs as they disembarked from the ice-crusted longships. The trip had been harrowing, to say the least. Hard rowing through one fjord after another . . . some narrow, and so shallow the vessels risked being landlocked, and others as wide as a river.

The weather had varied from rain to bitter winds, but was always intensely cold. They did not even camp for the night; it was dark a large portion of the day anyhow. Instead, they stopped for breaks at six-hour intervals whereby cold food was served—including the horrid *gammelost*—and bodily functions could be relieved in nearby bushes. All the time they were attempting to outrun the onslaught of full winter, which was apparently a disaster to be avoided when on the open waterways of the region known as the Land of the Midnight Sun.

What a harsh land, this northern section of Norway! Of course, she was seeing it for the first time under the worst of circumstances, but it was a mountainous, primitive terrain, more suited to wild beasts than men.

Alinor hadn't spoken with Tykir since he'd handed her the "gifts." He'd kept to the other longship most of the time, but she could see even from a distance that he was nigh crippled with pain. And Tykir wasn't the only one suffering. Many of the seamen were afflicted with the usual wintertime ailment of sneezing and running noses and eyes. Of course, they blamed it all on her witchly presence. Few had been convinced by Tykir's defense of her at Anlaf's court.

She intended to make them all a good, rich chicken broth once they reached Dragonstead . . . a guaranteed cure for the winter chills. And she would force it down their stubborn throats if they resisted it as witch's brew . . . yea, she would. She was sick to death of stubborn, superstitious men.

But now they'd come home for the winter. The timing was fortunate in that they'd arrived during one of the few hours of daylight. Many of the seamen were met by family members waiting for them on the wharves of Dragonstead. One by one, and in small groups, those men who did not reside in the main keep made for their homes in the nearby village.

Finally, the chaos of unloading the goods was completed, and Alinor stepped onto the wooden planks of the dock, getting her first good view of Dragonstead.

Then she gasped.

Dragonstead was situated in a bowl-shaped valley known as the Valley of the Dragons. Adam had told her earlier that the name came from an old legend that millions of years ago this valley had served as a dragon's nest. Now, there was a small lake forming the base of the bowl and dense, tree-lined mountains surrounding it. The lake was formed from melted snow and rain run-off from the mountains, which flowed into the fjord by which they'd entered. A small timber and stone "castle," in the Frankish rather than the Norse style, sat perched on the lip of one side, overlooking the lake. Viking longhouses making up the Dragonstead village were scattered in clusters around the bowl.

It was a land ill-suited to farming, but goats and sheep would do well here. She smiled to herself at that last. "Tykir the Great" as a sheepherder? She thought not.

With fat snowflakes billowing down on the scene, Dragonstead, with its valley and lake backdrop, presented an exquisite picture. Magical, even. A land where fairies and elves and other woodland creatures might very well reside, if one believed in such fanciful notions.

She was seeing it through winter's filter, of course. How much more beautiful would it be when spring burst on the valley with its greenery and wildflowers and native animals abirthing, like reindeer and beaver and great bears? Or summer, when ducks and other feathered fowl came to nest here?

Tykir came up to her then and took her by the forearm. "Come," he said tersely. "Don't stand about dawdling."

She would have reacted to his rudeness, but she was too engrossed in the scene before her. "Your home is wonderful."

"Huh?" His head came up alertly, and his eyes widened with surprise.

"If this was my home, I don't think I would ever leave."

She could tell her words pleased him, though he tried to hide his emotions from her. "Is this another trick of yours?"

"To what purpose?" she scoffed. "I give you a compliment so that I can gain . . . what?"

He shrugged. "To avoid your punishment."

"Oh, that! I thought you were serious."

"I am serious. You are going to be punished for your many crimes, in ways you cannot imagine."

"Ha, ha, ha!"

"Did you open my gifts?" he asked.

"Yea, I did. That was some grand jest you played on me."

" 'Twas no jest."

"Adam is laughing."

A look of disgust passed over his face. "You showed Adam?"

"Yea. He says you are perverted."

Tykir threw back his head and laughed. "That's truly a case of the pot calling the kettle black. I will have a talk with that guttersnipe if he is calling me names. Perverted! Indeed!"

"Well, actually, I'm the one who called you perverted, and he just agreed."

Tykir was shifting from foot to foot, gazing about his homestead with an expression that could only be described as unbridled love. Unbidden, a thought occurred to her. *What would it be like to be favored with such devotion from a man? Nay, not any man. What would it be like to be so loved by Tykir?* Alarmed, Alinor reined in her untenable mind-spinnings and turned her attention back to Tykir.

Without thinking, he stuck his tongue out and was letting snowflakes melt on his tongue.

"You are such a child," she said, but her heart turned over at the innocent gesture. "I can just picture you as a mischievous boy, throwing snowballs with your friends. Chasing the girls with icicles in a game of catch-me-if-you-can."

He cocked his head in surprise. "I had no friends as a child. We moved about too much, and had no real home, as such. Except later for a short while, mayhap, when I lived with my grandparents at Ravenshire. Nay, there was just me and my brother Eirik, and he was older, and much too somber in his ways for such trivial pursuits as snow-play."

He seemed to make a conscious effort to pull himself out of his wistful musings then, and added with a deliberate twinkle in his eye, "But, yea, I recall now that I did give more than one girling hot pursuit with many a cold icicle. 'Til one day the goatherder's daughter, Elfrida, upset with my harmless taunting, stuffed a handful of snow down the front of my braies. God's bones! 'Twas an experience I would not want to repeat."

She smiled at that image. "And did it teach you a lesson?"

He shrugged. "For a short while. But I got back at Elfrida, to be sure. I flipped up the back hem of her robe during a Michaelmas feast. Turns out she wore no undergarments. And everyone got to see her bare backside . . . as wide as a fat bishop's, I might add." He grinned at her, unabashedly.

"For shame!" she scolded, but only halfheartedly.

"Well, Wallace the Privy Builder proposed marriage to her the following sennight," he informed her with a continuing grin. "Must be he had a taste for overlarge backsides. Perchance it had something to do with his trade."

God above! The man is adorable.

Aaarrgh! Where did that thought come from? He is not adorable. Not, not, not!

"So, you like your first view of Dragonstead?" Tykir asked, changing the subject.

"Yea," she said with much enthusiasm. "It must be so beautiful here in the summer."

He shrugged. "I wouldn't know. I'm always gone by then."

Her heart went out to the lout—way too many times this day, actually. She could see how much Dragonstead meant to him, and yet each spring he tore himself away to wander on his various travels. There was something significant to be learned here.

But Alinor had no time for that. She had just noticed something more important. Tykir's face was flushed, and not from the cold.

"Are you sick?" she demanded, reaching up to place a hand on his forehead.

He was burning up with fever.

He tried to step back from her but swayed from side to side. The rigors of the trip, on top of his already sorry condition, were finally catching up with him.

"Bolthor!" she cried, and the giant came immediately to her side, taking in the situation at a glance. Just in time, he caught Tykir and picked up his lifeless form in his arms.

Tykir the Great was deathly ill.

It was a most auspicious beginning to Alinor's winter stay at Dragonstead.

The dumb cluck! . . .

Three days later, Alinor sat at the kitchen table chopping

a plump raw chicken, along with leeks and various dried herbs for yet another kettle of rich chicken broth. Later she would drop tiny dough balls into the soup pot, once the dish had been bubbling for three or four hours, when the meat began to fall off the bones in shreds. The dough balls were a secret touch she'd learned from Leah, a Jewish merchant's wife who'd passed through Graycote a year past. Leah had also suggested keeping the chicken feet, gizzard and heart in the brew for extra flavor, even though some cooks tossed them in the midden.

"Chicken *again?*" Bolthor asked, rolling his eyes heavenward. "'Tis past time to put a haunch of wild boar on the spit. Or a few rabbits. Men need red blood, lest their virility suffers."

Men need red blood? For virility? Where did that bit of male non-wisdom come from? "Chicken broth is good for the winter ailment," Alinor said defensively. "I know some of the men . . . well, most of the men . . . are stall-fed on my chicken soup, but—"

"You've been serving it three times a day since our arrival at Dragonstead," he pointed out dryly.

Alinor knew many at Dragonstead were still leery of her as a possible witch, but fortunately, they'd allowed her to minister to their master's illness. They watched her closely, though.

"I care not a fig for the finicky palates of you men if the liquid strengthens your sniffling systems, especially Tykir, whose fever broke only yestereve, praise be to God!"

"Finicky appetites! You are killing our appetites," Bolthor grumbled. "But, yea, 'tis good news that Tykir is finally on the mend."

Bolthor had paused to speak with her as he was passing through the scullery with a huge armload of firewood. It took a massive amount of wood to heat the three hearths in the great hall, the cook fire in the kitchen and the fireplaces in two of the upper bedchambers, from late autumn till spring.

Luckily, the woodmen had worked nonstop since last winter to set by a goodly supply.

As Bolthor left the kitchen, she heard him muttering something about a new saga, "Alinor the Witch and the Deadly Chicken Potion."

"Pay no mind to Bolthor," Girta the Round said. Alinor had forgotten Girta was behind her in the kitchen, rolling out circles of unleavened dough made of rye, barley and peas, to be baked on flat wheels with a central hole. Later the bread would be stored by threading on a pole near the hearth. "Men don't know what's good for them. Take Jostein the Smith, who has been smitten for years with Bodil the Ripe, our head dairymaid."

Huh? Alinor didn't even know half the people Girta spoke of. Alinor's gaze followed Girta's flour-covered finger to the open door of the buttery, where the voluptuous Bodil was making the Viking soft-curded cheese known as *skyr.*

"Jostein took her to bed, on more than one occasion, I might add, and never offered her the wedding vows," Girta rambled on. "Now Bodil is about to wed with Rapp of the Big Wind, and Jostein is heartsick. Moons about the keep like a wounded cow, and for the life of me, I cannot fathom . . ."

As Girta gossiped on, Alinor smiled at the jolly, talkative woman, with her distinctive blond-braided crown. Girta supervised the affairs of Dragonstead with an iron hand, along with her husband, Red Gunn, the steward, who was as slim as Girta was round. Dragonstead was a small estate, but it ran with remarkable efficiency due to this couple's combined efforts, both indoors and out, with the master in residence or not.

Alinor was impressed.

When Tykir was gone on his trading ventures, there were at least two dozen housecarls—freemen and women, not to mention a handful of children—living at Dragonstead, not including the village folks. When Tykir returned, that number often increased by a hundred or more. Not an overlarge populace, even for a small keep.

But Girta was still talking about the Dragonstead household whilst Alinor's mind had been awandering. Alinor interrupted her. "Why do they call him Rapp of the Big Wind?"

"Oh! You might very well ask that," Girta tutted. "Because he can break wind at will, and does so overmuch. Men think it is a great talent, foolish dolts that they are. In truth, Rapp can clear a room in a heartbeat, if you get my meaning."

Alinor had to laugh, despite her revulsion.

"Poor Bodil! Methinks she should whack that Jostein on the head with a butter paddle. Mayhap it would knock some sense into his dull brain. 'Tis not too late . . . not 'til the vows are exchanged. What say you?"

"I have no idea," Alinor said honestly. But then she brought up a subject that was bothering her more. "How soon do you think it will be afore Tykir is up and about?" she asked.

The barrel-bellied Girta shrugged and divided a new batch of dough into a series of balls, which she plopped onto a floured board. Before she answered Alinor's question, she began to roll the dough into a number of wide circles, the top and bottom crusts for the first of a series of eel pies that would be baked and served for the evening meal, along with Alinor's chicken broth. The men were going to be pleasantly surprised by the tasty menu addition.

"I would not expect too much too soon," Girta said. "The warm bricks you've been applying to his thigh have helped . . . not to mention the chicken broth you've been force-feeding him." She chuckled at that last. Even in his delirium, Tykir had taken to making grunting sounds of "Yeech!" through gritted teeth when she fed him her chicken broth. She'd resorted to pinching his nose till his mouth opened for her spooning.

"I've been so frightened," Alinor confessed. "Never have I encountered a fever so fierce, nor long-lasting."

"Well, the Master Tykir has had many a year to master his war wounds. He knows well enough not to be abusing the leg when it starts to ache. And, for a certainty, in the past he has always been back here at Dragonstead afore the cold weather set in. I don't know what the foolish man could have been thinking."

"His men blame me for all the delays."

"And are you at fault? Is it guilt that prompts your vigil by his bedside?"

"Nay! The clodpole kidnapped me. 'Twas not my fault it took him so long to find me, nor that delays happened along the way. But he did stay at Anlaf's court to defend me, and he did bring me here against his wishes. For that, I owe him plenty."

"Don't be beating your breast over this, dearie. You've spent way too many hours hovering over the man as it is. When did you sleep last? If you're not careful, Lady Alinor, you'll be getting sick yourself. And don't be thinking the master will be thanking you for your ministrations, or your lack of rest on his behalf. The way I hear it, the master is planning some grand punishment for you."

Alinor felt her face flame. "Adam has been talking."

"You could say that." Girta put a floury hand to her mouth and giggled. "But Adam would not give us any details. All he does is waggle his eyebrows and make suggestive remarks to tease everyone. The rascal!"

Alinor put all her broth ingredients into the large cauldron over the fire and added a goodly amount of water. Stirring it with a large copper ladle, she then covered the pot and moved the spider hook to the back of the hearth for slow simmering.

Having finished rolling the first of her crusts, Girta clapped her hand to remove the flour, then wiped her hand on the open-sided Norse apron that covered her from shoulder to ankle. Next Girta took the lid off the eel barrel on the side of the fireplace and reached into the murky water to retrieve a particular long, slimy creature—about the size of a battle pike. With nary a grimace, Girta pressed the squirming eel onto a cutting block and whacked its head off with a cleaver. Alinor flinched at the sight of the headless, still flailing eel, spurting blood.

With an economy of effort, Girta made a slit the length of the snakelike animal and peeled its skin back, all in one clean piece. As she chopped the eel meat into pieces, and dropped it into a bowl of thick cream and wild onions garnished with peas, Alinor was staring at the eel skin on the floor. An outrageous thought had occurred to her.

Do not be ridiculous, Alinor. Stop it right now. You are becoming as wild and unrestrained as these heathen Vikings.

Still, the mischievous thought persisted.

"Do you know where Rurik is?" Alinor asked tentatively.

"In the guard room, sharpening weapons, methinks," Girta answered distractedly as she worked to crimp together the crusts of the first eel pie.

The blue-faced Viking had been blathering high and low since they'd arrived at Dragonstead. Tykir may have defended her before Anlaf's court, but Rurik still proclaimed her a witch. At the same time, he was profiting mightily on her magic wordfame, selling wood crosses and holy water. Truly, Rurik was the biggest, most irksome thorn in her side.

Mayhap 'twas time to shake that thorn loose.

Oh, I couldn't.

Yea, I could.

'Twould be childish.

Yea.

Alinor leaned down to pick up the eel skin gingerly, between a thumb and forefinger. *It resembles a . . . well, tail,* she thought and smiled with wicked anticipation.

Before she had a chance to surrender to her more rational misgivings, Alinor hiked up the back hem of her gown and tucked the end of the eel skin into the waistband of her underdrawers. Then she dropped the gown back in place. Peering over her shoulder, she saw the eel skin emerging along the floor, like a tail.

"For the love of Freyja!" Alinor looked up to see a startled Girta watching her, mouth gaping open. Then the cook smiled widely as comprehension dawned.

Alinor sauntered off to the guard room, hips swaying, tail swishing. "Oh, Rur-ik," she called out.

"What in bloody hell do you want now?" the surly knight answered her.

Well, I certainly feel no guilt now.

At first he paid her no nevermind, just murmured something about wenches having no business in a man's workroom. So, she wandered around the room, examining the armor and shields and deadly weapons that lay about.

The rasp of a sword edge along the whetstone slowed, then stopped.

A bare instant later, Rurik emitted a loud masculine shriek, then a shout of "*Aaaaack!* Run, everyone! Run!" that reverberated throughout the castle. As Alinor scurried through the kitchen, tossing the eel skin under the table, paying no nevermind to a clucking Girta, she heard one of the young armor boys back in the guard room say, "The master Rurik 'pears to be having a fit. His mouth is sucking in and out like a fjord flounder."

Alinor hid in the buttery for more than an hour, laughing till tears rolled down her cheeks. What had possessed her? It was the most foolish, impetuous, uncharacteristic thing she had ever done in her entire life. And the most satisfying.

Roses gave him ideas, and they weren't about gardening . . .

The scent of roses drew Tykir from his deep sleep.

He tried to prop himself up on his elbows, but he was weak as dragon piss. His body weighed him down to the mattress, heavy and aching. Most of the ache was centered in his thigh, which throbbed painfully. But, in truth, he felt better than he had in days.

The roses pulled at Tykir's senses . . . a memory tugging at him that he couldn't quite grasp. Was he in an English flower garden? Or an eastern harem, where floral oils were often used by the *houris?* He opened his leaden eyelids slowly and realized he was in the huge bedstead in his upper chamber at Dragonstead. The air was chill in the room, though he was warm as a babe in the womb under the layers of bed furs covering his body. And there was some heat generated by the roaring fire he heard crackling in the fireplace, though the hearth heat did not fill the entire chamber. Sometimes the walls were covered with ice in winter, even as the fire blazed.

Tykir turned his head slowly on the pillow toward the hearth. *Ahhhh!* Now he recognized the source of the rose scent.

Lady Alinor, of the rose-scented hair.

He licked his dry lips and tried to focus. He was not really surprised to see the witch standing there. Every time he'd awakened during the past three days of fever, she'd been in his bedchamber, leaning over him, pressing cool cloths to his forehead, forcing spoonfuls of chicken broth into his mouth. It wasn't that the broth tasted vile; there was just so much of it. In his dreams, he'd taken to crowing like a rooster. At least he wasn't laying eggs. Yet.

Had she really pinched his nose to force his mouth open? She would pay for that.

He'd been barely conscious . . . seeing everything through a filmy haze . . . sometimes flailing and muttering sense-lessly . . . but he'd recognized her as a continuing presence during his illness. And been strangely comforted.

It was probably a spell.

Alinor was combing her wet hair in front of the fire . . . thus the roses. Damn his sister-by-marriage for giving Alinor the hair cream. Just how much had she given her? Hopefully,

Alinor would run out soon. Then again, mayhap he did not really want her to stop enticing him thus. *Aaarrgh! I'm being driven mad by rose hair cream. Could Eadyth perchance be a witch, too?*

Alinor must have just taken a bath because she wore a loose chemise, the type women usually donned after rising from their baths. Over and over, she raised the ivory comb— his comb, he realized by the by, with an odd tug in his chest—then pulled it through the waist-length strands. Each time she lifted her arm, the outline of her breast under the white linen raised, as well. Every time she followed through on the comb stroke, the breast relaxed into its natural, delicious shape.

Someday he would like to watch her perform this sensuous exercise nude. And he had no trouble imagining how she would look. He knew exactly how to picture the witch naked. It was an exercise at which he'd become adept.

He stared, mesmerized, at the rhythmic motion of her hand, and her body in profile.

And another part of his body reacted to the rhythm with a hardening rhythm of its own. Leastways the fever had not caused any permanent damage to *vital* organs.

He tried to smile, but his chapped lips cracked. He barely noticed, though, because his eyes were already fluttering closed. There must be some sleeping herb in that bloody chicken brew.

As he drifted off to sleep again, he began to dream. And they were very interesting dreams. Not just erotic, which were his favorite kind, but accompanied by their very own smell.

Roses, of course.

Torture by chicken, that's what it was . . .

It was an odor that drew Tykir out of sleep once again. But not roses.

Chicken broth, he realized sluggishly and gagged. "Yeech." Which gave the witch an opportunity to shove a wooden spoon sloshing chicken broth into his mouth, practically to his throat. He knew it was the witch because his eyes shot wide open.

It must have been some time since his last awakening because Alinor's hair was dry now and hanging in a single braid down her back. Her chemise was covered with a dark green, thick wool gunna, covered with an open-sided Viking apron.

Too bad! He much preferred her earlier attire. Or non-attire.

Oh, well, I can always imagine her naked.

"You're awake," she said cheerily. *I am not in the mood for cheerily.* She shoved another spoonful of the broth into his mouth. *I am not in the mood for more chicken broth.* This one had a glob of dough floating on top. *I am not in the mood for globs of dough.*

"Glpugglup," he sputtered as he attempted to choke and speak and chew at the same time. Then he grabbed the wrist of the hand dipping the empty spoon into a bowl on the bedside table and growled, "Yea, I'm awake. How can I not be awake with all that slop you are feeding me?"

She winced, but not from his tight fingerhold on her wrist, which he immediately released. Nay, she'd winced because he'd hurt her feelings.

Bloody hell! Why should I feel guilty for voicing a fact that should be apparent? She has been overdoing the chicken broth. But mayhap I shouldn't have referred to her good efforts as slop. He wasn't in the mood for apologizing, though.

"I want some real food," he said, sitting up suddenly, then immediately dropping back to the pillow when an invisible broadaxe cleaved his skull. He pressed the heels of both palms to his brow to stop his brains from spilling out. "Did you poison me again? Did you give me a potion to explode my head this time, instead of my bowels?"

She ignored his accusations and immediately reached

forward with concern, placing a cool palm on his forehead. *I am not in the mood to be placated, but her hand does feel good. Mayhap I will let it rest there for a moment.*

"What is amiss? Is it your head?"

"Nay, it's my arse." *Hell and Valhalla! I am in a vile mood.*

She made a tsk-ing sound as she adjusted the furs around him, tucking them in tightly at the sides till he felt like a corpse being dressed for the coffin.

He slapped her hands away. "Stop fussing over me."

"I'm only trying to help."

"Help me by fetching some bloody damn food."

"I don't like your tone."

"I don't give a damn what you like."

"My, my, you are testy today. Must be you are getting better when you begin to sound like Rurik. Grumble, grumble, grumble all the time."

He narrowed his eyes at her. "Was that Rurik I heard shouting earlier today?"

She examined her fingernails with blatant guilt. "I wouldn't know. I don't keep track of Rurik's doings."

"What did you do to him now?" he demanded to know.

"Me?" she asked, fluttering her eyelashes. "I have no idea what you mean."

He rubbed his bristly jaw. "God, my mouth tastes like a midden on a hot summer day."

"Your breath smells the same."

"Thank you for pointing that out. Chicken breath, that's what I must have. Now get me some food. Anything, as long as it doesn't have feathers. Mutton would be good. Or lamb chops. Baby lamp chops."

All that talking had worn him out, and he yawned widely, feeling his body closing down for sleep once again.

He thought he heard the wench giggle then as she eased herself off the high bed and asked, "How about some eel pie?"

"What's so funny about eel pie?" he grumbled.

"If you're lucky, Viking, I might just show you."

Who knew bathing could be so sweet? . . .

A smell drew Tykir out of his sleep once again.

It was a strong, pungent smell this time . . . not unpleasant, but different. Soap. That's what it was. Girta's homemade soft soap, used in the bathhouse.

He opened his eyes a mere slit and saw that Alinor was bathing him. The nerve of the wench! Bathing him like a newborn babe. But, nay, there were other possibilities. Immediately, he closed his eyes, hoping for "other possibilities." He was too weak to engage in any vigorous activity, but he wasn't so far gone that he couldn't enjoy laying back for a few lustful . . . possibilities.

He tried to regulate his breathing to emulate sleep, a hard task when she was lathering up his neck and shoulders and—Oh, my God!—his chest. He did have a fondness for touching . . . both being touched and doing the touching himself. There was an art to good touching. Alinor was an artist, if he did say so himself . . . or she would be once he'd given her the advanced tutelage of a touch master.

She used a damp, soapy cloth to wash his neck and shoulders, wiping the area off with the same cloth, which had been rinsed and wrung out. But she worked the soap into his chest hairs with her fingertips, over his flat nipples, skimming his abdomen and waist, over and into his navel.

He bit his bottom lip to hold back a moan. 'Twas a good thing his private parts were covered with a breechclout. Else he would, no doubt, scare her with the size of his appreciation.

She finished with the palate of skin from collarbone to groin, much too soon. But then she entered a different territory. Carefully raising his arms overhead, she began to lather the hair in his surprisingly sensitive armpits. He almost shot up off the bed at the intense pleasure her fingertips brought there. To be sure, he was going to make her play in that newly discovered erotic spot once they made love.

And there was no doubt in his mind that they would be making love sometime soon. She owed him.

Yea, he could picture the scene. He would be lying on the bed, naked, with his arms folded behind his head. She would be straddling his waist, naked. Or should she be lying on her side, naked? Regardless, he would have his arms upraised, and she would lower her head to kiss and suckle first one nipple, then another. He would have his eyes closed the whole time because he'd want to prolong the anticipation. That was another thing women loved about him . . . how he prolonged the anticipation. In any case, after she'd nigh melted his bones by suckling on his nipples, she, still naked, would trail soft kisses up to his armpits where she would . . .

Nay, nay, nay, he had a better idea. She could be wearing that little harem outfit he'd gifted her, and every time she moved, there would be a tiny jingling of bells.

"Are you awake?" she whispered.

Uh-oh. Had his heart lurched against his chest walls with all these imaginings? Or had he inadvertently grinned? He didn't think she'd noticed the tentpole in his breechclout. Otherwise, she would have no doubt slapped him with her damp washcloth. But wait till he got her naked. Then her goose was cooked . . . so to speak. Or was it her chicken that would be cooked? In all humility, she wouldn't be able to resist him, naked . . . her naked, not him . . . well, actually, both of them.

"Are you awake?" she repeated softly.

He said nothing to her question, just moaned softly, as if in deep sleep. He planned to do a great deal more moaning sometime later, and she would be moaning, too. That was one of his greatest talents, making a woman moan. And prolonging anticipation. And . . . well, he misremembered all his bedsport talents now, but there were plenty of them.

He could scarce wait to hear how a witch moaned. Or would a witch howl? He shrugged mentally. Moan, howl . . . either one would suffice. He planned to roar, himself. And moan and howl. And those other things he couldn't remember.

But wait, there were interesting events taking place whilst his mind had been wandering. Alinor had flipped the bed furs up to cover his chest and stomach, exposing his legs. She was using the cloth to wash the furred skin from loins to toes. He called on every bit of self-control his battered body still held in store as she skimmed the tense muscles of his inner thighs. A good warrior, forced to ride unruly destriers into battle, soon honed those inner thigh muscles, and with honing came heightened sensitivity. The unbelievably intense pleasure her soapy caresses engendered caused him to clench his fists and grit his teeth, but he could not stop a certain part of his body from rising to the occasion. Never had his staff felt so hard and long. Never had it throbbed with such wonderful pain.

But then her fingers worked in the lather, rather than the cloth, and that was his undoing. Much more, and he would humiliate himself.

With a roar of protest, oblivious to the pain in his head, he sat upright and shoved her hands aside. "Are you trying to kill me, woman?"

She blinked at him with surprise. "You're awake."

"Yea, I'm awake. I would have to be a cadaver not to revive after all that prodding and poking."

"Prodding and poking?" she exclaimed indignantly.

"Blessed Lord, Alinor, were you using a washup as an excuse for finding every blessed erotic spot on my body?"

"Erotic spot? What's an erotic spot?"

He couldn't help himself. He began to laugh. When he finally calmed down, he informed her, "Everyone—man and woman alike—has erotic spots on their bodies. Places that are especially susceptible to excitement. Some have more than others. Some have them in very . . . uh, different spots. The inner thighs are among my particular favorites, as you very well discovered. I thank you not to torture me so . . . leastways, not till I am well enough to follow through on your invitation." He smiled at her to soften the blow of his criticism.

She frowned, and he could tell that she did not really understand his words. A widow three times over, and she was naive as a virgin farm girl.

"Why, you ungrateful cad! Where is your appreciation for all my ministrations these past three days? Where is your thanks for my taking on the odious task of bathing your body? Where is . . ."

Her words trailed off as her eyes latched onto his midsection. He cupped his hands over himself, but it was too late. She'd seen enough. She narrowed her eyes at him, then began whacking him all over with her wet washcloth . . . his shoulders, his arms, his legs, his "tentpole." The whole time, she was berating him, "As if I would deliberately tempt you . . . or any other man! You lecherous lout! You odious oaf! You perverted puddinghead! You—"

She drew herself up suddenly, as if realizing the impropriety of beating a sick man.

He pushed his luck just a mite too far when he inquired with a grin, "Does that mean you're not going to finish bathing me?" He looked pointedly down at a part of his body that would really, really like to be bathed by her soft woman hands.

She answered by storming out of the room, slamming the door behind her. Instantly, the door opened again, and she was the one grinning now, except the grin never reached her flashing green, evil eyes.

"I showed Rurik my tail today."

"Really?" He grinned, never having believed that tail nonsense.

"If you're not careful, Viking, I'm going to show you my

tail—and a whole lot more." Then she slammed the door again.

I'm counting on it, witchling. With all my being, I am counting on it.

CHAPTER TWELVE

❦

How could one witch cause so much chaos? . . .
It was a cozy, familiar scene that met Tykir's eyes as he made his way carefully to the great hall the next afternoon, to the warm greetings of his men.

The burly warriors and seamen, dressed in leather tunics and braies, huddled close to the three roaring hearths for warmth as wind whistled through the closed shutters of narrow, arrow-slit windows. Other heartier souls, covered with cloaks of wolf, sealskin, bear and fox, sat about the hall in small groups. Some of them were drinking mead and playing dice, while others polished swords and armor. Two men in the corner squinted and cursed as they painstakingly sewed a tear in one of the longship sails spread over a trestle table.

From the kitchen came the chattering voices of housecarls and maids at gossip and the delicious scent of meat roasting on a spit. Tykir sniffed several times. Not chicken, thank the gods! Probably reindeer.

He sauntered over to Rurik, who was whittling shards of wood off a chunk of oak and forming them into crosses on leather neck thongs. Tykir shook his head in amusement at his friend, who appeared to be amassing a fortune off the back of Lady Alinor . . . or rather her tail.

Tykir was still chuckling over the tale Rurik had regaled him with the night before in his bedchamber, something about a grand jest the witch had played on him involving an eel skin. He had to give the lady her due. He had not thought she had a bit of humor in her bones.

Bolthor, who'd accompanied Rurik to Tykir's room, had then burst into a new saga:

> *"Slippery and slimy*
> *The rascal was . . .*
> *The eel,*
> *Not the blue-faced warrior.*
> *But the witch was*
> *Smarter than both of them.*
> *For she got the last laugh."*

"I swear, Bolthor, someone is going to slice off your tongue one of these days," Rurik had raged. "Your sagas get worse and worse. And I'd better not hear that particular one being recited belowstairs. I'll not be the jest of any more of your stories."

"Why should you be any different than the rest of us?" Tykir had remarked with a chuckle.

But now Tykir was making his first trip downstairs since his illness began. His fever was gone, and his leg felt better than it had in years . . . flexible and pain-free. He supposed he had the witch to thank for that.

"Where is she?" he asked Rurik as he dropped down to the bench beside him.

"Well and good you should ask!" Rurik growled and continued with his whittling.

A maid handed Tykir a cup of mulled ale, along with a trencher piled high with several slices of flat bread and some *skyr.* At least it was not *gammelost,* he thought, though he would not tell the Saxon wench that he, too, was sick of the smelly fare. Then he berated himself for always thinking about the wench. She was ever on his mind these many days, and he did not know why, nor care at all for the obsession.

"Where is she?" he repeated to Rurik.

"Walking."

"Walking? Where? The parapets?"

"Nay, not the parapets. That would be the choice of a normal woman."

A long silence followed. "Well, speak up, man. Where is she walking?"

"Around the lake."

"The lake! 'Tis colder than a witch's tit out there." He immediately realized the fitting nature of his choice of words when Rurik slanted him a look of approval and said, "Indeed!"

"Really, Rurik! Lady Alinor could get lost, or freeze to death in these strange surroundings."

"Oh, that we would be so lucky!" He continued his infernal whittling and added, "Beast is with her. Of course, Beast is *always* with her. The animal is no longer my pet. In truth, he gives me the same condescending, I-am-better-than-thou looks as the witch when he passes by. Furthermore, Beast laid a pile of dung in my bedchamber yestereve after I yelled at the witch for her eel prank. Methinks it was deliberate."

Tykir put a hand over his mouth to hide an unbidden smile. But, actually, Rurik's continual criticism of Alinor was starting to annoy him. Not that Alinor didn't annoy him, too. But it was not Rurik's place to . . . well, never mind. He cut those wayward thoughts short and took a long drink of mead. Once he wiped his mouth with the back of his hand, he commented, "I have been thinking . . . I am not so sure the Lady Alinor really is a witch."

"Easy for you to say! You have been lying abed these many days whilst she conjured up trouble hither and yon."

"Like what?" he scoffed.

"The chicken soup, for one."

He laughed. "Mayhap she was overzealous in her cooking, but her intentions were pure. And Girta tells me it cured the sniffles amongst the men, and helped bring my fever down."

"Girta is under the witch's spell, too." Rurik's mulish expression reminded Tykir of a little boy's stubborn whining. Next he would be sticking out his lower lip and pouting.

Rurik stuck out his lower lip and pouted. "'Tis true."

Tykir grinned. Then, more sober, he lectured, "Rurik! 'Tis unlike you to accuse someone without just cause."

"Well, mayhap Girta is not really ensorcelled, but there have been strange happenings. Inga, down in the village, gave birth to triplets. Three girls! Explain that."

Tykir nodded, giving serious consideration to Rurik's charge. "Dropping three babes at once is a rare occurrence, but not unheard of. And 'tis true, many a man would be disappointed in having not one girl child, but three. I suppose it could be within a witch's power to influence the birthing, but I cannot be certain 'twas Alinor's doing."

"She is e'er interfering in men's work and play."

"Like?"

"Like this morn, we men were engaged in a mere contest. The witch raised such a to-do amongst the women, we had to disband for all the shrieking."

"A *mere* contest?" Really, 'twas like pulling a plow-horse out of a bog to get a clear answer from Rurik.

"Oh, if you insist! 'Twas a pissing contest . . . who could spell the foulest word in the shortest time in the new fallen snow. Now, is that such a bad thing that the Lady Alinor would fly into a rage? Is that any reason for Girta to call me a crude oaf? It could have been called a learning situation . . . those who can read and write teaching those who cannot."

Tykir choked on his ale and spit out a shower onto the table as he attempted to swallow and laugh at the same time. When he finally wiped his mouth and the table with a linen cloth, he gave Rurik a level look. "Methinks you need to find a life-purpose. Methinks you dwell too much on a witch who is not a witch because you are idle too much. Methinks Girta is correct . . . you are a crude oaf. Methinks there is no proof of witchcraft, Rurik. Face that fact and get on with it."

"Nay, my friend. You are the one not facing facts. Those are only a few of the witch's crimes."

He exhaled loudly, then waved Rurik on. "Proceed."

"Three of the maids have refused to service us men, even though they always did in the past. Those that will are barley-faced and stiff as sticks in the bed straw. 'Tis like swiving a loaf of bread."

"Come now, Rurik. 'Tis a maid's prerogative whether she wants to sate a man's lust or not. Leastways, that has always been the rule at Dragonstead. You cannot blame that on a witch."

"Yea, I can."

"If Alinor interfered in that regard, it was no doubt as a high-born lady, not a witch. We have become accustomed to living the rough life here for overlong. My sister-by-marriage, Lady Eadyth, would have advised her female servants much the same, and you know it."

"Why do you defend the witch, Tykir?"

"I do not defend her. I am trying to be fair."

"Well, you cannot say that the witch is not responsible for interfering in the planned wedding of Bodil the Ripe and her intended, Rapp."

Tykir put his face into both hands, atop elbows propped on the table. If he had not been muddle-headed when he came down to the hall, he was fast becoming so.

"Bodil is rescinding her agreement to wed with Rapp because the witch told her it is every woman's right to change her mind. Can you imagine! As if women even have minds! And now Rapp suffers constantly from the gut rumbles. And that is not all. Jostein the Smith has been mooning about like a lovesick cow, and Bodil will not feel sorry for him."

"Jostein? What has Jostein to do with this?" Tykir peeked out betwixt his fingers, thoroughly confused.

"Jostein is the one Bodil really favors, but Jostein spread her thighs and enjoyed her charms aplenty without the offer of matrimony. Then Bodil decided to show him what-for and agreed to marry Rapp in retaliation. Now, Jostein moons and Rapp's stomach rumbles."

"Rapp? Are you speaking of Rapp of the Big Wind? His stomach always rumbles. Is he not the one who farted and belched to the tune of 'Three Maids and a Viking' at the yule feast last year?"

Rurik ducked his head sheepishly, but only for a second. "She does not act as a captive should, Tykir." He thought a moment, then asked, "She is a captive, isn't she?"

Tykir cocked his head. "Well, yea. I mean, nay. 'Tis hard to classify her as captive, nor is she a guest."

"The men ask when you intend to mete out her punishment. You have yet to discipline her for poisoning you back in Northumbria, not to mention her many crimes since."

Tykir drew himself up with affront. "The wench will be punished, but I will be the one making the decision how and when, and no one else."

Having lost that argument, Rurik tried again, "The lady pushes the bounds of impudence. Why, she whomped Bolthor over the head with a salmon just this midday when he was passing by the scullery. All he did was mention something about a saga involving trolls, witches and raspberry body parts."

Tykir threw back his head and laughed heartily.

"I can see you remain unconvinced," Rurik said with disgust. He sighed deeply, then informed him, "If the rest of what I've related does not weigh heavily against the witch, then hear this: The wolf packs have come down from the mountains. You must admit 'tis too early in the season for that. Some of the village folk claim the beasts howl all night long. I say they are the witch's familiars come to do the beckoning of their sorceress mistress."

It took several moments for Rurik's words to sink into his thick head. When they did, Tykir stood abruptly. "You fool! Are you saying that you let Alinor walk the lake, alone, when there are wolves about? Best you say a prayer, or twelve, on those bloody crosses you keep carving. I swear, if she is harmed in any way, I will hold you responsible."

With that, he grabbed a heavy fur-lined cloak and his broadsword, buckling it on as he stomped toward the double doors leading to the bailey and down to the lake. He could scarce breathe under the intense fear that overcame him.

It was he who prayed then. Not Rurik.

Please, God. Let her be safe.

Oh, the power of a woman's moan! . . .

No sooner did Tykir pass through the outer bailey than he saw Alinor approaching around the bend of the closer bank of the lake. Thank the gods, she was not far away. Though he was feeling much better and his leg hardly pained him, he probably would have been incapable of a long jaunt around the lake.

A quick glance back over his shoulder showed that Bolthor, Rurik and a dozen soldiers had donned light armor and weapons, about to follow after him. No doubt Rurik had told them of his concern about the wolves. By the wisdom of Odin! There should have been patrols guarding the area anyhow, if not for Alinor, then for the villagers who might be at risk.

He waved them back for now.

Alinor did not notice him yet, nor did Beast, who was racing up and down a slippery wooded path after a large rabbit. Alinor had stopped, her attention caught by the beautiful scene before her. Earlier that day it had snowed heavily. Now the lake and the snow-capped trees presented a vision of pure white under a bright blue sky. The air was chill and windy, but bearable. In truth, he could not blame Alinor for wanting this bit of fresh air whilst the light lasted. Although it was only early afternoon, it would be dark soon.

All that Tykir could see of Alinor was her face, in profile, covered as she was by his heavy, hooded, fur-lined cloak, which dragged on the ground behind her. For some reason, his heart constricted, watching her admire that which he held in such high regard, in his hidden heart of hearts.

He was thirty-five years old—a man of middle age—and still the old hurts stayed with him. It was foolish, really, how he could not let them go. The first eight years of his life he'd struggled like a scrappy pup, seeking affection from anyone who came within sight of him. Yipping, yapping, "Love me, love me." How many times had his hopes and heart been battered?

Oh, his father had never intended to wound him so. Staying away from him and Eirik had probably saved their lives, as intended. And his mother, who'd abandoned him as a babe . . . she would have been a poor mother if she'd stayed. And his stepmother Ruby had had no choice in leaving him. And Eirik had had every right to go off afostering in the Saxon court, leaving him at Ravenshire with two grandparents, Dar and Aud, who'd died soon after.

What a poor Viking he was with all these weak-sapped needs! Sniveling and yearning over emotions best left to women and children . . . and small dogs. Actually, he had learned good lessons from all that heartache. Never care enough to be hurt. Never let any other know that you are vulnerable.

But there was one small weakness he allowed himself: Dragonstead. If he could not trust his feelings to another person, he could at least harbor secret affection for a place. And, Lord, he did love Dragonstead . . . every stone and timber of the keep, every drop of water in its lake, every tree and animal that marked the forests, and from a deliberately kept distance, even its people.

"Well, the troll has come a-walking."

Tykir jolted to attention. Apparently, the lady had finally noticed him. He took the several more wide strides needed to reach her side. "Good day to you, as well, witch."

"What brings you out of your cave?"

"You."

"Me? Oh, God's tears! You're not going to start that captive nonsense again, are you? There's nowhere for me to escape here if I tried, lest you suggest I try swimming."

Tykir fought a grin. "Can you swim?"

"Of course I can swim. Otherwise, my brothers would have drowned me on more than one occasion as a child. They put the same worth on me as kittens and other small animals, subject to their cruelties."

Damn! I am going to have to wring the necks of those two Saxons one of these days. Mayhap when I return her to Graycote, I will teach Egbert and Hebert a few lessons, Viking-style.

"Don't you be looking at me with pity, you lout. Any man who owns paradise and punishes himself for some lackwit reason by staying away a good part of the year is the one to be pitied. All for the sake of a-Viking or a-wandering or a-trading or—"

"—a-raping and a-plundering?" he suggested, not even bothering to deny her assertion that he was a fool to stay away from a home he loved. She saw too much. Or mayhap he allowed her to see too much. Now that was a dangerous possibility.

"At least you have not neglected your home. I will give you that," she declared, sniffing haughtily. "The estate is run efficiently, inside and out, even in your absence."

When had he asked for her approval? The bold wench! "And how would you know about the workings of Dragonstead? Its fields are covered with snow. Its stores are locked up in outbuildings. Its animals are snug in their winter stalls."

They'd begun to walk side by side back toward the keep. Somehow his hand had linked with hers as they ambled along. Or had her fingers laced with his? Either way, she acted as if it was the most natural thing in the world. And, blessed Lord, it was. He could not remember any time in his life when he'd gotten joy from such a simple thing as holding a maid's hand . . . and she was well past the stage of being a maid.

Mayhap she did have witchly powers.

Mayhap he was besotted.

Mayhap he did not give a bloody damn, either way.

"I spoke with some of the villagers whilst I was walking," she said in answer to his question as to how she knew of Dragonstead's good care. "They have high praise for you. And Girta thinks you walk on water."

He shrugged. "And that brings us to the reason for my clomping through the snow after you. A lady should not be out walking alone, unprotected. There are wolves about."

"Wolves?" She shuddered, then waved his concern aside with her free hand.

He was holding on to her other hand like a lifeline. Even realizing that sad reality, he did not let go. It felt too good, and he had been feeling so bad lately. Hell, not lately, he corrected. Forever.

"But not to fear," she babbled on, "I have brought my protection with me. Beast."

They both turned as one to see the dog rolling playfully, side over side, in the fluffy snow.

"Some knight in armor your Lord Beast would prove!" he scoffed.

As if sensing that he was the subject of their discussion, Beast stood and shook his fur, then came loping toward them, tail wagging and tongue lolling. Without preamble, Beast stood on his hind legs, forelegs propped on her shoulder, and gave Alinor several sloppy dog kisses. Before he knew what the beast was about, the animal did the same to him, except that Tykir could swear he added more slobber.

Alinor laughed gaily.

He said, "Yeech," but he was oddly touched by the dog's demonstration. Beast dropped to all four legs and gave them each a long, considering look, waiting like a good dog to be told what to do next.

"Wouldn't it be nice if people could love us unconditionally as a dog does?"

He raised a brow at her.

"A dog does not say I will love you if you are beautiful. Or if you do what I want you to. Or if you have wealth. Or if you produce babes. Or—"

"—if you are good-mannered. Or more quiet. Or less troublesome. Or a strong fighter. Or a diligent student. Or generous with gifts. Or especially lusty in lovemaking." He waggled his eyebrows at her with that last remark.

She clicked her tongue in a familiar tutting sound he was coming to love. Nay, he was not coming to love anything about her. 'Twas just a sound he was coming to *associate* with her. There. He felt better having made that correction in his mind.

"Tykir?" she said softly.

He braced himself. The wench had a habit of boring her way into his personal life with her intrusive questions, and they most always started with a soft-spoken, "Tykir?"

"Why have you never settled here with wife and children?"

Intrusive did not begin to describe the depth of her probe this time. It speared the heart of him. He was about to say that it was none of her affair. Instead, some demon in his head said, "Why don't you tell me . . . since you seem to have an opinion on every blessed thing in the world?"

"Mayhap you never found the woman with whom you wanted to share Dragonstead," she said faintly. The expression that passed over her face could only be described as glorious.

Why should she look glorious?

He did not want to know.

Yea, I do. Why?

Females always think it is a woman who will make a man's life complete. A fierce fight, strong ale and a warm bed . . . that is all a man really needs . . . and mayhap an occasional wench, but for rutting only.

Could she possibly think she is that woman?

"Where do you get these fey ideas?" he snapped, dropping her hand from his clasp as if it were suddenly leprous.

"Testy today, are you? Perchance you should have stayed

abed another day. I know," she pronounced brightly, "you need another bowl of my chicken soup."

He put a forearm to his forehead in mock horror. Well, not really mock. He *would* be truly horrified if he had to slurp another drop of that soup.

"By the by, why has a lock been put on the chicken coop? Can you open it for me?"

He started to laugh then and began to walk toward the outer bailey.

"Answer me," she demanded to his back.

He didn't stop walking away, just kept on laughing.

"I'll show him," he thought he heard her mutter, just before something hit him on the back of the head with a wet splat.

He turned with disbelief. The wench was dancing from foot to foot, taunting him with a fat lump of snow in each extended hand. She had dared to strike him with a snowball?

He took two steps toward her, exiting the castle grounds again.

She backed up two steps. "Now, Tykir, I was just doing you a favor."

"A favor?" he hooted. "What kind of feminine illogic is that?"

"You said just several days past that you never had any playmates as a child . . . no one to have snowball fights with."

His eyes grew wide at that. Then he chuckled. "You wish to *play* with me?" He took two more long steps closer.

She dropped her snowballs and ducked behind a wide tree. Peering around, she replied, "Nay. 'Twas just a joke . . . because you were ignoring me."

"So, now you want my attentions?" He skirted around the tree and smiled.

"Not *those* kinds of attentions, you lout." She skipped to the other side.

He stalked her, feinting one way, then the other.

She turned tail and ran for the open gates of the castle ramparts.

He meant to grab her by the waist from behind but his foot slipped in the snow and he ended up tackling her to the ground, falling on top of her.

"I can't breathe, you big oaf," she said in a suffocated whisper.

He lifted himself slightly, allowing her to turn onto her back, then immediately pressed his body over hers, holding her fast to the ground. He took both her wrists in one hand and held her arms above her head. "Now you have my attention," he said, also in a suffocated whisper.

And she did have his attention.

Her hood had come off in the struggle and her bright red hair lay in cascades over the white snow, like silken flames. Her face was wind-flushed under her creamy, freckled skin. Her lips parted and she breathed heavily from their exertions. She stared at him through clear green eyes, framed with blondish-red lashes and brows.

She was the same near-homely woman he'd first seen on the Northumbrian moors tending her sheep. And she was different. Now she was beautiful to him. How could that be?

"So, the Saxon wench wants to play with a Viking, hmm?" he teased, taking a handful of downy snow in his free hand and rubbing it into her face.

She struggled and sputtered, to no avail. "You have me at a disadvantage, Viking . . . being as big as a war horse. Release me."

"Nay, not till you pay forfeit for your misdeed."

"Hah! And what might that be?" she said, sweeping her tongue over her top and bottom lips to remove the lingering flakes.

He felt that sweep over every nerve ending in his body, and one in particular.

"You have already refused my coin. And I am not going to gift you my prize ram, even though your land is well suited to raising sheep."

He laughed. "Never once did it occur to me to ask for a bloody lump of mutton as forfeit."

"What then?" she asked, still struggling against his hold.

He had not intended to say, "A kiss." The words just slipped out.

"A kiss?" she repeated. "That's all?"

All? That was everything, as he soon discovered.

She moaned before he even touched her. Oh, if women only knew the power of a moan, released at just the right moment, men would be slaves to their every whim. He was a man partial to a woman's moan.

First, he settled his warm lips over her icy ones, still cool from the snow bath. Gently, he pressed, testing for a perfect fit. It was.

"Do you like that kind of kiss?" he murmured against her mouth.

"I don't know," she murmured back, her breath sweet and her lips no longer cold. "I have naught to compare it with."

"Bold wench!" he chided, nipping at her bottom lip with his teeth. Now that he had her lips parted, he kissed her more forcefully, shaping from side to side, giving and demanding, pressing and sucking. When he pulled back this time, her lips were moist and her green eyes glazed over. "And that kiss?"

" 'Twas satisfactory, I suppose."

"Satisfactory? That is what one says about a batch of manchet bread. Or a business transaction."

"Well, I was hoping for another kiss, like that other."

"What other?"

"The one back at Hedeby."

Ah, now he understood. As he recalled, there were tongues involved. He smiled. "So, you remember my kisses from that night in the bed furs, do you?" he asked, twining a strand of her rose-scented hair around a forefinger, studying the change of colors as it was held this way and that in the sunlight, everything from pale blond to bright orange.

"Don't you remember those kisses?" she asked, tilting her head slightly to the side.

"Som man roper i skogen får en svar," he said with a laugh.

"What does that mean?"

"As you shout in the forest, so will the echo sound."

"Well, that's as clear as moat mud."

"It means, ask a stupid question and you get a stupid answer."

"Oh."

"Are we done jabbering?"

"I hope so."

Lord, the woman had no sense at all, tempting a man with such wanton insinuations. This time he burrowed his fingers into her hair, holding her face in place. He kissed her voraciously then, letting loose with all the pent-up longings of the past few sennights . . . or mayhap the past few years . . . or, God above, mayhap a lifetime.

He tongued her open mouth.

She gave him her tongue in return.

He whispered wicked words when he came up for air. And she whispered equally wicked things back—things she could not possibly comprehend from her own experience.

"Do you think I'm scandalous?" she asked, ducking her head shyly.

He put a finger under her chin, forcing her to look at him. When she did, he grinned and answered her, in a hopeful voice, "Not yet."

Neither one of them spoke after that as they came at each other with equally matched appetites. Who would have known she could be so eager? Who would have known he wanted her so much? On and on the kiss went, till he heard above him the ominous words, "Hear, one and all, this is the saga of Tykir the Great."

Tykir raised his head to see at least two dozen men arranged in a wide circle watching them with amusement, whilst Alinor hid her face in her hands and Bolthor recited the verse words:

> *"Kiss, kiss, kiss.*
> *It started with a snowball fight.*
> *It moved on to a kiss.*
> *Did the witch lure the Viking?*
> *Or the Viking lure the witch?"*

When Vikings come a-calling with lewd intentions . . .

The man kept watching her.

It was most disconcerting. Every time Alinor entered the great hall that evening, helping Girta and the other women serve dinner, she couldn't help but notice Tykir leaning back lazily in his chair at the head table, picking at his meal (and it wasn't even chicken), sipping at his cup of mead and watching her.

His smoldering, golden eyes followed her every move. And, sweet Mary, they *were* smoldering! Like a dangerous mountain cat, he was, waiting for the right moment to pounce on its prey. There was no doubt which body in this room he had marked as quarry.

What does it mean?

It was probably the kiss. Just because she'd succumbed to a wave of sentimentality . . . just because she'd waxed under the beauty of Dragonstead and imagined how her life at Graycote could be without her brothers' interference . . . just because she'd allowed the lout one kiss . . . or two . . . or five . . . that melted her bones and caused her eyeballs to go up into her head like a mad woman . . . well, now he must think she'd developed round heels and was anxious to leap into the bed furs with him.

Hah!

Well, he may think himself the mighty hunter and me just small game in the sights of his bow, but I do not intend to be any man's victim. Not anymore.

She slammed her tray of stuffed pigeons on a table, causing one soldier to jump and spill his ale. Then, walking to the side of the hall, she made direct eye contact with the watching Tykir, jerked her head to the right repeatedly, indicating she wanted him to follow her into the corridor leading to the storerooms.

Tykir put his cup down and frowned as if he did not understand. Well, mayhap she did appear as if she had developed a neck tic. So she tried crooking her forefinger at him.

He grinned.

Lord, spare me from a man with an overblown conceit. He must think I am inviting him for some lascivious play. If he thought she was going to let him kiss her again, she would clear his head in that regard, quickly.

She continued to crook her finger.

Tykir stood so abruptly he knocked his chair over. Which caused Adam and Rurik, sitting on either side of him, to notice the target of Tykir's attention. Understanding—or rather, misunderstanding—immediately, Adam smiled and gave her a little salute, while Rurik looked as if he'd swallowed a pigeon whole.

Red-faced, Alinor scooted down the hallway toward the food storage rooms, Tykir following. When she glanced over her shoulder, Alinor saw that the lout was staring at her backside.

Oh, Lord! This is not going to be easy.

She clucked her tongue in disgust, a sound that usually annoyed him. Now he just grinned.

Oh, Lord! This is not going to be easy.

She was just about to set him straight on a few important facts when he stepped up close to her, forcing her back against the wall. The smells of smoked meats, honey, fresh ground flour and spices surrounded them. Without warning, he asked, "Wouldst thou like to visit the bathing house with me?"

"Huh?"

He stepped even closer, so that his chest, under his heavy

woolen tunic, touched her breasts, under her heavy woolen gown. But it was as if they wore nothing at all, the way her breasts swelled and her nipples peaked. She'd never felt that way before, except maybe in the days just before her monthly flux. Never in the presence of a man.

"Wouldst thou like to visit the bathing house with me?" he repeated.

"Why?"

"To bathe." His eyes danced mischievously at some secret he was not sharing with her.

"Together?"

He laughed aloud then.

She was not so naive that she did not understand the lecherous lout's intent. Scooting under an outstretched arm that was aimed, unbelievably, for one of her breasts, she folded her arms across her chest, tapped a foot impatiently and said in the sternest voice she could muster, which was really difficult when her breasts were throbbing under her forearms, "I did not beckon you here to satisfy your lewd inclinations."

"You didn't?" He folded his arms across his chest, too, and leaned against the wall. Lazily. Like a wild beast stalking his mark, biding his time to ambush his unsuspecting victim. Well, she was not unsuspecting.

"Nay, I called you here because I could see by your manner that you suffer from a misunderstanding."

"Me?" he said with exaggerated horror, eyebrows lifted dramatically.

"I let you kiss me this afternoon because—"

"Forgive the interruption, my lady. A small clarification is called for here. Methought you were kissing me back."

"Well, be that as it may, what I am trying to say is that you should not put too much meaning into a mere kiss."

"Mere? There was nothing *mere* about the enthusiasm of your lips pressing on mine. There was nothing *mere* about the feel of your tongue in my mouth. There was nothing *mere* about—"

"Enough!" She stamped her foot on the stone floor. "You are deliberately teasing me when I am trying to be serious."

"'Tis hard to be serious when I am thinking of you naked," he said ruefully.

She followed the direction of his stare and saw that even under the heavy fabric of her bodice the outline of her distended nipples was evident. She moaned softly, then caught herself.

"God, I love it when you moan. Wouldst thou do it again?"

"You're impossible."

"Please."

"Listen to me, and listen well, you thick-headed fool. The kiss"—she saw that he was going to correct her—"the *kisses* were nice, but that is the end of it."

"Nice? You call my kisses *nice?*" He raised his chin with consternation, causing the light from the kitchen fire in the next room to glitter on his long golden hair, which was braided off to one side. "I am deeply offended. Come here, my lady, and let me try again. I promise you, this time I will do better than nice."

She put her hands out, barring his approach. "Stop harping on irrelevant details, Viking."

"I do not consider *nice* kissing irrelevant. A milksop gives nice kisses. A mother gives nice kisses. A lover does not give nice kisses, that I know for a certainty."

"You are not my lover," she declared hotly.

"Nay, I am not," he said. "Yet."

CHAPTER THIRTEEN

☙

He wanted to make her his WHAT? . . .

"Wake up, witchling," a voice said cheerily the next morning.

Alinor burrowed deeper into her bed furs. Girta probably wanted her to help with the soap making she'd planned for today. Apparently, it took a massive amount of soap to keep these huge Vikings clean.

"'Tis time for all slug-a-beds to be up and about," the voice continued with maddening brightness. The *male* voice.

'Tis Tykir the Troll.

He must be up to some mischief to address me in such a syrupy tone. Either that, or he wants some favor of me. Well, he can't have it . . . no matter what it may be.

Then another alarming fact crept into her sleepy head. *Good Lord! Is it possible the troll is actually blowing in my ear?*

Alinor's eyes shot wide open to see a cleanly shaven, freshly bathed Tykir leaning over her. His shiny hair, almost dry, stood out in a halo of burnished gold about his head, down to his wide shoulders, which were covered in a newly laundered tunic. *God, what a sight to awaken to! St. Michael the Archangel couldn't look any better! Or Lucifer on a mission of devilment.*

"Go away!" she said, and pulled the bed furs up to her chin, wondering how long the man had been watching her. The room was chill, the fire in the small hearth having burned down to embers. Thank the Lord she had decided to wear a linen chemise to bed, or the lout would have gotten more of a view of her endowments—or lack of endowments—than he'd wagered for.

Or was that what he'd intended?

Alinor shuffled to a sitting position, maintaining her full coverage of bed furs. She'd been sleeping soundly in a small bedchamber on the second floor of the keep. She usually awakened at dawn, by habit, especially with the roosters crowing their wakeup calls—but all the roosters seemed to have disappeared or been hidden away at Dragonstead. Besides, she hadn't been able to sleep much last night after all of Tykir's sexual teasing. As she yawned now, she realized that it was much later than usual . . . mayhap even late morning. It was hard to tell with the way Norway lost its sun for most of the winter hours.

"What are you doing up so early? And in my bedchamber?" she grumbled.

"We have a big day ahead of us."

"We?" Alinor's sleepy head suddenly became unsleepy.

"Yea, *we*." He chuckled. "Now, get up, Alinor. Time is a-wasting."

"What? You are going to help me and Girta make soap?"

He laughed, an ominous, deep-throated sound of mirth.

If she were a loose woman, inclined toward men with deep-throated, sensual laughs, she might be feeling a little tingle in the pit of her stomach now. Good thing she was far from loose. In fact, suddenly she was coiled tighter than a seaman's rope.

"Nay, we will be making something, but it won't be soap."

"Stop talking in riddles. I am tired to death of your constant teasing. And, frankly, whilst on the subject of teasing, I do not much appreciate your slick kisses either."

"Methinks slick is good when it comes to kissing. And you seemed to appreciate my kisses yestereve in the corridor and out in the snow, and back in Hedeby." He tapped his chin pensively. "Or was it some other wench licking my back teeth?"

"You are unchivalrous to remind me of my slips in sanity, but I will tell you—"

"Slips in sanity?" he hooted. "That is the first time I have heard arousal termed thus."

"Arousal? Ooooh, now you have gone too far. I was merely . . . um, curious. Yea, I was curious as to what all the fuss is regarding kissing. Maids and young men do make much ado about what amounts to naught, in my opinion. But now that I know, I have decided that I want no more."

"Oh-ho! *You* have decided? Be forewarned, my lady, there will be more kisses in your life. And you will like them, too."

Alinor inhaled and exhaled deeply for patience. "Listen, I am not such a muddlehead that I do not understand what this is all about. You have been insinuating for some time that you intend to punish me. It is apparent to me that your form of punishment involves coupling. Well, let us make a bargain then. I will lay back and spread my legs for you, and by the time I am done saying my Pater Noster, you will be done rutting and I can be about my soap-making chores."

He went slack-jawed at her offer. Most men were unaccustomed to women being straightforward with them.

"What say you? Is it a bargain?" she asked. "Then can I expect a halt to the veiled innuendos and sly threats?"

He snapped his mouth shut. "Alinor, Alinor. What an innocent you are for such a long-in-the-tooth female! When we make love, you will be too involved to be saying your prayers. And I guarantee it will last more than a few moments." He flipped the bed furs aside and prepared to drag her from the bed.

"Wait! Tell me what it is you want from me. What is all this gibberish about?"

"Your punishment," he said and lifted her by the waist from the mattress, setting her on her feet.

She scrunched up her bare toes against the cold of the

rush-covered floor. "There you go again with that punishment nonsense."

"'Tis necessary, Alinor. Your discipline has been put off far too long . . . first due to our trip to Dragonstead, then to my illness."

"Why is it necessary?"

"A man must be a man in his own house and before his followers. You poisoned me, woman. My soldiers, even my cotters and housecarls, will not respect me if I let you go without punishment."

"That's absurd. Dost not matter that *you* kidnapped *me* with no good cause . . . that I helped minister to you in your sickness?"

"Yea, it does. That is why you will not taste the lash. Nor die. But . . ." His words trailed off, and he studied her, as if weighing how much to reveal.

"But?" she prodded.

"But you must become my slave until that time when I release you to go home to Northumbria."

"Slave?" She was astonished. "You would have me scrub your floors and launder your clothing and carry firewood and such? I already do my fair share."

"Not *that* kind of slave." He grinned and leaned an elbow lazily against the mantel. Then he just stared at her, grinning.

"Well, are you going to share the jest?" she snapped. "What kind of slave did you have in mind?"

"A love slave."

Oh, the plans he had for her! . . .

Tykir had been holding his hands over his ears for a very long time—at least a minute—but still he was unable to screen out the sound of Alinor's shrieking. And the names she was calling him . . . well, a crusty old seaman might appreciate her repertoire of expletives, but he was not impressed.

"Enough!" he shouted finally. In one seamless motion, he

picked up the shrew and tossed her over his shoulder like a bag of barley flour.

"Oomph!" she said as he knocked the air from her gullet. Good. Mayhap she would quiet down a bit.

"Where's that rose hair salve?" he asked, spinning in a circle, with her kicking, flailing body slung upside down, as he scanned the small bedchamber.

"Why?" She was addressing his rump.

"Because I am taking you to the bathhouse, and I want to make sure you slather plenty of that cream on whilst you are bathing. I do favor a sweet-smelling woman."

She made a low, growling noise that probably indicated that she did not care what he favored, but what she said was, "I took a bath yesternoon. I do not need to take another this morn."

"Yea, you do," he assured her. Having found the cream on a corner shelf, he walked through the open doorway. Meanwhile, Alinor was back to shrieking and struggling. "When will you understand that you have no choice in this matter?"

She continued to struggle.

"If you insist on extreme measures . . ." he said with an exaggerated sigh, and reached under the hem of her long chemise, clamping a hand on her bare buttocks.

She immediately stilled.

And so did he.

Holy Thor! She was round and smooth and warm to the touch there. He was going to enjoy this "punishment" even more than he'd thought.

"Checking for tails again, Viking?" she remarked sarcastically.

His own overanxious "tail" wilted. Alinor did have a way of cutting off a man's lust at the quick. "Nay, I'm looking for a place to plant one," he said with a laugh.

"Put me down. Right this instant. I'm going to put a curse on you. Do you hear?"

"The whole of Dragonstead can hear."

"I mean it. If you don't let me go, I'll make your man-part shrivel. I'll turn your teeth blue. I'll make hair grow on your rump. I'll turn all your food stores into chicken broth. I'll—"

"I thought you said you weren't a witch."

"Mayhap I am, and mayhap I'm not. Dost thou want to take that chance?"

He didn't have to think for more than an instant. "Yea."

She gasped then, and he looked over his shoulder to see her peering to the side through the open doorway of his bedchamber. "Why are those housemaids cleaning the rushes from your room today? And putting juniper tops in the fresh rushes? That is a springtime chore. And they are putting clean linens on your bed. Today is not Girta's laundry day. And, blessed Lord, the fire in your hearth is big enough to roast a boar. What are you planning to do in your bedchamber, Viking?"

He could tell by the stiffening of her body that she immediately regretted her question.

"Use your imagination, my lady." He was already down the stairway, stomping through the great hall toward the bath-house.

"Where are all the men?" she asked. There were only a handful of his soldiers about and a scattering of servants performing their duties.

"They have gone on a hunting trip, to add to the supply of fresh meat for the winter."

"Why did you not go?"

"I have more important things to do here at Dragonstead."

There was blessed silence for a moment as she pondered that news, and he proceeded through the kitchen and into the roofed outdoor passageway leading to the bathhouse. Girta and Bodhil and the other kitchen maids, who had been chattering as they worked to prepare the day's meals, looked up, their conversations suspended. Then they burst into a giggling fit.

"I'm going to kill you for this humiliation," Alinor swore.

"I'm shivering in my braies," he said, dropping her to her feet in the steam chamber, where he already had a strong fire going and the rocks heated to red-hotness.

She glanced about her, then stabbed him with a glare. "How long did you say your men would be gone?"

"Two days," he said.

And he did not even try to hide his smile.

Take that, you lecherous lout . . .

"I love combing your hair," Tykir said as she sat on a stool before his bedchamber fire. He sat on a chair behind her, running an ivory comb through the thick strands of her wet waist-length hair.

Alinor rolled her eyes up into her head at his words, which he intended to be seductive. Hah! She was unseducable.

"'Tis a sensual experience, do you not agree?" he continued in a husky voice, unaware of her eyes rolling.

Sensual? Huh? "Oh, certainly," she said. Then, "Do you comb women's hair often?"

He laughed . . . a low, masculine rumble, which was not entirely unattractive. "Nay, this is a first for me."

"How fortunate for me," she remarked drolly. *Next he will want to pare my toenails, and deem it ecstasy.*

"You could say I'm a virgin of sorts," he chortled.

"*Of sorts* being the key words, I presume."

He rapped her on the shoulder with the comb. "Sarcasm ill becomes you, my lady." Then he placed one hand on top of her head and with the other hand continued to run the comb ever so slowly down the length of her hair. "Does the hair combing arouse you as much as it does me, witchling?"

This time she did not roll her eyes. Her eyes nigh popped out of her head.

The Viking had gone mad. And he would find a way to blame her for this latest calamity once he came to his senses.

Start harping on the witchcraft nonsense again. But she refused to take responsibility for his present bizarre actions.

Mayhap it was a long life of some pain that had been eating away at his brain. Mayhap it was an excess of lust in his bloodstream. Mayhap it was the fever that had pushed him over the dividing line from sanity to insanity. Mayhap it was just too much damn *gammelost*.

Hair combing! The man had requested that she comb her hair afore the fire in his bedchamber . . . *naked*. Now, if that was not mad, she did not know what was.

She had refused, of course

To which he had offered a compromise. He would comb her hair for her and she could wear the linen chemise, which was near transparent from the wetness of her recent bath.

Bathing and hair combing as the first installment of a punishment plan? Yea, the man was demented.

Being no fool, she'd acquiesced. After a lifetime of trying to argue with her dunderhead brothers, she knew how to pick her battles and when it was the wiser choice to yield.

Not that she intended to surrender to the brute's lascivious demands, unquestionably the next step in his punishment plan. Had he not mentioned his outrageous plan to make her his love slave? Blessed St. Beatrice! She was not even certain she knew what being a love slave entailed.

Well, that was not her immediate concern. Nay, she bided her time till the right moment. Then she would make a dash for the door and a hiding place she'd discovered these past few days at Dragonstead. She figured this madness that had overcome Tykir would pass, as surely as his fever had. Then she would be able to negotiate a more just "punishment," more in the line of reparations. Some logical arguments . . . a little groveling . . . a few coins . . . mayhap an ell or two of her prized woolen fabrics thrown in for good measure . . . and everyone would be happy.

She inhaled deeply for patience, screening out the droning sound of Tykir's chatter—something half-witted about punishment sometimes being sweet—and the surprisingly pleasant rhythm of the comb passing through her drying hair. *Concentrate, Alinor. You must come up with a plan for escape . . . how to get out of this bedchamber without the big oaf lumbering after you.*

Her eyes latched onto a high-backed chair on the other side of the hearth—the one Tykir had purchased in Hedeby—that matched the one on which he sat. It was a beautiful work of craftsmanship, with carved Nordic designs and a series of interlacing oval holes along the top.

Alinor smiled with sudden inspiration.

"Ty-kir?" she inquired in the giggly sweet voice she had heard the housemaids use with Rurik and Adam.

"Hmmm?"

"Would you mind"—*giggle, giggle, giggle . . . Lord, I feel like I'm going to upheave my stomach's contents*—"uh, would you mind if I combed your hair now?"

He stilled. "I already combed my hair."

She forced herself to giggle again behind a palm pressed coyly over her mouth. "Well, I was thinking that mayhap I could braid your hair because . . ." Her words trailed off in what she hoped appeared to be shyness.

Alinor did not know how females did this pretend dim-wittedness with men all the time. But she did understand why.

"Because?" Tykir prodded.

"Just in case you get particularly enthusiastic in the mating . . . well, you know, it would help if your hair did not get in the way."

"Jesus, Mary and Joseph!" Tykir exhaled.

Alinor hoped that his use of a Christian expletive was a sign of disorientation indicating that he liked what she'd suggested.

A short time later, Alinor threw the comb to the floor and ran for the doorway. "Do not be upset over being bested, Tykir. 'Tis for the best. Really."

"Aaarrgh!" Tykir roared like a trapped bear as he stood, intending to come after her, but found that his hair had somehow been braided to the back of his new chair.

She scurried down the second-floor corridor toward the small treasure room, for which Alinor had found a second key several days past while exploring the keep. The last thing she heard before unlocking the door and hiding herself away was Tykir's ominous message, as he clunked across his bed-chamber, the chair obviously being dragged behind him.

"Alinor, you will not have cause to worry over your freckles ever again," he shouted, "because I intend to skin you alive."

Hide-and-Seek was ne'er his favorite game . . .

Five hours had passed, and still Tykir had not found Alinor.

"Mayhap the lady really is a witch. Else how could she have disappeared from the castle unseen?" Girta commented with her usual garrulousness as she placed a trencher of cold pork sausage, leek pie and manchet bread before him on the table, along with a large cup of mead.

"She is not a witch," he said, surprised at his own firm conviction. "Just a foolhardy woman with a witchly disposition."

Girta frowned at that seeming illogic.

"There is a difference," he contended, but declined to explain.

"Bodhil says she saw a cloud of smoke pass over the midden this morn and it resembled a black cat. Some might say 'twas the witch's familiar come to rescue her. Best you consider the possibility of a curse having been placed on Dragonstead. Have you checked your manpart recently?"

He choked on his mead. "For what?"

"Curves."

"Alinor is not a witch," he repeated.

"But where could she have gone? You have had a dozen and more of us searching every corner of the castle, to no avail. Even Rapp. And you know I do not like him wandering about in my clean keep. He leaves a malodorous trail behind him, that he does. Methinks he does it apurpose, to avoid work. That's why I sent him out to scour the lakeside in hopes the lady was taking her usual walk. Even Beast would not go along with Rapp, such a stink does he make." On and on Girta went till Tykir thought her gossipy ways would turn his ears numb. Finally, she concluded her rambling with a question. "Wilt thou kill the witch when you catch her?"

"What makes you think I will catch her?"

"Oh, there is no doubt about that. Are you not Tykir the Great, as Bolthor always says?"

"Yea, I am feeling extremely great now," Tykir said dryly. "But as to your question, yea, I will kill her once I catch her, but there will be a massive amount of torture beforehand."

"As there should be. As there should be," Girta commented. "Not that I do not like the Lady Alinor. A fine lady she is. But we cannot have the master of Dragonstead bested by a mere woman, can we? What would the skalds say of that? What will Bolthor say in his next saga?"

"Don't you dare encourage Bolthor," he sputtered.

After Girta left him, Tykir picked at his food and let his gaze wander the great hall. He was alone. No doubt the few soldiers left behind from the hunt were hiding from his unpleasant self. For a certainty, the female servants would not come near him, except for the hearty Girta. He did not blame them, with all the roaring and shouting he'd done this half a wasted day, searching for the elusive wench.

It was just so infuriating. Like a puzzle that must be solved—but a piece was missing. What item had he overlooked in his search for the Lady Alinor?

The witch had to be somewhere inside the keep. There had been no time for her to escape the castle walls. And even if there had been the time, she would have been seen. Furthermore, dressed as she was in a thin chemise, she would not have ventured into the freezing outdoors.

So, where could she be hiding?

He raised his eyes to the stairway leading to the second floor, where he could see the open corridor circling the great hall. All bedchambers and storage rooms on the second floor opened onto the two-story great hall. But they had checked and rechecked every nook and cranny of the keep that was not already secured tightly under lock and key.

Tykir shifted in his seat, about to tip his chair back against the wall when his attention was caught by the jingle of keys on the ring at his waist. He looked down at the large metal keys, then up again to the second floor.

And then he smiled.

Gotcha! . . .

Something awakened Alinor from her light slumber.

Peeking out from under the precious furs in the treasure room where she'd hidden, she could see nothing in the pitch blackness of the windowless chamber. All she could make out was the outline of walrus tusks, bolts of cloth, pottery jars of wine, intricately carved wooden boxes that she knew from her earlier exploration contained jewelry, gems, gold and silver coins, and ornately embossed swords and sets of chain mail. And, of course, many bags and miniature caskets of Tykir's chosen product of trade—amber.

She squinted into the darkness. How many hours had passed? Was it afternoon or evening? All she knew was that she'd finally fallen asleep after becoming bored with just lying in hiding. Now her stomach was churning with hunger, not having eaten since the night before. You'd think with all that wine, the trader troll would have plundered some foreign soil for rare foods, too, like almonds or sugared dates. Even a boiled camel's hoof would hold some appeal at this point.

Maybe that was what had awakened her . . . the sound of her hungry stomach. No, it was another sound. A key was turning in the door lock.

Uh-oh!

She'd had hours and hours to second guess her hasty decision to run from the Viking. Now, it appeared that she would find out if she'd been wise or foolhardy. She'd also had plenty of time to hone her arguments against Tykir's punishment plan. For some reason every one of them escaped her now.

This was absurd. She should step forward before he detected her . . . take the offensive . . . brazen out her actions.

Instead, Alinor scrambled back under the furs and held her breath. She would be brave later.

She sensed a faint light.

"Alinor, I know you're here," he said. "Come forth. *Now!*"

Alinor didn't need to see Tykir to know he was stiff with outrage. No doubt he was clenching his fists. Gritting his teeth. Playing mental games of "Pick the Torture."

Ha, ha, ha, she thought then. *How fanciful of me! Despite being a vicious Viking when it comes to war or defending himself, Tykir wouldn't do great physical harm to a woman. Leastways, I don't think he would. Just that love slave business, which is almost more frightening than a good birching. The latter I am familiar with and can withstand. The former . . . well, what exactly does a love slave do?*

"You are making me angry, Alinor. Very, very angry. That is not a wise course."

She could hear him kicking aside chests and rummaging amongst bolts of fabric. A clanging noise probably indicated swords falling against each other. "Force me to waste more time searching for your scrawny hide. Go ahead. I relish the prospect of additional sins to add to your already staggering list of transgressions." His voice dripped ice.

Enough of this cowering! Alinor flipped aside one sable and two fox furs and stood clumsily. "Were you looking for me?" she asked with forced cheerfulness.

His only answer was a growl. His teeth *were* indeed gritted, as she'd suspected. She could see them, and his clenched fists, by the light of the smoking torch he held overhead. He reached down to pick up a broadsword in his path, then motioned with it for her to step out of the room in front of him.

She lifted her head proudly and squared her chin before proceeding to obey. Could he tell she was quivering inside like a bowl of calves-foot jelly? That her knees felt like butter?

As soon as she passed by him, she felt a hard whack across her bottom. Shocked, she glanced back over her shoulder, and realized that the brute had struck her with the broad side of his sword blade. And he was looking very pleased with himself, though the smile that creased his face was cold and mirthless, never reaching his eyes.

"You brute," she said, rubbing her buttocks as she hobbled out of the room. "So, that is your plan, then? To beat me?" Well, she could live with that. She'd been beaten by her brothers innumerable times in the past. 'Twas humiliating and painful but soon over.

"Nay, there will be no beatings. Leastways, not unless you rile me even further . . . which is a distinct possibility." He tossed aside the broadsword with which he'd smacked her. It landed with a thud on a pile of Persian carpets.

"What then?" She insisted on knowing her fate, even as he reached out an arm to drag her from the room.

"First off, I intend to swive you till your tongue curls and your eyeballs bulge. Then, mayhap, I will suckle raspberries till I get a rash. You will then lick my rash to ease *the itch*. By that time there should be several itchy spots, if you get my meaning."

Alinor didn't.

"Then I might swive you another ten or so times."

"Oh!" she said on a whooshy exhalation, reeking with disappointment. "Rape it is to be, then."

"Nay, it will not be rape."

A charged silence followed, during which Alinor was permitted to register the meaning of his words.

Rape? Tykir thought. *The lackbrained woman thinks I intend to rape her as punishment.* Even in his greatest fury in the past—and he was nigh approaching that level how—Tykir would never have raped a woman. What pleasure would there be in that? The shame afterward would have far outweighed the merits of any momentary physical release. Nay, he would not rape her, but he was so angry he feared that he might go berserk and accidentally kill her in his rage. He had to calm down. Think. Calm down.

He put the torch back in a wall bracket. Taking her by the elbow in a pincer-grip, he guided her forward and slammed the door behind them, then pushed her along the corridor toward his bedchamber. Did she deliberately take baby steps to his giant ones? Or was his stride that much different from hers?

From the open side of the passageway, with its waist-high stone banister, he could see at least two dozen soldiers and servants staring up at them from the great hall, wide-eyed and silent. Already the gossips would be churning out juicy tidbits about his being defeated by a mere wench. For a certainty, no matter how much he threatened, Bolthor would be sure to write sagas about a mad Viking bested by a witch with chair-and-hair-braiding skills. People far and wide would hear of this incident, even as far as Northumbria. His brother Eirik would never let him forget. Selik and Rain would be telling children's versions of the event to the orphans in their care. Adam would carry the saga to the Arab lands. He had to redeem himself in his people's eyes or he would be the object of so much jesting he would be unable to hold up his head.

The wench had forced him into this untenable situation. It was all her fault.

Instead of guiding her now, he moved ahead impatiently, dragging her along till they reached his bedchamber. Kicking the door open with one booted foot, he shoved her inside, then locked the door behind him, pocketing the key.

She stood in the middle of the room, staring at him

through wide green eyes glinting with resistance. *Holy Thor! Even when the ravens are circling overhead, the witch will not admit that she has lost the battle.* Her hair, mussed by her stay amongst the furs in the storage room, stood out like a wild red bush. *If such a bush exists, I would like to plant one in the herb garden to remind me of how she looks right now.* Skin, which was paler than usual, provided a white backdrop to her freckles. *Have the freckles increased, or are they just more apparent with the blood drained from her flesh?*

In truth, she was a mess.

In truth, she held much too much appeal for him.

She was afraid. But even so, the stubborn streak she rarely attempted to rein in was apparent in her jutting chin and pike-stiff body . . . a body that was a shadowy, tantalizing temptation to him through the thin linen shift, despite his anger.

"You must understand, Tykir—" she began.

"Do . . . not . . . talk," he said through gritted teeth, and picked her up by the waist, tossing her high in the air and onto his stout-timbered bed. She landed on her back, legs and arms splayed comically, as the mattress straw crackled beneath her. *Well, not quite comically*, he corrected himself. It was hard to smile when even more of her body was revealed with the chemise hitched up to her thighs, exposing exceptionally long and shapely legs, and with one shoulder of the undergarment draped down over her arm practically to her breast.

"It's not necessary for you to be so rough," she griped. Rising to her knees, she adjusted her gown and rubbed the upper arm, where his fingermarks were already beginning to show against her creamy skin.

"Do not move," he ordered, pointing a finger at her for emphasis as he turned his back on her and began to build up the fire once again. As he worked, he noticed that his hands were trembling with inner wrath. Or was it something else?

"Where would I go?" she said sarcastically.

He crossed his eyes at her lackwit refusal to obey his orders. He should lop off her head and be done with it. "I thought I told you not to speak," he answered icily. "And as to the where of it, you would no doubt fly through the window, witch that thou art."

"You don't for one minute think I'm a witch," she accused.

He turned to glare at her. She still knelt in the middle of his massive bed, looking smaller and more frail than he knew her to be. "Nay, I do not," he admitted. "But that does not matter. You are capable of a woman's sorcery."

"What does that mean?"

He shrugged and went to the corner, where he'd placed some boxes earlier—the "gifts" he'd given Alinor the day they'd left King Anlaf's court. From the next-to-smallest box he took four velvet ropes, each the length of a woman's arm. With slow, deliberate care, he tied one to each of the four bedposts. Through his side vision, he saw Alinor watching his every move, saying nothing but wetting her suddenly dry lips—a gesture that he found oddly arousing and guilt-provoking at the same time.

"That's not necessary, you know. I've been beaten dozens of times by my brothers and never had to be tied down." Her voice shook in spite of her best resolve.

Dozens of times! Nay, do not feel sorry for the wench. Do not feel sorry for the wench. Do not . . . "I told you that I was not going to beat you," he snapped.

"Oh," she said. "Well, I did not have to be tied down for the coupling with my husbands, either. I just closed my eyes and spread my legs."

He couldn't help but smile. "And said the Pater Noster," he reminded her.

"That, too," she agreed, casting a quick glance his way, no doubt thinking his mood toward her had changed because of his small jest. It had not.

"Give me your hand, Alinor," he ordered, taking one rope in his fingertips.

"I don't want to," she resisted.

"Give me your hand, Alinor," he repeated more firmly.

He saw the fear and stubbornness in her eyes war with the certainty that some battles were best conceded early on. She gave him her one hand, then the other, followed by both ankles. Soon, she was tied to the bed, spread-eagled and vulnerable.

But not vulnerable enough for his taste. Especially when he heard her murmur under her breath, "Troll!"

He took the small knife from the scabbard at his waist and approached the bed. She flinched involuntarily, obviously thinking he intended to cut her. Instead, he pressed the blade to her collarbone, holding her eyes the entire time . . . eyes that were green as the deepest ocean on a summer day and so fair they nigh took his breath away. Then he sliced her chemise from neck to hem, cutting away the shoulders, too. Now she was fully exposed to him.

Gods above! She's beautiful, freckles and all. In truth, I am beginning to love freckles. Yea, I am. Every blessed one of them. Especially the ones . . .

With a concerted effort, he raised his eyes above her neck.

The green eyes grew glassy with unshed tears, and she bit her bottom lip to keep from crying out. He sensed instinctively that this blow to her pride would be more painful than any cut to her flesh.

"Well, why don't you say it, Viking?" she spat out.

"Say what?" he said in a strangled voice.

"That I am the homeliest female this side of kingdom come. That I have so many freckles the devil must have been spitting for a sennight. That my breasts are too small to suckle a babe and my legs too long to cradle a man's hips. That my red hair would scare a heathen Viking." She turned toward the opposite side of the bed so she wouldn't have to face his scrutiny.

He smiled at the last of her statements, which she didn't even realize might be offensive to him. Sitting on the edge of the bed, he took her chin and forced her to meet his gaze. "Who told you those things?"

She blinked in confusion at the gentleness of his touch. It was a momentary lapse.

"My husbands. My brothers." She shrugged. "Everyone."

He trailed a forefinger down the length of her arm, tracing a path of freckles. "Is the leopard any less splendid because of its spots?"

She said nothing, but a shiver passed visibly over her body. He was fairly certain it was not due to the cold.

He tugged at a strand of her hair, pulling it down to lie over one breast, which was indeed small, but lust-provoking, nonetheless. Fighting the tight constriction in his chest, and in his braies, he continued, "Is the lion with its fiery mane not magnificent?"

Her mouth parted in surprise at his sweet words.

"As to your form," he said and had to cough away the raspiness in his voice, "none would fault the cougar for its sleekness. Those who would do thus with you have never really seen you."

She stared at him—bedazzled by his own brand of sorcery, he would wager. But then she shook her head, as if to ward off unpleasant thoughts. "What are you trying to say, Viking? Spit it out."

He rose and walked to the far corner again, choosing not to address her hurled words just yet. Returning to the bed, he placed another of the boxes atop the furs.

"You are beautiful, Alinor. Unbiddable, shrewish, foolish, for a certainty, but beautiful nonetheless. Never doubt it.

That is what I meant," he told her as he unlatched the long, flat box with its fancy carvings—a purchase he'd made from a sultan who had been disbanding his harem.

She narrowed her eyes at him, suspicious. As well she should be.

He opened the lid of the box, displaying the vast array of peacock feathers. All sizes and textures. And he smiled.

"Now, 'tis time to see if the she-cat can be made to purr."

CHAPTER FOURTEEN

*C*ould *a woman die of feathering? . . .*

What was the troll up to now?

After setting the box of peacock feathers on the bed next to her naked body and making the cat purring remark, Tykir had left her alone. And now he'd been gone for more than a half hour.

Was it a form of torture?

Of course it was.

Did he want her to contemplate her crimes and wonder exactly how he would punish her?

Of course he did. Not that she'd committed any great crimes, and certainly none that were not warranted. She was the aggrieved party here, not him.

Did he want her to be humiliated by her continued nudity?

Yea, he did. The troll!

But what remained a mystery to her, as he no doubt intended, were the feathers. Obviously he intended to torture her with them. But how? Did he intend to stick the quills into her body, like a bird? Or make her eat them?

Adam had inferred, when she'd shown him the gifts, that the feathers had some perverted sexual purpose, but for the life of her, Alinor couldn't figure what that might be.

"Oh, for the love of Freyja!" Girta had started to open the door with a load of freshly laundered linens in her arms. Her mouth went slack-jawed with disbelief. But then she scurried

off, giggling, no doubt to tell the world about Alinor's igno-
minious position. And that was probably Tykir's intent.

"Have you missed me, witchling?"

Tykir pushed the door open wider with his hip and carried in a pottery jug and a huge wooden platter loaded with
food—manchet bread, cold meats, cheese, apples and pears,
along with a honeycomb dripping its sweet nectar. He set the
jug and food on a low chest and locked the door behind him.

"Nay, I haven't missed you," she said sourly. Then she
made the mistake of adding, "Have you missed me?"

He grinned, though she could still see fierce anger in the
glittering gold of his eyes and the hard lines bracketing his
mouth. "Yea," he replied. "With a *passion*."

More innuendos! Alinor was tired, tired, tired of all the sly
words. And she was hungry. And embarrassed beyond belief
at the way the brute was staring at her with . . . well, hunger.
"Are we going to eat?"

"Not yet."

He walked slowly toward the bed, toed off his ankle
boots, then lifted his tunic up and over his head. His hair was
clubbed back at the nape with a leather thong. He kicked the
boots to the side. Then, with a careless flourish, he tossed the
tunic over his shoulder. It landed in the rushes.

Blessed Lord! The man had the body of a god. All
muscled contours and sun-toughened skin, he exuded mas-
culinity in a wide-shouldered, lean-hipped frame—a frame
that drew the reluctant eye.

"Have you had time to contemplate your fate, my lady?"
He crawled up onto the bed and knelt between her legs,
wearing only a pair of low-slung braies.

Oh, the mortification of her nakedness! And he was enjoying it all! "Get on with it, Viking. Lest I fall asleep."

"In time, in time," he drawled. "Do not be so anxious." He
leaned forward and tapped her playfully on the mouth with a
forefinger, cautioning, "You are a foolish, foolish maid to
challenge me with that remark."

She pretended to yawn. A foolish taunt that bolstered her flagging pride and naught else.

He grinned infuriatingly. "Are you familiar with peacocks, Alinor?" he asked, pulling the case closer.

"I am," she said hesitantly.

"I would wager you do not know the things that I do."

What? He is going to give me a lecture now? I really will fall asleep. And, oh, she wished he would cover himself. *I am not going to notice the flatness of his stomach or the deep ridges of his ropey abdomen. I am not going to notice the hotness of his honey eyes under thick fringes of golden lashes. I am not going to notice . . .*

"The male peacock, of course, is the more resplendent of the species. As most men are."

"And they both squawk in the most ungodly fashion during the mating season," she pointed out, then gave an imitation of the "Honnk, honnk, honnk!" noise the birds made for nights on end. A neighbor of hers had tried breeding peacocks at one time and soon gave it up.

He nodded his head in agreement. "Yea, and 'tis all to attract the female. The squawking and the plumage. See what you females force us males to do, all to gain your sexual favors."

So, that's where this conversation is leading?

"The most interesting thing about peacocks is their feathers, of course. So many different textures, everything from the spectacular eye feathers to the soft underdown, all on one bird. 'Tis why they are so popular in the eastern harems."

A long silence followed in which she presumed that he wanted her to contemplate how they would be used in the harems. She pretended to comprehend what she did not by prodding, "So?"

"So, I think we should experiment with them."

"Experiment?" This time her voice betrayed her calm facade by coming out as a squeak.

He smiled. "Yea. Look at this one." The quill itself was

not that long, but from it came an extended trail of tendrils—
azure blue silk threads intermingled with pure white.

As he leaned upward, Alinor felt the tightly coiled power
in him and tried her best not to cringe. He passed the feather
over her forehead, her exposed ears, then her cheeks and
mouth. Her lips parted in surprise at the tickly sensation.

Sitting back on his haunches, he employed his "torture
device" from her neck, along the fine skin of first one, then
the other, of her inner arms, still tied above her to the bedposts. She never would have suspected that her armpits could
be so sensitive to touch. Or her wrists. Or her elbows. These
were delicious, unnerving sensations, which caused goose-
bumps to arise on her skin and a dull ache to lodge in her
lower stomach.

"How does that feel, Alinor?"

"Terrible."

He chuckled. "Well, then, perhaps I am doing it wrong."

"I wish you would not do it at all."

"I know," he said, but he did not stop. Instead, he moved
his handiwork lower, swirling the feathery threads around
and around one breast, then another.

She felt odd. She wanted him to stop. And she wanted
something more. Soon she discovered what that "something
more" was as he employed the feather like a fan, back and
forth and back and forth across the nipples of her breasts.
She arched her back upward in protest and keened low in
her throat. Her nipples grew into hard points, and the breasts
themselves seemed to swell and throb.

"Tell me how it feels," he urged in a raspy voice.

She could not.

"Tell me," he repeated, "or I will continue."

And he did.

She clenched her fists. She braced her feet flat on the mattress. She bowed her back and tried to turn away, from one
side to the other. To no avail. He and his silken instrument
were merciless in their fine torture. Up the curve of one

breast, dragging over a nipple, down the valley, up the curve of the next breast, dragging over a nipple and down again. He repeated the procedure so many times she lost count. Alinor could have screamed with the sweet agony of it all.

When she thought she could stand no more, he squirmed backward so he knelt between her calves. Then he proceeded to employ the same soft torment to her abdomen, her flat stomach, her legs from hipbone to the arch of her foot. Then he did the most scandalous thing of all. He passed the feather, lightly, over her woman's hair, and the ache in her lower stomach dived downward and lodged in a hot pool between her legs.

"Tell me that you like it," he entreated.

"I do not," she said, and it was the truth.

Next, he took a shorter, broad-feathered quill in hand and informed her, "The most interesting thing about these are that they are called 'hot feathers.' Can you guess why?"

She soon found out. Unbelievably, these feathers seemed to hold heat, or create heat in their path.

He used the hot feather much the same as he had the first. Her skin was on fire now. The hot pool within grew even hotter and began to seep outside her body, much to her embarrassment.

She hoped he would not notice.

He did.

He placed the tip of a rich purple eye feather, splashed with tints of green and gold, against her there, and it came away glistening. She heard his soft intake of breath at the sight.

He was probably repulsed.

"Alinor," he whispered in a most appreciative voice.

He was not repulsed.

"Now, Alinor. Now we come to the true tail feathers of the peacock. They are stiff and shorter than the other more beauteous ones, but, oh, I think you will like them very much."

"Tykir, stop. Enough! You have proven your point."

"And what point might that be?"

"That you can humiliate me. That the greatest punishment for me is loss of pride. That I cannot abide loss of control."

"Ah, but Alinor, you haven't lost control yet. Not nearly."

She whimpered.

"Now me, on the other hand: I am in greater danger of losing self-control," he confessed, passing a hand brazenly over the erection that stood out from his braies. "I have endured a long period of self-denial these past sennights."

"Oh, God!" she whimpered again, accepting that he was not done with her yet.

Now he used the bristly strokes of the shorter feather to trace the outline of her mouth. "Soon I will kiss your lips, and you will kiss mine. Endlessly. With my tongue, I plan to re-enact the feather's journey. What say you to that?" When she said nothing, he added, "I do so like kissing, don't you?"

What could she say to that? In truth, what could she say at all when her lips were parting at the feather's tantalizing path? When she was already imagining Tykir's lips pressed to hers? Yea, she did so like kissing, too.

"I love your breasts, Alinor. Have I told you that afore?"

While she'd been only half-attending, he'd moved his feather to new, more dangerous territory. He was circling and circling and circling the aureoles with the feather, avoiding the rosy peaks.

"I cannot wait to taste your raspberry nipples," he declared. "But that will have to wait till the second stage of your 'punishment.'"

Alinor wanted to respond to several of the outrageous things he'd said, but she was unable to speak above a croak. Tykir had brought her nipples to life with a mere flick of the feather's bristles. And now he was vibrating the feathers back and forth rapidly over the pulsing peaks like the wings of a hummingbird.

"I wondered how your nipples would look when you are aroused," he confided in a voice raw with his own arousal.

"Would they be tiny and pink like unripe raspberries, or thick and succulent like the ripened fruit? I think they will be a mix of both. What do you think?"

Think? Think? She was a quivering mass, incapable of thought or reason. She bit her bottom lip to keep from crying out at the tantalizing torment assaulting her nipples and the private place of which chaste women never spoke.

"I am a wanton." She had not meant to speak the words aloud. They slipped out in the horror of her discovery.

"I hope so," Tykir said. "May all the gods intercede on my behalf. I certainly hope so."

But, wait, the Viking was up to some new mischief. Before she could blink, or say "Bloody hell!" the troll had spread her legs farther apart, then begun to assault a new region of her body. A totally virgin area, to her. When she tried to protest, rolling from side to side, he pressed the palm of his free hand on the bottom of her stomach, just above her woman's hair. With that palm, he established a pressing rhythm to match the feathery flutter in that other place.

As he intently worked his sorcery on her body, his ragged breaths and her mewling whimpers were the only sounds in the room, except the crackling of the fire. A strange inner excitement was overtaking Alinor. She was frightened and excited at the same time.

He stopped suddenly and glanced up at her. "Relax, Alinor. Your legs are stiff as pikes. Relax, and let it come."

Let what come? she wanted to ask, but no words would pass her pressed lips.

He waited till he felt the tension seep from her limbs, then resumed his assault on her *there*. "Reach for the peak, Alinor. It's there, witchling, just within your grasp."

"Peak? What peak?" she cried out.

"Don't tense up again. Let me give you this woman joy."

Oh, God, oh, God, oh, God! With each touch of the feather and each press of his palm, she was building and building toward some great event. She hated the not knowing. The vulnerability. Being manipulated beyond control. This shattering of the senses.

But wait. She tried to focus through the haze of passion that was clouding her brain. *Passion? Me?* Something different was happening now. Something . . . compelling.

At first there was a slight fluttering between her legs, inside. But then the fluttering heightened into spasms, followed immediately by sharp clenching and unclenching of her inner muscles. Her heart stopped, then thundered wildly as blood raced to all her extremities.

He made a rough sound. Was he, too, losing control of his faculties?

Too late! No more time for thinking. She screamed, "Tykir!" as she hurtled through a place consumed with swirling red light, intense heat and the most astonishing physical pleasure she had ever experienced.

Alinor must have swooned for a moment—something she'd never done in all her life, but then, she'd never experienced this peak or woman-joy either. 'Twas not an experience she ever wanted to repeat. What woman in her right mind would want to yield so much to a man? For what? A momentary pleasure? Even though it was an *amazing* momentary pleasure, she conceded to herself.

"You're smiling," Tykir observed from the side of the bed.

When had he left? What had he been doing while she'd been woolgathering? Her eyes shot wide, and she realized that while she still lay spread-eagled on the bed, with satiation of some sort, her ropes had been untied. Quickly, she scurried to a sitting position and grabbed for a bed fur to cover herself.

He tossed the furs to the floor.

She scowled at him and drew her knees up to her chest.

He laughed and leaned down to throw more wood on the fire. Why, she had no idea. It was roasting in here now. Or was it just her skin that was overheated?

"I think I'll go back to my bedchamber now," she decided.

His only response was a short laugh. "Good try." Then he began to peel off his braies, slowly. He wore no undergarments.

She tried to look away but couldn't. *Oh . . . my . . . God!*

She already knew he had a magnificent body. What she hadn't expected was the large erect staff standing out rampantly from a nest of dark golden curls at the joining of his thighs. She'd seen dangly manparts before, but . . . but . . . There were no words for her amazement. Apparently, there were manparts, and then there were *manparts*. This was one of the latter variety.

Amusement curved his lips upward as she continued to stare at him there. And, to her astonishment, *it* grew even larger under her scrutiny.

"Have you no shame?" she inquired, once she was able to speak. "Dost think I want to look at your dangly part?"

"Dangly? I am definitely not dangling, if you will notice. And, frankly, many women are impressed with my manpart, whether it be in its dangly state or otherwise."

"Hah! 'Tis just like a man to think big is better."

He laughed heartily. "Oh, Alinor, you really are a gem. Do you not know that betimes big *is* actually better."

"Hmpfh! Well, you are not putting *that* inside me," she asserted.

"Move over, wench," he ordered, ignoring her declaration. "'Tis time to begin your 'punishment.'"

"Begin? Begin?" she sputtered. "What was all that other . . . peaking business?"

"Peaking business?" He frowned with bafflement. Then grinned. She hated it when he grinned like that. It made her feel warm and melting inside.

She shimmied her body to the other side of the bed, but still the massive bed felt too small. His virile body crowded her, made her feel unsettled . . . afraid.

Nay, nay, nay! I will not cower in the face of a brute.

"That little peaking business, as you call it, just took the edge off my appetite. 'Tis time to begin the main course."

"I'm not a meal to satisfy some base appetite," she argued.

"A mutual meal and a mutual satisfaction, then." He nudged her playfully in the leg with a toe.

She almost jumped off the bed. "I have no idea what you're talking about." Then quickly added, "Nor do I want to find out."

"Come here, Alinor, and let me kiss you." He reached out a hand and took a strand of her hair between his fingers, rubbing sensuously, then bringing it to his nose to sniff. He did have a fondness for her hair . . . well, not really her hair . . . the rose-scented hair cream.

But what had he said about kissing? "You want to kiss me? That's all?" Hmmm. That wouldn't be so bad. In truth, she liked his kisses. As long as they didn't lead to that peaking nonsense. "Let me put a nightrail on first."

"Yea, I want to kiss you, Alinor. And, nay, that is not all. And, for a certainty, you are not donning any item of clothing for the next two days."

"Wh-what?" she choked out.

He took advantage of her momentary shock and dragged her across the mattress and into his arms. Lying on her back, she watched as his head descended ever so slowly. She could not believe she was succumbing so readily to his forceful domination. The only thing freezing her in place was the light touch of his fingertips on the pulse place at the side of her throat.

I am lost, she thought. *And I don't care.*

He settled his lips over hers, gently at first, and caught her cry in his mouth. Next, he shifted the kiss from side to side till she fit him perfectly. He encountered no problem at all working his magic on her, entreating her lips to open for his tongue, gripping her head with fingers tunneled in her hair. It was one unending kiss of many nuances . . . a tender pleading soon shifting into rapacious hunger. In the end, it was not a neat kiss, by any means. It was open-mouthed, wet and devouring in its fervor. In short, ecstasy. A kind of ecstasy Alinor had never imagined and did not welcome.

If it was only the kiss, she might be able to resist, but there was also the sensation of his crisp chest hairs abrading her breasts and the ever-present reminder of his raging desire pressing into her hip. And worst of all, he was moving lower, to new, unexplored territory.

"Nooooooo!" she keened as he took practically half a breast into his mouth and pulled upward with a suctioning force till he held only the distended nipple between his lips. Then he began to suckle her, alternately licking the tip with his tongue and drawing on the nipple with a fast rhythm.

It was the most horriblehorriblehorrible pleasure she had ever encountered. It was torture. And it was bliss.

"Stop!" she screamed and pushed at his shoulders.

He didn't budge. Instead, he looked up at her through passion-glazed eyes, which aroused her even more, and moved his onslaught to the other breast. The whole time he used a palm to massage the other already sensitized breast with wide circles. "I knew you would be like this. Oh, God, I just knew it."

She shouted. She flailed. She bucked her hips and kicked at him. She lashed him with every filthy name she could call to her fuzzy mind. "Loathsome lout! Bloody boar! Vicious Viking! Foul fornicator! Perverted pig! Son of a sinful barbarian! Hellish heathen!"

He would not stop.

The hot pool in her woman place turned scalding with heat, and that secret spot she'd newly discovered under the feather's duress seemed to swell and throb.

He nudged her legs apart with one knee and lay on one side, holding her in place. Regarding her hotly, he panted heavily. Why he should be exhibiting overexertion she could not say. She was the one who was being physically tormented.

"I don't want this, Tykir. Will you really take a woman against her will?"

His face turned stormy with anger at her insult. "You say me nay, Alinor, but I will prove you a sweet liar."

She raised her chin haughtily—a ridiculous gesture considering her position. And, damn the devil, she was panting, too.

Before she could guess his intent, Tykir took her hand and placed it on her own woman's place. "Feel the wetness, Alinor. That is your body saying its welcome to my body. Feel how hot and slick you are in your need for what only I can give you. So, do not say me nay when you really mean yea.

"Someday I will show you your own body with a hand mirror," he promised huskily.

She gasped in horror.

"But for now, touch this bud here." He held her own finger to herself.

Her hips jerked involuntarily at the flashfire ignited with that mere touch.

"'Tis the center of your woman-joy, the launching spot that will catapult your peaking."

She was not listening anymore because he was caressing her there with his own fingertips, whispering wicked words of admiration and promise. She became mindless with need, begging for release.

When he finally lay himself atop her and placed his huge erection at her woman-portal, he asked in a voice savage with raw distress, "Dost consent?"

She nodded, well beyond control of her battered senses.

"Will it be rape?"

She shook her head.

"Tell me," he insisted, looking as if he'd been pushed beyond the edge himself.

"Please," she begged. And that was all she could say.

It was enough.

With a groan through gritted teeth and head thrown back

on corded neck, he pushed himself slowly into her tight passage. "Al-i-nor!" he cried out. The Viking had buried himself inside her body, to the hilt. He stretched her and filled her.

And she shared his incredulity.

He was still braced on extended arms over her. Once his jaw was no longer clenched, he whispered, "You feel so good, Alinor. Am I hurting you?"

"Nay," she whispered, and her inner folds shifted, apparently pleased at his compliment. To her amazement, he grew even larger inside her body, which adjusted to fit him tightly.

"So good, so good," he breathed.

"You feel good, too," she admitted.

He smiled at her then, a wonderfully open, dazzling display of white teeth and pure male satisfaction.

"Thank you," he whispered against her mouth in a fleeting kiss before he began the serious business of mating.

"Is it time for me to begin the Pater Noster?" she teased, trying for a semblance of levity in an overwhelming situation.

"Don't you dare." He choked on his own laughter as he began his first long stroke—out, then in again with a maddening slowness.

She bent her knees, intuitively knowing that it would heighten the pleasure and give him greater access. With each of his long strokes, she keened her enjoyment, throwing her arms over her head in wantonness. He played her like the sexual creature she became, telling her what he liked, asking what she liked, taking her hips in hand to teach her the rhythm, and all the time pummeling her with prolonged slides of what felt like warm marble.

This had to be the best-kept secret amongst all womandom.

Did all men have this talent for bringing a woman to peak? Or just Vikings? Or just this one particular Viking? Whatever the case, Alinor was not such a fool that she did not recognize good fortune when it smacked her in the face . . . rather, smacked her in the . . . well, *there*.

Tykir could not believe his good fortune.

The woman was an uninhibited wanton. Arms thrown over her head in abandon. Legs wrapped around his hips. *When had that happened?* Hips undulating to the cadence he had taught her only moments ago. *A quick learner!* And her inner folds were clasping and unclasping his hardness. *That is something I did not teach her. Clever witch! Who'd have thought the lady would take to the bedsport with such enthusiasm?*

Of course, he had a history of woman-luck, due largely to his well-honed talents in the seductive arts and some gods-given natural endowments. However, he could not help but think Alinor had been smoldering with erotic embers for a long time, just waiting for the right man to come along.

His penetrations were so deep now that he could scarce contain himself, especially since she was rippling continuously around him. The short strokes were fast approaching. Too soon, but not nearly soon enough.

"Why is your jaw clenched?" she inquired in an oddly wounded voice. "Am I doing something wrong?"

"Nay, Alinor. My jaw is clenched because you are doing things too right," he choked out on a laugh.

"Good," she said.

"Witch," he answered.

She put her hands on his shoulders, drawing him down to her body. Then she did the most amazing thing. She rubbed her breasts back and forth over his chest hairs, and he could have sworn she purred.

He grinned. Two could play this teasing game. Disengaging her leg locks on his hips, his hands snaked out and grabbed her ankles. He pushed them up and out so she was even more exposed to him. And his deep, deep penetration moved even farther into her body, surely all the way to her womb.

She tried to move beneath him, but he remained immobile till he felt her peak begin—at first the gentle clasping motions, then fiercer and fiercer spasms.

A long, long keening wail came from her parted lips. Her

eyes were staring up at him, unfocused. Only when she passed her first peak did he start his short strokes. Hard, hard, hard, he pounded her, sensing she could withstand the erotic pummeling.

His groans and hers co-mingled. Desire roared like a waterfall in his ears. He had been the aggressor, but the witch who dug her nails into his shoulders was consuming him with her ecstasy. His erection became so huge—the stuff of boyhood dreams—that he feared his eyes were rolling in his head. Her soft sounds spurred him on even farther. He reared his head back and howled with the sheer elation of the feelings that inundated him. When he finally came with a roar of exultation and spurted his seed into her, he was as mindless and incoherent as she.

Tykir had started this day intending to "torture" the witch, but he wondered now if he hadn't been hoisted on his own instrument of torture.

You could say she was a Viking shish-ke-bob . . .

Minutes later, Alinor still lay stunned. The Viking, heavy as a small horse, reclined atop her, breathing heavily into her ear. In truth, she could not complain. The troll had given her more physical pleasure than she'd experienced, combined, over her entire life.

Still, she'd surrendered and revealed more of herself to this man than she ever should have. Not that she'd had a choice. Who knew what he would do with that dangerous information?

"Move, you big oaf," she demanded, pushing at his shoulders. "And stop snoring in my ear."

He raised his head and stared at her. *Good Lord, was that a bite mark on his shoulder?*

"I wasn't sleeping," he said, chucking her under the chin. "Just recuperating." He rolled them both onto their sides and lifted one of her legs over his thigh, as if to maintain intimate contact.

By St. Magdalene's sin! She needed no reminder with his male member still buried inside her, albeit quiescent now. Was he waiting to regroup, or had he forgotten to remove himself? Silly question! The self-satisfied lout was nigh gloating. He'd forgotten nothing.

This was all so new for Alinor. Her three husbands had been quick to disengage after a coupling. But then, there was no comparison between the swift three-thrust ruttings that her husbands had performed on her with their limp wicks and the spectacular event she'd just witnessed. Nay, she had to be truthful . . . the spectacular event she'd just participated in.

"You're smiling, Alinor," Tykir pointed out.

"You're gloating," she countered.

"I'm just happy." He waited for her to question why. When she didn't, he chuckled and continued anyway. "Because I've just been swived by the most sensuous woman in all England . . . hell, all the Norselands and the remainder of the civilized world, as well."

"I did not swive you," she asserted indignantly. "You swived me."

That answer seemed to please him.

"Well, move. Now that you've had your pleasure, I might as well go make soap."

"Dream another dream, witchling. You are not leaving this chamber lest I give you permission. And I can assure you that will not be for a long time yet."

She closed her eyes for a brief instant, praying for strength. Would she be able to withstand this rogue's allure if he "assaulted" her again?

"Thank you," he whispered huskily, running the pad of his thumb across her bottom lip.

"For what?" *The sly dog is up to some new trick.*

"For giving me more pleasure than I have ever received in the coupling." He brushed his lips lightly across hers. She felt the kiss all the way to her toes, and that mortifyingly wet place in between.

"You probably say that to all women."

He playfully finger-walked a trail from the side of her hip to the side of one breast. "Nay, I've never said it afore." His attention was focused more on the breast he was studying as he pushed it up from the underside, then fitted it perfectly in the palm of his big hand. "Have I told you how much I like your nipples?"

"About two dozen times. Stop touching them." She slapped his hand away.

"You could touch mine," he offered magnanimously.

She had to laugh at his false generosity. But then she wondered aloud, "Does it feel . . . uh, the same, when a man's nipples are touched as a woman's?" Her face flamed hotly at asking such an intimate question.

"Good, you mean?"

"Never mind," she said.

"Try and see," he urged, taking one of her hands and placing it over his chest.

When she grazed her fingertips over the flat male nipples, she felt that part of him still inside her jump.

"More," he coaxed.

She experimented with different touches on him. He seemed to like them all, especially when she flicked the nubs with a fingernail. The evidence of her success burgeoned to life again inside her. The final proof was when she leaned down and licked one nipple before suckling it wetly. He let loose with a moany exhalation and rolled onto his back, taking her with him. To her surprise, she found herself astraddle the man, impaled.

"Oh, my!" she gasped.

"Oh, my!" he echoed.

I am sitting bare-naked, skewered on a Viking manpart, she thought. Then she smiled. "Did you think up this trick yourself? Or do all men know about this?"

"I'm the only one." He winked at her then.

"Don't think that because I'm letting you do these things

to me that I like you," she declared, wanting to establish some pride in this unprideful situation she found herself in.

"Letting?" But then he told her, "I don't much like you, either, Alinor."

"But I do like your lovemaking," she admitted.

"That's good enough for me," he said with a grin. "By the by, can you ride, my lady?"

"Horses?"

"Nay. Vikings."

It turned out, she could.

CHAPTER FIFTEEN

❦

Who knew being a love thrall could be so... enthralling?...

Two days later, in the middle of the afternoon, Alinor was still in Tykir's bed.

Oh, he had taken her to the bathhouse late at night when everyone else was asleep, and to the privy when nature called. But mostly, he kept her under lock and key, with Girta putting fresh food and bed linens, along with clean chamber pots, outside the locked door several times a day. Alinor would never be able to face the Viking woman again. Or anyone else in the keep.

Worst of all, Tykir's men had returned this morn from the hunt, but he refused to leave his bedchamber, not even when Adam came knocking on the door. "Come down, Tykir. You must see the game we bagged on the hunt afore it is all dressed down."

"Later," Tykir had mumbled. Her face flamed even now to think what he'd been doing to her at the time. It involved floral-scented skin oils and a belly button stone.

Nor did Tykir budge when Rurik had come inquiring, "Are you alive, Tykir? Or blue? Has the witch snared you so securely that you cannot escape? Shall I break down the door?"

Tykir's only response to Rurik had been a foul expletive and the comment, "Go away!" At that time, he'd been in the midst of persuading her (*he was an expert at persuading*) to try a new position . . . something involving better access to a secret Viking erotic spot on *her* body. It was a very interesting spot, indeed.

Even Bolthor, now reciting a new saga outside in the corridor, did not move the infuriating Viking to release her.

"Came a witch with a talent for braiding.
Came a Viking with a vain disposition.
She bested him with a chair-braiding.
But some say he got his due
By braiding her maiden hair.
This is the tale of the braiding."

"Good Lord! He is awful," Alinor observed.

"Yea," Tykir agreed, quickly followed by "Hmmm." Apparently he'd gotten an inspiration—*the man had way too many inspirations!*—from Bolthor's saga and was busy trying to braid her maiden hair. Which was an impossible task. And it took him a long time. In the end, he never succeeded, his fingers being too large and clumsy and . . . well, it being an impossible task . . . but they both had a good time with the trying, accompanied by a great deal of laughter. And moaning.

"Do I hear moaning in there?" Adam asked, back again and now obviously pressing his ear against the door. How long had he been standing there? Maybe he'd never left.

"Best you come down soon, Tykir," he advised, laughing uproariously, "Bolthor just skipped belowstairs—well, mayhap he did not skip—more like lumbered. And I misremember his exact words, but methinks he is spinning a saga about how to make a Viking groan. Its title is 'When Norsemen Groan and Witches Moan.' Dost know what he means?"

They both moaned and groaned together.

"Be careful the witch doesn't grind your cock down to a nub," Rurik chimed in. *Merciful heavens! The two men must be standing with ears pressed to the door.* "I knew a witch once who could do that. 'Twas not the witch who struck me blue. 'Twas another witch."

"You know a hell of a lot of witches," Tykir remarked dryly.

Then Rurik addressed Adam. "I still say we should get a log and ram the door."

"Nay," Adam said. "Let them do a bit more *grinding.* Tykir hasn't had enough grinding in his life lately."

"I'll show that pup grinding," Tykir grumbled, getting out of bed and storming over to unlock the door. With no modesty whatsoever, he stood in the half-open doorway, bare-naked, and shouted down to Girta's husband, "Red Gunn, bring a bathing tub and hot water up here. My lady has worked up a mighty stink. Just jesting," he called back to Alinor, whose nakedness was fortunately hidden from view by his large frame. Then he added to her humiliation by shouting to Red Gunn again, "Make sure it's the *big* tub . . . the one large enough for two people."

The laughter rising up from the great hall must have come from dozens of men, by the sound of its volume.

"Ty-kir! Are those scratches and bite marks all over your body?" Adam questioned. "Oh, for shame! Look at that, Rurik. Do my eyes prove me false, or are those fingermarks on Tykir's manpart?" To Tykir, he added, "Does it hurt?"

"I told you she was a witch, but would anyone believe me? Nay!" Rurik snorted with disgust. "No doubt those fingermarks will turn blue. Blue, I tell you, Tykir. Blue!"

"Why don't you go heal someone, healer," Tykir suggested with a loud yawn. "And Rurik, best you go check your own manpart, for I am now convinced the witch has impressive . . . uh, powers."

A gurgling sound was Rurik's only response. He was checking the inside of his breechclout, she would wager.

"'Tis true I am a master healer," Adam boasted. "Is it

possible Alinor is covered with as many bruises as you? Mayhap you should let me come in to check. 'Tis not good to let these things fester."

Tykir laughed and slammed the door in both their faces.

Alinor was going to kill the clod. The problem was, she couldn't move. She was plastered facedown on the mattress—boneless, sated and sore in some important places. And, yea, she was covered with bruises, all gained from the enthusiasm of their bedsport, not from any intended pain on Tykir's part. Even the air touching her over-stimulated skin felt like a caress.

"Time to get up, witchling," he said, donning a pair of low-slung braises. "Come. Let us break fast and get about the day's work."

"False promises do you make, Viking. Seems to me you said that very thing to me two morns ago." She mimicked his deep voice then, "Time to get up, witchling."

"Do you make mock of me?" he inquired with a short laugh.

Before her fuzzy brain could come up with an answer, a feather tickled the back of her knees. She shot to a sitting position. There was no way in the world she could withstand another of his feather tortures, though she had to admit to having reversed the torture on him a time or two last evening. Or was it the evening before?

He was leaning against the bottom bedpost, arms folded over his naked chest. His eyes swept her nude body ever so slowly—a maddening habit of his that she had become accustomed to. She did not hide herself in modesty, having learned he would not allow such. Besides, she was not ashamed of her body now. Tykir had succeeded in one thing, at least—making her feel beautiful. Well, he had succeeded in many things, but not all of them so commendable.

"You *are* bruised," he observed with concern, stepping forward to run his knuckles over the top of one breast. "I did not mean to hurt you thus."

Thus being the key word, Alinor thought. She accepted that he'd meant her no physical pain, but he certainly cared not a whit if she was hurt in other ways. She was beginning to suspect that he had kept her overlong in this bedchamber today, even knowing he was needed below, to make a point with her, his soldiers and all his people. Her status was to be thrall from now on. Oh, not a castle drudge or scullery maid. Nay, he had something more loathsome in mind. What had he called it? A love slave. Yea, he was establishing her status firmly for all to see. His own personal whore.

And that hurt Alinor more than any bruise.

The suspicion was reinforced a short time later when they had both finished bathing and Tykir held out the last of the gift boxes for her.

"Nay," she said, shaking her head vehemently, knowing its contents even before he pressed the latch and the red silken harem apparel spilled forth.

"Yea, Alinor. You will wear it."

"There are many things you can make me do, Viking. That is not one of them. I will kill myself afore I parade about in that scant costume for one and all to see. Believe me when I say that. I prefer death to that public humiliation."

"You will wear the garb, but only for me."

"Wh-what do you mean?"

"You will wear the outfit for me alone in our chamber—"

Our chamber? The fine hairs stood out on her body. So, this intimate confinement with the Viking was to continue? For the entire winter? *Oh, my God!* she thought. *Oh, my God!*

"—and you will wear it belowstairs, but under your gown."

She arched a brow in question.

"*I* will know it is there." His voice was husky with meaning.

A short time later she was attired in the scandalous garment which pushed her breasts up and gave them the appearance of greater size. Vast amounts of skin were left bare—her shoulders and abdomen—and even more skin was visible through the almost sheer fabric. Worst of all, the only way she could avoid the tinkling of her bells was to take tiny steps, like a humble thrall. She blinked her eyes several times to keep the tears that scalded there from welling over. "I will hate you for this, Tykir," she declared softly. "I think I was beginning to love you a little . . . fool that I am, but now—"

"Love?" he scoffed in horror. "I never asked you for love. Nor do I want it."

She saw a momentary flash of regret in his eyes and knew that he lied. But it was too late now. The die was cast.

Could a woman ever really tame a wild Viking? . . .

The days passed, and they were not so bad for Alinor.

Still, Alinor's pride could not be reconciled to her less than honorable position at Dragonstead. She fought Tykir at every step, even on the reasonable requests he made of her, like the mending of a favored tunic or trimming his over-long hair. And she took offense at even the slightest insult.

Right now she was refusing to speak to the troll because he'd failed to introduce her, at first, to a visiting Viking jarl who'd passed through that afternoon by horse-driven sleigh on his way to a neighboring reindeer farm he owned. Tykir had been puzzled by her feelings of being slighted. "Jarl Jorund is a boorish lout," he'd explained, trying to defend himself. "I was trying to protect your sensibilities."

"A likely excuse." She'd sniffed indignantly and slapped away the placating hand he'd set on her arm.

"Why would you want to meet another lout? Am I not lout enough for you?" he'd teased.

"You forgot I was even there."

He'd grinned sheepishly then. "Is that such a great sin?"

Nay, it was not. But it was part of a pattern that bothered Alinor tremendously. A pattern that said she was a small part of his life, and that one less than honorable.

"Why do you fight your fate so?" Adam inquired now.

"Because I deny it is fate."

She and Adam were seated before a roaring fire in the chilly great hall after dinner. Dozens of others sat about in groups in front of other hearths, drinking, conversing, dicing. A scene that was reminiscent of those taking place in noble Saxon homes she was familiar with.

"He treats you almost like mistress of his castle," Adam argued as he watched her grading the poor wool she'd found in Tykir's storerooms. It was not near the quality of her own sheep fur, but she was carding, spinning and weaving it nonetheless . . . a familiar task that gave her comfort. She would use the finished wool for servants' clothing

Alinor gave Adam a skeptical look on considering his words. *Mistress of Tykir's castle?* "In all ways except one," she pointed out.

Adam quirked a brow at her.

"That exception is when he takes me by the hand and draws me peremptorily to his bedchamber with clear sexual intent." 'Twas odd that she felt comfortable discussing such matters with this young man who'd become a friend to her, but she was so frustrated that she needed to vent her fury somewhere.

Adam grinned at her blunt confession, clearly thinking Tykir was not such a bad fellow. "It does happen often."

If he'd intended to make her feel better, he was sorely mistaken. "It matters not to Tykir whether it be mid-morning and I am in the midst of setting the day's menus with Girta, or afternoon helping Bodhil churn butter, or evening before the hearth fire in the great hall. The man is . . . insatiable."

"Alinor, Alinor, Alinor," Adam said, laughing heartily. "There are some women who consider such demands for their company a compliment. Mayhap you do too good a job in providing for his bed pleasure."

"Oh, you just don't understand. He gives me no choice."

"A wife would have no choice either," he noted.

"Wife? Who said anything about a wife?"

Adam frowned. "Methought we were discussing the difference in respect given to a leman, compared to a wife." He studied her intently. "What really is at the heart of your complaints?"

She took a deep breath. "Tykir makes his joy in our coupling too evident," she disclosed. It was a deeply personal thing to confess to a mere friend, but she had no one else who might conceivably be able to advise her. "He wants me with a bottomless hunger, and he doesn't care if anyone knows."

That's why she felt pegged as mere bedmate, rather than respected lifemate. It was not that she wanted that kind of permanent relationship with the Viking. At least, she did not think she would want that. But surely a man did not stare at a wife so lasciviously all the time, but especially when she walked fast all of a sudden, causing one of her bells to jingle ignominiously. Nor did a normal husband feel the need to touch his wife incessantly, whether in passing, with a light caress of her hair, or in assaulting her with a sudden exuberant hug.

Adam's mouth dropped open. He did not laugh at her again, though. Instead, he shook his head with disbelief, and took both her hands in his. "Alinor, my dear, what you describe is a woman-blessing. A man loving a woman beyond all reason."

"Oh, nay, nay, nay! I never said aught of love."

He shrugged. "I know I am young, but I am well traveled, and I can tell you that God has laid a gift in your hands. You can toss it aside or tend it with care. Mayhap it is not love, precisely, but who knows what it could be? Tykir's a good man, Alinor. Look beyond his actions to their cause."

"The man is a troll," she argued.

"Some would say you are a witch," he countered. "Troll, witch, Viking, Saxon, man, woman . . . they are all just words."

Adam walked away then, leaving her to her hand-spinning.

She used the time to ponder Adam's words and her own niggling suspicions. In the end, she came to an alarming conclusion. *God help me, but I love him.* How that disastrous situation had come about, she could not say. The simple answer could be that the lout brought her incredible sexual pleasure. Or that he was bone-meltingly handsome, especially when he smiled or winked at her. Or that his roguish teasing actually brought her joy. But the truth was, he touched her in a more elemental way. There was an invisible bond connecting them that seemed to have an almost mystical basis.

Was it possible that fate, or some celestial being, had destined them to be together? Did God want her to tame the savage Viking? Now that was a daunting prospect, she thought with a silent laugh. And amusing, really, to think that the blessed Lord would use a Viking king's crooked manpart to gain his ultimate ends with her.

She had no more time to ponder her fate then, because the bane of her life arrived . . . well, the *other* bane of her life. Rurik. He slumped down onto a bench near her, elbows braced on his widespread knees, and stared glumly into the fire.

"Now what?" she finally asked. "Didn't the chicken dung ointment I suggested for removing your blue mark do the job? Never mind. I can see that it didn't."

He cast her a sidelong glare. "I'm not as dumb as you think I am."

"Nobody is." She thought a moment. "Don't tell me; let me guess. You have run out of women in all of the Norselands to lure into your bed furs."

His lips turned up reluctantly, and she had to admit he would be a tempting bit of manhood, if she was the type of woman attracted to his particular brand of arrogance. "There are a few left, but those are old crones . . . not worth the effort."

"You could start over again."

"I could."

"So that's not the source of your sour mood? Could it be your favorite part has shriveled up and died from overuse?"

"Enough!" he said. After several moments, he revealed his dilemma. "I need your help."

Uh-oh.

"People are starting to believe you are *not* a witch."

"And that's a problem?"

"Yea, it is. No one wants to buy my crosses or holy water anymore. You have to do more witchly things, Alinor."

At first, she just gaped at him, slack-jawed with surprise. "You don't believe I'm a witch anymore?"

"Nay. Well, leastways, not every day. Come, Alinor. 'Twould be a small thing to do a few witchly acts betimes."

She hooted with laughter.

"It's not amusing. Would it hurt you to waggle your fingers at some other men's private parts on occasion? Can't you pretend to boil up a cauldron of bats' wings and snake eyes? Or"—he grinned at her—"dance naked in the forest?"

"You are impossible," she stated and soon sent him on his way, grumbling with dissatisfaction.

It was getting late. Deciding to end her chores for the night, she put her spinning materials inside a wide basket, then looked up to see Tykir watching her from across the hall. The usual smoldering glint in his honey eyes struck a spark in her, which she tried mightily to resist, despite the instant sexual fire ignited in her belly.

He crooked a finger at her.

She sat up stiffly. *The arrogance of the man, demanding I come to him. I will show him.* Alinor crooked her finger back at him, thinking to prompt some adverse reaction.

Instead, Tykir smiled and stood immediately, making his way toward her. How could she hate a man who could be so demanding one instant and so willing to bend the next? Apparently he didn't care which one did the coming, him or her.

When he stepped close to her, he took her by the upper

arms and pulled her to her feet. She felt the heat of his body and the even greater heat of his need of her. 'Twas a heady, heady aphrodisiac, being wanted so much by such a virile man. Mayhap for now that was enough.

"I missed you, sweetling," he murmured.

Sweetling? "I missed you, too, troll," she conceded.

He smiled widely, a wonderfully open display of gratitude for her simple concession . . . a smile that caused her toes to curl and her heart to expand with joy.

Yea, 'tis enough for now.

Then he pinched her buttock playfully as they made their way to the stairway and whispered in her ear, "Have I told you of a bed game I just remembered? 'Tis called 'The Flaming Lance.' "

She stumbled, then righted herself, causing her bells to jingle. She flashed the grinning oaf a glare.

On the other hand . . .

It was the best Christmas present ever . . .

It was the best yule season Dragonstead had ever witnessed, and they owed it all to Alinor.

With great satisfaction, Tykir looked about his great hall festooned with holly and evergreen branches—decorations more akin to Saxon homes than Viking. But his people seemed to like them. In truth, his estate had been well run for years, even in his absence, but Alinor had gone one step further and turned his castle into a home.

A dangerous, dangerous turn of events. One he could not dwell on. Best to turn his mind to the merriment around him.

Vikings welcomed any excuse for feasting. And it was a rare good feast Alinor had put on to celebrate the coming of the Christian God-child. There were Saxon and Norse foods alike, and some he could put no nationality to. Plum pudding and Yorkshire pudding, which was really not a pudding at all, but a bread baked in roast meat drippings. He'd insisted with an exaggerated horror that no chicken be served, though they did have many boiled eggs sprinkled with rare eastern spices. Some were even sliced into a jellied aspic rendered from reindeer hooves. No doubt Alinor would make everyone as sick of chicken eggs as she had of chicken broth. Then, too, there was an abundance of the pork sausages and soft cheeses favored by the Vikings . . . a necessary fare at any feast. But not a speck of *gammelost* was in sight, he noted with a smile. His Alinor would not permit that.

Tykir stopped his mind-meanderings on that unsettling thought. *When did I start thinking of Alinor as mine?*

As much joy as there was in his heart these days, there was also turmoil. He felt as if he were caught in a whirlpool and could not escape his swirling emotions. The only remedy was to wait out the storm and see what happened once the waters settled.

Not that he was planning to drop anchor with any woman. Not even Alinor. Besides, she'd probably heave the anchor onto her shoulder and stomp off into her own destiny in Northumbria.

It was just an interlude they were sharing. A pleasant one. But that was all it was, or could ever be.

He knew Eirik and Eadyth failed to understand his resistance to love and marriage, even to a mistress of any long-standing. But the soul-deep hurts he'd sustained as a child and the defenses he'd erected as a result were part of his very nature now.

Imbedded in his brain were unsavory images of himself: as a needy, pathetic boy searching every passerby's face for his long-gone mother; as a youthling standing at one roadway or dock after another waving farewell to his Jomsviking father, and later standing at his bedside when he died far too young from battle wounds; as a tearful eight-year-old shattered by his brother Eirik going off a-fostering to King Athelstan's court; not to mention the disappearance of his stepmother Ruby; then, finally, the loss of his grandparents, Dar and Aud, at Ravenshire.

Oh, he knew there were many who had suffered as much or more. His own brother Eirik, for one, who'd had a finger chopped off as a boy by Ivar the Terrible, the same villain who had killed their father. But Eirik was half-Saxon, a different bird all together. Plus, he'd been a few years older than Tykir and certainly more mature when all these events had taken place.

Being a scrappy young Viking through and through, Tykir had learned to survive his hurts by building an invisible wall around himself. A man—or boy—couldn't be hurt if he didn't care.

Except . . .

Tykir glanced to his side and watched Alinor, whose rapt attention was caught by the saga Bolthor was telling. He'd already advised the giant skald, on threat of a detongueing, that there were to be no "Tykir the Great" sagas or poems at this feast. So, Bolthor was now relating for those assembled the tale of Tykir's paternal grandsire, Harald Fairhair.

Alinor looked at him and smiled. "Your grandsire was quite a man. All those wives and mistresses. And, blessed heaven, twenty-two sons and a comparable number of daughters."

"Your sarcasm ill-suits you, wench," he growled.

She laughed gaily, something she did far too rarely.

"You share his blood, Viking. Do you share his nature?"

"Nay. As you well know, I have not even one wife and only one mistress at the moment." He immediately regretted his hasty words when he saw the quick flash of pain on her open face. He knew she did not like her designation as mere mistress. Would she be any more pleased to be called wife of a heathen Viking?

Aaarrgh! Where did that traitorous thought come from?

"Some say King Harald was inspired to greatness by the

taunts of Gyda, daughter of the king of Hordaland," Bolthor was relating. "Gyda was an ambitious wench, and she declined to wed with Harald till he ruled all Norway. So, Harald made a solemn vow: He would not comb or cut his hair till he had won all Norway and the fair Gyda. Ten years it took Harald to achieve his goals. Thereafter, the man known as Harald *lúfa*, or mop-hair, became known as Harald *hárfagri*, or fairhair. And a finer set of tresses were never seen in all the Norselands. Further, some say that a great swiving took place that day in the chamber of Gyda, once she yielded to Harald's great feats. This is the saga of Harald Fairhair."

"Did you ever meet your grandsire?" Alinor asked, reaching to take a drink of wine from Tykir's cup. The wine was from the private stock he'd traded for in Rhineland last year and was reserved for special occasions. Tonight felt special.

He liked the way she put her lips to his cup on the very spot where he had been drinking. It was probably a coincidence, but he preferred to think otherwise.

"Did you?"

"What?"

"Meet your grandfather?"

"Yea, I did. He came to King Sigtrygg's Norse castle in Jorvik when my father lay dying."

She tilted her head, waiting for him to disclose more.

"He was a majestic old man, massive in size, not shriveled and bent over like some graybeards. His long hair had gone completely white by then, but was luxurious just the same, and held in place by a gold circlet around his forehead. He was wearing a black velvet cloak embroidered with gold thread and studded with precious jewels. Odd that I should recall those details." Sighing deeply, he added, "I saw him a. few times before he died about ten years ago. He was a hard master, to his underlings as well as his family. I cannot say he ever loved any of us. Though, I must admit, the old man deeded me Dragonstead on his death, much to my surprise. It was one of his lesser garths, 'tis true. Still . . ."

"Mayhap he was like many men, unable to show his affection."

"Mayhap." He turned to address Alinor directly. "These are not pleasant memories you prod in me, Alinor. Why so curious?"

"I just want to know more about you."

He felt a tightness in his throat at her words. She was starting to care, just as he was. Best he put a stop to that nonsense right away.

"The only thing you need to know of me is betwixt my legs," he said crudely.

She jerked her head back as if he'd slapped her.

Guilt tugged at his conscience, but he shoved it aside. At least she was not looking at him with caring now.

He could not hold himself apart from her for long, though. When she attempted to get up off the bench beside him and stomp away, he put an arm around her shoulder and pulled her close. "What think you of the marriage plans that abound at Dragonstead? Bodhil the Ripe and Jostein the Smith?" The couple had announced earlier that evening that they would be wed afore spring.

Her stiff demeanor relaxed. "Well, 'tis about time Jostein declared his intentions. He almost lost Bodhil, you know."

"Yea, and Rapp of the Big Wind is none too happy about it, I understand. Overcome with melancholy, he is. See him over there in the corner even now, alone, working on a mead-head."

"He is alone because he smells," Alinor noted wryly.

Tykir laughed. "That, too. Tell me, Alinor, did you have aught to do with the marriage plans?"

Her cheeks bloomed with an attractive blush. "I merely told Bodhil that she did not need to settle. She should be strong, and—why are you smirking?"

"Not smirking. Smiling," he corrected, chucking her under the chin. "You are so vehement in your feelings. And perchance 'tis time for you to be strong with your brothers, too."

"There's naught wrong with a woman seeking what she wants."

"And what do you want, Alinor?"

"Certainly not you, troll."

He tweaked her hair in punishment. "Not even if I have a special gift for you?"

"I've been presented with that gift a hundred times."

"Not *that* gift," he chided her with a tapping forefinger against her pursed lips.

"And I want nothing more in the vein of feathers, oils, ropes or dancing costumes. My reputation is ruined as it is by those scandalous presents. I wouldn't be surprised if news of them has already reached King Edred's court in Wessex."

He smiled at her. "Not those kinds of gifts, either."

Later that night, Alinor lay beneath him, sated, after the most tender loving he'd ever given a woman. The tenderness of his bedsport with her came not from caring, he told himself. It was just that the mood had struck him for a more gentle wooing.

He thought he heard laughter in his head. Probably the mischievous Loki poking mirth at his delusions.

It was then that he presented her with his Christ-gift. "You said one time that you had never been given a present. Here, then." He put his hand under the pillow where he had hidden the flat, blue velvet case, then shoved it into her hands.

"Tykir, I have no need of gifts. And certainly not a pity gift. Besides, I have no gift for you." She tried to return the box to him, unopened.

He insisted that she take it in hand. "There is naught of pity in this gift. Vikings love to give gifts. Accept it for what it is, and no more. A man's pleasure."

She nodded and began to undo the latch. She was sitting in his bed now, propped against the backboard, a bed fur pulled up to her waist, leaving her breasts bare to his pleasure. He loved her breasts—small, raspberry-tipped, swollen from his recent attentions.

"Oh, Tykir!" she whispered when she saw the box's contents. It was the amber neck ring he'd shown her at Hedeby. "I can't accept this." Her green eyes welled with tears, and her voice sounded choked with emotion.

"Yea, you can and will." His voice was equally choked.

Brushing a tear aside with the back of one hand, she reminded him, "You told me that the Arab trader who bartered it with you said it was intended for a bride on her wedding night, as a charm ensuring marriage-luck. Since you do not intend to wed, you said you would give it to one of Eirik's daughters on her wedding day."

He shrugged. "I changed my mind."

"About marriage?" she asked, wide-eyed with surprise.

"Nay!" he retorted way too quickly and loudly.

But she just smiled at his impassioned response.

"Do not look for hidden meanings in this gift, Alinor. I wanted to give you something special, but not—"

She pressed her fingertips to his mouth, halting further words. "It is special."

She let him put the neck ring on her then. Its thick gold band fit snugly around her slim neck, just above the collarbone. From it were suspended many tear-shaped amber stones, starting with a large one in the center and decreasingly smaller ones on either side, going back, till they were the size of tiny human tears. She resembled a magnificent Viking princess, garbed thus. A goddess. The yellowish stones set off her breasts and the creaminess of her skin. They made her eyes sparkle green fire.

"Thank you, Tykir," she whispered. "It is a gift I will always cherish. Always."

She thanked him then by being the aggressor. And she reversed the tables on him in other ways, too, by giving him the most tender loving of his life. In the process, something precious happened between them.

Mayhap the amber neck ring did indeed have magical powers.

Or mayhap the magic was in them.

CHAPTER SIXTEEN

⬥

*H*ow could he just let her go? . . .
   Springtime arrived way too soon, and they were
leaving Dragonstead.

Oh, it was not a true spring. There was still snow on the
ground in the mountains, and the air was chill. But the ice had
broken in the fjords, which allowed the longships to move out
for their trading and a-Viking ventures.

Jubilation filled the air as the bearlike Vikings, many with
huge beards and fur cloaks, came out of winter hibernation,
eager for new adventures. Blood thickened by the cold season and lack of exercise suddenly thinned and roared to life.
These virile men were not made for inactivity or bucolic
work, and exciting exploits awaited them in the Westlands,
beyond Norway.

Not everyone was jubilant, however.

Finally, Alinor was going home. But where was home now?
She'd become so fond of Dragonstead and its people . . . and
one infuriating Viking, in particular. She was so confused.
This was not her home, and yet it felt like home.

She'd always thought that her only dream was to live in-
dependently on her own estate in Northumbria. No mar-
riages. No greedy brothers. Just a peaceful, solitary life.

What a foolish maid she had been!

"Why the tears, my lady?" Tykir inquired softly. All the

trading supplies and foodstuffs had already been loaded. He'd come up to her side where she stood on the dock waiting to board the longship. She noticed that he barely limped, having pampered his leg all winter long with hot bricks, massages and rest.

"I'm not weeping," she said, swiping at her cheeks with the sleeve of her gunna.

He raised his brows in contradiction. "I would think you'd be happy to leave this 'prison' and return to your homeland." There was an odd vulnerability on his face as he spoke.

"I *am* happy," she lied. "These are tears of happiness."

It was the wrong thing to say. She saw that immediately when his expression went flat. What did he expect of her? He hadn't asked her to stay. And, frankly, she didn't know what she would have done if he had.

"Well, then, there must be a keepful of happy people here at Dragonstead. I have not seen so much weeping amongst the womenfolk since the widows came to claim the bodies after the Battle of Brunanburh. 'Twould seem you have touched a few hearts here, Alinor."

She nodded her head at his kind words, unable to speak over the lump in her throat.

"You must be stronger with your brothers when you return to Graycote," he advised her then. "Do not let them dictate your life, as they have in the past."

"Yea. I have taken a vow to withstand their assaults on my private life in future. What think you," she asked, flashing a mischievous smile his way, "of my threatening to curl their manparts if they try to force another husband on me?"

"That should handle them good and well," he said on a laugh. Then, suddenly serious, he declared, "I will miss you, Alinor." He put up a halting hand when she opened her mouth to speak. "I do not utter those words lightly, sweetling. Know this: I have never said them to another woman in all my life."

"Oh, Tykir," she murmured.

Then, on a lighter note, he teased, "But I will not miss your chicken soup."

"Nor I your *gammelost*."

He smiled gently down at her. "Mayhap we will meet again someday."

"Mayhap."

He didn't believe that any more than she did. Once Tykir's longships reached the juncture of fjords and sea near Anlaf's court two days hence, they would all be going their separate ways—Tykir and Bolthor to the Baltic lands for amber harvesting; Adam to the land of the Arabs, where he would continue his healing studies; Rurik off to Scotland in search of a dye-wielding witch; and Alinor back to Graycote and her sheep.

"One thing is for sure," he said, handing her up onto the landing board that spanned the distance from dock to ship, "I will never forget you, Alinor the Witch."

"And I will never forget you, Tykir the Troll."

In the background, aboard ship, she heard Beast barking madly, Rurik cursing about one thing or another, Adam flirting with a hersir's wife, who was going with him to Birka, and Bolthor reciting a new poem:

"Dumb, dumb, dumb.
Some Vikings are smart.
Some Vikings are dumb.
Some Vikings see with their eyes.
Some Vikings see with their hearts.
Some Vikings are so bewitched,
They cannot see at all.
This is the tale of
The dumb Viking."

On the morning of the second day they arrived at Trondelag and Anlaf's castle.

At least a hundred longships of all sizes, including the

large knarrs, or trading vessels, were lined up along the docks or anchored a short distance out to sea. Alinor was walking along the quayside, waiting for Tykir to return from paying his respects to the king. Then he would put her on an England-bound vessel with Rurik before making sail himself for the Baltics. He wanted to waste no more time, since the winds were good today.

Even Bolthor's one good eye had seemed to well up with emotion. "We will see each other again, Lady Alinor," Bolthor had said gruffly before going off to perform some ship chores. "I feel certain of that."

Alinor didn't share that certainty, but Bolthor's final words had brought a slight smile to her face.

"There once was a lady from Graycote.
On her many sheep she did dote.
Then came a Viking on his boat.
And with love she was smote.
But to him she did not quote.
Thus he had no vote.
Now on a ship she will float.
Back to her own lonely moat.
Over this sad tale, no one will gloat.
Thus the skald wrote."

"It rhymes," had been the only words she'd been able to come up with. But Bolthor had taken that as a compliment, saying, "Yea, those are the best kind."

While Tykir had gone inside the castle, she chose to stay outside, wanting no repetition of the witchcraft charges levied against her. Besides, Tykir had not invited her to accompany him. Was he ashamed of his relationship with her, which had no doubt spread through the Viking gossip chain? Or was he protecting her sensibilities against any mean-spirited be-smirching of her reputation?

"Pssst! Pssst!"

Alinor turned this way and that before she recognized that it was King Anlaf's older sister, Gudny, who was standing behind some barrels of salted herring, trying to get her attention. Jerking her head sharply, she indicated that Alinor should join her in hiding.

"What?" she asked, looking up at the woman, who was tall as a man, wide-shouldered, thick-boned, and buxom as a ship's prow.

"I need a love potion," Gudny said furtively, shoving a few coins into Alinor's hand.

Alinor tried to give the money back. "I have no knowledge of love potions."

"Yea, you must. Witches know things we mortals do not."

"But I'm not—"

"I'm desperate," Gudny moaned. "Dost know what it is like to live on my brother's sufferance? He makes my life miserable. And everybody laughs at me . . . to think I could not keep the attention of a husband, especially one as worthless as Alfrigg. But I want him back. There's a ship going to the Irish lands that I could board, if only I was carrying a love potion with me to ensure that he will return with me." Gudny exhaled loudly after that long-winded exhortation, then added, "Please?"

Alinor racked her brain for advice she could give the poor woman. For a certainty, she knew how Gudny felt living under her brother's thumb. Suddenly, she inquired, "Have you tried bells?"

Gudny swiped at her tears and brightened. "Bells?"

And Alinor explained a most unusual costume that Gudny could make for herself to entice her wayward husband home. Alfrigg was either going to be overcome with lust or surprise when he saw the big woman adorned like a harem houri.

Alinor was still smiling over that picture long after a wildly thankful Gudny had left her. That's when Signe, King Anlaf's daughter, approached her.

"Uh, Lady Alinor, um . . ." Signe began awkwardly. "I was . . . uh . . . speaking with Gudny, and . . ."

Uh-oh! "Signe, you're young and beautiful and you've only been married a few months. Surely you don't need a love potion."

"But I do," Signe wailed. "I saw Torgunn talking with a Rus slave trader this morn. And ogling a young Slav girl, he was. I suspicion he is going to take her as a bed slave."

The pig! Alinor thought. In the end, she suggested, hesitantly, "Have you tried feathers?"

When she was done giving her brief explanation, Signe was staring at her with such admiration you'd have thought Alinor had invented gold . . . or sex. "I don't know if we have any peacock feathers about. Dost think goose feathers would suffice?"

"I daresay any kind would do," Alinor said on a laugh. "'Tis the texture, not the looks of the feather that matter."

"Ooooh!" Signe cooed and shoved a piece of gold into Alinor's hand.

A number of other women showed up next, but Alinor put up a halting hand. Enough was enough. "I am not a witch!" she'd asserted firmly, and they'd gone off grumbling.

"Have you gained a witch following now, Alinor? A coven, mayhap?" Adam asked, coming up to embrace her in leavetaking.

"Don't even hint at such a thing."

"What is the cause of your sudden popularity then?"

"You do not want to know," she said with a smile.

"Well, I am off then." He gave her another fierce hug.

"Godspeed," she answered. "Someday I will expect to hear news of your great fame. The Healing Knight. It has a good sound to it, does it not?"

He smiled warmly down at her. "Alinor, I hate to see you traveling back to Britain alone. Is that really what you want?"

"We've had this conversation afore. I have no choice."

"But you love the oaf . . . I mean, Tykir . . . though why I cannot say, he is such a homely beast, unlike me who—"

He ducked when she tried to swat him on the side of the head for his devilment.

"You do love Tykir, don't you?"

She exhaled loudly. "Yea, I probably do, but—"

"Have you told him?"

"Of course not! Never would I embarrass him or myself so."

"Embarrass?" Adam frowned with confusion. "He loves you. You love him. You are going to Britain alone. He is going to the Baltic alone. What is wrong with this picture?"

"Tykir does *not* love me. Oh, I concede that he has formed a fondness for me. Mayhap that's the best any woman could hope for with him . . . but he does not love me. That I would know."

"Just as he would know, without the telling, that you love him?"

"I don't want to discuss this any longer with you, Adam. It's over. Painful as it is, I have resigned myself to the fate God has given me."

He shrugged hopelessly, then tried a different tack. "Come with me, then."

Her mouth dropped open in surprise. "With you? To the Arab lands? Why?"

"My lady, how you insult me!"

"Hah! Your conceit is much too great for you to take offense at my refusal of your overblown charms."

"Was it my charms you thought I was offering?"

She blushed.

"Nay, I just thought you might like to come along as a fellow adventurer. A friend. Think of all the exiting new places and people you would meet. Think about—"

"What? Do my ears play me false?" Tykir asked in a voice reeking with consternation. "What are you up to, Adam, that you would invite the Lady Alinor to accompany you?" Then he turned to Alinor. "And you, what a fickle lady you have become, that you would go from my bed to Adam's with nary a second thought."

She and Adam both gasped at Tykir's misunderstanding of the situation . . . and at the vehemence of his wounded pride.

"If you are going anywhere with any man afore returning to your homeland, you may as well come with me to the Baltic," Tykir said and stomped off.

She and Adam exchanged a stunned look at Tykir's uncalled-for reaction, followed by the less-than-complimentary offer. Not that she was about to refuse. No matter how ungracious the invitation, Alinor was not so lackwitted as to fail to realize she'd been given a reprieve. A temporary reprieve, but a reprieve just the same.

Adam smiled widely and bragged, "I am *so* good!"

She smiled back and gave her thanks where thanks were due. Certainly not to Adam. *Thank you, God.*

Dumb and dumber just got dumber . . .

Alinor was once again alone, momentarily.

Bolthor was on one of Tykir's ships, helping him rearrange the goods in the six longships he would be taking to the Baltic. These last-minute changes were necessary to accommodate the special Saracen horse, Fierce One, that Anlaf had gifted to Tykir, previously, along with some mares the king wanted him to sell in Hedeby on his way back.

The air was cool, but the sun was warm on her face as she leaned against a narrow tree near the docks. Tykir gave a silent signal to her that they would be a little bit longer and soon was gone from sight on one of the far boats.

Suddenly, she was grabbed from behind. Alinor squirmed and tried to see who it was, but she was being held firmly with one hand clamped over her mouth and another wrapped round her waist from behind. Lifting her off the ground, the person proceeded to edge backwards toward the forest and a number of outbuildings. Her eyes darted this way and that, but no one seemed to be looking her way. She squirmed and flailed, to no avail.

Was it a jest someone was playing on her?

Nay. The only person she could think of who would do that would be Adam, who was gone, or Rurik, who was working alongside Tykir and Bolthor.

Was it King Anlaf's way of getting back at her? Nay. Alinor knew that Anlaf would enact his revenge in public, not in a clandestine manner.

Her questions were soon answered when she was dragged into an empty woodshed where Egbert and Hebert stood with a half-dozen ruthless-looking men of various nationalities. Mercenaries, she would wager. A few looked to be Vikings, and a sorry lot they were, hard-eyed and scruffy in attire, though Norsemen just the same; probably Viking outlaws.

"Are you two mad?" She pulled out of the grasp of her captor and, storming at Egbert and Hebert, stood in front of some large object lying on the far side of the woodshed. "To come into Norse country . . . surely you have lost your senses!"

"You ungrateful bitch!" Egbert's face turned purple with rage, and he raised his hand to strike her across the face . . . a familiar ploy of his.

"Nay, Egbert," Hebert cautioned, putting up a hand to halt his brother's arm. "We can have no visible marks on Alinor if our plan is to work."

Egbert paused, saw the wisdom of Hebert's words and kicked her in the shin. It was a sharp, brutal blow that caused her to stumble backward and almost fall. She was saved by the burly chest of her captor, who still stood behind her.

"What is this all about?" she asked, trying to hide the pain in her wobbly voice. "Surely a mere woman like me is not worth all this trouble."

"Actually, you are," Egbert informed her icily. "'Twould

seem that news of your witchcraft has spread throughout
Britain. And, surprisingly, there are some men who see
value in that. Do you really have a tail, Alinor?"

"Mayhap these smitten men think you can perform some
magic in the bed linens," Hebert added with a lascivious
snicker.

"In essence, your bride-price has gone up substantially,
tail or no tail," Egbert announced. "Methinks that your being
leman to a Viking jarl—yea, news of that disgrace traveled,
too—will add even more coins to the marriage purse." He
shook his head with wonder, studying her. "I cannot see the
attraction myself, but apparently you must have some talent
that would hold the interest of a fierce Viking. There are a
few Saxon noblemen who consider that a challenge . . . to
taste what has been thawed by a heathen barbarian." He shivered with distaste at the thought.

*Demented! My brothers have gone from bumbling idiots
to full-blown demented bumbling idiots.* "Tykir will never
allow you to do this to me," she asserted, though she was not
so sure he wouldn't consider himself well rid of her. Nay,
that was not true. Tykir was a man who set high standards
for the treatment of women . . . even one who was a mere
leman . . . or former leman.

"Yea, he will," Egbert declared, puffing out his chest and
smirking with some secret satisfaction. "He will when you
convince him that you come with us of your own choice."

She snorted with disbelief. "And why would I do that?"

"Because of this," both brothers said at the same time,
and stepped aside to reveal the pile of clothing that lay on
the bare ground behind them. Nay, it was not a pile of clothing, Alinor realized. It was . . .

"Oh, my God! What have you done?" Alinor rushed forward and dropped to her knees before the tortured, muti-
lated body of a young boy. At first she did not recognize
him, so swollen was his face with bruises and his eye half
out of the socket. One leg lay askew, having been broken

midcalf and left unset. The chest area of his tunic was sliced and bloody. Then, horror filled Alinor as she realized that it was Karl, the young boy who had been serving customers at Tykir's stall in Hedeby.

She looked up at her brothers through teary eyes. "Why?"

"The lackwit wouldn't tell us, at first, how to find your Viking lover," Egbert complained sulkily.

"You fools! He probably didn't know. He's not a Viking."

"And he was insolent, the whelp was. Called us the devil's get, he did," Hebert added defensively. "How were we to know how much information he withheld without the torture?"

Tears streamed down Alinor's face as she studied the boy, not sure where to start, and whether she would do more harm handling him. "Hurry. Get a healer to come at once. Tell Father Caedmon inside the castle that his presence is required."

"There is no need of a healer. The boy died this morn." There was disgust in Egbert's voice, not remorse.

Hebert motioned the six mercenaries to the doorway and whispered some orders to them. They left with haste, and Hebert came back to her.

"I always thought you two were fools, and I sometimes thought you cruel, but I never thought you evil. This is an utterly evil act." She motioned to the lifeless body before her.

"We didn't do it," they exclaimed at once.

"Dost think the mercenaries *you paid* are at fault? Nay, you are the ones who will suffer eternal damnation for this ruthless act."

"Be that as it may," Egbert said. "We do not have much time. Will you come with us voluntarily, or will we order the same treatment for Thorksson?"

"Tykir? Are you threatening to do the same to Tykir?" She laughed mirthlessly. "You two dimwits are in the middle of Norselands, a hairsbreadth from a castle housing hundreds of soldiers, and you threaten a high-placed Norseman? You truly are mad."

Hebert grabbed Alinor by the upper arm and pinched hard. "Watch your tongue, sister, or you may follow the same fate, eventually."

"Nay, we would not attack your lover in his own lands. We have given orders to the six mercenaries Hebert just dispatched," Egbert informed her with relish. "If either of us disappears, or is captured, or has any harm done to him, there are five hundred marks of silver awaiting the delivery of Tykir's tortured body, or his head, to my steward in Wessex."

"And what makes you think Tykir couldn't defend himself?"

"Oh, I daresay he could defend himself in a fair fight, even if the odds were against him . . . as they were when he attacked us outside the Norse palace in Jorvik last fall," Hebert said.

Apparently, Hebert had forgotten who had attacked whom, but that was not the important issue. He was right: Tykir was not immune to a devious, backstabbing attack. Still . . .

"I could scream now, and you two would be dead within minutes."

"Ah, 'tis true, 'tis true," Egbert agreed, smiling maliciously. He had one front tooth missing, whether from the rot or some misbegotten escapade, she did not know . . . probably the latter. "But where are the six mercenaries, my dear? Already they have blended with the hundreds of men hereabouts. They may have even left on one of the departing ships. Could you identify them, for certain?"

Alinor's shoulders slumped. She hadn't paid them heed once she'd seen her brothers, and then the poor boy.

Could she take the chance of Tykir being harmed?

Should she trust in his greater strength and intelligence to handle the situation?

Would strength and intelligence matter when dealing with blackguards?

In the end, Alinor had no choice.

"What do you want me to do?

* * *

Betrayal cuts deeply when love wields the knife . . .

"There she is!" Tykir breathed a sigh of relief. Finally, he'd found Alinor.

She was walking toward him, easy as can be, as if he hadn't been worried sick about her whereabouts when he'd discovered her missing a short time earlier. Too many people still considered her a witch and would relish naught more than a witch burning.

But wait. Who were those two men flanking her? Two *red-haired* men. Oh, Holy Thor! It was the dimwit twins.

He put up a hand to signal his men to hold their weapons till he could discern what devilment Egbert and Hebert were up to now. He could handle the two no-brains himself, if need be. And if they'd done even the slightest thing to harm Alinor, he would wring their scrawny necks like the chickens they were.

"Alinor," he said with barely controlled patience, "I have been searching for you." He ignored her brothers as he spoke.

Alinor licked her lips nervously. "You know my brothers, Egbert and Hebert."

"I know them." His greeting was rude, but he did not care. Something was amiss, and he had no patience for niceties when directness was called for.

"I need to speak with you, Tykir, *alone.*" Alinor's chin was lifted high with determination. Or was she trying not to weep? God, he was going to kill those brothers of hers if they'd done anything to harm her.

He motioned to his men to stand in place and keep guard over the brothers. Then he took Alinor firmly by the upper arm and pulled her toward the trees.

"Well?" he demanded. "What are Cain and Abel up to now?"

She smiled at what she must have considered a jest. Blessed Lord, could she not see how little in the mood for humor he was? But he then noticed that the smile did not reach her sad eyes. "What's wrong? Have they harmed you?"

She shook her head.

"Threats?"

She shook her head more vehemently. "I've decided to return with Egbert and Hebert to Britain," she blurted out.

In his surprise, he had no time to hide his gasp. "But just a short time ago you agreed to go to the Baltic with me."

"Nay, Tykir, I did not agree. You said I may as well go with you if I was even considering going elsewhere with Adam. You never asked my opinion. Besides, 'twas a forced invitation."

"I meant it."

"I know you did."

"I do not think I ever intended to let you go to Britain," he admitted grudgingly.

Her eyes went wide at that news. "'Tis too late," she told him, regret clear in her voice.

He tilted his head in puzzlement. "Why is it too late?"

Her jaw clenched into rigidness. He recognized stubbornness when it stared him in the face, and, oh, he was suddenly very, very fearful that she was determined to leave him now.

"I just meant that I have decided that it is best for me to return to my homeland. It's where I belong. Egbert and Hebert have promised that I will not have to wed again. And I have my sheep and Graycote and . . ." Her voice broke. "Do not make this difficult for me, Tykir."

"Why? Why must you go?" The shrillness of his voice shocked him. It reminded him of . . . oh, my God! . . . it reminded him of the exact same words he had exclaimed numerous times as a boy when others had left him, too. His father, mother, Ruby, Eirik, Dar and Aud. Oh, God, it was happening again. He had somehow opened himself up to the excruciating pain *again*.

"Oh, Tykir." The pity in her voice rocked him to his soul. *Pity? Is this what I've come to?* He lifted his chin, but not because he wanted to keep tears from welling over in his eyes. He refused to believe he actually had moisture welling there. Nay, he wanted to show her that he could be stubborn, too. He wanted to show her that he could be as heartless and uncaring as she was now. He wanted . . . so many things.

Dashing his pride aside, he inquired, "Are you sure this is what you want, Alinor?"

She nodded, her eyes huge with unshed tears. Tears of pity, no doubt.

"You have other choices, sweetling." *God, I am pathetic.*

She tried to smile at his endearment but could not. "Nay, I do not. It is my final decision . . . mine to make, not yours."

He swallowed over the lump in his throat. "And you will be safe from your brothers' machinations?"

She nodded again. "Try to understand. It's for the best."

Best? Whose best? he roared inside. *I am dying, and she says it is for the best.*

She put out a pleading hand, as if to touch his arm. He could not stand that now. It would be his undoing. So, he slapped her hand aside.

She put the hand to her mouth to hold back a sob. But he could see that she was not going to change her mind.

"So be it," he said finally. Before he spun on his heel to walk stiffly away from her, he took Egbert and Hebert by the necks and cracked their heads together, just for the pleasure of it, for all their past misuse of Alinor and to ease this wild need to go berserk. "Hurt her and you hurt me," he murmured under his breath to the two whimpering brothers.

Then, without another word to her or even one final, lingering look, he turned his back and stomped away.

As he left he thought he heard her murmur, "I love you."

But he must have been mistaken.

On the heels of tragedy came a blessed . . . event? . . .

Alinor arrived on British soil a mere two sennights later,

and she was not in a good temperament. Her brothers probably wished they'd never come after her.

She'd done nothing but vomit with the seasickness, despite
the placid seas. When she wasn't emptying the contents of her
stomach, she'd been eating everything in sight.

Or she'd been rushing for the chamber pot in a screened-
off area to relieve herself. There was something to be said
for the male anatomy, which allowed men to just whip out
their manparts and take care of matters over the ship's side,
she'd thought on more than one occasion. And crying . . .
Blessed Mary, she'd done more weeping and sobbing than
ever before in her entire life. If she hadn't been making
water from one end it had been the other. Good thing she
was inclined to sleep so much.

Furthermore, she'd taken every free moment to berate her
lackwitted brothers for every infraction they'd levied against
her in the past twenty-five years. And she had a long list.

They were walking through the Coppergate district of
Jorvik now, heading toward the horse stables, where Egbert
and Hebert intended to buy some steeds to take them to
her—their—estate in Wessex and an eventual parade of prospective bridegrooms. 'Twas enough to make her vomit again.

Suddenly, Alinor came to a screeching halt, causing
Egbert and Hebert to run into her back end, which had grown
decidedly wider of late, she'd noticed. It was a smell that had
drawn her attention. She glanced to the side and smiled.
Gammelost. It was a Norseman's booth in the craftsmen's
district of Coppergate. Amongst the intricately carved bowls
and furniture, there was a linen cloth heaped with the smelly
Viking cheese intended for the man's midday meal. Alinor
pulled a coin from the cloth flap at her waist and smiled.

A short time later, as she stood gobbling the cheese down
as if it was ambrosia of the gods, Egbert and Hebert approached her with the horses in lead reins. They looked at her,
then at each other, then blurted out simultaneously, "Are you
with child?"

"Huh?" Alinor said, setting aside the cheese, which suddenly appeared disgusting. "Do not be ridiculous." As she fought off the urge to vomit, or make water, or weep, all at the same time, she stared at Egbert and Hebert as if they were even more demented than usual.

Then she thought, *Could I be?*

Nay. I am barren. Three husbands have I had and never quickened before.

But what if Tykir's seed were more potent? Or my womb more receptive? What if . . . oh, praise God! . . . what if I am carrying Tykir's child?

But she would have known, wouldn't she? Well, actually, she would not. Her monthly fluxes had always been irregular . . . 'twas why she had reasoned in the past that she could not conceive. Plus, she had told Tykir once when he commented on her weak or nonexistent monthly fluxes that her body was probably affected by the cold, or the change of place, or all that lovemaking.

She felt foolish now, not to have suspected.

Then she put a hand over her stomach and remembered a night—'twas Christ's Eve, less than four short months ago—when Tykir had made tender love to her after gifting her with the magical amber neck ring. Hadn't she felt afterwards that something special had happened?

It had.

She burst out with joyous laughter. "Yea, I am pregnant. I have conceived the troll's child. Isn't that the most wonderful news in the world?"

Egbert and Hebert gaped at her with horror and disgust.

"Pregnant? How can we sell . . . uh, betroth . . . you to an English nobleman with a heathen whelp in your belly?" Egbert stormed, pulling madly at his mop of red curls.

"And do you say the babe will be a troll?" a terrified Hebert squealed.

"Now you have ruined everything," Egbert wailed.

"Nay, this is the best thing that has ever happened to me. I am not barren after all."

"No man will want her now," Hebert told Egbert.

"'Tis true. 'Tis true. And the Viking would surely come after us for vengeance if he finds out about this," Egbert told Hebert. "If we were to rid her of the babe, or fob it off on some cotter after wedding her to another, that vengeful monster would follow us to the ends of the earth. I know he would."

"Forget about the Viking. I would rip your eyes out with my own fingernails if you dared take my babe from me," Alinor said vehemently, only slightly surprised at how protective she was feeling already toward the seed growing inside her.

"We wipe our hands of you then, ungrateful wench," Hebert spat out. "Never did you appreciate all our efforts on your behalf. Now find your own fate. We care not if it be in a Viking midden or hell."

With that, the two stomped off, already concocting new brainless schemes, leaving Alinor standing in the middle of the busy city. Alone.

She hooted with laughter then, drawing a few curious looks from passersby, but she did not care. For the first time in her life, she was free. She could go to Graycote and be an independent woman. Or she could find herself a husband of her own picking. Or—and her heart skipped a beat—she could make her way back to Dragonstead and wait for Tykir to return.

She did not even hesitate.

Dragonstead it would be.

We are fam-i-ly. His brother, and his sister, and me? . . .

Rurik was ambling along Coppergate, enjoying the sights, including a Saxon maid with a pair of swishing hips that would make a Norseman blush. Well, some Norsemen. Not him, of course. He was too much a man of the world.

Beast was temporarily sheltered at Gyda's house. He was

headed toward the king's garth, where he intended to pay his respects to Eric Bloodaxe, then make his way north to Scotland and a certain mischievous witch. But then he stopped in his tracks when another bloody witch caught his attention.

Lady Alinor! What is she doing here? She is supposed to be off in the Baltic skipping along the beaches, collecting amber with Tykir. Could she perchance be in two places at once, being a witch and all?

Nay, Rurik decided, having long ago accepted that Alinor wasn't a real witch. Just witchly.

She was jabbering away at a tall Norseman with long blond hair and a huge, finely groomed beard. A mercenary, by the looks of him. In fact, Rurik seemed to recall seeing him one time at King Haakon's Vik court on Oslo-fjord. And, oh, Holy Thor! Was the woman daft? Now she was jabbing the big Viking in the chest with a finger to make some point whilst she talked his ear off.

Amazingly, the man didn't lop off her head, as any sane man would. Instead, he listened intently and his face got paler and paler at whatever news she was imparting.

Meeting up with her will mean trouble for me, I wager. Should I pretend I haven't seen her and escape? No one will even know. While he pondered his decision, Rurik moved closer, his curiosity getting the better of him.

"I have a child?" the man was asking. "For the love of Freyja! Tell me more, Lady Alinor."

"Yea, Toste, you have a child. His name is Thibaud, and he has seen only four winters. Good thing I overheard the craftsman over there address you by name, or you might never know the glad tidings."

"A son?" Toste said with wonder. "A son?"

Alinor smiled indulgently, apparently no longer angry with the man. "Yea, and a beautiful boy he is, too."

"I have thought of Rachelle many times these past years since we were together in Rouen. But she was married, or so

I thought." He shrugged. "And you say the boy lives in Hedeby with his mother? Why, I was in the market town just last year. How could I have missed seeing her?"

No doubt he'd spent his time in an ale house, or visiting the loose women who sold their favors there. That was Rurik's opinion. Leastways, 'twas how he spent his days there.

"I do not think Rachelle goes about much, Toste. You see, before her husband divorced her, he performed a brutal mutilation on her." Alinor explained, and Toste's face grew red with rage.

"That matters not to me," he asserted. "I will go to her and my son forthwith, and make right all she has suffered for being with me. And I will take revenge on her former husband, Arnaud, as well. That I forswear."

Well, there's naught here for me to do, Rurik thought, and was about to creep away, unnoticed.

"Rurik! Is that you?" he heard a male voice call from behind him.

Too late! Trapped!

"Eirik," he groaned aloud, seeing Tykir's brother coming forth. Then he groaned mentally as he noted the rest of Lord Eirik's party. "Lady Eadyth, Selik, Rain . . .'tis good to see you again. And all your children." *By the gods, these two couples breed like rabbits. They must copulate enough to populate the entire countryside. 'Tis best that Tykir has never wed if his brother and sister and their spouses set such an example.* That was what he thought, but what he said with a sweet smile of admiration was, "What nice families you have!"

"Who is that you are watching over there?" Eirik pointed so that Eadyth would look, too. "Oh, I see, 'tis Lady Alinor. Where is Tykir? I daresay he would not let the witch escape, so he must be about somewhere."

"He is not here, as far as I know," Rurik disclosed. "Last I heard he was on his way to the Baltic."

Alinor glanced up, and Rurik groaned aloud again. He was trapped, good and proper, now.

Everyone was introduced all around, including Toste.

Eadyth embraced Alinor in the way womenfolk often did, as if they were longtime friends. 'Twas their lesser brains that caused them to act so, in Rurik's opinion. Rain embraced her, too, stating, "You are the one that Eadyth has told me about . . . the one she predicted would capture Tykir's hard heart."

Alinor burst into tears then and was blubbering noisily about a number of nonsensical things, like braids and feathers and lusty trolls and *gammelost* and cravings and piss and vomit. But only one of them caught his attention. *With child.*

Rurik threw his hands in the air. *Well, that does it! Now I will never get away. The witch will be foisted on me. Everyone will think me uncaring if I just traipse off without caring for my best friend's babe . . . and the mother of my best friend's babe . . . and the sister and brother of my best friend . . . oh, hell, the whole bloody world.* He sighed deeply, though no one was paying attention to him. Everyone was doting on Lady Alinor.

"I know Tykir probably does not want me, even with a babe," Alinor explained on a sniffle, "but my only wish now is to find someone with a longship to take me back to Dragonstead."

Everyone turned to him. *Me? Why me? Oh, this is just a wonderful turn of events. I should have followed the maid with the swishing hips when I had a chance.*

"Does your face hurt, Rurik?" Rain inquired, turning him from side to side with a firm grip on his chin.

"Nay. Why?"

"Because it's blue."

"Oh, have you not seen Rurik since he turned blue?" Eadyth spoke to Rain, but everyone in the bloody world was listening, including many a passerby. "He got it whilst swiving a witch."

"Ead-yth!" Eirik remonstrated. "Where have you heard such language?"

"From you." She wiggled her nose at him.

"Men!" Eadyth and Rain exclaimed, sharing a communal look of disgust. Alinor was too busy blubbering still.

"Rurik, do you have a longship here?" Eirik asked.

Uh-oh! Blindsided whilst woolgathering. "Yea, but I was going to Scotland for a time."

Everyone stared at him as if he was the most selfish clod in the world. "I suppose I could postpone—"

Eirik had already assumed he would help them and was off on another subject. "The ships that Selik and I own are off being repaired. We have not much heed of them, being land-locked as we are these days. Ouch," he said, as Eadyth jabbed him with an elbow. "I wasn't complaining, sweetling," he told her with a reassuring pat on the arm; then he addressed Rurik again. "I suppose the one longship could take us all to Dragon-stead?"

"All?" Rurik squeaked out, and his single word was echoed by everyone else in the group. Toste was nodding at everyone and making his escape. Lucky fellow!

"Yea, *all.* You did not think we would let you go alone, did you? And, of course, Eadyth and I will want to bring our five children. Some of them have never seen Dragonstead."

"And Rain and I will bring at least four of our children and some of the orphans, though our oldest, Mary, and Adam's sister, Adela, could stay with the greater number of the orphans. On the other hand, they want to come, too. Mayhap we could set them all to rowing. Ha, ha, ha. What do you think, heartling?" Selik asked Rain.

Rurik thought he might go mad and wondered if he might have been cursed by Alinor the Witch, after all.

There was no maybe about it, Rurik decided a short time later when Alinor looked up at him and wheedled, "Rur-ik?"

'Twas always best for a man to run like the wind when a woman asked something in a wheedling voice, especially when accompanied by the batting of eyelashes. Alinor should know that he was immune to her charms, or lack of charms. Tykir was the only one who thought her winsome. "What?" he snapped.

"Can I bring my sheep with us on your ship?"

"Nay!"

"Please?"

"Nay! Nay! Nay!"

"Ple-eee-ase?"

"Well, mayhap one. Or two. But that's all."

The huge smile she flashed at him then told him he had been bested good and proper. There would be more than two sheep.

Alinor turned to the others then. "Since Rurik is willing to take me back to Dragonstead—"

Hah! Who said aught about "willing"?

"—'tis not necessary for all of you to accompany me."

Well, finally, someone has an intelligent thought here.

Everyone demurred, though. Lackwits, all!

"But why do you all need to come?" Alinor asked.

"Good question," Rurik piped in quickly.

"Do you think we would miss Tykir's wedding?" they all said, except for a slack-jawed Rurik, who thought Tykir might have something to say about that important event, and except for a slack-jawed Alinor, who began to cry again.

CHAPTER SEVENTEEN

⊗

What he needed was a good country she-done-me-wrong song . . .

Tykir had been on the Samland Peninsula of the Baltic coast for only three sennights and he was driving everyone as hair-pulling mad as he himself was.

Flesh was melting from his body from lack of appetite, and even when he tried to drink himself senseless as an ale-head, the brew could barely pass over the lump in his throat. Drumming through his brain with an incessant refrain were the selfsame painful thoughts.

Alinor. Gods, how I miss her!
She must have bewitched me.
But she's not really a witch.
How could she have left me?
How could I have let her go?
I should have told her how I feel.
How do *I feel?*
Aaarrgh!

He was so racked with confusion over his turbulent emotions that he could not think or work or sleep.

Gods, I miss her so!

Then Adam arrived to add to the madness. He'd changed his travel plans, claiming a concern for Tykir's well-being.

By the gods, who named Adam and Bolthor his protectors? Even as he'd strived to hold people at a distance all these years, some seemed to have ignored his signals. He did not need them. He did not need anyone, not even the fickle Alinor. That was what he told himself. What he thought was: *I am dying inside.*

"I got off my ship at the first watering stop on the way to the Arab lands," Adam told him. The fool, who'd been sleeping on a makeshift pallet in the single bedchamber in his Rustic longhouse near the Baltic beach, had heard him rise at dawn. Now he professed a yen to ride alongside him and the amber harvesters on the Baltic shores. That, after being up half the night . . . tumbling half the maids in all the Baltic, no doubt. He'd surely hit the first half the night before.

"Like a thorn in my privates, you are, Adam. Go back to snoring and leave off with your nosing in my affairs."

Ignoring his advice, Adam continued to dress . . . in his ridiculous Arab robes, at that. Tykir would like to see him astride a horse in a good wind. Some of the female amber gatherers would like that, too, he would wager. "Something told me you were going to make a muddle of things with Alinor," Adam continued to blather while he tied a rope around the waist of his flowing robe and grabbed a hunk of manchet bread topped with a slice of cold sausage to break his fast.

"Well, *something* should tell you to just blow away. Mayhap I like being in a muddle."

"I just knew you would need my expert advice in love matters." Adam had an annoying habit of screening out any words he did not want to hear and talking over a person. Apparently, he was screening him this morn because the jabberling went on blithely. "And see, I was right. Here you are. Alone. Smitten. And dying of a broken heart. Methinks I got here just in time."

"Methinks you think too much," Tykir countered, shoving the young know-everything in the arm. He then proceeded to suggest that Adam do something he presumed was physically impossible. But then, one never knew with Adam.

The lackwit just grinned at him and danced away to

avoid his second shove. "I could give you advice on how to hold a woman's attention . . . a sort of reverse bewitching," Adam said, munching on his cold repast.

Tykir slanted him a sideways glance of disgust, then dunked his head in a bowl of water, drying off with a rough linen. "Brrr!" was his only response to Adam—or the quick cleansing.

"Really, Tykir. I know *things*," Adam continued, waggling his eyebrows. "Things I learned in the Arab lands. Those desert princes have naught to do out on the dunes except count sand particles and chase camels; so, they have become adept at—Hey! Be careful!" Tykir had thrown the wet cloth at him, mussing his hair, which was clubbed back off his too-handsome face.

"It wasn't my lovemaking skills, or lack thereof, which caused Alinor to leave."

Adam seemed to ponder that assertion. "I could have sworn that she loved you . . . and you know how women are once they are bitten by that particular bug. There is no getting rid of them. What did she say when you told her you loved her?"

"Adam! Your intrusiveness passes all bounds. You have no right to ask such personal questions of me."

Adam studied him for a moment, a frown creasing his brow. "Do not tell me that you never told her how you feel. Surely you are not *that* inept in the love arts."

"How I feel! How I feel!" he exclaimed, pulling at his own hair. "How the hell do I know how I feel?"

Adam's face brightened, as if a candle had been lit behind his eyeballs. "Ah, there is the rub, then. At last we have arrived at the crux of your problem. Now I will be able to prescribe a solution."

"What problem?" Bolthor asked, coming in, unannounced. "Oh, are we speaking of *Tykir's* problem? Didst thou tell him of the solution we conjured yestereve over our horns of ale?"

Tykir put his face in his hands.

"I was even inspired to write a poem about it."

Still with his face buried in his hands, Tykir groaned.

"Pride is the downfall
Of many a man.
And a Viking most of all.
Lord of the swordplay he may be.
And sing his weapon does.
But when it comes to the music
That fills his heart,
Pride stands in his way.
Rather than sing of his own true love,
The proud Viking bird goes mute,
And falls on his less-than-feathery arse."

With a cough, Bolthor concluded, "This is the Saga of Tykir the Great, also known as 'The Saga of the Proud Viking.'"

"More like, 'The Saga of the Viking Who Fell on His Arse,'" Adam muttered under his breath.

Tykir was about to tell Bolthor how awful his poem was and to snarl at him, as he had at Adam, to stay out of his life. But Bolthor stared at him with such obvious need for encouragement that Tykir found himself saying, "That was excellent, Bolthor. I really think you are improving."

"Thank you." Bolthor's good eye seemed to fill with tears of appreciation. "I was afeared you would not like it. Even laugh." Then he confessed, "I could not think of a rhyme for arse at the end. In truth, I have a terrible time with rhyming, which is surely a failing in a good skald."

Adam commented, "I think you are a good skald," and Tykir could have kissed the young lout.

At the same time, if he hadn't thought it before, Tykir did now. *I am going mad.*

Tykir rode his horse a good part of the morning till he and his steed were both exhausted, sweeping low with a specially designed basket scoop to rake the sands for loose amber. Then he plagued his amber workers in their sheds along the shores as they sorted and polished the raw amber.

Some days they brought in hunks of amber as big as a man's head, especially after a storm had churned up the ocean's bottom, but most often they were small pieces. It was luck that determined their hauls for the day, not the workers' misdeeds, and he had no right to take his mood out on them.

Adam and Bolthor had kept up with him in the amber harvesting, in fact, relishing the outdoor exercise as they galloped along the foam of the low tide. But finally, the two confronted him at the end of the day.

"Tykir, this has to stop," Adam declared. They were seated at a table in his lodging, sipping at huge goblets of ale. "You are driving yourself too hard, not to mention your workers. Have you looked in a mirror lately? You have dark shadows under your eyes. Your face and frame are becoming gaunt."

"Since when have you cared about my appearance?"

"I care about you," Adam said gravely.

"And so do I," Bolthor added gruffly.

"I do not want you to care," Tykir roared, slamming his fist on the table, then softened his voice. "I do not want anyone to care."

"Be that as it may, Bolthor and I have been talking, and we think you should go to Northumbria and bring Alinor back."

Tykir gaped at them. "Bring her back? To where?"

Adam and Bolthor shrugged.

"Here," Adam offered.

"Or Dragonstead," Bolthor recommended.

"Anywhere *you* are," Adam and Bolthor urged as one.

"And if she does not want to come? Are you suggesting I take her captive again?"

"The idea has merit," was Adam's opinion. "Have I told you about the sheik who captured—"

"A hundred times, at least," Tykir said dryly.

"Nay, I do not think kidnapping would be necessary this time," Bolthor opined.

"I am *not* going after Alinor," Tykir asserted firmly. "She made her decision, and it was final." Besides, the heart-pain he endured now would be naught compared to how he would feel if she rejected him again. 'Twas time to reinforce his old defenses. A man could not be hurt if he did not care. Everyone leaves . . . eventually. It was a fact of his life.

"But she didn't have all the facts," Adam argued. "If you—"

Tykir put up a hand, barring further debate. "I will not go after Alinor, but you are correct. I cannot go on this way. I have made a decision."

Both men looked at him expectantly.

"I am going back to Dragonstead."

Home is where the Viking heart is . . .

Two sennights later, in mid-May, Tykir was arriving back at Dragonstead.

It was the right decision to have come back, Tykir realized as he gazed about him at the verdant paradise that was his home. *Home*, he repeated to himself. Yea, that's what it was. He'd been denying it for years, denying himself the pleasure of it in its best seasons. Alinor had been correct in that, at least. He'd been a fool to stay away from Dragonstead.

As his longship turned a bend in the fjord, the valley and lake in all their springtime splendor came into full view. And something else, too.

Tykir came instantly alert. There was a dragonship tied to the bollards of his wharf. He drew his sword from its sheath. Adam and Bolthor, at his side, did likewise.

"Is that not Rurik's vessel?" Bolthor questioned, squinting, as they came closer.

"But I thought he was headed for Scotland," Adam said.

"And who are all those people about?" Tykir murmured. There were men and women up near the lake. And sheep, even a curly horned ram . . . nay, he must be mistaken about the curly horns. It was probably an illusion of the bright sunlight. But it was Beast who was chasing some mangy sheepdog that resembled . . . but, nay, that was impossible. And look there. Children. Lots of children. "Oh, good Lord! Is that Eirik and Eadyth?"

"And Selik and Rain. She must have had the baby," Adam added, noting her flat stomach. "I should have made for the Arab lands when I had a chance. They will be cajoling me to come back to Northumbria, *where I belong.*"

Soon, his longship was anchored and tied to the wharf, and Tykir was surrounded by his family.

"What are you doing here?" Tykir asked Eirik.

"Well, that is some welcome, brother! Can we not come to visit Dragonstead when the inclination calls?"

"When I am not here?" Tykir inquired, his eyes narrowed suspiciously.

"Have you been ill, Tykir?" Rain's healing instincts leapt to the forefront. "You are much too thin, and there are bags under your eyes, and your pallor is—"

"I am fine." He laughed whilst she prodded and probed him with a forefinger here and there. She even lifted his eyelids—to check his eyeballs, he presumed.

"For shame, Adam!" Rain said then, hugging him tightly as she spoke, then passing him on to Selik, his adopted father. Both Rain and Selik were tall as a tree. Adam would no doubt have bruises on his ribs when they were done with him. "What kind of healer are you becoming that you would let Tykir waste away so?" Rain continued to berate her "son."

"Methinks Adam would be a better healer if he were back in Northumbria . . ." Selik started to say.

And everyone finished for him, ". . . *where he belongs.*"

Adam groaned.

They all moved up toward the keep, after Tykir instructed his seamen about the chores to finish up before heading for a cup of cool mead in their own homes or in the castle's great hall.

"Who do all those children belong to?" Tykir grumbled, an arm looped around the shoulders of Eadyth and Rain, on either side of him. Everywhere he looked there were children, of all ages, from babes barely out of swaddling clothes toddling along in front of maidservants, to youthlings with first beards and young girls in first bloom.

"Me," Eadyth, Rain, Eirik and Selik answered as one . . . then beamed with pride, as if begetting were some great feat.

"I thought the same thing you're thinking about the number of whelps when I ran into your family on the street in Jorvik," Rurik confided, coming up to them with two twin boys hanging on to each of his ankles, like puppies, and another little girl sitting on his shoulders, tugging on his hair.

"Rurik!" Tykir exclaimed. "I thought you went to Scotland. But, nay, I see you still have your blue mark; so I guess you never made it that far." He stared at him in puzzlement. "What are you doing here?"

"Trapped," was Rurik's only response as he spun on his heels and hobbled away with his human cargo.

Tykir shook his head slowly, totally confused.

"What you need is a cup of mead," Eirik said, and everyone agreed. They all exchanged the oddest looks with each other as they nodded in agreement. Bolthor, Adam and Rurik were grinning like lackwits as Selik whispered something in their ears.

Something very strange was amiss at Dragonstead.

But first he would have a cup of mead to clear his head.

Tykir shrugged off Eadyth and Rain, who were clinging to him like a long-lost swain, and began to walk through the bailey toward the keep door. Once he glanced back over his shoulder, then looked again. "Good Lord, the bunch of you are following after me like a herd of ducklings after a goose."

"Quack, quack!" Eirik opined.

"Do not be laying any eggs," Selik advised him. "Or anything else."

"Some people are so immature," Tykir remarked. Then,

"Phew! What is that stink in here?" He was about to enter the great hall when the stench assailed his nostrils. "Has Rapp of the Big Wind been hereabouts?"

"Nay, it's the *gammelost*," Eadyth announced gaily from behind him. He could hear giggles and male guffaws as well, but he had no time for wondering about their behavior. He was too busy staring at the most wonderful sight in the world.

"Alinor!"

She looked up, and the joy he saw there made his heart leap. All the pain of the past few sennights melted away. Mayhap he'd been wrong. Mayhap everyone didn't leave him after all. "What are you doing here?"

Her face fell.

Had his voice been sharp or less than welcoming? Oh, Gods, he wanted to say the right thing, but he couldn't think. He could only feel, and what he felt was the most intense happiness and relief.

"Eating *gammelost*."

"Huh?"

"You asked me what I was doing here, and I told you. I'm eating *gammelost*."

"Willingly? No one is torturing you?"

"Notice that I am not amused by your jest." She put another hunk of cheese into her mouth. Cheese with a golden syrup on top, which she licked off her fingers.

"You are eating *gammelost* with honey?" He gagged at the prospect.

"Yea, and horseradish, too." She glared at him, as if waiting for him to laugh at her.

He forced himself not to laugh.

"Would you like some?" she asked softly.

"Nay, I just ate on the longsh—"

Someone jabbed him in the back and hissed, "Lackbrain."

"Actually, I might try a bite," he said, but before he sat down he turned on his following and gritted out, "Get out of here! All of you!" He heard muttered oaths and the scurrying of footsteps behind him, followed by the slamming of a door. Then silence, except for the sounds of Alinor's munching.

She stopped for a moment and put a slab of *gammelost* on his palm, oozing honey and topped by a dollop of horseradish.

"I missed you, Alinor," he blurted out.

She looked up at him. Was she pleased or just surprised by his blunt words? Mayhap stunned, because she seemed unable to speak.

"Did you miss me?" he inquired. *Gods, I am pathetic in my need for her. Why doesn't she speak and put me out of my misery? Is her throat clogged with that bloody cheese?*

"Well," she said hesitantly, "I missed Dragonstead."

"Then why did you leave?"

"Because you did not ask me to stay, you dunderhead."

Now, this was interesting. He cocked his head to the side, studying her. And for the first time he noticed the changes in her. Her face seemed fuller—all that cheese, no doubt—but the skin under her freckles had a certain bloom to it. A lovely hue, actually. Mayhap she had been out in the sun. Yea, that was probably it. And her breasts, were they fuller? But it was hard to tell with the full gunna of green wool she was wearing.

"Stop staring at me."

He smiled. "I like staring at you. But, Alinor, I would know this: If I had asked you to stay at Dragonstead, would you have?"

"I don't know," she wailed, and big fat tears filled her eyes and spilled over onto her cheeks.

"You're crying! Why are you crying?" He started to take her hand in his, but he still held the cheese in his palm.

"Because that's what I do," she keened. "That, and sleep."

Sleep? What has sleep to do with aught? This was the most ludicrous conversation he'd ever had in all his life.

She stood suddenly, pulling her hands from his grasp.

"Where are you going?"

"To the garderobe."

He stood, as well.

"Where do you think you're going?" she snapped churlishly.

"With you?"

"Do not be ridiculous," she chastised him, walking off. Over her shoulder, she added, "I make this visit about fifty times a day. Willst thou accompany me each time, my lord of the privy?"

"Didst the wench need to slice me with her sharp tongue? All she had to say was she wanted to go alone. Men go to the privy together. Why not men and women?" he muttered to himself as he sat there staring at the loathsome concoction on the palm of his hand. Quickly, he dropped it to the rushes at his feet and scraped the sticky remains against the edge of the table. Beast and Alinor's sheepdog, Beauty, ambled up, sniffed at the cheese, then turned up their noses and ambled away. *Smart dogs!*

Soon Alinor returned and sat down across from him with a long sigh.

He had no idea what the sigh meant . . . probably some offense he'd inadvertently committed. "Dost thou want more to eat, dearling?" he inquired, trying for a more tender tone and pushing the trencher closer to her.

She shook her head, shoving the trencher away with repugnance. "I would vomit if I took a bite of that now."

Who wouldn't? But, oh, she looked so beautiful sitting there with her hands folded in her lap. He wanted to take her into his arms and hug her and kiss her and tell her that he lo—lo—how he cared, but first he wanted to know what the hell was going on.

"Where are your brothers?"

She shrugged. "Wessex, I presume."

"Why are you not with them?"

She stiffened at that terse question and would have left his clumsy presence if he hadn't leapt over the table and sat beside her on the bench, forcing her to stay. "I can always go to them now," she sobbed. She was back to weeping again.

"Alinor, you are never leaving again . . . not Dragonstead . . . or . . . or me." There he'd said it . . . *almost*.

"I'm not?"

"Nay. Now, tell me why you went with your brothers if that was not your desire."

"Because . . . oh, Tykir, they killed Karl. Well, leastways, their mercenaries did."

"Mercenaries? Karl? Dost thou mean the young boy who works for me in Hedeby?"

She nodded, and the tears kept flowing. Like a waterfall, they were.

"I'll kill those two, I swear I will."

She told him the entire story then, and he got angrier by the minute. To think that her brothers would threaten Alinor so, in his very presence practically. To think that they had killed Karl. And to think that Alinor trusted so little in his expertise in protecting himself and those under his shield. But that was a bone he would pick with her later.

"And then they released me when they found out," she finished.

He shook his head like a wet dog. So much information she had hurled at him, and still he was baffled. "Found out what?"

She looked at him through huge green eyes, like pale green emeralds, and waited for him to understand. He recognized the vulnerability in her quivering lips and wringing hands; he shared it. But . . .

Suddenly, everything came together in his thick head. The *gammelost*. The frequent visits to the garderobe. The vomiting. The need for sleep. And the weeping.

"Are you with child, Alinor?" he asked, and could not believe the words came, unbidden, from his lips.

She nodded. Oh, God, she nodded.

"With my babe?" He was incredulous.

She slapped him on the arm. "Who else's, troll?"

"Lord, how I love it when you call me troll," he said with a hoot of laughter and pulled her upright into his arms, swinging her around and around with the sheer joy of the moment. "You are carrying my babe!" he kept saying over and over as he hugged her and kissed her wet cheeks and hugged her again.

"Put me down, you lunkhead," she finally cried out, "or I will be spewing *gammelost* all over your shoulders."

He set her on her feet and knelt before her, pressing a palm to her stomach, which was barely a little hillock at this point. But his babe grew there, and tears filled his eyes at the wonder of it.

"Oh, Tykir!" she said softly, and he hugged her about the hips, laying his cheek against her belly. He imagined he felt a heartbeat there. A fanciful notion, that!

"Do I take it that you are happy at the prospect of fatherhood?" she asked as he stood once again and stared at her with amazement.

"Ecstatic! What a talented woman you are, to take my seed into your body and make it grow."

"Did I have any choice?" she observed drolly.

That gave him pause. "How do you feel about your pregnancy, Alinor?"

"Ecstatic," she echoed his word.

A heavy load lifted from his heart. "Will you be content to live here at Dragonstead?" His breathing stopped as he waited for her reply.

"Ecstatic." She repeated, never hesitating in her answer.

He let out a whooshy breath. "You will marry me, of course."

"Is that a proposal?" She lifted one brow.

He laughed. "Yea, 'tis. Was I putting the ship afore the ocean?"

"Something like that." She was smiling, but the smile did

not reach her eyes, and Tykir knew he had other words that needed to be spoken.

He sat down once again on the bench and pulled her onto his lap. "Alinor, all my life everyone leaves me. Nay, do not think to argue with me on this. I have known from a young age that everyone leaves. I learned early on how to survive, though: Do not care. Let no one get too close, not even my family or friends, though they have been nigh pestsome in that regard of late. And it worked for all these years. Until . . ."

She was weeping again. "Have I been pestsome, too?"

"The most pestsome of all," he informed her, "because try as I might, I could not stop myself from loving you. There. I have finally said it. I love you. Are you happy now?"

"Yea, I am happy." And she *was* happy. He could see that by the way she was laughing and crying at the same time.

So he repeated the words, just to see how they would feel. "I love you." It was easier this time.

"I love you, too, Tykir." She said the glorious words with a fervency, holding his eyes the entire time, and cupping his face tenderly with one hand.

"You do?" he choked out. Who knew those words would feel so good, in the telling and the receiving? All these wasted years when he had missed them. Nay, deep inside he suspected he'd been waiting for just the right woman to say them to. Alinor.

"Yea, I love you, troll that you are. And I will tell you this one time and one time only, so listen well, Viking. I will never leave you. Never."

He could not speak, so overcome with emotion was he.

Then elation filled him and he scooped Alinor up into his arms. Life was good. He was home, at Dragonstead. His babe would arrive in a few short months. And . . .

He grinned and headed toward the staircase.

"Tykir! What are you doing?" Alinor said, clinging to his neck as he rushed up the steps, three at a time.

"I have never made love to the mother of my child afore,

Alinor," he told her with a husky growl, slamming the bed-chamber door behind him with the kick of one booted foot. "And that is something I intend to remedy right now, heartling."

And he did.

Twice.

At the end, a well-sated Alinor was heard to murmur, "You've got to love a Viking."

Truer words were never spoken.

Later that night, Bolthor regaled the gathering with one of his poems in the continuing Saga of Tykir the Great.

> *"There once was a Viking smitten.*
> *By a witch the troll was bitten.*
> *Some say love comes to those*
> *Who need it most.*
> *Some say love comes when*
> *Least expected.*
> *Some say love is a gift*
> *From the gods.*
> *But mayhap 'tis just*
> *A form of bewitching."*

EPILOGUE

❧

Everyone loves a wedding, especially Vikings . . .

The wedding at Dragonstead of Jarl Tykir Thorksson and Lady Alinor of Graycote was a rip-roaring Viking event.

It was a Friday, or Friggs-day, in commemoration of the goddess of marriage. The heavens reciprocated by smiling down on them with warm weather and bright sunshine.

People came from far and wide, filling the hills and the valley surrounding the lake, where gaily colored tents had been erected. Among the guests were Tykir's Uncle Haakon, the all-king of Norway, a fair-haired handsome man a few years younger than Tykir. Haakon brought with him his best friend, Sigurd, the jarl of Lade. Only slighter in size than Haakon's royal entourage was that of King Anlaf and his many wives and concubines, not to mention his ebullient daughter Signe, who was trailed by a perpetually grinning husband, Torgunn, and his sister Gudny, who cared not if anyone noticed the jingling noises beneath her gunna as she held on tightly to her bewildered husband, Alfrigg, walking beside her.

Alinor was a sight to behold in her soft wool gown and surcoat, tailored to hide her slight stomach, both of a cream color embroidered with Byzantine gold thread. At her neck was a magnificent neck ring of amber teardrops. Atop her flaming rust-colored hair, left loose in the Norse bridal fashion, was a garland of Dragonstead's own lilies of the valley, mixed with tiny rosebuds.

So beautiful was she that some said rusty hair and freckles became a favored attribute for women of the North that day.

People generally accepted now that Alinor was not a witch, but they took no chances. Many of the men were seen in her presence with their shields placed casually in front of their manparts ... most obviously, King Anlaf. And more than a few spectators were seen checking the back hem of Alinor's gown, just in case a tail was seen falling off now that she'd wed-locked a mortal man.

Besotted was the only way to describe Tykir as he gazed at his beloved approaching the bridal canopy on the arm of Bolthor. Eirik, standing at his side, squeezed his arm, and the two brothers exchanged a look of understanding. Both knew the profound effect the women in their lives had on them and how hard in coming that knowledge had been.

Tykir was dressed all in black, from leather ankle boots to braies and tunic. The starkness of his rich attire was broken only by a thick gold-looped belt at his waist and his usual star-shaped amber pendant. As always he wore at his one ear, exposed by blond hair left loose, but braided on that side only, his father's silver thunderbolt earring.

After the Christian marriage vows performed by Father Caedmon, they proceeded to the Viking wedding rituals.

"Who accepts the *mundr*, or bride-price, on behalf of Alinor of Graycote?" King Haakon's lawspeaker, Ketel, asked."

"I do," Bolthor said, stepping forth to take in hand a chest of magnificent jewels from Tykir. 'Twas a task Alinor's father, or other family members, would have undertaken if they were about, which, thank God, they were not.

Rumor was that Tykir's *Morgen-gifu* for Alinor—the "morning gift" to be presented the next day, following that night's consummation—was to be a strangely shaped piece of polished amber that seemed warm to the touch and pulsed. What an odd *Morgen-gifu* that would be! one and all proclaimed in hushed whispers, and wondered at its purported erotic purpose.

"And dost thou have a *heiman flygia* for your husband?" Ketel asked the bride.

"Yea, I do. I give to my husband half-share in a flock of two-dozen prize sheep and a rare curly horned ram."

Tykir was heard to chuckle then, and his bride was seen jabbing him in the side with a sharp elbow, murmuring something that sounded like, "Behave, troll!"

"Who acts as witness to the *handsal* that thus seals this wedding contract?" Ketel inquired, and six men stepped forth: Eirik, Selik, Bolthor, Rurik, Anlaf and Haakon.

King Haakon handed to Tykir the ancestral sword, Millstone-biter, which had belonged to the famed King Harald Fairhair. Legend said that Harald once cleaved a millstone to the eye with it. Placing a plain golden finger ring on the tip of the sword, Tykir offered it to Alinor, stating, "I give you this ring to mark the continuous circle of our unbreakable vows, and this sword to hold in trust for our sons."

She nodded, with tears filling her eyes as was her wont of late, and repeated the ritual words with a male finger ring for her groom.

With one hand each on the hilt of the sword and their other hands joined, Tykir motioned for their witnesses to step forth. Then the lawspeaker said, "We declare ourselves witness that thou, Alinor of Graycote, and thou, Tykir of Dragonstead, do bond to each other in lawful betrothal, and with the taking hold of hands, dost promise one to the other, love, honor and fidelity, as long as blood flows through your veins." The lawspeaker then made a small slit in each of their wrists, pressed them together and proclaimed, "With the blending of their blood, Tykir and Alinor are one."

It was not exactly the traditional Viking ritual, handed down through the ages, but close enough, if the smiles on hundreds of the faces were any indication, followed by rowdy Norse whoops of congratulations to the newly wedded couple. Besides, calling on the goddess Freyja to bless the couple with fertility would be an indelicate reminder of the bride's already fertile condition.

"Are you ready, wife?" Tykir said with a wink.

"Yea, I am ready, husband," Alinor replied with a wild shout that did a Viking maiden proud. Then she ran for the keep, lifting her gown calf-high as she made her way across the grassy knoll for the castle. It was the *brudh hlaup*, or "bride-running"—though it looked more like "bride-lumbering" due to her condition.

Tykir chased after her—albeit slowly, though his leg was feeling better these days—followed by the entire wedding party, laughing and cheering. In the end, it was Tykir who awaited her at the keep door, grinning, with the sword laid across the entryway. If she stepped over the sword, it was the final proof that she accepted her change of status, from maiden to wife.

She did, to the raucous cheers of all.

Some said Tykir then whacked her across the buttocks with the broadside of the sword. Viking men were trollish like that betimes.

Once inside the great hall, Tykir plunged his sword into the rooftree, putting a deep scar into the supporting pillar of the house. The depth of his cut was an indication of virility and good family-luck.

With the ceremonial drinking of the bridal ale, Alinor presented mead to her new husband in a two-handled bowl and recited the traditional words:

"Ale I bring thee, thou oak-of-battle,
With strength blended and greatest honor;
'Tis mized with magic and mighty songs,
With goodly spells, wish-speeding runs."

After sipping, Tykir made the sign of Thor's hammer Mjolnir over the cup and presented the same to Alinor, saying:

"Bring the Hammer the bride to bless:
On the maiden's lap lay ye Mjolnir;
In Frigg's name then our wedlock hallow."

After that was much feasting and drinking of the honey-mead, which would be imbibed for a month during the "honey-moon" period. Some said that honey was taken into the bridal chamber that night as well. But who can say if that is true?

Bolthor did write a poem about it, though, to no one's surprise.

"The troll got honey
On her feathers,
So the witch proclaimed.
'Am I complaining?'
Laughed the Viking.
'There is honey
On my quill, too.' "

Three months later, Thork Tykirsson came howling into the world, a blond-haired, green-eyed babe of winsome disposition. Some say he is destined to win the world, not with his sword, but with a wink and a smile.

READER LETTER

❧

"The girl with ash-smooth arms
is already getting used to
my bad ways."

—EGIL'S SAGA

Dear Reader:

I hope you liked this revised reissue of *The Bewitched Viking*. I must say that Tykir ages well. Don't you agree?

One of the most common questions that readers ask writers is: "Where do you get your ideas?" Well, there's a funny story related to where I got the idea for this book.

My husband, Robert, came home from playing golf one afternoon and told me, "Craig's you-know-what took a right turn." (Craig is, of course, a fictitious name, and you-know-what is not the term my husband used. Plus, it makes you wonder what exactly men discuss when hitting a little ball with a stick if subjects like this come up.)

After we had a good laugh at Craig's expense, I said, "This would make a great story element." Thus was born my Viking king whose "manpart" took a right turn.

My husband's reaction was, "See. There *is* a benefit to playing golf."

Laughable, I know, but then laughter is a survival skill in today's modern world, as so many of you readers have told me. "You made me laugh out loud at a time when I really, really needed a smile in my life," is a common refrain.

And apparently that was the case in early times, as well. Don't you just love the fact that some Viking skald hundreds and hundreds of years ago referred to old Egil's "bad ways"? I like to put my own particular spin on this stanza and imagine Egil as an overconfident, handsome rogue who has his eye on a fair maiden with ash-smooth arms. And, Lordy, that damsel had best pull up the drawbridge before she is tempted by this guy's "bad ways."

Like my very own Tykir with his "bad ways."

All writers want to touch their readers in some way—sometimes with strong emotion, sometimes to teach historical facts or an important life lesson, sometimes to share empathy or common experiences. (Erma Bombeck did this so well.) But I have come to believe that readers can be touched just as deeply, and no less importantly, with humor.

And it doesn't have to be only those who are in dire need of a laugh, like the lady whose husband had just undergone a kidney transplant, or the disabled trucker, or the young girl with a learning handicap. It's enough sometimes to entertain, period. And sometimes those books are remembered most of all.

We hope you agree that laughter can be an important part of romance, and that the best sex in the world has a smile in there somewhere.

If you'd like to know more about these Vikings and their sense of humor, try *The Long Ships: A Saga of the Viking Age* by Frans Bengtsson; or any of the books of Viking sagas or eddas in your public library. Or check out the research of Christie L. Ward (Gunnora Hallakarva) at <http://www.realtime.com/~gunnora/>; some of the wedding rituals in my epilogue are adaptations of ones listed on her website, or exact in the case of the ritual words themselves. And, of course, if you're looking for gorgeous Vikings with a wicked sense of humor, note that *The Bewitched Viking* is the fourth book in a series of loosely linked novels (which can be read out of order), following on the heels of *The Reluctant Viking, The Outlaw Viking* and *The Tarnished Lady*. Its sequels are *The Blue Viking, My Fair Viking, A Tale of Two Vikings, Viking in Love,* and *The Viking Takes a Knight*.

Please let us know what you think of my brand of Viking humor.

Sandra Hill
PO Box 604
State College, PA 16804
shill733@aol.com
www.sandrahill.net

GLOSSARY

Althing (or Thing)—an assembly of free Viking men from a wide area that made laws and enacted justice, fore-runners of a legislative body

Berserker—ancient Norse warrior who fought with frenzied rage in battle

Blód hel!—Bloody hell!

Braies—slim pants worn by men, breeches

Brudh-hlaup—the bride running

Castellan—one who oversees a castle in the absence of the castle's lord.

Churl—peasant, or freeman of the lowest rank

Danegeld—forced payment of money, food, lands, or trea-sures that Vikings demanded of their enemies in return for not attacking them.

Drukkinn (various spellings)—drunk in Old Norse

Ell—a measure, usually of cloth, equaling 45 inches

Futhark—runic alphabet

Gammelost—a pungent cheese once a staple of Norse diet

Garth—yard or open courtyard

Halberd—long handled battle axe

Hectares—unit of land measure equal to 2.471 acres

Hedeby—a market town located at the head of the Schleswig peninsula in Viking Age Denmark

Hersir—military commander

Hide—a primitive measure of land, equaling the normal

holding that would support a peasant and his family, roughly 120 arable acres

Hird—permanent troop that a chieftain or nobleman might have

Hirdsman—one of the third

Hospitium—name for a medieval medical facility usually tended by monks, such as the one associated with the minster of Viking Age York, or Jorvik

Housecarls—troops assigned to a king's or lord's household on a longtime, sometimes permanent basis

Jarl—a high ranking Viking, similar to an English earl

Knarr—a Viking merchant vessel, wider and deeper than a regular longship

Lutefisk—dried cod

Mead—honeyed ale

Minster—a church

Mjolnir—Thor's hammer

More danico—having more than one wife

Motte—high, flat-topped hill on which a castle or fortress was located

Norselands—what are referred to today as Scandanavia, in particular Norway

Northumbria—one of the Anglo-Saxon kingdoms, bordered by the English kingdoms to the south and in the north and northwest by the Scots, Cumbrians, and Strathclyde Welsh

Odal rights—rights of heredity

Orphrey—gold- or silver-threaded embroidery

Pennanular—circular, usually referring to brooches which held a shoulder mantle in place or the straps of a Viking apron

Sennight—one week

Skald—poet

Skyr (various spellings)—a type of Viking soft cheese

Sulung—equal to two hides

Surcoat—an outer garment often worn by men over armor

embroidered with heraldic arms, or a sleeved or sleeve-
less garment worn indoors over a gown or other apparel

Sword dew—blood

Thing—see Althing

Thrall—slave

Trondelag—A geographical region in Central Norway

Tun—252 gallons, as in ale

Valhalla—heavenly hall in which Odin welcomed those soldiers slain in battle

Vapnatak, or weapon clatter—At a Thing or an Althing, the
men indicated their votes by banging swords against
shields.

Wergeld (or wergild)—a man's worth

Witan or witenagemot—the king's council of advisors, pre-
cursor to the English Parliament

Wound dew—blood

Can't get enough of *USA Today* and
New York Times bestselling
author Sandra Hill?
Turn the page for glimpses of her amazing
books. From cowboys to Vikings, Navy
SEALs to Southern bad boys, every one
of Sandra's books has her unique blend of
passion, creativity, and unparalled wit.

Welcome to the World of Sandra Hill!

The Viking Takes a Knight

❀

For John of Hawk's Lair, the unexpected appearance of a beautiful woman at his door is always welcome. Yet the arrival of this alluring Viking woman, Ingrith Sigrundottir—with her enchanting smile and inviting curves—is different . . . for she comes accompanied by a herd of unruly orphans. And Ingrith needs more than the legendary knight's hospitality; she needs protection. For among her charges is a small boy with a claim to the throne—a dangerous distinction when murderous King Edgar is out hunting for Viking blood.

A man of passion, John will keep them safe—but in exchange, he wants something very dear indeed: Ingrith's heart, to be taken with the very first meeting of their lips . . .

Viking in Love

✧

*C*aedmon of Larkspur *was the most loathsome lout* Breanne *had ever encountered. When she* arrived at his castle with her sisters, they were greeted by an estate gone wild, while Caedmon laid abed after a night of ale. But Breanne must endure, as they are desperately in need of protection . . . and he is quite handsome.

After nine long months in the king's service, all Caedmon wanted was peace, not five Viking princesses running about his keep. And the fiery redhead who burst into his chamber was the worst of them all. He should kick her out, but he has a far better plan for Breanne of Stoneheim—one that will leave her a Viking in lust.

The Reluctant Viking

❧

*T*he self-motivation tape was supposed to help Ruby Jordan solve her problems, not create new ones. Instead, she was lulled into an era of hard-bodied warriors and fair maidens. But the world ten centuries in the past didn't prove to be all mead and mirth. Even as Ruby tried to update medieval times, she had to deal with a Norseman whose view of women was stuck in the Dark Ages. And what was worse, brawny Thork had her husband's face, habits, and desire to avoid Ruby. Determined not to lose the same man twice, Ruby planned a bold seduction that would conquer the reluctant Viking—and make him an eager captive of her love.

The Outlaw Viking

&

*A*s tall and striking as the Valkyries of legend, Dr. Rain Jordan was proud of her Norse ancestors despite their warlike ways. But she can't believe it when she finds herself on a nightmarish battle-field, forced to save the barbarian of her dreams.

He was a wild-eyed warrior whose deadly sword could slay a dozen Saxons with a single swing, yet Selik couldn't control the saucy wench from the future. If Selik wasn't careful, the stunning siren was sure to capture his heart and make a warrior of love out of **The Outlaw Viking**.

The Tarnished Lady

&

*B*anished *from polite society, Lady Eadyth of Hawk's* Lair spent her days hidden under a volumi- nous veil, tending her bees. But when her lands are threatened, Lady Eadyth sought a husband to offer her the protection of his name.

Notorious for loving—and leaving—the most beautiful damsels in the land, Eirik of Ravenshire was England's most virile bachelor. Yet when the mysterious lady offered him a vow of chaste mat- rimony in exchange for revenge against his most hated enemy, Eirik couldn't refuse. But the lusty knight's plans went awry when he succumbed to the sweet sting of the tarnished lady's love.

The Bewitched Viking

◈

*E*ven fierce Norse warriors have bad days. 'Twas enough to drive a sane Viking mad, the things Tykir Thorksson was forced to do—capturing a red-headed virago, putting up with the flock of sheep that follows her everywhere, chasing off her bumbling brothers. But what could a man expect from the sorceress who had put a kink in the King of Norway's most precious body part? If that wasn't bad enough, Tykir was beginning to realize he wasn't at all immune to the enchantment of brash red hair and freckles. Perhaps he could reverse the spell and hold her captive, not with his mighty sword, but with a Viking man's greatest magic: a wink and smile.

The Blue Viking

❧

For Rurik the Viking, life has not been worth living since he left Maire of the Moors. Oh, it's not that he misses her fiery red tresses or kissable lips. Nay, it's the embarrassing blue zigzag tattoo she put on his face after their one wild night of loving. For a fierce warrior who prides himself on his immense height, his expertise in bedsport, and his well-toned muscles, this blue streak is the last straw. In the end, he'll bring the witch to heel, or die trying. Mayhap he'll even beg her to wed . . . so long as she can promise he'll no longer be . . . **The Blue Viking**.

The Viking's Captive

(originally titled MY FAIR VIKING)

⟐

Tyra, Warrior Princess. She is too tall, too loud, too fierce to be a good catch. But her ailing father has decreed that her four younger sisters—delicate, mild-mannered, and beautiful—cannot be wed 'til Tyra consents to take a husband. And then a journey to save her father's life brings Tyra face to face with Adam the Healer. A god in human form, he's tall, muscled, perfectly proportioned. Too bad Adam refuses to fall in with her plans—so what's a lady to do but truss him up, toss him over her shoulder, and sail off into the sunset to live happily ever after.

A Tale of Two Vikings

⊗

Toste and Vagn Ivarsson are identical Viking twins, about to face Valhalla together, following a tragic battle, or maybe something even more tragic: being separated for the first time in their thirty and one years. Alas, even the bravest Viking must eventually leave his best buddy behind and do battle with that most fearsome of all opponents—the love of his life. And what if that love was Helga the Homely, or Lady Esme, the world's oldest novice nun?

A Tale of Two Vikings will give you twice the tears, twice the sizzle, and twice the laughter . . . and make you wish for your very own Viking.

The Last Viking

☙

He was six feet, four inches of pure, unadulterated male. He wore nothing but a leather tunic, and he was standing in Professor Meredith Foster's living room. The medieval historian told herself he was part of a practical joke, but with his wide gold belt, ancient language, and callused hands, the brawny stranger seemed so . . . authentic. And as he helped her fulfill her grandfather's dream of re-creating a Viking ship, he awakened her to dreams of her own. Until she wondered if the hand of fate had thrust her into the loving arms of . . . **The Last Viking**.

Truly, Madly Viking

⚭

A *Viking named Joe? Jorund Ericsson is a tenth-*
century Viking warrior who lands in a
modern mental hospital. Maggie McBride is the
lucky psychologist who gets to "treat" the gorgeous Norseman, whom she mistakenly calls Joe.

   You've heard of *One Flew Over the Cuckoo's Nest*.
But how about *A Viking Flew Over the Cuckoo's Nest*?
The question is: Who's the cuckoo in this nest? And
why is everyone laughing?

The Very Virile Viking

Magnus Ericsson is a simple man. He loves the smell of fresh-turned dirt after springtime plowing. He loves the feel of a soft woman under him in the bed furs. He loves the heft of a good sword in his fighting arm.

But, Holy Thor, what he does not relish is the bothersome brood of children he's been saddled with. Or the mysterious happenstance that strands him in a strange new land—the kingdom of *Holly Wood*. Here is a place where the folks think he is an *act-whore* (whatever that is), and the woman of his dreams—a winemaker of all things—fails to accept that he is her soul mate . . . a man of exceptional talents, not to mention . . . **A Very Virile Viking.**

Wet & Wild

⊗

What do you get when you cross a Viking with a Navy SEAL? A warrior with the fierce instincts of the past and the rigorous training of America's most elite fighting corps? A totally buff hero-in-the-making who hasn't had a woman in roughly a thousand years? A dyed-in-the-wool romantic with a hopeless crush? Whatever you get, women everywhere can't wait to meet him, and his story is guaranteed to be . . . **Wet & Wild**.

Hot & Heavy

❧

*I*n and out, that's the goal as Lt. Ian MacLean prepares for his special ops mission. He leads a team of highly trained Navy SEALs, the toughest, buffest fighting men in the world and he has nothing to lose. Madrene comes from a time a thousand years before he was born, and she has no idea she's landed in the future. After tying him up, the beautiful shrew gives him a tongue-lashing that makes a drill sergeant sound like a kindergarten teacher. Then she lets him know she has her own special way of dealing with overconfident males, and things get . . . **Hot & Heavy**.

Frankly, My Dear . . .

☙

*L*ost in the Bayou . . . *Selene had three great passions:* men, food, and *Gone with the Wind*. But the glamorous model always found herself starving—for both nourishment and affection. Weary of the petty world of high fashion, she headed to New Orleans for one last job before she began a new life. Little did she know that her new life would include a brand-new time—about 150 years ago! Selene can't get her fill of the food—or an alarmingly handsome man. Dark and brooding, James Baptiste was the only lover she gave a damn about. And with God as her witness, she vowed never to go without the man she loved again.

Sweeter Savage Love

&

*T*he stroke of surprisingly gentle hands, the flash of fathomless blue eyes, the scorch of white-hot kisses . . . Once again, Dr. Harriet Ginoza was swept away into rapturous fantasy. The modern psychologist knew the object of her desire was all she should despise, yet time after time, she lost herself in visions of a dangerously hand-some rogue straight out of a historical romance. Harriet never believed that her dream lover would cause her any trouble, but then a twist of fate cast her back to the Old South and she met him in the flesh. To her disappointment, Etienne Baptiste refused to fulfill any of her secret wishes. If Harriet had any hope of making her amorous dreams become passionate reality, she'd have to seduce this charmer with a sweeter savage love than she'd imagined possible . . . and savor every minute of it.

The Love Potion

☿

*F*ame and fortune are surely only a swallow away when Dr. Sylvie Fontaine discovers a chemical formula guaranteed to attract the opposite sex. Though her own love life is purely hypothetical, the shy chemist's professional future is assured . . . as soon as she can find a human guinea pig. But bad boy Lucien LeDeux—best known as the Swamp Lawyer—is more than she can handle even before he accidentally swallowed a love potion disguised in a jelly bean. When the dust settles, Luc and Sylvie have the answers to some burning questions—can a man die of testosterone overload? Can a straightlaced female lose every single one of her inhibitions?—and they learn that old-fashioned romance is still the best catalyst for love.

Love Me Tender

ॐ

*O*nce upon a time, in a magic kingdom, there lived a handsome prince. Prince Charming, he was called by one and all. And to this land came a gentle princess. You could say she was Cinderella . . . Wall Street Cinderella. Okay, if you're going to be a stickler for accuracy, in this fairy tale the kingdom is Manhattan. But there's magic in the Big Apple, isn't there? And maybe he can be Prince Not-So-Charming at times, and "gentle" isn't the first word that comes to mind when thinking of this princess. But they're looking for happily ever after just the same—and they're going to get it.

Desperado

☙

*M*istaken *for a notorious bandit and his infamously*
scandalous mistress, L.A. lawyer Rafe San-
tiago and Major Helen Prescott found themselves
on the wrong side of the law. In a time and place
where rules had no meaning, Helen found Rafe's
hard, bronzed body strangely comforting, and his
piercing blue eyes left her all too willing to share
his bedroll. His teasing remarks made her feel all
woman, and she was ready to throw caution to
the wind if she could spend every night in the
arms of her very own . . . **Desperado**.